MW01126031

Tale of the Sharp-Dressed Man

Jon M Michaels

~*~
Dark Fruit Publishing
~*~

This is a work of fiction. Names, characters, places, and incidents are either the product of the author's imagination or are used fictitiously, and any resemblance to actual persons living or dead, business establishments, events, or locales, is entirely coincidental.

Tale of the Sharp-Dressed Man

COPYRIGHT © 2017 by Jon M Michaels

Dark Fruit Publishing
All rights reserved. No part of this book may be used or reproduced in any manner whatsoever without written permission of the author, except in the case of brief quotations embodied in critical articles or reviews.

Published in the United States of America

Cover Art by *Jason Zaloudik*

Dedication:

To my Uncle Brownie. He was the uncle with the colorful stories and jokes, that us kids weren't meant to hear—or repeat. He once told a story about a stranger who came to visit him as he lay in a hospital bed fighting for his life. That story is my inspiration.

Uncle Brownie, for the record, made a miraculous recovery and carried on.

Acknowledgments:

My lovely, patient wife. She stood by me, believing and supporting my dream of writing a book. Thank you, my dear.

Many, many thanks to Alicia Dean, a talented writer and editor. She was my lamp. I couldn't have made it this far without her.

Chapter One

No Fishing Today

Mid-Spring, Wetumka Oklahoma

IT WAS 1976, and me a thirteen-year-old knee-skinner living a fairy tale life on my grandpa's farm in Oklahoma. I didn't care to care, too much. Just living the *good* life.

Boredom? Never heard of it.

Worry? Scratch that off the list.

Fun? Now we're talking.

Excitement? I'll come back to that later.

I fished. I climbed trees. I ate from pecan trees, peach trees, and apple trees. You get it. A real Huck Finn life.

The countryside was a stirring landscape of rolling green hills, and when the wind mixed with the grass and trees just right, it sounded like a pounding surf. Trees dotted the property like fixed buoys, swaying and creaking. All such wonders lay beneath a blue canvas of floating clouds that cast lazy shadows upon the land. It was magical.

Grandpa—my hands-on helpful mentor—had me in the hayloft stacking sacks of feed when he called from below.

"Luke, you got a minute?"

I wiped sweat from my brow and gazed down at him, hoping he was going to cut me loose of my chores. Maybe let me do some fishing. "What's up, Grandpa?"

He took off his straw cowboy hat and fanned his face.

"C'mon on down and get a drink of water. It's too durned hot."

"Okie-doke," I said, already headed for the ladder.

I climbed down, and he handed me a thermos of ice water, which I greedily drank from.

"Don't drown on me," he said, chuckling. "I might need ya for more chores."

I hoped he was joking.

He swept his long white hair back and put his hat back on his head and pointed to the southwestern portion of the sky. "We've got a storm brewin'. I imagine it's goin' to be a gulley washer."

I looked and saw a distant, growing darkness take root on the horizon. Anything could happen in an Oklahoma thunderstorm. They tended to lean toward the extreme. Sometimes throwing a *gulley washer* at us.

"Have ya checked the cellar for water?" he asked.

"Yep, first thing this morning."

"How about snakes? Did ya check for snakes?"

"Yep," I answered. I *always* checked for snakes.

Grandpa rubbed his jaw and looked at the sky once again. An odd expression of surprise spread across his face, but it was quickly replaced with dread.

"What's wrong?" I asked.

He blew out some air and shook his head.

"What is it?"

He put his arm around me and pointed straight due west. At first, I wasn't sure what he was pointing at, as it was away from the storm clouds. Then I saw it. Blackness moved and writhed above the treetops, like a thick shadow trying to pull away from itself. It was a good five miles from where we stood. Birds flew from the blackness as if shot from a gun, separating and going their own way.

"Wow, what is it?"

"You can see it? Is that what you're sayin'?"

"Yep. I can see it."

Grandpa suddenly looked sad. "Luke, ya know who

lives over yonder. Right?"

Of course, I knew. He was referring to the backwoods freaks of the county, otherwise known as the Plume family. I personally had never seen them before, but depending on who you spoke to, they were a scary bunch. Grandpa never said too much about them, but he dropped faint hints of keeping my space, along with comments such as, *"They've got a different way of thinkin' than most folks."* My schoolmates made a bigger drama of my neighbors than did Grandpa. Most had never laid an eye to the Plumes, so the tales grew into legendary horror without anyone actually knowing a damn thing about them. The only thing about the Plumes that most thought to be true and undeniable was they were a family built upon an incestuous foundation.

My school chum Eldon tells a story about the time he and his two older brothers, Melvin and Cotton, was coon hunting close to the Plume property one night. It was a scary time according to him.

Here is the way Eldon tells it.

One summer evening, he and his brothers were running like madmen through a pasture chasing their dogs. You see, a coon hound has differing barks, depending on what the dog is barking about. If the dog is on a coon's scent it barks differently than when it is actually treeing a coon. A coon hunter waits for the changeover bark, a noticeable change from trailing to treeing. Sometimes, it takes a long time if the dog is a babbler. A babbler is a hound that opens up barking when there is no scent, driving the owner into fits.

Eldon's brothers had babblers.

They never knew for certain if the hounds were trailing, or barking for the hell of it. They lucked out every now and then, which is why the trio was trekking through the woods on this particular evening. They trudged across pastures with their spelunker lights bouncing like glowing yo-yo's, hoping and praying for a coon. Three hours later, their hoping and praying paid off.

Melvin's dog sounded off on a coon.

"Hot, damn. Ole Ace has got 'em one treed," Melvin bragged. "Let's keep goin' this way."

Ace was an old hound, with most of its ear chewed up from a tangle with a coon. Ironically, it was one of the few times Ace was in actual proximity of one. Possum, armadillos, and gophers were more to his liking.

"Wait." Cotton reached for Melvin.

"What?" Melvin asked.

"Well, ain't we kinda' close to the freaks?"

Melvin twisted his face into a look of disgust. "C'mon on, son. There ain't nothin' to be scared of."

"I don't know…"

"Oh, *Gawd.* You know what your prob—"

A yelp sounded out from the dark, freezing Melvin. It was Ace.

Eldon began looking around and backing up. "I think we ought to get the hell out of here."

"I ain't leavin' Ace out there, and watch your damn cussin'," said Melvin.

"Why don't ya holler for him? Maybe he'll come," Cotton suggested. "I ain't all fired up to go traipsin' around close to those freaks."

"Yeah," Eldon piped in.

Melvin thought about it and agreed with his brothers. He began shouting Ace's name and whistling for him. He did this for several minutes, fully expecting to see ace galloping to him from the darkness at any moment.

Silence. Not even a cricket or bird offered up a song. Stillness fluttered down upon the woods like a sticky membrane.

"All right, I'm goin' in after him." Melvin shone his light in each of his brother's faces. "Anyone goin' with me?"

"Shit, no," Eldon said.

Cotton looked at the ground and sighed. "I'll go with

you."

"What? Ya'll are leaving me by myself?" Eldon sounded shocked.

"Don't worry, Eldon. Ace probably just fell in a creek bed." Cotton swallowed nervously. "There ain't no bogey-man goin' to get you."

"You ain't sounding too convincing," said Eldon.

A high-pitched whine of pain broke the quiet, followed by a yowl that abruptly stopped.

"Oh, damn." Eldon's voice shook.

Quietly, Melvin said, "Watch your mouth, Eldon."

"Well?" said Cotton.

"Well, what?" Melvin's breathing had become labored.

"What are you goin' to do?"

Melvin took his spelunker hat off and ran his fingers through his hair, then plopped it back and walked resolutely into the unknown to search for Ace. "There ain't nothin' to be afraid of. My dog needs my help, man."

Cotton looked at his youngest brother and then left to join Melvin in his rescue effort. He took several steps and stopped, suddenly aware of the opaque nature of the dark that awaited them. It was *so* much darker toward the Plume property, so…unnatural. He went against his instinct and marched into the smothering gloom.

Eldon watched the pair of lights move up and down. It helped to settle his nerves and keep his imagination from running rampant about monsters in the dark.

Keep looking at the lights, everything's cool as a cucumber.

His brothers' lights suddenly winked out. Like they had been, indeed, swallowed by a monster.

"Oh, crap," Eldon said.

A high-pitched bawl, similar to what a baby might make, echoed in the woods before switching to a wicked, awful laugh. A human scream quickly followed, which dropped Eldon into a bucket of incommunicable fear. His crotch became warm and wet with urine, but pissing his pants was the least of his concerns. The primary concern was getting as far away from the woods as he could. He turned and ran for the open pasture like it was his mother's love.

Somewhere along the way, his light fell from his head. For the briefest moment, he considered letting the light stay where it was, but he pushed that idea away—it would be ridiculous to run blind in this darkness. So, he slowed to retrieve his light and heard heavy breathing, and the unmistakable sound of something running at a high-speed. Running toward him.

Eldon attempted a snatch and run technique, but failed miserably, losing his balance and falling flat on his face. His panic level raised a considerable number of notches. He tried screaming, but all he was able to rally was a raspy whimper.

The unknown runner was nearly upon him now, so Eldon stumbled to his feet without the aid of a light. With his arms flailing, he twisted and bawled in his way into the night. He risked a look behind only once.

It was once too many.

He ran into a pecan tree just as he turned his head, sending him prone. His courage and energy went out the window. His world became dazed and confused, full of stars and color. But he was still able to hear and feel, as he was physically lifted from the ground.

"Kill me fast," Eldon slurred.

"There ain't nobody goin' to kill you," Melvin said. "But, we'd best keep movin'."

"Don't worry, Eldon. We've got you," Cotton said.

Relief swam through his fog, settling him into a stone, cold sleep. It was better this way, the two older brothers told one another. Why put Eldon through the added horror of explaining the blood and gore that dripped from Cotton's clothes? No need to recount how the remains of ole' Ace rained on Cotton like warm bathwater from the trees.

Eldon would ask them later about what they saw, and they didn't lie. They saw nothing. It was too dim to see anything. They recalled a mood of evil that bore into their brains like a carnivorous worm. Evil that haunted the brothers in their sleep for many years after the event.

Ace was eventually replaced, and Cotton's dog eventually found its way home. It hid under the house for several days before finally peeking its nose out.

Eldon and Cotton gave up coon hunting, but Melvin kept at it. Just as long as it was in another county and at least fifteen miles from the Plume property. Eldon's crucial concern after the incident was that nobody knows of his pissing himself.

I STOOD WATCHING the strange blackness in the sky and ran Eldon's tale of terror in my brain. "Do you…uh, think that the Plumes are causing it?" I asked.

"It ain't exactly *them*. But, they ain't innocent neither. Somethin' caused the land to turn sour years ago, when I was a youngster."

"I still don't understand."

He gently patted the top of my head and gave me a short smile. "It's okay if you don't understand. I ain't sure I understand it."

I studied the blackness in the sky again, hoping for clarity to slap me in the face. It grew darker, looking like a black hole full of twisting snakes.

"Luke," Grandpa said, "don't stare at it. Don't let it…reach you."

I didn't have a clue as to what he meant, but a shiver went through my spine nonetheless. I broke away from the twisting anomaly and looked toward the gathering storm clouds instead. At least thunderstorms were familiar, and I knew what to expect from them. It was creeping closer, assembling its power as it moved along. I took a deep breath in through my nose, savoring the storm's aroma.

"C'mon to the house with me," Grandpa said.

"Am I done with chores?"

"Oh, yes indeed. You're done with chores."

Visions of fishing lures spun in my head.

"But, I'm thinkin' you'd best pass on the fishin' this afternoon," said Grandpa.

"Why?" I guessed I had at least an hour or more before the storm arrived. There was plenty of time for me to fish.

He pursed his lips in thought and looked at the oddity that hovered over the trees, then ruffled my hair like a German Shepherd. "I'll have to explain later."

"Is it the thunderstorm?" I asked. "Is that why you won't let me fish?" I pointed to the spectral darkness. "Or *that*?"

He paused a few seconds. "Well, I ain't goin' to lie. It's *that*."

I quickly wished for idyllic ignorance.

I began to fear what Grandpa had warned me about. That it had *reached* me. A trickle of fear found its way into my mind. My fear, strangely enough, was not of the unknown or the coonhound bogeyman. It was deeper than all that. I was most fearful of having my wonderful, storybook life stolen away from me.

"I don't feel like fishing anymore," I said.

"I'll explain some things to ya down at the house. Maybe eat some pecan pie." He smiled.

"Will I feel better?"

"Well, ya like pecan pie, that'll make ya feel better."

He had a point. I am a big fan of pecan pie and Grandpa's was the best in the county. He had a drawer filled with blue ribbons serving as proof. "Are you going to tell me what's going on?" I asked.

"Yep, we'll talk whilst we're eatin'."

A strong wind arrived, stirring barn-dust and hay in the air. The storm's scent clung to it, but there was something else in the air that I couldn't place. Whatever it was, Grandpa smelled it too. "Let's get to the house," he said.

Chapter Two

A Crazy Story

I TOOK A heaping bite of pie and chased it down with a gulp of ice-cold milk, dribbling a little on the table. As usual, the pie was like a slice of buttered heaven, but it did little to erase my edginess. I wiped my mouth. "So, what's the deal with that *thing* in the sky?"

Grandpa tilted his glass of milk, downed it in smooth fashion, and belched. "Well, I was about your age, thirteen if I'm recollectin' properly, back durin' the spring of 1916."

"Wow, that's…old," I said.

He laughed. "Yep, pretty durn old." He took his cowboy hat off and laid it on the table, allowing his long, white hair to tumble about his broad shoulders. "Well, anyway, I was livin' here on the farm, and I was out in the pasture throwin' hay to the cattle from a wagon that was bein' pulled by Millie, our mule…

…when he heard a commotion in the woods. His first thought was maybe some of the cattle were loose in the trees, but a head count quickly dismissed that notion, and it was the wrong time of the year for deer movement. His concern rose when the trees began to shake, and the sound of breaking tree limbs grew louder.

"What's goin' on, Millie?" he asked. He expected no response, but she snorted and moved her legs nervously, nonetheless.

The western part of the trees suddenly erupted with

wildlife that spilled into the pasture. Coyotes, squirrels, raccoons, and even deer ran in all directions from the tree line at breakneck speed. Snakes glided along the ground looking like shiny bull whips, while birds took frenzied flight.

Thinking a fire must have set the animals running he looked for smoke along the tops of the trees, but saw none. However, he did spot a large, spinning, shadow above the trees with a slender tendril of black attached to it like a string on a state fair balloon.

"What in tarnation…"

A shrill scream, jagged and violent, sounded off from the trees, chilling his bones. Millie didn't care too much for the noise either. She decided to take off on a dead run for the hay barn, which toppled him from the wagon. He yelled, "Millie, get your butt back here!"

Wasted breath. Millie had made her mind up to leave and nothing was going to change her thinking on the matter.

"Stupid, ole' mule," he muttered.

He found himself sitting in a pile of wet cow manure and quickly sprang to his feet. He was fuming and fearful at once. Copperhead snakes slithered close by, freezing him in place until they passed, which was no easy task as the cattle began to scatter dangerously close to him. Another scream wailed from the trees, rattling in his head like a loose marble. He looked to the house—an easy two hundred yards—and measured his chances of making it home without being snake bitten.

Maybe, fifty-fifty.

A snake bumped into his foot, but continued with a sinuous grace toward some unknown destination. The tall grass swayed and jerked with its movements.

Less than fifty-fifty.

Another crawled across his work boots, pushing his bodily functions to the threshold. He had to get the hell out of there.

"How are ya goin' to do that, Theo?" he asked himself. "This is a fine pickle."

A few straggling cattle trotted dead-on in his direction, threatening to knock him to the ground. He had to think fast. An old Hereford cow sped up, leaving him with seconds to act.

He sidestepped the charging beast and wrapped his arms around its neck, careful to keep his feet off the ground, splaying them wildly as he was roughly carried across the pasture. The cow bellowed and picked up the tempo, but Grandpa grabbed handfuls of hair and swung a leg over the cow's back, hanging on like a rat on a gut wagon.

"Lord, I need ya. I need ya *real* bad," he prayed. It was at this moment he found himself suddenly holding a tuft of cow hair in each hand and hurtling through the air.

There was a defined separation between man and beast.

Apparently, the cow set off in a northerly direction, while Grandpa's wiry frame went south. The result was him tumbling like a rag doll across the landscape. He ended up flat on his back and unable to breathe, with his head lying in a pool of wet manure. Mercifully, his breath came rushing back to him, which he inhaled like a greedy drunk. He was still alive, but he liked his chances of survival better on his feet. He had to get off the ground.

Screaming like a madman, he flung himself up, expecting nothing less than the direst of circumstances. He faced due west and saw no cattle. They appeared to have gathered some instinct, shifting their movements southward toward the hay barn.

He collected his wits and thanked the Lord for sparing his life, and then began looking south. The large, two-story house revealed itself through a veil of elms and pecan trees, while the barn sat more in the open, fifty yards to the southwest. It was a long walk, considering the circumstances.

Looking again to the west, he stared at the dark movements in the afternoon sky. He focused intently on the weird thing, studying it. Something was moving within the blackness. He dug into it closer, scrutinizing. Something began to form. It was a figure of a man. Yes, he was certain of it.

He strained his eyes harder, trying to shake something out of it. The blackness suddenly began to swell. It grew and widened and became a gaping pit in the sky. And as it grew, it revealed its secrets.

The darkness slowly peeled away to show the back of a man walking down a winding dirt-road that led to a village. The man was tall, made even more so by the shiny, black, top hat that sat upon his head. He wore a jet-black suit that glimmered with each step he took. Suddenly, the man stopped and spun around, revealing a strikingly handsome face. However, his smile was sorely lacking charm. He had a mouthful of black teeth. "Theophilus. Right?" The man spoke with a tongue made of silk. "Or, do you prefer *Theo*?"

Grandpa stood stiff as an oak tree. He was too terrified and stupefied to do much else.

"Right. Then, *Theo* it is."

Then, finally from Theo, "Am I dreamin'?"

"Damn good question."

"I'm dreamin', I must be dreamin'."

The man folded his arms and moved toward Theo. "Nope, you're not dreaming. And, I'm going to prove it to you."

Theo screamed as the man reached from the sky with an arm like rubber that stretched to grotesque lengths to snatch at Theo.

"Don't be such a crybaby," the man said. "You're already here."

A numbing realization came over him. He was no longer standing in the middle of a pasture. He was suddenly standing in the middle of a dusty dirt-road next to the strange man.

The man stepped back from Theo and spread his arms wide. "Welcome to a new reality."

Theo's mouth hung slack.

"You don't say much, do you?" The man widened his black smile.

"Could I have a peek at your eyes?" Theo asked. "I can't see 'em."

"Whatever for?"

"Someone once told me that to make a nightmare go away, you had to look at whatever was scarin' ya straight in the eyes. Your hat's makin' a shadow over 'em."

More laughter.

The man took off his hat and held it loosely to his side. His hair spilled forth like an overturned inkwell. Black and velvety, it cascaded across his shoulders.

"Well," the man lowered his head, "have your *look.* Tell me what you see, lad."

Scared out of his mind, Theo leaned in for a good look. It was an action that did nothing to soothe him. It only heightened his angst. An infinite well of blackness reflected back at Theo from black, mirrored eyes. Cold and devoid of humanity. It chilled Theo to the bone.

"So," the man said, "you looked me straight in the eyes, and I didn't disappear. So, you're either *not* dreaming, or someone gave you a piece of ridiculous advice."

Theo turned to look for his sane world. He remembered it well. He was born there, had a mother and father. All he had to do was leap from the sky and pray he didn't break his neck. However, when he turned to look down on the farm, it was gone. There was no sign of his world. His customary scenery of soft, rolling hills was replaced with something very different. The only land beneath his feet was the stranger's land, and it stretched for miles in every direction. Mountains appeared as faraway borders, flexing beauty and strength. Two rivers roared along embankments held up by mammoth trees.

"I ain't sure which is right," said Theo.

The man twirled the hat like a Vaudeville character and deftly placed it atop his head. "I was not expecting an eloquent response. You didn't disappoint. But, please," he playfully clapped his hands, "*please*, do indeed tell me what you thought of my eyes. What did you see?"

"It made me sick at my stomach. I've never felt so awful in my life."

The man smiled, then placed an arm around Theo's shoulders. "Here, lad. Let's stroll on down to the village. They're gathering for a feast." As they walked, the man pointed. "Do you see? Look at the bounty of flowers. *So* much color…it takes one's breath away."

Indeed, there was such vivid color, that of which Theo had never seen. Not even his mother's flower garden could stand against such beauty. The village itself was beautiful, nestled in a valley with snow-peaked mountains on either side and quaint cottage-style homes billowing smoke from chimneys.

A chorus of children, shrill and excited, could be heard. It made Theo think of tiny bells being chimed. It was such a pretty sound.

"Ah, yes. The sound of innocence," the man said. "Sounds like they're having a splendid time."

Theo wished he was having a good time.

The man picked up the pace, dragging Theo along. "We mustn't hasten or we'll miss the fun."

"I ain't concerned about missin' any fun. I just want to go home."

"That's because you don't know any better. You're still clinging to the idea that this is all a bad dream."

"It *is* a bad dream."

"No, no, lad. None of this is a dream, and as I stated earlier, I'll prove it to you."

Theo's sanity was unraveling like an old sweater. Retaining the few remaining threads hinged upon his bizarre adventure being an outlandish dream. "You keep sayin' you'll prove it. Well, I'm waitin'."

The man drew them to a halt beneath a tree. It was the weirdest looking tree Theo had ever seen. The branches were pinkish in color, kind of like the underbelly of a pig, and lacking anything resembling a leaf. Strange fruit hung like bats from the limbs, round and furry.

"You would be incorrect in thinking this is a persimmon-tree." The man plucked one of the pods. "Here you go, lad. Take a bite of this and you'll soon...see the light."

"It's got hair on it," Theo said in disgust.

"Yes, it does have hair. However, it's delicious despite the appearance. Sweeter than honey, I *promise*."

Theo cautiously reached for the fruit and took it into his hand, feeling repulsed by its feel. He instinctively dropped it.

"It was warm. I don't like it."

The man shook his head side to side, and then stooped to pick up the hairy fruit. As he wiped the dirt and grass away he said, "Theo, I expected more from a lad such as you. You've worked and tilled the land like a grown man for an impressive number of years. You've butchered farm animals and been sprayed by their blood, and yet you're squeamish about *this*. You remind me of a little girl."

"I don't care. I ain't eatin' that."

The man's mood darkened. Theo felt it.

"Are you certain of this decision?"

"Yep, I'm certain. I just want to go home."

With impressive swiftness, the man grasped the back of Theo's head with one hand and used the other to force the fruit into his mouth. Theo gagged against it and tried to fight the man off. It was like being in a vise.

The fruit's skin broke against his teeth, releasing a thick juice that ran down his throat. It was hot and sweet.

The man released Theo, sending him tumbling to the ground. "Look to the village. Look and see with your new eyes."

Theo did look. He saw an old-world community. He saw people gathered at wooden tables in a courtyard. Food was heaped on the tables in anticipation of being consumed and enjoyed. The children sat at a table away from the adults, laughing and smiling. Theo saw the same familiar blackness thrashing about in the sky. A thin vine streamed from the mass, reaching a house and entering through the roof.

"It's been called many things, from many different cultures, but it is most commonly known as a spell-cloud. It never appears unless summoned," said the man, as he pointed to the sky.

Theo vomited.

Smiling, the man said, "I told you the fruit was sweet. I never said it would be agreeable."

Theo began to hate the man.

"I found it interesting that you were able to see me." The man helped Theo to his feet. "Ordinarily, the only way to see to the other side is if you've eaten of the fruit, or someone in your bloodline has. Sometimes it gets passed on to other generations. I made you eat the fruit out of simple curiosity. I wanted to see your reaction to its essence. Clearly, you've not sampled my wonderfully wicked tree."

The man sat on the ground beneath the tree and crossed his legs. "Of course, if a human's soul is dark enough, and knows how to invoke or conjure, then there is no need to eat the fruit. But, I don't sense that you are the evil sort—I would assuredly know—which makes me spin with wonder about how you were able to see me in the sky."

Theo spit and wiped his mouth. "What's it do? I'm meanin', besides takin' me from home."

The man leaped to his feet and thoughtfully stroked his chin. He nodded toward the village. "Keep watching."

Without warning, the blackness promptly descended

upon the village. Flowers lost their glow and withered. The sun became a pale ball in the sky. Shrieks of confusion could be heard, mostly from the little ones.

Theo lowered his eyes at the man in the top hat.

The man grinned. "Oh, it gets better."

A black fog began to move about the ground with a sinister intelligence, darting and rolling. It tore at the villager's clothing, stripping them naked before dragging them down into the shadows. Livestock bellowed in the mix. Then the children.

The man licked his lips. "Are you worried the mist will take the children?"

"Yes, and I ain't goin' to just sit and watch it neither," Theo said.

The man raised his eyebrows and cocked his head. "That's heroic and ridiculous. But, you need not worry about the wee ones."

He didn't believe the man.

"You're such a skeptic. Look," the man gestured with his head, "look upon the tables, lad."

The children were huddled together atop the tables like kittens surrounded by a pack of jackals. The food was smashed and wasted, much of it covering their bodies.

Theo balled up his fist. Rage and fear burned his insides.

"See? Do you see?" the man said playfully. "They can't have the children. It is forbidden." He rubbed his hands briskly. "But, the mist would *relish* the chance to taste their sweet and succulent flesh. I have it on good authority, they taste a bit like chicken."

Pointing a finger, Theo said, "Mister, you're plum wicked."

"Yes, I am *most* wicked. It is my essence." He bowed.

"Well, I ain't like you. I ain't a coward," Theo said. "I'm goin' down there to help them kids."

"By all means, *go*. Play the part of the knight in shining armor."

Theo turned away from the man and ran to the village, stopping just outside the walls. He was on the edge of the madness. Almost nose to nose with it. The nightmare seemed confined to the village. The fog crawled along the edges of the town, never going beyond a wall or entryway. It reminded him of what a black-widow spider looked like in a jar. Trapped, but nasty nonetheless.

Theo moved closer.

The mist had grown even thicker, giving it a greasy look. It disgusted Theo.

"*Brave heart*, indeed," the man said.

Theo closed his eyes. "Lord, I'm pretty sure I'm dreamin'...or I'm crazy. I ain't sure what to think to tell ya the truth. But, I'm goin' in there and I aim to trust in ya..." He paused. "It'd be nice if this was just a dream."

"Pathetic." The man brushed at something on his coat sleeve.

Theo said, "I wish you'd a left me alone."

The man smiled.

Theo looked at the frightened children, let out some air, then crossed into the other world. He was in the jar with the spider.

He experienced a most foul odor as he crossed over. It smelled like several hundred head of rotting cattle. It hit Theo in the gut, bending him over. As the vomit spewed, he looked down into the mist, watching it spin circles around his feet, wondering why it had not already attacked. The others were taken down in haste. Maybe the mist didn't want to be puked on. Theo laughed at such a silly notion.

When it attacked, it was fast. It quickly draped its coldness around him, stinging him with feelings of despair. It clouded his mind and clogged his heart. He felt as if the eyes of God were turned away from him, which made him recall the man's eyes.

Horrible, unimaginable thoughts began to spot his mind. Awful things. Things about the children. Things he wanted to do to them. Yet, his faith remained strong as oak pressed against a storm. Something pure, something inside him, waited for the Lord to intervene. To ride into town on a white stallion with His host of angels. He believed this even while his flesh was fondled by sticky, unseen hands. A sensation he found to be ashamedly delicious.

"Take my hand," said a silky voice. The voice was unfamiliar. It immediately soothed him and cut through the darkness, like a reaping hook clearing away weeds.

The mist released him, dispersing as smoke in the wind. He lay on the ground among scattered chunks of flesh and bone, his body slick with blood. Standing over him was a beautiful woman with emerald-green eyes, her hand extended to Theo, while in her other she held a garment.

Theo quickly realized he was naked.

"Take my hand, Theophilus," she spoke.

Theo covered his crotch, mortified.

She turned her head. "I will not look, but you should get out of the filth."

He took her hand, and she pulled him upright. Keeping her eyes averted, she handed him the garment. He quickly wrapped it around his body, immediately feeling its warmth. It was made of a strange material, soft and luminescent. The woman wore similar attire.

He looked for the children and saw they were gone.

"Do not worry. They are safe," said the woman.

"Who are ya?" he asked.

"Not *who*, dear boy. You should ask her *what* she is." It was the man. He walked toward Theo and the woman.

Smiling, the woman said to Theo, "I was sent to help you."

"Are you an angel?"

"No," the man interrupted. "She's an interfering whore."

"I'm taking him home, Apollyon."

Apollyon. He had a name.

Apollyon pointed a finger at the woman. "Wait. There is more to this little shit than faith. He was failing miserably in his faith, yet you still came to his aid. And his most clever trick? He was able to *see*."

"You are wrong about his faith. As your demons seduced him he believed he would be protected." she said. "But, you are proper in thinking he holds more than faith. He is from a lineage of holiness, marked many years ago. He has a gift for seeing what most cannot. He has been unmindful of his power, as have many." She motioned to the carnage that lay about their feet. "This is why he did not meet the same fate as these people."

A small, guttural sound passed through Apollyon's lips.

"I tell you, your demons were fearful of him."

"I think not, whore."

"I do not wish to debate this with you. I am taking him away."

Apollyon moved menacingly toward the woman. Murder gleamed in his eyes.

"You realize there would be consequences if you carried out your cruel thoughts," she said.

"Yes, I am *abundantly* aware," he replied. "But, if I might, I would like to share my thoughts."

She dismissed him with a wave. "There is no need."

"Maybe the lad would like to be indulged."

"No indulgin' needed here, mister," said Theo. "I just want go home, or wake up."

"Oh, yes. Go back to shoveling shit on the farm," said Apollyon.

A howling sounded from one of the cottages. The same sound Theo heard from the woods.

"Come, we should go," the woman said.

"I have to see," Theo said.

"I do not agree. We must take leave," said the woman.

Apollyon smiled. "Come, come, now. Let the boy see. I've promised him I would prove this is a reality, and I fear

I've failed miserably."

A scream followed the howling, full of pain and fear. It was a man's plea.

The woman gently took hold of Theo's shoulder "It is too late for that person. He is the one responsible for bringing Hell upon these villagers."

Theo, having never been accused of listening to good sense, ran to the cottage. He had come this far, and he wanted answers to his questions. He ran with imaginary blinders, trying to avoid the butchery. This tactic nearly had him down in the bloody mush. His foot slipped on a piece of glop, sending him into less than acrobatic movements.

"Yes, grace to compliment bravery," Apollyon goaded.

Theo arrived at the home, and noticed the absence of a door. In its place was a darkened maw. He thought of a dark hole, full of snakes.

He was wrong. What lived in the hole was far worse.

Wet, croaky sounds reached his ears.

I have to see.

Movement. Something sliding along the floor.

I have to see.

The man inside screamed and cursed.

Lord, help me. I have to see.

"Theophilus." It was the woman. She stood behind him.

"What's in there?" he asked in a shaky whisper.

The woman reached into her clothing and retrieved a dagger. The blade glistened as if made of diamonds, radiating and glowing. Without speaking she knelt at the doorway and drove the blade into the ground. This illuminated the darkness, revealing to Theo what he so desperately needed to see.

What he saw was abhorrent and disturbing. An old woman lay in a corner, her eyes turned slate-gray and lifeless. Theo figured it was probably for the best. From her womb crawled scaly creatures the size of month-old pups. They had no eyes. What he assumed was a nose was two, raw openings with a yellow discharge. Most discernible was the mouth. Freakishly large with a jutting chin. Rows of jagged teeth gnashed. As they made their way out of the woman they crawled along with elongated, bony arms, for they had no legs. It was understandable as to why the man was screaming. They were feeding on his flesh in growing numbers.

Apollyon laughed, spraying malice as he brayed. "Now, *that* is loyalty. He gave his life for eternal damnation. All for me and my undeniable greatness." He walked into the dwelling and kicked the old woman. He shook his head. "Poor dear. It was his mother. What would you be willing to wager she did not foresee this happening?"

The creatures began to wail, sounding like sickly new-born babies.

Apollyon looked at Theo and then said to the little beasts, "Still hungry? Maybe I can talk our accidental tourist into offering up a small nibble."

Theo backed from the doorway. The creatures laughed, high-pitched and raspy.

"Enough." The woman snatched her dagger up and turned to Theo. "Have you seen enough?"

He had seen enough. It was all a tattoo on his brain. "Yes, ma'am. I'm more than ready to go."

She put her arms around Theo and walked him away from the rankness.

Apollyon called out to her. "How is it that I was unaware of his *distinction*? I knew his name from the instant I set my eyes on him, but nothing else. It certainly is news to me that he is marked as holy. Why is that?"

"I am not able, nor am I willing, to answer your questions," she replied.

"Well, I certainly know of him now. I'll make certain to keep a watchful eye on his kin."

The thought of Apollyon watching his family hung in his belly. Terrified him.

"Continue walking," she told Theo. "Do not let him provoke you, and do not look back."

He nodded his head and obeyed.

"It's been a scant few that have escaped me," Apollyon said. "I'll remember you, boy."

That's fine, Theo thought to himself, *I ain't likely to forget you neither.*

Chapter Three

Mountaintop Madness and Death

THEY WERE BEYOND the village and walking up the dirt-road. Several minutes passed before a word was spoken.

Theo broke the silence. "You're an angel, ain't ya."

"Yes, I am an angel."

"That's amazin' to me."

"I have been familiar with you since your birth."

"Protectin' me and such?"

"Yes, but I can only do so much. If you decided to fling yourself from a cliff, the most I would be able to do is nudge your common sense." His angel gave a slight smile. "Which is no easy task. You rather enjoy crushing barriers."

"But, you helped me back yonder. That wasn't just you nudgin' my common sense."

"I can physically aid you, yes. But, only within this realm and circumstance."

"I don't understand."

She stopped them next to the tree that Theo had experienced earlier. "You stepped into a supernatural realm, conjured by a sorcerer. I am a supernatural creature."

"Supernatural?"

"The simplest example would be what you are currently experiencing. Something otherworldly."

Theo studied the unusual tree. "This tree is otherworldly, right?"

"Yes. Most, certainly."

He put a closer eye to the tree, studying it. The tree had no bark. The pinkish color was the result of having skin, instead of bark. Veins, blue and stringy, ran through it like worms. It served as a proper summation of everything Theo experienced on this day.

Theo looked behind his angel. "Where are your wings?"

She took his arm. "Theophilus, we must keep moving."

"All right," he said. "But, don't ya have wings?"

"Yes. I have them beneath my clothing."

"That's amazin'. Would you mind show—"

With a burst of mystifying speed, the angel grabbed Theo and ran up the road. They glided as if they were a pair of Arabian stallions caught in the throes of a full-on stride. The scenery whisked past them in a messy collage of colors. Small vibrations tickled and ebbed throughout Theo's body, rattling his teeth. He began to worry less about Apollyon's village of horror, and more about what lay ahead.

And then, they suddenly stopped.

They now stood on an outstretched cliff, extending from a mountain top. It was one of many mountain tops. All of them stabbing upward, bullying their way into the clouds. It was all there was to see. Just gray, stark mountains. Snow-peaked and craggy. It was beautiful.

"I ain't ever seen anything like it," Theo said. "I was once in Colorado, but this here is somethin' else."

"It is where my kind gather."

He walked a few steps toward the edge of the cliff, wondering if he had the courage to look down, then decided that he had seen enough. Enough for a lifetime. "You and other angels? Ya'll gather here?"

"Yes," she said.

He wondered what angels talked about.

Wings suddenly appeared from behind the angel, springing loose of their confines. Glowing feathers, white as snow, adorned the powerful wings.

Theo stood in awe. "They're bigger'n you."

"Theo, it is time to send you home."

He took the angel's beauty into his mind. He wanted to lock the memory away for safe keeping. Something to reminisce over. But, that was for later. He was eager for home.

"Walk to the edge of the cliff," said the angel.

He had no reason not to trust the angel, so to the edge he went. A stairway lined with gold descended down into the mix of mountains. The stairway disappeared into giant clouds. A plunge into the unknown.

It was a mighty long way to the bottom. If indeed, there was a bottom.

"The stairway will take you home," said the angel.

"Looks like a long walk. How long of a walk is it goin' to be?"

"Not long."

Theo eyeballed the stairs and raised a skeptical eyebrow. "Well, if you say so."

He turned to offer his thanks and bid his farewell. He was surprised to see a multitude of other angels standing behind his angel. Their wings shone like a full moon on a cloudless night. Some wore a golden armor that covered most of their body, with swords tethered to their legs. Theo thought it made them look like biblical gunslingers.

"I still ain't sure this ain't a dream." He looked at his Heavenly audience. All of them glowing and majestic. "Folks'll think I'm touched in the head if I tell this story."

"That would depend on to whom you told the story," his angel said.

A roar, full of menace, moved like hot steam through the air. It came from beyond the mountains, echoing a baritone ferocity. Theo felt the mountain tremble beneath his bare feet. The angels spread their wings and unsheathed immense swords. The flapping of their wings became a strong wind in Theo's ears. Gone from the angel's faces were the peaceful expressions of love and grace. A warrior's mask was instead present, showing gritted teeth and narrowed eyes.

"You must go," his angel said. "Go, now."

With no hesitation, he ran down the stairs, gripping the railing with anxious hands. Another roar bounced from the mountain tops, causing the steps to shake.

A trumpet blast came about as an ear-splitting arrow of pain, ice-picking into Theo's head. He checked his ears for blood, fearing he would surely go deaf. This fear became smoothed away, as he was able to hear the second blast just as clear.

He began taking the steps three at a time, hopeful he wouldn't stumble. A fall from such a height would be a long death. All that time to think about what was coming. Waiting for your guts to pop open and your head to split like a melon. This was the image of death that surfaced.

He was fifty yards away and closing in on the cloud that was hogging the stairway, when a metallic clash rang out, sending a vibrating din upon Theo. It disoriented his whereabouts. He stopped and shook his head.

"Lawsy," he said under his breath. "I ain't goin' to have a lick of hearin' left."

Thunder shook the stairway, and a white light shone upon his back, prickling his skin and warming his clothing, casting his shadow across the awaiting cloud. More light and sounds came. Clearly, something explosive was going on behind him.

Screams came next. Screams filled with enough pain and sorrow to make the day's earlier escapades seem unexceptional. It stopped him in his tracks. He turned to look.

He once again beheld a sight that ripped at his sanity. It was becoming a case of old hat.

Angels lay littered upon the rocky landscape, their clothing stained with blood. Several had spears protruding from their broken bodies, and some were decapitated. Not all were the shiny, beautiful angels Theo was familiar with. Black-winged creatures, pale and dark-haired, joined the others in the ugly display. Many bodies lay stacked together in some instances. It was a morbid portrait of death.

He looked to the sky and saw the angels battling, swinging their swords and shouting in voices that shook the air. As an angel perished, it unleashed the pitiful screams he heard, then fell onto the rocky terrain. The explosions and flashes of light occurred when their weapons met, or when two bodies smashed headlong into one another as flesh and blood battering rams. It was violent and disturbing. It brought tears to Theo's eyes.

He turned, ready to stay on his path to home, but he stopped and looked back again. It was, after all, his accursed nature.

"Holy, shit," he muttered.

One of the black-winged creatures had broken away from the mass, zeroing in on Theo. Its wings were pinned back, and it was moving with the grace and speed of an airborne predator. Theo felt like a rodent, ready to be gobbled up by a hawk. Like any rodent, he turned and ran. Unfortunately, his footing gave way and became entangled within his new clothing. He fell roughly down the stairs, headfirst and in painful fashion. He threw his arms out in front, trying to protect his face, which for the most part worked. But, he still rolled and bounced down the stairway, his arms and legs bearing the brunt. All the while he tumbled, he readied himself for the creature's attack. Fear stuck to the back of his head, provoking a scream that sounded like that of an excited school girl.

He reached blindly for the railing, and surprised himself as he was able find it. His grip was precarious, three outstretched fingers, but it was enough stop his descent. This allowed him to place himself so that he might look his attacker in the eyes.

His new perspective did nothing to stall his fear.

He could see the creature's features clear as crystal. A pale, crooked face with deep-set eyes that were surely borrowed from Apollyon. They bore the same blackness and corruption, shining like obsidian from a sun-bleached skull. It had a flowing black mane, flickering as if it were a flame. No top hats.

Theo figured he had seconds of life left. The dark figure grinned and withdrew a sword. It spoke to him in unintelligible gibberish, discharging a yellow spittle.

Theo steeled himself, hoping for a quick end. Then something unexpected occurred.

The demon's head became detached and quickly plummeted, a trail of blood chasing its host like a gory comet. The demon's body remained aloft, thrashing blindly with the sword, its wings continuing to beat the air. Theo managed to steady himself and back away, moving several steps. A shining blur passed before his eyes and traveled to the headless being. It was a spear, long and effective, as it entered the armpit area and came out through the gaping wound between the flapping thing's shoulders. The creature ceased to move and dropped like a sack of rocks, disappearing into the abyss.

"There comes a point when bravery and curiosity, simply become nonsensical acts of stupidity," said a new voice. It was soft yet authoritative, not a woman's voice.

Air left Theo's lungs as if he were in a vise. He whipped his head in both directions, expecting the usual array of blood and death. "Good, Lord. Who wants to kill me now?"

"Certainly not me," said the voice.

"Where are ya?" Theo's voice became ragged with anxiety and mental exhaustion.

A strong breeze blew through Theo's hair, cooling the gathered sweat on his forehead. Then a magnificent angel appeared from overhead, landing just a few feet away. A heavy armor clung to its body, brandished with several weapons, mostly arrows and swords, but Theo was certain he saw what looked like guns of some sort.

"Did you chop that thing's head off?" Theo asked.

"Yes, I did."

"I surely thank ya."

"I should tell you to think nothing of it," the angel said. "But, in your case, I am advising that you remember this event. You are far too inquisitive."

"That ain't the first time I've heard that."

"I am inclined to believe you," the angel replied.

Battle sounds washed down upon the two, pulling their eyes skyward. The angel pointed at Theo. "The Evil One is curious about you, which is the cause of the current conflict."

Theo wanted to ask the angel *why*. Why would Apollyon want to know anything about the son of an Oklahoma farmer? But his being tired, dazed, and crazed, superseded his inquisitive nature.

The angel pulled a gun with a flared barrel from an aged, leather holster and fired it toward the middle of the carnage. A wide spray of fire and smoke blasted forth, smearing the sky like crumbled charcoal on linen. Small flecks of black emerged from the blast and moved as a swarm, streaking into the overhead fray. More horrid screams quickly ensued as the demon's bodies began to fall apart, dripping as wax from a burning candle. The angel holstered his weapon and looked at Theo. "Have you had your fill of adventure for the day?"

"Yep," he said.

"Good. Turn around, and you'll see a cloud coming to greet you."

Theo was surprised to see the same cloud he was chasing earlier. However, it was now rolling up the stairs to *him*. "Is that cloud goin' to get me outta' here?"

"Yes," said the angel. "It most certainly will."

Without warning, the angel grabbed Theo by the arm and tossed him in the air. He fell into the clouds, flailing his arms like a bird that has suddenly forgotten how to fly.

Why had his heroic angel saved him from a demon if he intended to throw him to his death anyway?

Theo's world turned to white as he entered the clouds. Wind whipped at him, while his mind became crazed with images of splattered road kill. He was helpless and terrified. He screamed a prayer at God. Faith had kept him alive thus far, albeit, he had a growing suspicion he was probably terminally mad.

A light, bright and out of place in the clouds, was blinding him. He turned his head and covered his eyes with his arms and kicked at the light. His cheeks stung with light blows, and he heard his name being shouted. His nightmare would never end it seemed.

Theo.

"Leave me be, damn it!"

Theo...Theo...Theo...

A familiar smell jostled his senses.

Another blow to his right cheek, much harder this time.

"Theo!"

Cognition came rushing like a river. He uncovered his face and squinted against the light.

"Boy, just what in tarnation has got into you? You're wallerin' around in cow shit, son."

So, *that* was the familiar smell.

"And why are ya wearin' a sheet out here?"

"Daddy? Is that really you?" asked Theo.

"Uh, *yeah*. Who else would I be? Are ya drunk, boy?"

Theo quickly understood he was on the ground. He sat up and looked around, first at his father holding the lantern, and then at the pasture. The sun was gone, so he saw little of anything outside the lantern's glow.

"What time is it?" Theo asked.

"Just nigh of midnight." His father shook his head in disbelief. The lantern made a sweep of Theo's head. His father suddenly jerked away, his mouth shaped like a donut. "What the...your hair. What in blue blazes is goin' on, Theo?"

Theo reached up and felt his hair, finding clumped cow manure. "It's cow crap."

"No, not the crap. It's your hair. It's turned white as a porcelain tub."

Theo frowned quizzically. "What do you mean?"

"I mean your hair is white."

Theo stood and began brushing at his garment, which had lost most of its ethereal glow. Then, it all crashed together. All of it was real, everything he went through. The garment authenticated his experience.

"Daddy, you ain't goin' to believe what happened to me," he said, his voice filling with emotion. Tears formed in his eyes.

His father's eyes softened in concern. "What is it, son? I been searchin' the pasture and woods for hours. Been by this very area more than once. I didn't see hide nor hair of you. And your clothes, your hair..." He shook his head. "You can explain later. Let's get you home. I don't imagine it's any fun havin' cow shit all over yourself."

Theo wiped his eyes and sucked in the aromas of home. The grass, the many different trees, the sweetness of the turned soil. The manure.

"I reckon a bath would be nice," Theo said.

"Yep. I reckon it would, son."

"Daddy?"

"Yeah?"

"I ain't crazy."

"I never said you were."

"Yeah I know it, but..." Theo felt a cramp rising in his throat, so he paused and gathered himself before continuing. Finally, he said, "You might want to smack me in the head after I tell ya my tale. It's goin' to be the craziest thing you ever did hear of, I'm promisin' ya."

"C'mon," his father said. He lead them through the dark with the lantern. "I ain't goin' to smack ya, but I'm sure goin' to throw some water on ya. Bless your heart, but, you smell like you fell out of a cow's ass."

Theo stopped and touched his father on the shoulder. "Look out for snakes, they were all over the place earlier today."

His father reached into a front pocket and pulled out a pistol, waving it. "I got the snakes covered. Your mama mentioned somethin' about snakes earlier today."

"I ain't surprised. There was plenty of 'em crawlin' around."

"Let's go on to the house, get you cleaned up, then you can tell me everything that's on your mind."

Theo looked to the Victorian home that lay at the bottom of the hill. An amber glow spilled from the windows, creating pools of warmth and surety. A welcoming beacon. "I sure did miss this place."

"I ain't even goin' to try to figure what you mean by that." Theo's father raised the lantern higher.

"Well—"

"Hold that thought, Theo. I'm thinkin' it would be best to tell this story to your mama and me at the same time."

"All right, then."

They trudged across the pasture on a moonless, dark night in silence. Theo had things to tell. Things that *had* to be told, and the silence was like needles under his skin. But, he held his tongue and waited, allowing the house to guide them along.

Theo trailed his father to a horse tank on the north side of the barn that hunkered beneath an elm tree. His father hung the lantern from a limb and pointed. "Get on in. I was plannin' on gettin' in there myself tomorrow mornin', but I reckon you need it worse than me. I'll bring out some clean clothes for ya. Let's get ya halfway presentable for your mama."

Theo stripped off his garment and almost let it fall to the ground. There was something special about it, this strange *sheet*. It would be blasphemous to intentionally soil the cloth, so he hung it near the lantern before sliding into the cool water.

He submerged his head and scrubbed his hair, working on the manure. It was an action that thoroughly disgusted him, but knowing he had the stuff fixed to his scalp and hair was much more disturbing, so he scrubbed harder. Upon resurfacing, he blew the water away from his lips and rubbed his face. He closed his eyes and leaned back, letting his body go slack. His arms became floating pieces of drift wood, while his mind tried to slow its shrew's pace of musing. The shrill serenade of crickets and tree frogs set him in a trance, threatening to induce him into a much needed sleep. His arms quietly ached from the scrapes and bruising he had collected, furthering his belief that his experiences were no mere nightmares or tricks of his imagination. He was *not* insane.

He slipped into a dreamless sleep, deep and dark. Perhaps it was his body's way of healing mind and soul, to send him to such depths. It certainly felt healing, until his slumber abruptly dissipated. His eyes popped open, while his brain took account of his surroundings. Something had disturbed his sleep.

The crickets and tree frogs had stopped singing. An eerie silence occupied the air. Theo grabbed the sides of the tank and raised himself up to look around. His heart pounded. What had silenced the night-time chorus? A twig snapped from the tree that hung over him. He was preparing to jump from the water and streak to the house, when he heard the screen door bang against the door frame. His father's silhouette moved toward him, then the crickets came back for an encore performance.

The thirty or so seconds it took for his father to reach the horse tank seemed an eternity.

"Lordy, I'm jumpy," Theo said.

His father placed the clean clothes into the crook of the tree, along with a towel. He held something else in his hand, something with a long handle. "Well, I imagine this here ain't goin' to help with that."

"What is it?"

His father held the object out to Theo and grimaced. "It's a mirror, son. I'll get the lantern."

"Do I still have crap in my hair?"

"Nah, it looks like you got it all." He swung the lantern around to Theo's face.

"Oh, you said my hair was...white. Is that it?"

"Uh-huh, that's *it* all right." His father handed him the mirror, then held the lantern next to Theo's face, dramatically illuminating his new hair. "Are ya feelin' any less jumpy?"

"Holy, shit," said Theo.

"Kinda' my sentiments, too."

Theo rubbed a hand across the damp hair. "It's white as snow."

"Yep."

Theo frowned. "How'd that happen?"

"Why are ya askin' *me* for?"

"I can't explain it." Theo handed the mirror back to his father and asked for the towel. "Maybe Mama will have an idea after I tell ya'll everything."

His father looked up at the stars. "Son, I ain't all that sure I'm ready for that."

Theo followed his father's eyes. "Do ya see something up there? In the sky?"

"Nope, just stars."

"Well, stars ain't all that's up there."

His father ignored the comment and tapped the horse tank. "C'mon, get dressed. Your mama wants to make sure you're all right. I'll walk with ya back to the house."

Theo quickly exited the water and dried off, then slipped into the clothes. As he walked to the house he became excited and hungry for home. He reached the front porch and turned to look up at the sky. A backdrop of diamonds thrown against a black canvas. A large patch of darkness glared among the stars, and it didn't allow for diamonds in its realm. Theo saw it as plain as a daisy in his mother's garden.

"What are ya lookin' at?" His father stood at the front door, his hand on the knob.

"Never mind," said Theo. "Let's go inside."

His father breathed out a heavy load of air and opened the door. "Well, honey," he said to his wife, "brace yourself."

Theo walked into the front room and immediately drank of its comforts. His mother's knick-knack shelves filled with trinkets. The ceramic dolls. The oil paintings that hung like stoic sentinels. His mother sat on a divan wearing a night-gown, her eyes wide. She kept her composure and remained sitting with her legs crossed and her hands resting upon a knee. Her lovely, black hair hung loosely about her shoulders. To see his mother's hair loose was rare. Unless she was sleeping, it was drawn in a ball against her skull. "Theo, what happened?" she asked.

"Can we sit at the kitchen table?" said Theo.

His mother moved toward him, her face frozen. She stood back and looked at her son's hair, then hugged him. "Theophilus, let's go to the kitchen."

Theo and his father followed her into the kitchen, watching her as she daintily sat at the table. They each joined her, with Theo being the closest.

"Well," his father rubbed his eyes, "this ought to be good."

Theo abruptly left the table and walked to a water basin in the corner of the room. He splashed water on his face and ran it through his hair. He was suddenly feeling hot. With his back to them, he said, "I've been chompin' at the bit to tell y'all this, but now that it's come down to the nitty-gritty I'm afraid to."

"Why?" his mother asked.

He turned to them and dried his face with a shirt sleeve. "Cause ya'll are goin' to think somethin's wrong with me, mostly."

She looked at his father before saying, "No, we most

certainly will *not* think something's wrong with you. Isn't that right, Chester?"

"Nah, of course not."

"Ya'll say that *now*. But, just wait 'til I'm done," Theo said. "It's a humdinger I'm tellin' ya."

Chester widened his arms and gestured for Theo to get on with it. "Don't worry about us thinkin' you're crazy. We're happy that you ain't layin' in a gulley with a broke neck. I looked high and low for ya all damn day, and we got a bit worrisome for ya. So, go ahead and get this out of your system."

"I'm goin' to have to stand."

"Then don't sit," said Chester.

He looked at his parents, trying to read what was on their minds. His father's brow was a veneer of worry. If it came down to the guts of things, Theo figured his father could live without knowing. However, his mother was the flip side of the coin. She sat composed and cool, wanting to know. Maybe their perspectives would change.

Theo opened his mouth, stalled a moment, then let the tale surge forth. His words were like water jetting from a fractured dike.

Chapter Four

No Storks Here

A WHISTLE ESCAPED his father's lips, while his mother sat with her chin resting upon a petite fist. Neither said a word.

Theo folded his arms and nodded. "Yep, ya'll think I'm crazy."

"Lordy, Lordy, son," said Chester.

"Theo," his mother asked, "did you bump your head? Your daddy found you...passed out in the north pasture."

"Yes, I *did* bump my head, but that don't mean it ain't true."

"And you weren't drinkin'?" Chester asked.

"You're the only one who drinks around here, Chester," his mother snapped.

Chester raised his arms in surrender. "Shit, I'm just tryin' to think of an explanation. Do you got anything better?"

"Chester, I've never heard of liquor turning one's hair white. Have *you*?"

"Nope, can't say that I have."

Theo slammed his palms on the table and leaned on it. "I've already told ya what happened. I cain't explain my hair, but everything I said was true."

"Settle down, son. This is a lot to take in." Chester pointed a finger at Theo and nudged a chair with his foot. "Have a seat."

Theo sighed and sat.

Chester looked across the table at his wife, his eyes pleading. "Lucille, you ain't said an awful lot. What do you think happened?"

She took Theo's hand. "Theophilus, what did you do with the...sheet?"

"It's hangin' on a tree behind the barn."

She turned to her husband, giving him a strange look. "You two stay put. I have something to show you, Theo."

"What?" Chester asked. "What are you *talkin'* about? Why can't we all get some sleep and worry about this in the mornin'?"

Ignoring her husband, she left the room. They soon heard her small footfalls upon the staircase.

"What do ya reckon she wants to show me?" asked Theo.

Chester shrugged. "Son, I ain't got the foggiest idea."

Theo cleared his throat and fidgeted his hands. "Daddy, I was thinkin' that I ought to tell the preacher about this."

"Preacher John?"

"Yep."

"Son, you just cain't go tellin' folks a story like this."

"But Preacher John ain't like other folks. He's a preacher."

"Listen." Chester leaned toward Theo. "That don't make a bit of difference. Preacher, doctor, or school teacher. It'll sound crazy to all of 'em. Are ya *wantin'* a room at the looney bin?"

Theo folded his arms and leaned back in his chair. "Preacher John wouldn't say nothin'."

"Son, do your mama and me a favor and....cool your heels on this."

A muted clatter of noise scratched at the kitchen ceiling, followed by a quiet thud. The woman of the house was moving furniture.

Theo and his father tilted their heads up. "I honestly don't know what your mama is up to."

"Daddy?"

"Yep."

"Do ya believe me at all? Maybe, just a *tiny* bit?"

Chester scratched his head. "Well, Theo, I believe that somethin' strange happened, and that's about as far as I'm willin' to go."

"So, ya don't think I'm crazy?" Theo asked.

"Nah. I've seen crazy, son," Chester said.

"When all of that was happening, I figured I was either dead or off the deep end. I almost hoped I *was* dead."

"Don't ever say that," Chester said. He grabbed Theo by the collar, looking him in the eyes. "Your mama and me would be haunted forever. You ain't supposed to die before us."

The staircase squeaked a protest as Lucille descended. Chester and Theo slumped into their chairs and waited for her arrival.

She entered the room carrying a wooden box. It was small, about the size of a bread-box, resembling a chest. She set it on the table and opened the lid, then retrieved a shiny white cloth. "Is this what Theo was wearing, Chester?"

Theo answered for his father, his voice brimming with excitement. "Yep! That's it. Ain't I right, Daddy?" He took the material into his hands and rubbed it with his fingertips, then held it out and dangled it.

Chester gaped at his wife, but said nothing.

"Where'd you get this, Mama?" asked Theo.

Casting a sidelong glance at Chester, she said, "It was your baby blanket."

Chester shifted uneasily in his chair.

"What?" Theo said.

Chester buried his face in his hands, mumbling.

"Boys, let's look at the other one," Lucille said. A light twinkled in her eyes, like a child's on Christmas Eve.

Finally, Chester spoke up, waving a hand in the air.

"*Lucille*, what are ya doin'?"

Making little of her husband's protests, she grabbed Theo by the arm and hurriedly left the room. Chester, saying his wife's name over and over, chased after the two, stopping them at the front door.

"Lucille...*look* at me." Chester reached and stroked her left cheek.

"Chester, it's worth looking into," she said.

Theo saw worry seep into his father's eyes, an emotional characteristic that seemed alien within his father. The man, for the most part, was continually humorous and sensible.

"What are ya'll talkin' about?" asked Theo. "Daddy, what's wrong?"

"Theo," his mother asked. "Would you please fetch the sheet?"

Theo nodded and opened the front door. He paused, as if to speak, then ran across the porch and leaped from the deck. The strange cloth could be seen from where Theo stood, its luminance returning to shine like white fire.

He stole a fleeting glimpse of the blackness in the sky. It had fattened into an immense cancer, choking the life from the stars. It moved like a living thing.

He quickly averted his eyes away from the blackness, fearful of its power. It occurred to him that someone was conjuring the blackness. According to Apollyon, this is how the blackness is born.

Straight from the devil's mouth.

But, *who? Who* would know of such a thing as conjuring?

No one lived in that direction. It was a mass of trees that stretched for miles. Not even the most ambitious land owner would want to undertake the task of excavating so many trees. Their closest neighbors, the Millers, lived four miles in the opposite direction. Theo and his family were alone for the most part. Not a neighbor within shouting distance for certain.

The air became frozen, as a spooky quiet settled in. It was the same quiet Theo experienced while he bathed in the horse tank.

Theo ran to the hanging cloth, his footfalls sounding hollow among the eerie silence. He snatched it from the tree and draped it around his shoulders, then ran toward the house. He prayed nothing was behind him, gaining ground. Some drooling demon, wanting nothing more than to gorge itself on his flesh.

He jumped as he reached the front steps, clearing them, then burst through the front door. He slammed the door, still feeling as if unseen eyes were boring into his back.

"Here," Theo said, pulling the cloth loose, "this here is the same as what you've got, Mama."

Theo held the cloth out to his mother. She reached for it and hesitated. It was a split second, but Theo noticed.

"What's wrong?"

His mother took the cloth and held it against her cheek. She closed her eyes, just as a tear surfaced. It moved down her cheek in a perfect line.

Chester let a sigh. "Son, your mama and me have somethin' to tell ya. You'd best sit down for this."

Theo didn't want to know. They could keep this information to themselves forever.

"Son," his father started, "do you know how much you mean to your mama and me?"

"Well, yeah."

"We love you more than anyone could ever love a son," his mother said.

"And nothing will ever change that. Not ever," said his father.

Lordy, just get to it.

"There ain't no easy way to say this to ya," said his father. "So, I'm goin' to just spit it out."

Here it comes.

"You...ain't...." His father stopped and took his

mother's hand, squeezing it.

"Chester, go ahead," said his mother.

Chester groaned. "Theo, you ain't *really*...uh, from us."

Theo tightened his face. "What does that mean?"

"It means, we found you on the front porch, wrapped in this here strange material, layin' in a wood crate."

"Wait." Theo shook his head side to side. "I don't understand."

His mother stood and embraced Theo, kissing his cheek. "Theo," she said smiling, "you're our miracle child."

"Mama, what are you talkin' about? I ain't no miracle child."

He twisted free of his mother's embrace, blindly backing away, overturning a lamp. The lamp broke against the wood flooring, scattering delicate shards of china and splashing lamp oil.

Chester opened the front door and pointed first to Theo, and then outside. "Let's go out to the porch. It'll be all right, trust me."

Theo stared at the lamp's broken pieces. It was once a family heirloom, ages old.

"I'm sorry about the lamp," he said to his mother.

"I'm not worried about the lamp, Theo. I'm worried about you, my son."

Chester said, "Let's go outside. It's just a lamp."

Theo gingerly stepped across the ruined lamp and went outside. He grabbed a weathered wicker chair and dragged it across the deck, then collapsed into a heap.

His father shut the door and lit a lamp, placing it at Theo's feet. He leaned against a pillar and folded his arms. "Well, first of all...I'm sorry you found out like this. I reckon it would have happened eventually, but not like this."

"What does Mama mean, sayin' I'm a *miracle* child? And what do you mean when you say I ain't from ya'll?"

Chester rubbed his lips together, thinking. "About thirteen years ago your mama gave birth to a child. It was a boy, but...it was born dead. Stillborn they call it."

Chester slid his back down the pillar until he was sitting. "It was just your mama and me. There weren't no doctor to help out, and we were pretty choked up if ya can imagine. It was a horrible night for a while, I promise ya son."

Chester closed his eyes, as he replayed the events.

"Then a storm came around, real sudden like. A real crazy kinda' storm. Thunder and lightnin' like I ain't ever seen and winds like a twister." He licked his lips and brought his knees close to his body. "And then...there was a loud knockin' at the front door. I mean, it sounded like someone was working the door over with a sledge hammer. So, I tell your mama I need to find out who was wailin' on our door. So, I run downstairs."

"I'm standin' at the bottom of the stairs, catchin' glimpses of the front door in between lightnin' strikes. I swear to ya, ever time the door was struck it shook the house. The door was bowin' against the force, just strainin' to hold tight, ya know. I looked across the room at the shotgun hanging above the fireplace, then I ran to it."

"About the time I reached the middle of the room, there came a bolt of lightnin' that lit up the world. It blinded me for a bit, but not before I looked out the window. When I looked out I seen...these shadows. They were long and such, and I guess I sorta' figgered some folks were out in the yard. But, I don't know. There was somethin' strange about it."

As Theo sat and listened, a small seed of hope tried to take root. He was unsure as to *why*. He was, after all, attentively listening to the story of his not having shared a drop of genetic blood with his parents.

"Then, all of a sudden, the storm stopped. No wind, no thunder or lightnin', just real quiet. My sight was startin' to come back, so I pulled back the hammers on the shotgun and walked toward the door."

Again, the inexplicable aroma of hope wafted.

"I wasn't sure of what I was goin' to see when I opened that door, but my first inclination was to blow somethin' to Hell and back." Chester paused and scratched absently at his neck, grinning at Theo. "But, I opened the door and there ya were, wrapped up and layin' in an ole' crate."

Theo began to understand the odd spark of optimism he felt. It was because knowledge and understanding was driving itself upward, moving into place like a well-oiled gear.

"Daddy," Theo said. "This all makes sense now. What happened to me earlier today, and with what you're tellin' me. It's addin' up."

"Oh?" said Chester, raising an eyebrow. "You understand all of this? Addin' up ya say?"

Theo pushed himself out of the chair and ran to the front yard. He looked up and stared into the night sky. "Yep, I think I do. And I ain't even bothered too much about it. That's what 's weird, Daddy."

Chester got up and walked down the porch steps, his face full of joy upon hearing *Daddy*. He joined Theo on the lawn and looked into the sky. "Since you seem to know so much, how about explainin' it to me. 'Cause son, this is all a big heap of madness, there ain't none of it that makes sense to me. I knew somethin' was wrong when I found ya layin' in the pasture. Somethin' just kept naggin' me, and I reckon I was tryin' to pretend that your...arrival was normal and that you'd never find out. Your mama and me always planned to tell ya, but not like this."

Theo looked over at Chester. "It's all right. I ain't mad at ya."

Chester slowly nodded, obviously relieved.

"Can you see that?" Theo pointed to the west. "Up in the sky, right there?"

Chester squinted and shook his head. "I don't see

nothin', except for the stars."

"Well, there's somethin' up there and it's spreadin'." Theo pried his eyes away, once again fearful of its power.

"Theo, what's goin' on? You said you understood."

"Well, I'm pretty sure that I was brought here by angels."

"Angels?"

"Yep, and I know it's crazy soundin'."

"Well, crazy is startin' to be normal around this family."

A smile beamed across Theo's face, preceded by a chuckle. It felt *good* to still have mirth available.

The smile became infectious, and spread to Chester. His eyes watered and he reached out to his son, embracing him with sinewy arms.

"Let's go inside," said Chester. "Your mama will want to see how well you're takin' this."

Theo flashed another smile.

Chester pointed to Theo's mouth, moving his finger in a small circle. "You've got somethin' stuck in your teeth."

"Huh?"

"Your tooth, close to the front and over on the left side of your mouth. There's somethin' black stuck there."

Theo worked his tongue around his teeth, feeling for the object.

"A little more to the left...," Chester advised.

Theo managed to locate it and get it dislodged. He spit it into his hand and rubbed it between his fingers.

"What is it?" asked Chester.

"I don't know, but it feels sorta' slimy." Theo went to the lamp and eyeballed the thing closer.

"Well?"

Theo's eyes became excited. He knew exactly what he had in his hand. "It's a seed from that awful fruit I ate."

Chester cleared his throat.

Theo shook his head, grinning. His father still doubted him, even after spilling his own tale of strangeness. Of course, even if his father did believe him Theo was certain it would not be easily admitted.

"I'm goin' to show this to Mama, then I'm goin' to put it in a jar," said Theo.

Chester looked over Theo's shoulder. "Let me take a gander at it."

Theo flattened his hand against the light's glow, taking stock of his father's reaction.

"Well, I got to admit that it's strange lookin'," Chester offered.

"I think it looks like an egg-seed."

"Let me touch it," said Chester.

"Go on, then. Just be careful."

Chester wiped his hands on his clothes, then poked at the seed with an index finger. His eyes widened in surprise, and he jerked his hand away.

"Why'd ya do that for," Theo said.

"It's...warm. Damn near hot."

Theo quickly felt the heat burrow into his palm, burning like a barb from the sun. He held the seed tightly in his fist.

"Shit, drop the damn thing!" Chester said.

"Nope, I need to put it in something."

"Lordy have mercy, boy." Chester searched his overalls and found his leather gloves. He slid one of his hands into one and held it out to Theo. "Here, hurry up."

Theo let it fall onto the glove, and then rubbed his palm. He felt a small blister begin to blossom

"Well, that's interestin'." Chester scratched his head. It was a habit he often displayed when he was perplexed.

The front door opened and Lucille poked her head out. "Is everything all right out here?"

Theo went to his mother and hugged her, delighting in the smell of lilac powder.

"Well," Chester said, "I reckon it's as good as it can be, considerin' the circumstances."

"I need to run my hand under some cool water," Theo

said to his mother, showing her his wound.

She looked at her husband. "How did this happen?"

"Well," Chester glanced at his gloved fist, feeling the heat, "I'll show ya here in a minute. I need a mason jar in a hurry, darlin'."

"A mason jar? Whatever for, Chester?" She led Theo into the house and stopped to blow on Theo's hand.

"I said I needed it in a *hurry*, sweetie," urged Chester.

She reached at a small shelf next to the door. It was filled with an eclectic mix of curios, such as cows, sheep, and a family of ceramic honey bees. There was also one shot glass, which she snatched and held out to her husband. "Here you go. I'd rather it be used for something other than liquor."

"Afraid I cain't say the same." Chester dropped the seed into the glass and gently shook it. "Of course, I ain't likely to drink out of it anymore."

"Follow Theo and me into the kitchen. I've got to put some butter on his hand," said Lucille. "I want to know what happened."

Chester sat the shot glass on the kitchen table. "Lucille, that little seed is what burned him. It was lodged in his teeth. He's lucky it didn't brush against his gums, but it sure burnt the dickens out of his hand."

Theo walked to the water basin and submerged his hand. The coolness immediately reined in the sting.

Lucille leaned over the table, peering into the glass. She reached as if to touch it, but Chester stopped her. "No, no. I don't recommend ya do that. Just trust me on this."

"Where on earth did it come from?" she asked.

"From my mouth. It's from that nasty fruit I told ya about," Theo said.

"Well, isn't that interesting." She walked to her son. "Theo, did your daddy tell you...everything? You know, about the way you came to bless our lives?"

"Yep. Don't worry about nothin', Mama. Everything's goin' to be all right."

She kissed Theo on his ear. "Honey, it does my soul good to hear you say that."

Theo pulled his hand out and studied it. He slowly moved it, stretching it slightly. The blister appeared to be shrinking, and the pain was following suit. "I think my hand's gettin' better."

"Are you sure a little butter wouldn't help?" she asked.

"He don't need no butter, Lucille. But, I could use one of your cannin' jars...if ya don't mind."

Lucille began searching in cabinets for a jar, and Chester plopped down in a chair. He stretched his arms and legs, then yawned. "It's *way* past bedtime ya'll, and we've got to get up early in the mornin'. The chores ain't goin' nowhere, and I ain't done a proper head count of the cattle."

Lucille located a jar and brought it to Chester. "I don't know how you expect us to just fall asleep after all that's happened."

"Everything that's happened is the reason I'm wore out," Chester said. He poured the seed from the shot glass into the jar.

"I'm wore out too," Theo said. "I could sleep standin' up."

"You've dealt with a lot of news tonight. Are you certain you're going to be fine?" asked Lucille.

"Yep, Mama. I reckon I'll do fine."

She kissed Theo on the forehead and smoothed out his hair. "Maybe I'll sleep better knowing that." She lit a lantern and left the kitchen to ascend the staircase.

Theo watched his mother disappear into the gloom. Looking at his father he said, "Daddy, make sure ya lock the front door. Lock it down tight."

"I got it taken care of, son. Don't ya worry none."

"Daddy?"

"Yep."

"I swear, on a stack of bibles, that I ain't made none of this up. I couldn't come up with a whopper like this."

Chester screwed a lid down on the trapped seed, then stared at it through the glass. "I don't think you're lyin' to us."

It was a sufficient enough answer for Theo. "I'm headin' to bed myself. I'll see ya in the mornin', Daddy."

Still captivated by the strange little seed, Chester waved at his son. "Go on. Get some rest and I'll wake ya in the morning."

Theo nodded and left the kitchen, hesitating for a moment to glance at his father. He was still studying the seed, mesmerized by its alien appearance. Theo left him alone with his curiosity and climbed the staircase, feeling as if sand bags were tied to his feet. As he reached his bedroom, fatigue overpowered him. He fell face forward onto his bed, and was immediately into a deep well of sleep.

Sometime later, his sleep was interrupted by the sound of footsteps upon his bedroom floor. He rolled over onto his back, expecting to see one of his parents. But, he was wrong.

"Hello," said Apollyon. Blackness crept from his mouth as he smiled. "Nice hair."

Theo's initial reaction was to scream, but he stymied it out of fear for his parents. He shuddered, as a ghoulish picture show of his parents being murdered flickered in his brain. He shook his head, trying to clear the thoughts away.

"Don't worry, boy. I don't intend on harming your hayseed parents tonight." Apollyon walked to the foot of the bed. "However, I *could* have. Oh, yes."

Theo sprang to an upright position and moved backward, ringing his head sharply against the wall. He spoke to Apollyon in a strained whisper. "Get out of here. Ain't nobody invited ya."

"Always the eloquent speaker. Do you eat with that mouth?"

"What do ya want with me?"

Apollyon placed his long arms on the bed and leaned toward Theo. He was smiling, but his eyes glowered with ageless malice and hate. "What I want, my dear little hick, is *you*. Yes, that's what I want."

"You cain't have me."

Apollyon winced as if struck. "Listening to you speak, is like having a red-hot poker shoved up my ass." He pushed away from the bed and adjusted his stove-pipe hat. "I've brought some company with me. I hope you don't mind."

A scratching and shuffling could be heard, coming from several different spots in the room. Theo's eyes flashed to darkened corners, searching for the source. He caught a glimpse of something moving along the floor. It might have had hair, but he couldn't be for certain. It moved with a sluggish gait, but was still quick. His bed began shaking as it was slammed by the unseen shapes, then something from beneath the bed pushed against the mattress.

Theo kept a skinning knife in the top drawer of his nightstand. He leaned and reached for the drawer, already planning to throw it at Apollyon's head, hopeful it would find its way to the space between his eyes. He was able to open the drawer, but his attention was drawn to something on the floor.

It was one of Apollyon's pets from Hell, and it was truly, quite hellish. It had several legs that sprouted from a lolling head, as if its neck were broken, and at the end of each leg was a three-fingered hand with long nails. Long, stringy hair was draped over the legs, like a skirt.

Theo instinctively jerked his hand back, but he wasn't fast enough. The creature was able latch onto his wrist with one of its freakish hands. Two more creatures came up through the mattress, creating an explosion of feathers. They grabbed his legs and gazed at Theo through milky-white eyes. Their heads moved side to side, seemingly beyond their control, while their tongues spilled out of deformed mouths, limp and lifeless.

"They're usually shy little things. I guess it's possible they find your bumpkin ways...charming."

Theo still had his left arm free. He swung at the beast that was clamped down on his other arm. It was an awkward punch, lacking the impact he was hoping for, but it found its target, landing directly on an eyeball. The creature widened its mouth and hissed a protest, clearly displeased at being struck. Theo cocked his arm again, intending to pummel the grotesque thing, but found his arm suddenly pinned to the bed by another. Its legs coiled and tightened like a throng of snakes.

"You should learn to be more gracious to your guests." Apollyon sat on the bed next to Theo's legs, caressing one of the creatures that had him bound. "Now, let's see...where were we? Ah, yes. I came for you, my dearest yahoo. Do you feel special?"

Theo spat at his tormentor. "Nope, not particularly"

"You're an idiot. But, you've not heard the entire story. I'm certain you'll remain an idiot, but...."

Theo stared into the ceiling, trying to carve a tunnel through the roof with his eyes, trying to see his way to Heaven.

"Don't even think about praying to *Him*," said Apollyon, wagging a finger.

"You cain't stop me."

Apollyon shook his head and stood up. He took his hat off and turned it upside down, peering into its darkness. "You are truly the epitome of an *idiot*. Have you not been warned of tempting the devil?"

"Our Father, who art in Heaven..."

A growl, low and baleful, emanated from Apollyon. He thrust his hand into the hat and retrieved a wriggling thing.

"...hallowed be Thy name..."

"This is not, I assure you, a white rabbit I've pulled from my hat."

"...Thy Kingdom come..."

Apollyon burst toward Theo, quickly snapping his mouth shut with long fingers. He waved the hat prize in front of Theo's eyes, holding it inches away. It was a shiny, yellow spider, about the size of a man's hand, with twitching fangs.

Theo's eyes widened, and his heart quickened.

Apollyon forced Theo's mouth open, dangling the spider by a leg. "You've every right to fear it. A single bite causes horrible madness, then a deliciously painful death."

Theo struggled, trying to break free of the crushing pressure against his jaws.

Wasted energy.

"I'm going to drop the spider into your mouth. Let me end that particular drama for you," Apollyon said. "But, you need not fear a thing if you listen to what I have to say." He licked his lips with the tip of his forked tongue.

"The key to your survival is to keep your tongue from wagging. In fact, be mindful of your breathing, keep it from becoming too laborious. The spider is *most* sensitive to movement."

Apollyon grinned and let the spider drop. Theo stopped breathing, listening as the spider's legs ticked and scraped against his teeth. It felt cold as death.

"Now, shut up and listen," Apollyon said. He gently closed Theo's mouth and stretched out his long legs. "I was curious about you. It's, as I've said before, quite rare that one is able to see beyond the veil. And you were—*are* such a rube, which only added to my curiosity. Now, understand this—I know all things that are of this earth. Just as I knew you were a pitiful dirt-farmer the instant we met. But," Apollyon sprang to his feet and began to pace, "I was unaware of your extraordinary protection, and that is just *impossible*. Do you understand, boy?"

Theo was unable to respond, but he was listening. He was also silently praying. He prayed for his parent's safety, and for this to end. He prayed that Apollyon would die, and that the Lord would let him be the one to kill the son of a bitch.

"Well, I paid close attention to you. I watched as you..." Apollyon giggled in a baritone, "regurgitated your misadventure to your hayseed parents. Oh yes, that was pathetic. However, Chester's tale had me positively enraptured with suspense right to the end."

Apollyon stopped speaking and began to laugh. He clapped his hands and showcased his dark smile, then pointed a finger at Theo. "*You* are a bastard. Found on the doorstep in the middle of the night, comparable to a character found in a fable."

Theo needed to swallow and it was becoming difficult to breathe. The spider had moved closer to the back of his throat, partially blocking his air flow. He wondered if he might crush the spider with his teeth without effect to his health.

"Our dear Chester's description of the evening in question rang a familiar note. The rogue storm, as an example, erupting suddenly, and the beings that brought you can only impart a single truth." Apollyon jumped onto the foot board and squatted like a toad. "You were taken from me. A promised first born, stolen away by *His* soldiers."

Theo was clueless.

"Yes, you are *mine*. I should by all rights own your soul, boy," said Apollyon. "Unfortunately, I do not know the identity of your actual father. You've been protected and hidden from me, away from my agents. Which, I cannot express enough, is quite impossible. Yet, here we are."

Things were still quite difficult for Theo. He tried to absorb every word he was hearing, but it seemed the spider was spinning a silken home within the confines of his mouth. He was close to screaming.

"So, it appears that you are *special.*" Apollyon left the foot of the bed and approached Theo, leaning in close.

"You have no idea how much angst I am feeling at the moment, having to admit such a thing."

Theo's eyes bugged and he gagged. The spider began to crawl down his throat, effectively shutting his wind off.

Apollyon opened Theo's mouth then snapped his fingers twice. A loyal pet, the spider scuttled from its moist confines and into its master's waiting hand. The master then flipped his hat off and dropped the pet into the darkness. He grinned at Theo. "You were turning blue."

Theo gagged and coughed, sucking in air like an emerging pearl diver. He worked his tongue feverishly, attempting to dislodge the sticky mess in his mouth. He fired hateful daggers from his eyes, aiming for Apollyon's face.

"Understand me well, boy. I will have you under my vigilant eye, and I *will* find the identity of your father." Apollyon flicked Theo sharply on the nose. "Whether he be alive or dead, it makes no difference. If he is alive, then he will be an affluent man, that's assured. It's always the same contract when dealing with a man or a woman's soul. I give them riches and I take their soul...or I take their children." He smiled and continued, "This is, of course, the abbreviated order of things, as I am fully aware of my current audience's lack of intelligence." He raked a fingernail across the bridge of Theo's nose, slicing through the skin. "I am the devil, and I can be found in every quarter of the earth."

Blood spilled in rivulets, running to Theo's eyes. Theo's tongue managed to push enough webbing aside to utter, "If it's the last thing I do, I'm goin' to figure a way to hurt ya."

"You've got moxie, boy. That much I'll give you. It might have been a welcome challenge to groom you, but it's far too late for that. You've been tainted by *His* words of love." Apollyon abruptly moved backwards, gliding as if on unseen wheels. He stopped at the bedroom door and opened it, then lightly clapped his hands. The beasts loosened from Theo and scampered to their master. They massed at his feet like starving dogs awaiting a scrap for work well done.

"We'll be leaving now. As you can imagine, I am quite busy. But don't worry your little heart. I'll be back." Apollyon moved an index finger in small circles over his creatures. As he did this, each one morphed into smoke, dissipating like morning mist against a hindering sun.

"Oh, yes. Before I go, I've a bit of irony to convey. As you may recall, when we first became acquainted, I did my damnedest to convince you that you were not dreaming. Do you remember? Surely, you must." The devil smiled and opened his arms. "Well, *this* is an actual dream. All of it. It's hardly the same as a flesh and bone visitation, but it was all I had time for. Busy, busy, busy."

The devil then tipped his hat, and was gone.

Chapter Five

Murder Plans and Pecans

"....AND SO, I opened my eyes to the early morning light pourin' in through the window. The devil never came callin' again," Grandpa said. "Not in a dream, or otherwise."

My chin weighed ten pounds and my mouth hung open, like a baby bird awaiting its morning worm. But I wasn't chirping. I was rendered speechless.

"My folks had the same look," Grandpa said. "You're thinkin' ole Grandpa has lost his marbles. Cain't say I blame ya none."

Finally, I said, "You're kidding, right?" I tried smiling, but it felt ugly on my face.

"I wish I was, Luke."

"The devil?"

"Yep, I'm afraid so. If I was kiddin' ya, that black thing in the sky wouldn't be there. I imagine there ain't nobody outside of you and me that can even see it there."

"I need to look at it again," I said.

"Nope, it's too dangerous. We need to wait."

"Wait for what?"

"For it to drop."

"Is that what happened the last time? Did it drop?"

"I'm pretty sure that's what happened. I peeked at the sky the next mornin' and it was gone. I know for sure it dropped on that village I visited, 'cause I seen it happen."

"How do you know we're the only ones who can see

it?"

Grandpa put a hand up. "Trust me, there ain't no one else that sees it."

"But, how do you know that?"

"Well, if any of the neighbors was seein' it, I'd a had a phone call by now. There ain't none of 'em that would mistake it for a rain cloud."

He had a point. It wasn't that the neighbors were nosy (maybe a few), rather it was the search for something out of the ordinary. Something to nudge them from their mechanical day. A reason to travel two or three miles to pay a neighbor a visit. A reason to be *neighborly*.

"What if the party line is tied up?" It was possible, but doubtful. Grandpa didn't answer my question, but instead gave me a look that imparted his thoughts. *I understand your fear of the truth, but bein' stupid ain't goin' to change nothin'.*

I absently wiped a finger at a sticky piece of pecan and stuck it in my mouth. It was delicious, and it was magical in the way it comforted me.

"Ya like the pie?" Grandpa asked.

I thought it a casual question, considering all things. "Uh, yeah."

"There's a special type of pecan tree that helped in makin' that pie."

I raised my eyebrows, not at all concerned with pecans. "Grandpa, I'm not trying to be rude, but what does that have to do with anything?"

"A lot more than you'd think," he said, smiling.

I was becoming more confused. I stood up, exasperated. "Grandpa, I still don't understand."

He stacked our empty pie plates and laid them in the sink, then stood with me. "I'm fixin' to show ya."

I found myself empathizing with Chester. We both knew in our guts that something had changed, but preferred to go the way of the ostrich. Stick our heads into an imaginary hole of infinite peace and ignorance.

I leaned against the kitchen counter and watched Grandpa reach into a cabinet, stretching for the top shelf. Glass and metal clattered out a tune as he blindly felt around, until he finally found what he was searching for. An old coffee can, rusted and beat to hell. He grinned at me and set the can on the kitchen table. "Go ahead and grab a pecan, tell me what ya think."

I took one in my hand. It had a soft texture, like a bruised apple, which didn't feel like any pecan I'd handled before. But the most glaring characteristic was the hair. Not prickly hair, as in a kiwi or coconut, but soft and silky. And it was warm in my hand. Had I been blindfolded, I would have sworn I was holding a mouse.

I dropped the pecan back in the can. "Those aren't pecans."

"Yep, they're pecans. But they've been cross-bred with something else."

"With what?" I said. "I'm totally creeped, Grandpa."

He laughed and slapped me on the back, as if we weren't talking about demons and hairy pecans. "Well, ya remember me sayin' that my daddy put the seed in a jar?"

I nodded.

"Yep, well he decided to plant it. I reckon his curiosity got the best of him, seein' how he'd been plantin' and growin' off the land since he was a youngster. It wasn't much of a chore for him to figure out how to cross-breed it."

Faint thunder rolled in the distance, followed by a strong gust of wind that swept through the house, rattling open windows and screen doors. I took a deep breath of it, and let it out slowly, tasting the storm's aroma. It was a familiar distraction. Something *real*.

"I might as well tell ya you've been eatin' them for a month or so," said Grandpa.

My stomach did a somersault, and I almost gagged.

"If you'll recall, I made a pie that made ya sick here awhile back," he said. "I cracked a joke about ya getting' a bad pecan."

I recalled with perfect clarity the moment he alluded to. It wasn't pretty, but vomiting never is.

"It has that effect at first. But it goes down easier the next time." He rubbed his stomach.

True words. His pecan pies were much richer than I had remembered, which is a considerable admission, as his pies have taken home more blue ribbons than a prize hog. Nonetheless, my gorge shivered at the thought of allowing such a strange food into my body. "You could have told me, you know."

"Yep, I know. But, I had to know if it would affect ya."

"Why?"

More wind gusted, furiously flapping the curtains that hung from the windows, as if it were queued up to delay the answer to my question.

"Well, I'd been ponderin' on whether to let ya have a taste of the tree. I finally decided that ya deserved to know what sort of things was loose out in the world," said Grandpa. "It's best ya be prepared, 'cause I'm pretty sure Apollyon has had an eyeball on ya."

"What?" I said, quite freaked out. "Are you serious?'

"As a heart attack."

"That's scary," I said.

"Yep, I reckon it is." Grandpa worked his hat, fanning the sweat that had beaded on his face. "Soupy out today, ain't it?"

"Yeah, real sticky," I said, not in the least concerned with the day's humidity.

"I'm goin' to set fire to the land over yonder. Burn it out," Grandpa said. "I'm goin' to need a little help from ya."

I didn't expect that. "Won't you get in trouble?" I thought about it. "Wait, *I'll* get in trouble."

Grandpa dropped his hat back on and laughed. "Shoot, I wasn't plannin' on tellin' anyone else."

As I conjured images of being handcuffed for burning the countryside to a smoldering crisp, a small tremor rumbled through the house. An entire family of ceramic bees fell from their dusty shelves, smashing against the wooden floor.

I felt sad for Grandpa. He'd grown up around them for all of his life, and now they were broken and gone. But, he hardly seemed aware of their demise. His attention was focused on something beyond.

"Was that an earthquake?" I said.

"Nope, I'm afraid not. I'm fairly certain that the spell-cloud over yonder dropped, and it's on the ground."

I ran outdoors and searched the sky. The blackness was gone, just as he'd said. "Aren't you concerned about the Plumes?" I said.

"Well, I understand your concern. But them Plumes over yonder...they ain't right. I've always suspected them of bein' somethin' like caretakers. Ain't nobody ever recalls seein' em move in. It's like they sprouted or somethin'."

I thought about that. Sounded insane. "But, they're still people. We can't just, you know, burn 'em up."

"They ain't people, Luke. Or, at least not like you and me. I've got a feelin' that we'll find proof of that soon enough."

He surely must have gone mad. I decided to humor him, and hope that a better idea came to me. "How are we going do this? Spread gasoline around their property and light a match? I figure that'll work pretty good."

"Maybe," he said. "But, I'm bettin' plenty that the Plumes are the protectors of that land. There's a reason animals go missin' around their property."

Poor ole Ace.

"It ain't gonna' be an easy thing," he said. "They'll try to kill us when we get there."

I was officially bothered by this talk. I was considering making a run for it.

"C'mon, follow me to the barn. I've got some stuff

yonder," he said, shaking his head and smiling.

As we walked, the temperature dropped. Dingy clouds, looking like low-hanging pouches, were beginning to overpower the overhead sky. The weatherman called them *mammatus clouds* because they look a bit like drooping mammaries. Folks around Wetumka weren't as technical in referencing them. *"Always have your eyes to the sky when there's bad weather approachin'. You gotta' look out for them titty-clouds."*

When we entered the barn, Grandpa walked to the northwest corner below the hayloft. The corner was buried beneath thick layers of shadows. It was an area I always avoided. The lights in the barn were never able to penetrate the corner's universe of discarded farm equipment, and pitch darkness. Lots of rusty sharp things in that collection. There was also an enormous spider web that served as a dissuasive device. I had never seen the actual spider—thank God. It was always absent from its web, presumably lurking in the dark.

Grandpa showed no bother to any of these things, as he brushed the right side of the web away with his hat and went into the gloom. I soon heard metallic clanks as he began moving around.

"What are you looking for?" I asked.

"Weapons."

We had guns in the house, so it struck me as odd that he was digging around in the barn. But, I didn't bother asking him why he chose to rummage in a darkened, tetanus pit. It helped kill time, which further delayed Grandpa's mad plan.

"Well, I found what I was lookin' for," he said, still hidden from me. *"And* I found somethin' I wasn't lookin' for." He emerged from the corner, walking slowly. When he came into full light he was holding two burlap bags, one in each hand. Each bag appeared to be stuffed with objects that stuck out at varying angles. Grandpa's snowy hair, coupled with the bags, projected a Santa image into my mind. But then, the imagery changed from Christmas to Halloween.

At a quick glance, I would have guessed there were possibly hundreds of spiders covering Grandpa. "Don't be spooked, it ain't that big of a deal. Trust me," he said.

"Holy shit, holy shit," I said. "Where'd they come from? Oh, *holy shit!*"

"Cussin' ain't goin' to help, Luke."

He was right. Cussing was not going to whisk the spiders away, but it somehow helped me to process the picture that was before me. "Try not to talk, they might try to crawl in your mouth," I said. I quickly covered my own mouth, fearful a spider would somehow fling itself down my neck.

"I'll be fine," he said. "But I need ya to grab the insecticide can and spray me down." He said this, as half of his face darkened with spiders.

Horrified and fearful for my grandfather, I wasted no time in retrieving the poison. It was kept in the barn with the rest of the various farm toxins, in a cylindrical can. I ran to him and began pumping the can, working my arm like a piston. A rubber hose ran from the can and attached to a wand with a trigger-sprayer. I pointed the business end of the wand at Grandpa and screamed. I didn't wait for instruction. I knew how to pull the trigger, and that's what I did, spraying insecticide directly into his face. "Keep everything closed! Oh shit, shit, shit!" I said.

The spiders became agitated, moving faster, but not fast enough to escape the heavy mist of death I was dealing. They fell around his feet, curling their legs into their abdomens. Grandpa threw his hat at the open double-doors and moved in a slow circle, informing me to keep spraying. I tried fighting against tears, but lost the battle when I saw the spiders in his hair and the angry welts on his face.

"Motherfuckers!" I screamed. Then, "Sorry..."

It was a variety of spiders. Small and spindly, to large

and hairy. The shiny black ones with the orange hourglass on their bellies worried me. Black-widows.

I shouted. I wished. I prayed. I cussed some more.

Grandpa moved toward the doors calmly. I followed closely, still dousing. "Where are you going?"

"The horse tank."

"You got bit, didn't you?" It wasn't really a question.

"A few times, but don't ya worry," he said.

Don't worry.

He approached the horse tank and began stripping off his clothes, prompting me to stop spraying. Normally, I would have felt uncomfortable at seeing my granddad's naked form, but the current crisis swept such feelings aside. I understood what he was doing. He was going to submerge himself and wash the poison from his body, and any other unwanted residuals.

"I need some clean overalls, Luke. Would ya go get me some?" he asked, just as he stuck a leg into the water. The angle of his leg and his bent over posture revealed more than I was able to withstand, and the feelings of embarrassment issued forth.

"Uh-huh, and I'll get a towel," I said, already running to the house.

It was easy finding a clean pair of overalls. It was his preferred attire, and it dominated the closet space. He owned two suits. Very nice suits, that were worn alternately on Sunday mornings. One suit was black, the other was blue. He believed in looking sharp for the Lord, but never bothered with the trouble of getting *gussied up* for anything else. I grabbed the first pair of overalls in line and gave them a yank, bringing the hanger along for the ride.

I was halfway to the barn when I realized I had forgotten to bring a towel, but I also realized that my grandfather had already exited the water, and was standing nude. His farmer's tan was on full parade, showcasing a startling contrast of skin color. A snowman wearing a mask and gloves.

Rather than go back in the house for a towel, which would only prolong the matter, I ran a little faster. Grandpa was standing thirty yards from the dirt road by our house, which meant he was well within eye-shot of a neighbor who might drive by. The phone lines would glow with the chatter. A real *party* line.

"Here." I tossed the overalls. "Sorry, I forgot the towel."

"I ain't worried about it." He backed his words up as he dried his deathly pale skin with the overalls, sparing nary a nook or cranny.

My thoughts suddenly clicked. I chucked such trivial substance as an old man's nakedness aside. My grandfather was attacked, and bitten by spiders. *My God, this really and truly has happened. Really. Truly.*

I turned to him and watched as he latched the last buckle. His hair was a tangled veil of cotton, hanging over his face. I began to quiver with worry.

"Grandpa, we've got to get you to the doctor..." I blubbered. "Oh shit, it's gonna' be bad."

He swept his hair back and gathered it in a fist. His face was an ugly mass of festering bumps. Red and angry injuries. Poisonous.

I began screaming, quite hysterically. I told him, "Fuck it...I'm sorry for...but *fuck it*! I'm runnin' to call for help!"

Grandpa grabbed me by the collar and smacked an open-hand stinger across my left cheek. The palm of his hand felt like hard-packed clay. It was the first time he had ever struck me, and he saw the hurt and shock on my face. "I'm sorry, Luke," he said. "But you were fixin' to lose your mind. I wasn't tryin' to be mean to ya."

I turned my head, hiding my tears. "Grandpa, you're flat out going to die if we don't get you some help. You keep on saying stuff like, *"There ain't nothin' to worry about,"* or *"It'll be all right,"* but it ain't all right. Nothing is *all right*. You're going to die and leave me alone!"

Yes, the underlying fear. I spat it out like a wad of phlegm. I didn't want to be left alone. Both of my parents were deceased. Grandpa was all I had.

"I ain't leavin' ya just yet," he said to me. "Ya got to trust me for a minute. The tree will keep me goin'."

"What tree is that?"

"The pecan tree. It's got a healin' power."

"Healing powers? It doesn't look like it's working very good to me," I said. "We've got to—"

Grandpa hugged his guts and fell to his knees. His face twisted into a wrung out rag, and his mouth became a spewing hole to which dark fluid erupted and flowed. He retched and gagged horribly. It sounded like a lung was squeezing past his throat. The smell was repellent, to say the least.

The putrid discharge suddenly stopped, and Grandpa started hacking and spitting. Wiping his mouth with the back of his hand, he said, "Lawsy, that was nasty."

"Yeah, I bet."

"I'm already feelin' better," he said.

With an incredulous pitch to my voice, I said, "You just got done puking half your guts out, Grandpa. How is that better?"

He leaned back and sat Indian-style, then smoothed his hair away from his face. "How's my face lookin'?"

I made a grimace and forced my eyes onto him, afraid to see his suffering. But I was wrong to worry at all. The swelling and blisters were receding. I was overjoyed. "Oh my God, Grandpa. It's a miracle!" I was a human pogo stick.

"Maybe. Maybe not." He leaned on the tank, using it as a crutch for climbing to his feet. He looked around, obviously seeking a particular item or detail. "Ya know where my hat went?"

"Yeah, it's over by the barn doors." I pointed. My eyes traveled from the hat and stopped at the two mystery bags of treasure that lay in the dirt. "What's in the bags? Guns?"

"Amongst some other things," he said, retrieving his hat. "I ain't exactly sure of what *everything* in the bags is. But I figure they're weapons."

"Where'd they come from?"

"They just started showin' up here and there." He snugged his hat on. "Just layin' on the property. I once found one in the pond, it was shinin' through the water."

"That's weird." He was truly leaping into the deep end of insanity. My mind was running in circles, trying to cope with it.

"Ordinarily, yep. Pretty weird," he said with a soft laugh.

"You sure you're all right?" I said.

He lightly patted his face. "Pretty as a picture. The taste in my mouth ain't so good, but I'll live." Then he grabbed the bags and turned them upside down, letting the contents spill into a pile. It looked like the bag was being emptied of sunlight. Large chunks of it.

"Holy cow," I said. "This is crazy."

"Yep, gold sure is pretty."

I knelt down and studied the shimmering assemblage, and was impressed. It was some type of weaponry, I was certain of that, but not like any I had ever seen. I saw what I thought were more than likely guns, but the barrels were flared at the end, giving them a trumpet look. There were several baseball-sized balls of gold, each having strange etchings. And there was a dagger. "Is it the same type of dagger your angel had?"

Grandpa knelt on the ground with me and picked the dagger up. He stroked it softly with a calloused finger. "Actually, I've always thought that this one here is the same one that she was holdin'. She was able to get it to me some way or another."

It was beautiful. "Can I hold it?"

He was surprised by my question. "Well, sure. Why wouldn't ya be able to touch it? You're goin' to be usin' it...and everything else. I'm pretty sure that we're goin' to have to take a few lives today, and them guns and such are goin' to be aidin' us."

Take a few lives. It was a nicer way of saying, *"We're going to murder a few folks today."*

"Here," he said, holding the dagger out to me. "Take it, and get used to the weight of it. It's got some heft."

As soon as I took the dagger, I became wracked with sharp vibrations that tingled my fingertips and traveled into my spinal cord. I dropped the dagger, and the sensation stopped.

"What's wrong," Grandpa asked.

"It felt weird, like I had hold of a live hornet."

"I ain't ever had that happen to me. Go on and pick it up again."

I picked it up and was once again zinged, but I held on to it this time, gripping it tightly with two hands. I waited for something sinister to occur. But all was uneventful, unless one counted the thunderstorm that barked its approach. The vibrations in my body quickly became less fierce, settling into an electric thrum that seemed to actually invigorate me. "Man, this is...sort of groovy."

"Groovy?"

"Yep," I said, nodding to him. *"Groovy."* It was not a normal feeling. I knew it was something *otherworldly.* It was enough to make me rein in my skepticism, just a bit.

"I'm hopin' that's a good thing."

"Yep, it means *cool.*"

"Cool." He stared at me with his faded blue eyes. I could see that his mind was working on something.

"What?" I asked. "What are you thinking about?"

"I figure there's a reason the dagger reacts to ya, but I ain't sure why." He pulled a leather sheath from the pile of weapons and handed it to me. "Keep it in this, and keep it on your body somewhere. You might need it."

I sheathed the blade and picked up one of the balls. I bounced it like a baseball in my hand. "I'm not feeling anything strange with this," I said. "What do you think these things do?"

"I don't rightly know what any of it does, but my guess would be that we're supposed to throw the balls." He shrugged his shoulders and began putting the weapons back into the bags. Then he added, "We're already under attack."

"Under attack?" I said.

"Yep. Those spiders bitin' on me wasn't part of the normal order of things. I figure the devil must've had one of his demon-kind devise 'em to do such to me. He's tryin' to scare me off, on account he knows what we plan on doin'."

I tried to wrap my head around what he'd said. "Wait…that sort of thing can happen? The devil can do that?"

"Yep, but we ain't lettin' that stop us. He ain't Lord Almighty, though he sometimes thinks he is. He cain't be everywhere all the time." Grandpa spoke with a growling ferocity, which was rare. He was the kindest person I'd ever known. "It's time we took the fight to him."

A raindrop, big as a penny, plopped next to my foot. I looked up and was suddenly hit in the face by a torrential downpour. Otherwise referred to as *a real turd floater.*

"It's time we got goin'," he said. "We've lost too much time. Ain't any way of startin' a fire in this rain."

"So, what's the plan?" I asked, hopeful he would end it.

He motioned toward the truck. "Let's get out of the rain. You run on to the truck, I'll be right along."

I hurried to the truck, glad to be out the rain. Regardless of what I did later, I had enough sense to come in out of the rain. I could at least say that.

Chapter Six

A Death, A Freak, and A Little Boy

I SAT IN the old pickup truck, listening to the raindrops thump out a careless tune on its faded roof. It was a *Rambler,* and its beauty queen days of cruising down Main Street were long gone. Grandpa said it used to have a bright red finish, but what was left of the original paint was now a pale pink. The truck generally rested in the shade of the large mimosa tree in the front yard, blending nicely with the tree's pinkish blooms.

The screen door to the house slammed shut. I watched Grandpa walk toward me, a shotgun in one hand and a pistol in the other. The bags that held the unusual weaponry were tied to a rope, and hanging from his neck.

"You need some help?" I asked.

"Nope."

He handed me the shotgun and pistol, but placed the bags in the back. He hopped in and cranked the old truck to life. "Hang on tight, Luke. We've got some time to make up."

"What's the plan?" I was certain he had a plan *b*. He was always two steps ahead of any problem, no matter the circumstance.

"Well," he replied, pulling onto the dirt road. "I ain't really thought out a new plan."

So much for superior forethought. It seemed we were flying blind, but I had been doing that for the last two hours.

"We're goin' to wing it and just have faith in the Lord." He accelerated, pushing the truck through the road, which was becoming slick. "Yep, keep your faith."

Keeping the faith was easy for Grandpa. He never failed to open his Bible in the evenings, and read until his eyes turned red with fatigue. He never missed a Sunday service, which meant *I* never missed a Sunday service. Back then, I couldn't get a handle on why he held on so tightly to faith. His wife died due to complications of giving birth to my father. And my father was murdered alongside my mother years later. One would understand if he were to flinch. But his faith only grew stronger.

I guess I believed in God, but how much? If I was willing to believe there was a devil, why wouldn't I have a belief in God. Or, maybe Grandpa was shithouse crazy, and the two of us would soon be rotting in jail for murder and trespassing.

A brilliant bolt of lightning, thick as God's arm, struck home somewhere to the west. A batch of thunder followed its trail, punctuating the storm's power. Part of the sky ahead of us had turned a strange green, superimposed over a bruised sky.

"Whew-ee! It's a doozy of a storm, Luke." He looked like a kid at his first county fair.

"Grandpa, I'm a little nervous about everything," I said, looking into the clouds.

"Well, I figure that's normal considering the way the day went so far. And I'd be surprised if ya didn't think I was crazy. That's all right."

I sighed. "Well, I'm sorry but...it *has* crossed my mind."

He chuckled. "Ain't no reason to apologize. I understand your feelins."

"I sort of wish that you *were* crazy. I'm feeling freaked out."

"Yep, I reckon I feel the same way."

"You're feeling freaked out?" I was surprised by this.

Not because he shouldn't be freaked out, but rather he never let it show. "Do you know what being freaked out means?"

"I was referrin' to the crazy part, but I guess I'm feelin' somewhat freaked out."

"I'm not sure why, but that makes me feel a little better."

He grabbed my shoulder then patted it. "Glad I could help ya."

I forced a smile, nodded, and turned to the flashing fence posts that blurred the sides of the road. I tried to let my mind go white. Just to escape to someplace in my mind. But, I didn't find any such solace. There was no *Never Never Land*, damn it.

The truck's engine geared down, rattling the exhaust. The rusty sound shattered my daydream, delivering me back to reality's crowded doorstep. We were stopping.

"What's going on? Did you change your mind?" I asked. *Please, please, oh please.*

"Nope."

I closed my eyes. "Then *why* are you pulling over?"

"We're a mile out from the Plume's place. This ole truck ain't goin' to let us sneak up on 'em. She's too rickety."

"So we're walking?" I asked.

"Yep, I reckon so."

"In the rain?"

Grandpa smiled. "You'll be all right, unless you're made of sugar."

He acted as if we were standing in line for a movie. Like it was all make believe.

"I figure to run up into the woods, while you move along the road. I want to keep ya at a distance from everything for as long as I can."

"By myself? Grandpa, I don't know what to do." My stomach, was a mass of fluttering moths. "I don't think I can do this."

"I *know* you can. You're a special kid, Luke. Just like your daddy."

I ignored the *Daddy* pump, content to carry on with my cowardice and whining. "So, I just walk up the road to their house and knock on the door?" The very thought made it hard to breathe.

"You ain't got to knock of their door. Just kinda' lag along, bein' quiet as ya go. There's a bunch of brush along the ditch as ya get closer to their house. Creep along and pay attention to everything around ya." He pointed to the leather scabbard tucked into my pants. "Pull that dagger out and hold it in your hands."

Earlier, the dagger had been a warm charge of confidence and calm. I was desperate for calm.

I unsheathed the dagger and almost dropped it as it buzzed me, but I increased my grip until the sensation became nothing more than a slight throb. However, my insides were on full tilt, feeling electric and powerful. "Man, that's *weird*."

"Keep holdin' it if ya have to."

I definitely felt emboldened. Not enough to numb me to what I was doing, but enough to get me through it.

Grandpa brandished a snub-nose .38 and spun the cylinder, then held it out to me. "Put this here in your pants, and don't hesitate to use it if ya get in a fix."

I put the dagger back beneath its leather hood and took the gun. The gun's weight was perfect for me. I had fired it a few times in the past, mostly blasting away at soup-cans and wild rabbits. I was a deadly soup-can-killer, but not much of a rabbit-killer.

"Well," said Grandpa, "I'll take the shotgun and the stuff in the bags. By the way, I'm working on a plan."

"What *is* the plan?"

"I ain't done thinkin' on it. I'll finish workin' it out as I head through the trees."

"How am I supposed to know what the plan is if I'm out here on the road?"

"If things go like I want 'em to, you'll know."

It was more of his mystifying logic, but I surrendered to it.

"The rain's slowin' down a little. I reckon we ought to get the show on the road," he said, as he took off his hat. He placed it in his lap and brushed at the crown. "Luke, I'm awful proud of ya. You're a good boy, growin' fast into a man. Folks in town speak highly of ya, your teachers and such."

"Uh, thank you."

He gave me a wink, then chuckled. "And I'm hearin' that the gals at your school think pretty highly of ya."

"For real?" It was a newsflash to me.

"Yep, for real I reckon."

"Not the best timing to find out," I said.

"Why ya say that?"

"I'll be dead, or in prison after today. That's why."

Grandpa grimaced and put his hat back on. He looked at me. "Luke, this ain't goin' to be easy. That much surely is a fact. But, I don't see any reason for ya to be worryin' about goin' to prison...or dyin'."

"How can you be so *sure*?"

"Faith."

Oh boy.

"I don't have that kind of faith, Grandpa." I felt ashamed and guilty. After all, this was the man who had been dragging me to church for much of my life.

"That's okay. I've got enough for the both of us."

Keeping my head down, I said, "All right. I believe in *you*, Grandpa."

"Good, then. Let's get this done, eh?"

I raised my head. "Let's get it done."

I stood in the rain and waved to Grandpa, just as he began his journey into the suffocating arms of the woods. He waved back with his cowboy hat, looking like a hero from a western movie. Then he ducked into the trees. I withdrew the dagger and started walking up the road.

I had been footslogging in the mud, against a hill, for twenty minutes or so when I heard a sound. I stopped and listened. It was the unmistakable sound of someone running in the mud. It was coming from the other side of the hill, faint but growing louder.

"Grandpa?" I said.

The footfalls increased, moving with much more speed. A determination resonated in the sound. Then I heard a laugh, high-pitched and crazy.

Nope. Not Grandpa.

I stood glued to the road. I didn't know what to do. My first instinct was to look for a place to hide, but a quick glance was all I needed to flush that thought away. Nothing but weeds and scrubs. With only one option left, I trusted the power that thrummed in my arm and ran up the hill, prepared to confront what awaited me. Regrettably, the dagger wasn't able to aid in my footing or balance, as my left foot slipped and I went spilling face first. The dagger flew from me, cresting the hill and beyond.

After spitting a gob of mud from my mouth, I got to my feet, anxious to locate my blade of courage. I topped the hill and saw the dagger, shining like a new dime in a puddle, and impaled in the soil like Excalibur. I was also able to see what was running down the road.

It was a nightmare made of gangly arms and legs. Arms so long that the knuckles were skimming and dragging across the mud, slinging it into the air. It had feet the size of snowshoes, which sounded like beaver tails smacking water with each footfall.

Whap-whappity! Whap-whappity! Whap-whappity!

I was unable to see it's face clearly. The rain and distance made it too difficult. But from where I was standing, it was a clock stopper. Narrow and misshapen, with a wide grin.

It was a Plume.

My first authentic sighting. The *real deal* was right in front of me, strutting in technicolor. And as it came closer,

I realized that it was naked. Its maleness was prominent and flopping.

"Oh, my God."

I pulled the dagger from the ground and wiped it clean on my soaked jeans. I held it out in front of me and pointed it toward the freak. I was surprisingly calm considering that a naked and crazed monstrosity was barreling toward me. Not the ordinary circumstances for calm, but miraculously, I was submerged in a pool of it.

The freak was within thirty yards when it laughed again. It sounded like an insane horse's whinny. Its breath was labored and wheezing, tinged with a madman's mirth. Then, it began to growl and scream and slap at its face. It was a terrifying madness, full of violence and venom.

Twenty yards.

It could see its face clearly now. Drool, long and stringy, flew from its grinning mouth, smearing across its cheeks and ears, like a drooling dog. A pus-riddled tongue slipped out of its mouth and began licking a lumpy snout that sat between its tiny eyes, solidifying the dog comparison.

Ten yards.

I had as much knife-fighting skills as a person born with no hands. I should have been scared shitless. But I wasn't. That's not to say, I was naive to my circumstances. My grinning neighbor from the west was a neon reminder. I could die. Horribly.

It sprang at me. One of its fingers brushed my right shoulder, which is when I yanked the pistol from my jeans with my left hand, and pulled the trigger. There was a flash and my ears rang from the gunshot. The freak yelped and wheezed in a gulp of air. I fell backwards and began sliding down the hill. My freaky neighbor was moving too quickly to stop, and somersaulted past me.

I rolled over and got to my knees, frantically searching for the freak. I found him, lying on his belly and staring at me. Hating me.

"Good Lord, you're ugly." I pointed the gun at his head and sheathed the dagger. I wouldn't be needing it for what I had planned.

He reached a long, sinewy, arm and bounded to his enormous feet, quick as a cat. I saw where the bullet had wounded him. A hole, just below his right collarbone was pouring a stream of blood. I was surprised I had shot him at all, considering I was right-handed and had drawn and fired with my left. This time I held the gun in my shooting hand and fired the pistol again, hoping to lodge a bullet in his brain and get this surrealistic event over with.

The freak must have sensed me squeezing the trigger, because he lunged a split second before I fired. I missed his forehead, but his right ear bloomed a brilliant red. I fired a second time, but he had closed the gap between us and was able to knock my arm astray, sending the bullet skyward and the gun skidding across the mud. A hand made of steel cord seized my throat, instantly cutting off my air supply. The freak pulled me to his slavering mouth and licked me across the eyes with his blistered and festering tongue. I thought my head would explode.

A blast of his breath blew my hair back, then he released me. I fell to the ground, coughing and sucking wind. I reached for the dagger and was woefully disappointed to find that it was no longer in my possession.

Crap.

I was expecting the freak to put a caveman pounding on me, but I was being spared for the moment. Maybe he wanted to toy with me. I got to my feet and ran a few yards in the opposite direction, and then whirled around, expecting to be bludgeoned to death. But the freak was lying on his back, the dagger buried in his belly. No rise or fall of his chest. No nut-ball utterances. Just the sound of the rain.

I surely did not recall sticking the bastard.

I quickly trotted over to the gun, continually cutting

my eyes at the freak. The gun was drowning, barrel first, in a puddle of mud. I grabbed it by the butt and wiped it down the best I could, which wasn't much, considering the saturated state of my clothes. I worried it might not fire.

I stood several feet from my neighbor, the freak. I looked for signs of faint chest falls, any sign of life.

Nothing.

All the same, I put another round into my neighbor's head. Temple shot.

He was dead. The gun still fired. Good news all around.

I knelt and pulled the dagger from the freak's belly, wincing as it made a sickening suction sound. Without bothering to wipe the blade clean, I sheathed it in the leather and looked up the road. I was not far from the freak's home.

I crept along the side of the road, using black-jack trees as cover, curious about Grandpa and how his escapade in the woods was progressing. I hoped he wasn't having to deal with any naked neighbors. But, if that were the case, I was thankful for not having to view such an event.

A hair-raising chorus of screams floated from the house, sounding strange and animal. I reached for the dagger, my courageous companion. But I stopped short of touching it. I didn't need it for courage anymore. All one needed for courage was to accept death as inevitable. Unavoidable destiny.

The wind blew harder, flaunting its raw power. Raindrops became needles. I ran beneath a tree, not much for shelter, but it was better than standing in the torrent. The western horizon was black, stretching miles across as far as the eye could see. The worst of the storm was almost upon me. I had zero ideas. Zero plans. Grandpa said I would know what to do. He was wrong. I was a babe lost in a fantastical, nightmare world.

Another wail cut through the storm's din, rising above

the thunder. It prompted me to leave my flimsy cover and continue my journey. I trudged forward for about five minutes, until I spotted a little boy standing in the middle of the road. He looked to be around five years old. My first inclination was to help him, but I was not in a position to help anyone. I thought maybe I would send him down the road to the truck. At least he would be dry until someone stumbled across him.

But, I had a problem with him. The boy gave me the creeps. He was smiling and rubbing his hands together and kicking his feet as if he were dancing.

Yes, he *was* dancing. And his mouth was smeared with something dark. Chocolate, perhaps.

"What are you doing out here?" I asked, creeping toward him. "You ought to be inside."

Inside where? Where the hell did you come from?

The Plume house of course. Where else could he have come from?

He giggled as if tickled, and ran from my view. I pulled the hammer back on the gun and followed the little tyke, grateful for a smaller Plume family member.

I followed him to the house and stood in the road, facing the house. It was a three-story Victorian monstrosity. The roof sagged and the wood was dark with age. The windows were boarded, and vines covered most of the surface. Definitely, spooky. But what was most spooky, was the black fog that writhed on the lawn and around the house.

The boy didn't seem to mind the fog. He sat on the porch in a rocking chair, eating something from a bucket. I was pretty sure it wasn't chocolate. Too slimy.

I waited for the hordes of freaks to emerge. All of them armed with machetes, butcher knives, and pitchforks. But, thus far it was just the kid and me. No hordes.

Grandpa, where are you?

I pulled the dagger free and walked toward the property. I stalled when I reached a pair of stone-carved pillars, marking the entryway onto the land. They were easily ten feet tall, seeming much bigger as they loomed down at me. Sitting atop each column's neck were sculpted faces of evil. I wasn't able to see the faces clearly, but I saw enough to feel their dark gifts. An overgrown path passed between the columns, inviting me to cross the threshold. The fog seemed held at bay by an invisible force, keeping it within the confines of the property. I was sure it was waiting for me.

So, just as my grandfather had done, I stepped into the smothering fog.

Chapter Seven

A Growing Nightmare

THE SMELL WAS awful. I gagged, feeling like my throat was clogged with maggots. I let loose with a stream of vomit that came from deep within. Very hardcore. Fortunately, it was short-lived, and I was soon in control of my stomach. This allowed me to begin to move around.

I walked with the dagger held out before me, which cleared the fog away and created a path in any direction I moved. I was positive the Plumes would spill from the house, but nothing stirred. Nothing except the little boy. He was still dancing his jig, and eating from the bucket. Something thin and ropey hung from the boy's grinning mouth, swinging back and forth like it was stuck between his teeth.

The moans and screams returned. Thunder joined the fray. I heard unidentifiable sounds coming from the woods. Then a shotgun blast.

Grandpa.

The fog acted agitated, swirling and streaming in circles. It cried and spoke in a strange language. Thousands of voices, full of hate and fury. Very unholy and vile. It took my breath for a moment.

Another shotgun blast. I heard Grandpa's voice. "Luke, where ya at?"

I ran to his voice, shouting, "Grandpa, hurry up! I'm coming around to the east side of the house."

I was certain the Plume clan would exit the house.

Surely, our shouts would draw them out. But I was wrong. However, the boy jumped from the porch and started dancing toward me, smiling like it was Christmas morning. The kid unnerved me. I found myself trying to keep a manageable distance between us. I didn't want the little creep in my space.

A beast roared from the woods.

The fog moved like rolling eels, slithering in the direction of Grandpa's voice. I churned my legs, thinking I could get ahead of the fog and warn Grandpa of what was coming. A foolish notion. The fog was an all-encompassing blanket.

I slashed at the fog with the dagger, a clumsy act of frustration at best, but something unexpected happened as the blade passed through the blackness. It struck on a solid object. I felt hot liquid spray my arm. A cacophony of complaints arose from the mysterious fog, savagely roaring in unison. I was fairly certain the fury was directed at me, which I hoped would draw them away from Grandpa. I gave another swipe with the dagger, and got the same results. Thick rivulets of blackness dripped from the blade.

The fog collected around me, and I began to see forms in the murk. Flashes of needle-point teeth gnashed at me, and clawed hands jutted for a second or two, then returned to the cover of the fog. I swung again, but the fog moved from me, still circling, but keeping its distance. Behaving as if it feared me.

Or, it feared the dagger.

I felt a sharp pain in my left calf. It was the creepy little boy, wrapped around my lower leg, biting and clawing me. I tucked the gun and grabbed a handful of his hair, tugging and yanking. But the little bastard was dug in like a tick, biting through the jeans and deep into my flesh. I shook my leg and screamed at him, but he hung on. I finally rapped him in the head with the blunt end of the dagger. Not as hard as I would have clubbed a mad dog, but enough to get his attention. He cried, sounding just like any other five-year-old child who had just been clubbed with a blunt object. I felt bad, but the burning pain in my leg helped to dull empathetic impulses. Another shake of my leg, and he went sprawling.

I heard a door being thrown open, or rather, a door being ripped from its hinges. It was the Plumes. Finally exiting, pouring like cockroaches from a peeled away wall. Maybe seven or eight of them, each having a hideous appearance.

I pulled my gun, aimed and fired at a freak that looked like it was cross-bred with a bull. Blood splattered from its chest, but it didn't go down. It slowed and backed up. I fired at another freak with huge swinging breasts. It was the lone feminine characteristic she carried. She was bald, with a lipless mouth that overflowed with rotting teeth. The bullet found her throat, and she dropped.

Two bullets left. I was in trouble.

From the corner of my eye I saw a shimmering blur move through the air and land in the middle of the fog. It was one of the strange, golden balls that Grandpa had stashed in his bags. An amber flash followed, illuminating the fog and throwing aside the veil that hid the demonic horrors within.

Horrible creatures with faces twisted in evil. Reptilian eyes, seething with unnerving wickedness.

The fog became a blue flame, blazing and incinerating. The demons were turned to ash, and the fog was no more. The rain and wind swept away what might have been left of the supernatural beings.

A shotgun roared from behind me, and a Plume fell to the ground. I fired a round at a mongoloid with wispy hair, but missed.

Grandpa appeared on my right side, his shotgun raised. "I've got 'em, don't ya worry."

The mongoloid's head sprayed into tiny bits of flesh and bone. Down to four freaks.

I had one bullet left, I tried to make it count as I squeezed off one more time, planting a bullet in the bullish looking one. It hit him in the gut, he fell to his knees, then onto his face.

No bullets left. "Uh, Grandpa I'm empty."

"Me too."

"Aw, crap."

An epiphany came to me. It concerned fear, and how fear was actually a friend. It helped prod primitive instincts of survival. Regardless of how I tried pushing fear aside, it kept crawling back. The dagger didn't extinguish my fear, but it settled me. Death was inevitable, but I'd be damned if I was going to die at the hands of this abominable tribe of killers.

Grandpa ran at one of the Plumes, swinging the shotgun. The butt slammed against a jawbone, knocking teeth loose. He then hastily fished around in one of the burlap bags and withdrew one of the shiny balls, tossing it at our assailants. The ball bounced around on the ground and collected mud, but the light show never arrived. The Plumes were not burned, or destroyed.

"I was afraid of that, but ya never know unless ya try," said Grandpa. He continued his assault, swinging the shotgun like a medieval ax. It struck a squat, toad-like Plume on top of the head, splintering the stock of the gun. Blood gushed darkly, streaming into the toad-man's eyes, but the damage was not enough to drop it to the ground. It reached and grasped for Grandpa with dirty hands, blindfolded by the sheet of dark fluid. Grandpa kicked it in the face with one of his clod-hoppers, then brought the barrel of the shotgun down onto the wound.

I thought I would help him out, end it with a good stab into toad-man's chest, but my head filled with stars and pain. I became dazed and fell. I looked up and saw the bottom of a dirty foot closing in on my face. I felt the awful impact, and heard my nose *crunch*. Sounds became muffled, and I couldn't keep my eyes open.

Then my eyes finally did open, and I found myself lying on my back in the mud and rain. Grandpa was leaned over me. "C'mon, get up. We're almost done."

I grabbed his arm and let him pull me up. "What happened?"

"Ya got worked over pretty good."

I gently touched my nose and face, finding pain and swollen parts. I then looked at the yard and my neighbor's strewn bodies. "So, they're all dead?"

He handed me the dagger. "Yep. Deader'n three in the mornin'. Ya dropped the dagger."

The dagger's onrush pulsed through my body. The strange charge was becoming less alien to my senses, but still comforting. I turned my attention to the Plume that lay at my feet. Its head was nearly free of the neck. Stretched sinew and gristle were all that prevented a proper decapitation. "Is this the one that was stomping on me?"

"That's him all right. It put up a decent fight."

"It don't look like it."

"I had to take the dagger to 'em"

"Yeah, I see that." I sniffed at the air, catching a whiff of blood. It made me queasy.

"We ain't quite done yet," said Grandpa, pointing to the house. "We've got to make sure the house has been cleared out."

"You think there's more?" I immediately thought of the young boy.

"Well, I don't think the house is empty."

Something sparkled, catching my peripheral vision. I yanked my head in the direction of the gleam, feeling my neck crack with pain. I was starting to feel more injuries from my beat down.

Grandpa bent and reached for the shining object that distracted me. It was the golden ball that misfired. "I wasn't sure if these weapons would work on normal flesh and bone. I reckon they must not."

"The dagger works just fine." I nodded to the body

that Grandpa had put the butcher job on.

"I cain't explain why that is. But I'm pretty certain a regular sort of knife wouldn't have harmed the demons. It's a special weapon."

A marble-sized hailstone bounced off the rim of Grandpa's hat. Then the winds stopped, and all became quiet. Grandpa tapped me roughly on a shoulder and motioned for me to run to the cover of the dilapidated porch. I was four steps into my run when the sky opened its mouth and drooled sheets of hail upon us.

"Keep on comin', son!" shouted Grandpa.

I protected my head with my arms, letting them take the brunt of the icy blows. I also noticed a sharp stitch from my right side, like maybe I had a cracked rib. I began to suspect that adrenaline was buffering a significant amount of my injuries.

Grandpa helped me up the steps and then flattened his back against the house. He slowly inched his way toward the splintered front doorway. He held the ball in his left hand. "Stand back. I'm goin' to do some clearin' out."

He tossed the ball into the mouth of darkness, and the effect was immediate. An amber flash was followed by screams and cursing. The house shook with rage, causing parts of the veranda's roof to fall away. I hugged a spot close to Grandpa, narrowly escaping the falling debris.

The hailstorm suddenly stopped, and the wind came to life. A heavy roar accompanied the late afternoon air, sounding like a freight-train rolling down a set of rails.

"That's a twister," said Grandpa. "It's close."

"Well, isn't that just *great*."

Grandpa grabbed a piece of wood from the collapsed roof. It was as long as a bat, and the business end was ragged with nails. "Get behind me with your dagger, Luke. We're goin' in."

There was no hesitation. He entered the darkness, and I played along, limping half a step behind. The gloom was smothering and heavy. What little daylight managed to crawl into the house was instantly enveloped. The reek of fecal matter, urine, and something unknown did a fine job of provoking my gag reflex.

"It's hard to breathe," I said in a low voice.

"Yep."

"What are we looking for?"

Grandpa pulled one of the strange guns from a bag, and another ball-bomb. "We're lookin' for demons. We're goin' to clear this house out."

"What about the tornado?" The rumbling outside was intensifying.

He handed the gun to me and said, "I reckon we've got time if we cut down on the lollygaggin'."

Lollygaggin'?

"It's pitch black in here," I argued.

"I think we got that problem licked."

"How's that?"

Something wet and heavy sloshed somewhere in the house. It sounded like guts slinking down a staircase.

Grandpa stabbed at the murk with a finger. "Take your dagger and walk into the dark."

"Do what?" Surely, I misheard him. "Walk into the dark?"

"Trust me. It'll light up like a Christmas tree."

Evidently, my hearing was just fine.

I shrugged my shoulders and gimped a couple of tiny steps into the dark, listening to the slippery sounds ooze closer. I held the dagger with my left hand and the strange gun in my right. Then, just as Grandpa promised, the dagger lit up. Like a Christmas tree. Like *Times Square*.

And the things that slithered were uncovered.

The darkness was a comfortable womb in which the awful things could nest. But the darkness was gone. Ripped away like a bandage. They were a frightful lot, scurrying blindly into walls, obviously perturbed by the light sweeping across their bodies. They squealed like fiendish, newborn babies, snapping at the air with barbed tongues and needle-teeth. Scaly creatures with jutting jaws. The squishy sounds were the result of the nasty things stumbling down the staircase on long arms, leaving a slick of blood and mucous.

Hellish slugs.

"It's the same little bastards I saw as a youngster," said Grandpa. He tossed a ball into the fray, and we watched as the amber light destroyed them. I could feel their darkness reaching for me as they died.

"Someone birthed these things, and I imagine that there's more of'em pouring out," said Grandpa. "I recall them eatin' on the person that conjured them."

I quickly searched the hallways with my widened eyes. I didn't feel up to uncovering more vileness. "So what do we do?"

"Finish up and leave," he said, approaching the staircase. "But, I'll need ya to light the way for me."

The wind outside yowled mockingly. I heard pieces of the house being bent and broken. I wasted no time. I ascended the steps hobbling like a bent, old man.

It was a three-story house, and I was not enthusiastic about the possibility of having to climb another flight. You can imagine my twisted relief, as I happened upon the source of the little monsters soon after reaching the second floor. They were creeping from a pile of flesh and bone that was heaped in front of an open door. A blue-flannel dress, barely visible through the redness, made a strong case for the pile being human. A dead human, as was obvious to me.

Without any forethought, I pointed the gun at the body and pulled the trigger. The result was a small explosion that hammered my eardrums. The body disintegrated into a bloody spray of meat particles. To my surprise, the kick was not too extreme. I was able to retain possession.

"So are we done?" My voice sounded like it didn't belong to me. It was too old and worn.

A voice, husky and liquid, rolled like smoke from the

open doorway. It was unmistakably feminine. "Not yet. None of us has finished our work."

I swung my gun toward the stranger's voice, keyed up and primed to kill. It was getting easy.

A figure emerged from the room. Long and sensuous, dressed in a shimmering black dress. Ink-black hair against alabaster skin. Oh, so beautiful.

"You," she spoke, and pointed a black talon at Grandpa. "You must be...Theo."

"I know your name too, Lilith," said Grandpa.

She walked toward us with feline grace, artfully avoiding the widespread mess. Her hips swayed and seduced with a sexual energy that had my budding hormones in an uproar. A large amount of blood rushed to my groin, invoking a marble-hard erection.

"Keep your gun pointed at her," said Grandpa.

"Oh, he has his *gun* pointed at me." Lilith snickered wickedly through succulent lips, flashing her exquisite, black, smile at me. The dress was low-cut, rising just above her nipples. It glistened with a wetness, clinging to every curve and bump.

"Luke, snap out of it! She's a demon!"

The temptress stopped walking. "I'm a bit more than that. Apollyon warned me of your stupidity."

Grandpa ignored the insult and stretched out his gun arm, aiming it at the she-demon's face. "How come the devil sent a tramp like you?"

"He was busy." She laughed, and it was a horrible sound. It made me want to rip free of my skin.

"Who conjured all of this up?" asked Grandpa.

She smoothed her hands against her breasts, and then tweaked a nipple that quickly resembled a hidden thimble. Her black tongue flicked across her lips like a serpent's. She grinned at me and spoke to Grandpa. "*I* conjured this."

"Well, too bad it's wasted effort on your part."

"How, so?" Her voice raged with contempt.

"Cause' your demons are dead, and so are the Plumes.

Pretty soon, this house will be gone and you'll be gone with it. The Lord will see to it."

She spat a stream of blackness at Grandpa. It splashed the front of his overalls, adding one more stain to its collection. Demon spittle was a rare addition.

"Do not bring *Him* into this!" Her face flickered like an eight-millimeter film clip, revealing snatches of her true nature. It was just for an instant, but I saw the demon's beauty replaced with a horrifying wickedness.

"Nice manners on ya there, ya stinkin' harlot," Grandpa said.

The train outside roared. The tornado would be on us very soon, ending all drama and suspense. We were all going to be dead.

Grandpa grinned. "That's God out there, demon. He's comin' for ya."

She snorted. "Do you *really* believe that, Theo?"

Grandpa cocked the gun and took aim. "Amen, I surely do."

Out of the corner of my eye, I saw movement to my right. A small figure was running toward me with a shining blade, raised high by two tiny hands.

The dancing boy was back. That little bastard.

Grandpa also saw him and swung the gun at the boy. He pulled the trigger. *Click.*

"Your Holy toys of death won't work against him," said Lilith. "He's one of you."

I moved to avoid the boy, just as the hallway became filled with wind and stinging debris. The roof of the house disappeared and floated Grandpa into the air, then threw him down the stairs like a rag-doll. The little boy-demon was not spared the storm's wrath, as he was stolen away and blurred into the sky. I felt my body being pulled, but the demon was on me with alarming deftness, slamming me onto my back. My arms came to be pinned against the rotting wood, my weapons rattled from my hold.

She straddled me, rubbing her naked crotch against

my fevered area, then sneered and leaned her face to mine. "I'm going to bring you back with me," she said, grinding against me passionately. "Think of the fun we'll have."

Her voice moved along my spine like a lover's fingertips.

"I know you want me, Luke. I can *feel* your longing pressing into me like a stone," she said. "You'll never have to fantasize about those school girls again."

Despite my awful worry for Grandpa, lust was winning the battle of interest. It made me sick.

She pressed her lips against mine and parted them with a hard, cold tongue that felt like an eel. She breathed into my lungs, filling me with her rancid breath. She let go of her kiss and began fumbling with the belt on my jeans.

"I *must* have you," she said. In a fit of passion, she bit into my right shoulder, reaching bone and searing it with awful pain.

I screamed, as you might have guessed.

My arms were free, but I had no weapon, nor the strength to wield one if I did. I tried to move and twist away, but pain ricocheted across the tips of every nerve ending in my body. It seemed that fate had me bound. I was to be raped by a beautiful demon with bad breath, and then dragged to Hell.

The storm's bellow increased, blowing more ferociously, whipping the debris in circles. I narrowed my eyes against the wind and saw the dagger swirling in the air like a boat prop. It gleamed, even though the sun was locked away behind the storm.

Just as my zipper opened, the dagger helicoptered downward, as if riding a rogue stream of air. The demon had my young manhood in her hand when the dagger struck her face. Amazingly, and thankfully, she didn't rip my penis from my body. She instead loosed me from her grip and screamed in a strange language.

The dagger had inflicted a nasty wound to the left side of her face. A slice of skin flapped in the wind, flinging wet blackness. She stood over me and roared, sounding like the unearthly beast that she was. Her beauty started to peel away.

"You stay away from him, demon!" It was Grandpa. "Take me on! I'm who ya want!"

I zipped my trousers and shouted to him. "Watch out! She's pretty pissed!" My ribs cracked with pain.

The demon's face was now covered in festering blisters and blackening veins. "Child, you have no comprehension of my anger and contempt." Her voice was thick and hoarse.

Grandpa had crawled his way back to the top. He rested on his forearms, while his legs trailed down the staircase. A heavy flow of blood poured from his head. His hat, remarkably, was still in place.

"You old fool." The demon glowered at Grandpa and chuckled. "Your time of usefulness has long passed. You're...*measly*. The power that exudes from this plot of land is *much* more significant than your entire hog-slopping life."

"I ain't the fool." Grandpa grabbed the rotting bannister and pulled himself to a knee. "You still think you're goin' to win."

Lilith's cheekbones sharpened, and her mouth widened like a python's. She seized my ankle, lifting me into the air, dangling me upside-down in the wind. "I'll win."

"Nope." Grandpa removed his hat and flung it like a plate at the demon. "You ain't."

The hat landed square in the demon's face, clinging snugly. Obviously, it wasn't a damaging blow, but it blinded her to a large cluster of debris that was hurtling toward her. It was as big as a Chevy and solid. It slammed into the demon with fantastic force. I didn't get the chance to see the aftermath, because I closed my eyes against the stinging rubble. But, I heard the demon's protest.

"Luke!" Grandpa's call was barely audible. I started to

shout back when my body became weightless, and I felt myself being lifted into the sky. My eardrums popped with insane pressure. Then, darkness cocooned me, and I became deprived of all senses. No sounds. No smells. No pain.

Chapter Eight

Despair, Eyeball Recipes, And A
Really Bad Old Lady

MY WITS RETURNED as tumbling bits of data. First, I heard snippets of voices, and then I saw blurred light. Unfortunately, pain was the illuminating sense that slapped my senses awake. I moaned a gripe as my ribs exploded with agony.

"Luke? Can you hear me?" It was a woman's voice, wading through a fog. It sounded muffled and excited.

"I'll be damn...someone needs to..."

My eyes fluttered open, and I found myself in a dark room. I was lying in a bed with several faces staring down at me. I didn't know any of them.

"Get the doctor, and hurry your ass!" The person speaking was a man wearing a tan uniform with a shiny star over his left breast. He leaned over me and patted my chest, cutting his eyes at the woman in the room. She wore a nurse's uniform.

I tried to sit up, but found I was strapped to the bed. It freaked me out. I thrashed against my restraints and began to scream. I found it to be instantly therapeutic.

A bespectacled man in a lab coat was quickly by my side, accompanied by another nurse. He was gray-haired and kindly looking. He spoke to me in a soft voice, somehow cutting into my commotion of noise. "Luke, I'm Dr. Amos. I really need for you to try to calm down. You're going to be fine. Nobody here means you any harm."

I wasn't done.

The doctor showed me a syringe. "Promise me you'll calm down. Otherwise..."

I knew what *otherwise* meant. I didn't want to be stabbed with a needle. I was done.

The man with the badge stood at the foot of my bed, his arms folded. He tried to smile at me. "Trust the doc, kid."

The pair of nurses loosened my straps while the doctor spoke. "Son, we had to buckle you in because you kept throwing yourself from the bed, bad dreams I'd guess." He dragged a wooden chair across the floor, grinding everyone's nerves. He sat to my left and leaned in. "You're a patient of the Hughes County hospital, and you've been injured pretty badly, son. Been sleeping for eleven days...counting today."

"Wait," I said. "Did you say eleven days?"

"That's right, son."

"Was I in a coma?"

"No, you were not."

"Wow."

Grandpa came to my mind, and I began looking around the room for him. The last memory I had of him was him struggling and injured, and somehow clinging to the top of the staircase.

A bad feeling welled in the pit of my stomach. "Where's Grandpa," I said.

The lawman cleared his throat.

"Has anyone seen him? You've got to go to the Plumes'! He's there!"

The lawman walked to the left side of the bed. His holster squeaked of polished leather. "Son, I'm afraid I've got some bad news...your grandpa—"

No.

"Was killed in the storm. I'm so sorry for you, son."

I immediately corrected him. He was wrong. I bawled out my point. I informed them that we were at the Plumes' and they needed to look for him there. He was injured, and needing medical attention.

"Luke, we've been all over the countryside. The Plume property got hit hard. The house is gone, not even a board left."

"So, you haven't actually *seen* his body?" I said.

"That much is true, but his truck was found on the side of the road, not far from the twister's path." He didn't try to press the issue. "Why would you be at the Plumes' anyway?"

"Because—" Whoa, wait a minute.

"Because, why?" he said.

Well, because we were killing the entire Plume family. And by the way, we also killed quite a few demons and I was nearly raped by one.

"I don't know. It was Grandpa's idea."

"Sheriff, this boy's been through a lot. This news is a hell of a thing to wake to," said Dr. Amos.

The lawman nodded his head in agreement. "Yes, but he has the right to know these things, Doctor. And I have an obligation."

The doctor held out a hand, splaying the fingers. "Five minutes. I'll give you that much time, and then I have to speak to my patient."

"I'm fine with that, thanks. I won't need five minutes."

Doctor Amos left the room with the two nurses and closed the door behind him. The sheriff sat in the doctor's chair and made a comment about the seat being warm. "Were the two of you hunting?"

Yep, we certainly were.

"No." I worried I might have answered the question too energetically.

"Was there anyone else with you?"

"No. It was just us."

"Okay." He stood up and shook his head with sympathy. "Well, we found you in a field of mud that was about three miles from the Plumes'. You're awful damn lucky to be alive. Lots of injuries." He moved his mouth like he wanted to ask me something else, but he paused whatever he had on his mind. "Look, we'll keep our eyes open for anything or anyone. I promise you that."

It had to be the toughest part of his job, telling people that their loved ones were gone. He spoke with genuine compassion, which probably helped to soften such dreadful news. I felt my own sorrow begin to swell in my throat.

"I'm going to look around the Plume property. But, don't expect any miracles," he said.

I thought of the dead freak lying in the road, and the rest of his freak family riddled with gunshot wounds. The tornado must have scattered the corpses, or so I hoped. The sheriff would be back to arrest me. This I was sure of.

"I'm going to run on out of here, Luke. You take care of yourself, and if there's anything you need just call the station and ask for Sheriff Jake Sanford."

I nodded to Sheriff Jake, as my throat stung with sadness. The probability of Grandpa surviving the incident was not good. It was time to stop kidding myself.

Sadness ripped into me, pummeling me with waves of pain. I wanted to die.

My sobs were aching and fierce, each one feeling like a sledge hammer to my injured ribs. Then, I suddenly could not breathe.

Sheriff Jake screamed for someone to help me, and help was immediate as two nurses and Dr. Amos arrived. The doctor barked something about ccs and a syringe.

"You've got to breathe, just relax." I felt the sting of the needle, but it was a pale discomfort. The drug raced through my blood quickly, effectively sending me back to a mindless chasm of sleep.

A sound nudged me back into awareness. My eyes opened to the same room, except it was darker. The antiseptic smells of the hospital swam with a lingering staleness, seeming sharper as I lay alone in the darkness. I noticed a pain in my left arm, a tube taped into place, dripping numbing concoctions into my body. A dim slash of light wandered in through the blinds in my room, probably from a street light. My head felt as if it was stuffed with cotton, and my sadness was still suffocating. I wanted to find sleep again. There was nothing in the world of reality that I wanted.

The shuffle of a shoe whispered from the darkened room, the rustle of clothes. "Who's there?"

Footsteps, slow and easy, grew closer. A figure emerged from the shadows and stood at the foot of my bed. He was tall, dressed in a shining suit and wearing a top hat. He had long, black hair that glistened like a snake's skin, and a face made for Hollywood. "Do you know who I am?"

"Yes." My voice was a whisper. "You're the devil."

"Well, give the hillbilly a chicken dinner. You must be the genius in the family."

The devil had a black cane topped with a small human skull, approximately the size of an infant's. He leaned forward on the cane and smiled at me. His teeth were glazed pieces of coal. "I go by many names, but you can call me Nick. I've been called that for some time in these parts."

Dreadfulness emanated from the devil, pushing against me with a smothering force. I scooted into my pillow and drew my legs tight.

Nick sighed and spun his cane with spider-like dexterity, walking in and out of the shadows, grinning. "Luke, Luke. You might have been an agent of spectacular ability. But, alas, you were protected by *Him*, which placed you beyond my influence. *Your* loss as much as it was mine."

I was scared. More scared than I had ever been in my young life—which is a rather significant statement, considering the horrors I'd recently endured. Things slithered and bumped in the room. I heard raspy whispers speaking in a strange tongue. And the devil himself stood in front of me.

Scared shitless, I was.

Nick stopped the twirling and sat on the left side of the bed. "I don't have much time to waste on you, so this will be brief. I just wanted to pop in for a chat. Is that fine?"

I nodded my head. I figured I didn't have much choice in the matter.

"You've got pluck, boy. Not unlike good ole' Theo." The devil tapped his chin, thinking. "Yes, the dearly *departed* Theo."

A jolt of anger filled my head with blood.

The devil laughed and stood up. He walked into the streaming light and tilted his head in a way that allowed me a brief look at his eyes. They were like black glass. "It seems all of your loved ones *depart*."

The words were hurled razor blades, angering and wounding. Tears formed in my eyes, which angered me even more.

"Yes, your father and your mother. They too have *departed*." He pointed the end of his cane at me. "I watched as they died. It was not a pleasant experience for either of them, I assure you."

I didn't know much of their death, only that they were murdered. I didn't want to know anything else about it, and I didn't want to hear it from the devil. "Why are you here? What do you want from me?"

"Just like ole gramps, you get straight to the point." Nick reached inside his jacket and withdrew a pocket-watch. He hooked the chain with a claw from his pinky and suspended it in front of his face. "And that is a good thing, as I do tend to get rather long-winded, and I have plans to meet with someone in this very hospital. Yes, an old woman who happens to be a patient, or in your case, a hospital neighbor. This woman has earned my company, and I do not wish to disappoint."

I closed my eyes, wishing he would reach the end of his say, or turn to smoke and disappear. He surely did enjoy the sound of his own voice.

"At any rate, it is a wonderful stroke of fate that this woman and you are in the same residence. I may now tell you, face to face, that your life from this moment on is going to be noteworthy. You've been marked, boy. Your grandfather was stolen from me. A debt is still owed."

Words dipped in hate.

"But, the hayseed—your grand pappy—possessed a faith so strong it garnered him worthy of His protection, which was passed down to you." Black spittle sprayed from his mouth. "So, I may not harm you."

If I trusted him, those would have been relieving words. But, he was the devil.

The devil took a long step to me and grabbed my chin with a clawed hand. He pressed his nose against mine. "But, that deal does not hold water with others. Only *I* am rendered impotent as a cause of your destruction."

His breath stank of decay and death. I gagged as I caught a strong whiff, and was on the verge of vomiting into his flawless face.

"My agents are everywhere, and they will track you down, and the others like you. All of you, stolen from me by those damning Overseers. It's bullshit."

He released me and began twirling his cane over his head, smiling viciously. Then he tossed it into a darkened corner. An arm, white and willowy, fired from the shadows and plucked the cane from the air, then disappeared into a shadow. "Adding to my misery is the moronic blunder made by my beautiful demon. She bit you."

I gently touched the wound through the hospital gown. It was tender and sore, but nothing to cause me much discomfort.

"This puts you in rare company, indeed. However, please understand you are so *very* undeserving of this gift.

It makes me want to rip your eyeballs from their sockets."

Glowing eyes emerged from the darkness. Rows of blinking orbs, accompanied by baritone growls. The devil held a hand to the unseen beasts and spoke to them. "I was merely expressing my thoughts, stay back. No snacks today."

"Friends of yours?" I said nervously.

"Don't be stupid. They are my slaves." His face constricted into a hideous smile. "Human eyeballs are second only to human hearts, as a desired meal. The beasts became excited, as you can imagine, when they thought a morsel was to be had. My personal preference is an eyeball marinated in a chalice of ancient cognac." The devil closed his eyes and sniffed the air. A wicked grin crept to his ears. "Yes, a rather gamey zest."

"Grandpa was right about you," I said. "You're a butthole."

"Ah, taunting the devil."

"Nope, not taunting. Just fed up with you and your kind."

"You are such a stupid, pitiful creature. You know absolutely nothing about my *kind*. And let us also be clear that you do not confuse *my* kind with the imps and demons that are scurrying around this hospital tonight."

I had struck a nerve.

"I am the most beautiful and perfect being to ever be created. That is my kind."

"You got kicked out of Heaven. Right?"

The devil smiled and rubbed his chin. "Your dear, old granddad would have known the answer to that question. He had the faith of the old ones. You only believe because of what you've seen with your eyes. That is not faith, bumpkin boy."

It was all true, what the devil was saying.

Old Nick once again pulled his watch out. He eyeballed the time, arcing an eyebrow dramatically. "My time with you is done, I must move along. If you should ever need me, I'll know."

"I'll *never* need you. I'll only hate you."

"Hate is good," said the devil. "Hate is strength. Perfect your hate, whenever possible."

The room was already crammed with hate. The reek was like rotten, hanging sides of beef. It made me ache for the days of goodness. All the years spent with Grandpa, on the farm.

"I thought you had an appointment." I wanted the devil to be moving along.

"Indeed, I certainly do." The devil smiled and tipped his hat. "I came to your grandfather in a dream once. We spoke, just as you and I have. Did he tell you about it?"

"Yeah, he told me."

"No more stories from Theo," said the devil. "You can stew about that while you lay alone in the dark."

"Why don't you fuck off," I said.

The devil chuckled and walked to the door. He opened it and paused, looking at me over his shoulder. "It will be entertaining to see how you manage the rest of your life."

I gave him both middle fingers.

The devil sneered and then walked out of the room, leaving me in the dark—although not nearly as dark as when he occupied the space. Darkness receded on account of his absence. Even my punctured spirits were lifted, which only moments ago were drowning. Anxiety and fear subsided. Sleep ambushed me.

Chapter Nine

New Friends and a Dead Lady

I AWOKE TO the smell of bacon and coffee, and to the sound of rumbling voices. The breakfast smells were from a steaming plate atop a TV tray with wheels. The voices were from somewhere down the fluorescent hallway, beyond my open door.

Holy shit, is that biscuits and gravy?

I attacked the plate of food. My body was sick of liquid nourishment, demanding a meal with flavor and texture.

"That's a good sign." Doctor Amos stood in the doorway, folder in his hands. "A good appetite is generally a sign of good health."

Startled, I jerked my head toward the doctor, and somehow was able to sling a glob of white gravy from my mouth. It spattered on the linoleum floor, creating a greasy mess.

"That's embarrassing," I said.

Doctor Amos waved me off. "Get as sloppy as you like. I imagine you're famished."

I ran a napkin across my mouth and swigged down a glass of orange juice. An acidic belch followed.

"Luke, some people are here this morning to see you," he said.

"Who is it?" I almost stopped chewing.

"Well, a lawyer and a few others. It's regarding who's going to be taking care of you from now on. Oh, and the sheriff is here."

I stopped chewing and swallowed a chunk of bacon. It stuck on the way down, inciting a coughing spasm. Doctor Amos rushed to my side, slapping me on the back.

"You might want to slow down a just a little bit. We wouldn't want you choking to death after surviving a twister," he said.

I shook my head in agreement. Maybe I was more inclined to be alive than I gave myself credit.

"Luke, I've not had the chance to talk to you much about your injuries. You had several broken bones, most of them ribs."

I felt the bandage wrapped around my torso, but my ribs didn't give an inkling of pain during my coughing spell. "They feel fine now."

"Yes, that's what I want to mention. You healed in roughly two weeks' time, which is a medical mystery, or a miracle."

"I guess I have good bones, and I'm real lucky," I said.

"I'd say you're correct on both accounts."

I was more concerned about my future and where I'd be living than my miraculous recovery. "Who do you think will be getting me?"

Doctor Amos shook his head. "I don't have that answer, Luke. Those answers will be forthcoming soon." He patted my foot with the folder. "I don't know you very well, but I'd be willing to stake that you'll be all right."

A light knock against the doorframe interrupted our conversation, and an old man in a wheelchair entered. He was being pushed by a broad-shouldered, stern looking man in a suit.

"Luke Morgan, I presume?" The old man smiled and surprised me with the brilliant glow his teeth had. The rest of him had not fared as well. He was bald, wore eyeglasses thick as a windshield, and had a face heavy with dangling wrinkles.

His attendee parked him to the left of me, and then stood by the doorway.

"I'm sorry for your loss." He stuck his hand out to me. "I've known Theophilus for a great number of years. I've never known a better person."

I took his hand and shook it. The old man had an impressive grip.

"I'm Thomas Bird, your grandfather's lawyer."

Doctor Amos excused himself and shut the door behind him, leaving me with the old man. "Your grandfather wanted you to be taken care of, and you most certainly will be." He slid a slim attaché case from beneath his suit and rested it in his lap. "The sheriff should be joining us soon."

"What's going to happen to me?" I said.

"Well, I have documents explaining all of this—"

Someone knocked on the door and slowly opened it. It was Sheriff Jake and another man wearing a suit.

"Would you leave the door open?" I appreciated the light as it came into the room. I looked to the lone window. "And would someone please open the blinds?"

The sheriff obliged, and we finally got down to the business of me. The suit with the sheriff was from the child welfare department, and he quickly began explaining my new guardianship. I would be moving to Oklahoma City.

"So, who's this guardian?" I said.

"Ruckus McGraw," said the suit.

A frown flickered across Mr. Bird's face. "Interesting."

"Have you met him?" I said.

"Yes, I have met him."

"What's he like?"

Tommy thrummed his fingers on the case, thinking before he answered. "Seems to be a good man, he must be if Theophilus chose him. He's somewhat…gregarious."

"What's that mean?" A fancy word for my neck of the

woods.

"Well, he's quite expressive."

"Oh."

"You'll also be coming into some properties and a substantial amount of money, once you've turned eighteen," said Mr. Bird. "Theophilus was planning for you, just as he did for your father."

"Did you know my father?" I surprised myself with the question.

"Yes, I knew your father, or at the very least, met him on several occasions."

Doctor Amos came in with a nurse, who began wheeling away the empty plates and glasses. He had some good news. "Luke, you're being released from the hospital's care. You're too damn healthy to be stuck here."

"How soon can I leave?"

"Within the hour. Some ladies from the Freewill Baptist church are on their way with some clothes for you. The ones you arrived in were covered in mud and blood."

"What did you do with the clothes?" asked the sheriff. "Do you still have them?"

"Maybe we have them, but it's doubtful. Like I said, the clothes were rather beat up."

The sheriff pursed his lips, thinking. "Any chance you could get someone to check for me?"

"Of course."

Sheriff Jake looked at me, grinning. "Well, I'm goin' to shove off. I've had a busier morning than usual. Luke, I'll be staying in touch."

"I believe I'll be leaving as well. Everything seems to be in order here," said the suit. "Good luck to you, Luke."

Within a few ticks it was just Mr. Bird, his silent wheelchair-driver, and myself left. Mr. Bird seemed to have been waiting for the moment. He dug in his attaché case and presented me with an old book, leather bound and cracked with age.

"You should read this when you have the time. It will

answer most of the questions you have spinning in your head."

I seriously doubted his claim. I set it aside on a nightstand.

"Tell me, Luke," he said. "Did the devil pay you a visit last night?"

Not a common question. I was stunned.

"I know more than you think," he said. "So, did he visit you?"

"Seriously?" I asked.

"I am quite serious."

"If I say yes, you won't have me locked up in a nuthouse?"

"You have my word. No nuthouse."

"Okay, yeah. He was here last night." Thinking about it made me shiver. "I've never felt so…"

"Hopeless, and alone?"

I began to tremble. "Yes."

"The devil is evil beyond words, young man."

"How did you know the devil was here last night?"

"The sheriff mentioned his busier than normal morning. That's because a patient here, found dead in her tangled sheets this morning, was quite a monster."

"What do you mean?"

"She was a murderer of children," he said. "This woman carried out these murders in hopes of one day gaining favor in Hell, according to notes and diaries the old woman kept. Dark souls have been known to influence some ranks down there. She was admitted into this hospital yesterday morning for a mild heart attack, which as it turns out, was not so mild after all. Her gardener found her face down in a mesh of red roses, unconscious and bleeding. He ran into the house to phone for help and happened across a little girl's decapitated head, defrosting in the kitchen sink."

"Holy crap."

"Yes, quite horrific. Upon further investigation of the

premises, authorities found more body parts and bones buried beneath the crawlspace of the home. They are still digging."

"How did you know the devil would visit me?"

"I didn't know for sure. But, after learning of the woman's wicked behavior...I wondered. I suspected he would be tempted to pop in on you, even before I'd heard of the murderess. He would want to taunt you because you are Theophilus' grandson, and he would want to test your mettle."

I didn't know what *mettle* meant, but I let him keep talking.

"Such unrepentant sins are a guarantee of a personal escort to Hell. I merely put two and two together, and voila." He made a *poof* gesture with his hands.

"So you know *everything* about Grandpa?"

"Indeed, I do. But, we'll talk more later."

I lay back against the pillow, looking at the ceiling. I soaked up his words. It was all so damn crazy. "How do you know all of this?"

"My father, John Bird, was the pastor of your grandfather's church. One day after service, Theophilus, still a young boy, confided to him about the strange events that turned his hair white. He was convincing enough to get him to talk to Chester and Lucille." He pointed to the book on the nightstand. "Much of what you want to know is in there. I've not read it in years, which is another way of me saying that I may not recall all of the details. Besides, it's Theophilus' story and it is rightfully yours to inherit."

"So, neither one of us is crazy?"

"Not in the legal sense." Tommy shifted in his wheelchair and coughed. "But you would be wise to keep this secret. Outsiders would, undoubtedly, think you insane."

"Is there anyone else that knows?"

"Yes, but you'll meet them in time, after you've

settled into your new surroundings."

"How long will that be?"

"Very soon." He squinted through his pop-bottle lenses to look at his watch. "In fact, I must be leaving to make certain your transition is smooth."

The stern suit came forward, ready to steer Tommy out. I looked closely at him, seeing chiseled Native American features.

"I'll be by next week," said Mr. Bird. "I'll have more time to talk."

Hearing this bolstered my spirits. I had questions growing like weeds.

He tapped a ring against the wheelchair, and then motioned to Mr. Stern Suit. "Bear, we must be moving."

"That's a cool name." I couldn't resist.

Bear smiled at me and nodded, then silently spun Tommy from the room and into the cold glare of the hallway. I was alone with no television or radio to drown the quiet, all the while trapped in a gown that didn't even cover my skinny ass.

I cried like a baby, wallowing in my excruciating grief to pass the time. This went on for a time, until I finally became fed up with being bedridden, and decided to take a walk.

I got out of bed and stood with my hand on the nightstand. My legs felt a bit shaky, but I was able to stand. I left the room and walked into the middle of the hallway, my left hand futilely trying to hide my backside. To my right were double-doors with rectangular windows at the end. Sunlight streamed in and I saw people milling around outside, some of them wearing police uniforms. So, I decided to join them and get some fresh air and sunlight.

The doors swung open with ease, and I stepped into the world of real light. It was wonderful. I closed my eyes and breathed in deeply, smelling flowers and churned earth. I heard voices mingled with the crackle of static coming from cop radios. I opened my eyes and noticed a black hearse parked next the hospital beneath a tattered cedar-tree. Painted on the doors was *Hughes County Coroner*.

"Holy, crap. It's her." I quickly looked around to see if anyone was paying attention to me. I was practically invisible. I scooted to the hearse and peeked in a window. Through a set of small drapes, I was barely able to make out a black body bag. Then I noticed the back of the hearse was wide open.

I had to get a closer look.

I approached the bag and saw that it was not fully zipped. A small tuft of gray hair poked through the opening, which was apparently the head. Her feet were closest to me, which meant I was going to have to crawl inside to get a better look.

What is wrong with me?

Knowing full well how absurd my actions were, yet unable to stop myself, I clambered inside and made my way to the protruding hair. I was a foot or two away from her head when it started to wiggle. In fact, the entire bag wiggled like it was full of vibrators. Gurgling sounds were coming from within the bag.

The door slammed shut behind me. "Damn it!" I pawed at the latch, but it wouldn't budge. And then the old lady cackled and sat up. I could see her face, the zipper stopped around her chin. Her eyes were black.

I balled up a fist and smacked her in the nose, knocking the corpse back. It was all I could think to do.

I immediately began fiddling with the door, kicking it with my bare feet. "Oh, God! This was stupid, stup—"

"Look at me, boy," said the old woman. Her throat sounded like it was crammed with mud.

I didn't want to look at her. But I did. Her mouth was widening, stretching. I heard her jawbone snapping. I saw spindly fingers creeping over her toothless chops. Something was crawling out of her, pulling itself up.

I screamed and pounced on the old woman, straddling

her. I connected with her nose again, raining knuckle upon knuckle on her face. My assault was stopped when the strange hands sprang at me and grasped my wrists with superior strength. Whatever was inside of her was using me to pull free of her guts.

I saw the top of the creature's head as it began to crest. It was narrow, elongated and covered with shiny orbs that blinked.

Holy shit, oh my God, it's got eyes on its head!

I wiggled my legs around in front and hammered both heels into the sickening maw, repeatedly working them like pistons. I thrashed my arms the best I could, but my tugging and pulling only aided the thing's progression.

I decided to ram my left foot as far into the old lady's mouth as I could, in an effort to push the monstrous thing back into her stomach. This took an enormous measure of courage. Never mind that I'm sticking my foot into an orifice with a monster—that was *way* bad—but the squishy wetness that seeped between my toes was disgusting.

My hard work produced a growl from the creature and it actually backed away from me, slinking back an inch or two. But as soon as I tried to pull away, the cord-like fingers tightened around my wrists. So, I bit down on one of its fingers and sawed my teeth back and forth, grinding away. The skin's texture was similar to sandpaper and smelled like bad bologna, but was not impervious to my teeth. I was able to bring forth a stream of putrid liquid.

I fought back the vomit.

The thing let go and hissed, showing me a mouthful of yellow fangs, and then slid back into the throat. I frantically yanked the zipper to the top, hoping to trap the bastard long enough for me to get the hell out of this mess. I threw my shoulder against the back door, and, unbelievably, it opened. I tumbled out and rolled from the hearse until a tree trunk stopped me. I got up and stood several feet away, my back against the tree, my heart set to explode into a million bits of meat. I didn't see any movement from within. In fact, nothing inside the hearse looked disheveled. It looked like nothing out of the ordinary had occurred—such as a young lad fighting off a demon while his foot was wedged inside a corpse. I walked to the open door, and slammed it shut.

An elderly woman spoke to me from behind, a stranger's voice. "Honey, your ass is hangin' out."

I turned and saw two gray-haired women. They were easily into their seventies. One of them held a large paper bag packed with clothes. I happened to know her, as she used to run the local café when I was younger. Eunice was her name. She waggled a finger at me. "And your tally-whacker is showing too."

I looked down and saw that my gown was torn. I also saw my tally-whacker.

I can only imagine the different shades of red my face must have suffered. I felt like I was going to melt into a pool of embarrassment. I covered myself in front, painfully thumping a testicle as I did so.

"Oh my goodness, honey," the lady without a bag said. She grabbed a pair of gray sweatpants and handed them to me. "Are you Theo's grandson?"

"Yes, ma'am," I said, looking at the ground.

"So sorry, about everything." She put her arms out to me and gestured for me to come in for a hug. "C'mon, honey."

I appreciated her kindness, but I didn't feel comfortable having an old woman pressed against my naked boyhood. I wrapped the sweatpants around my waist, effectively hiding my offensive flesh. I started to slide toward the hospital entrance. "I'm not feeling that hot, I think I need to go back to my room. I surely do appreciate the clothes."

"We'll drop the clothes off to the front desk, Luke," said Eunice. "If you ever need anything you holler, okie-doke?"

"Thank you." I nodded to the other lady.

"My name is Ginny, should you need me." Bless her heart. Ginny still had her arms held out to me.

"All right, thanks." I scooted through the door and padded up the hallway in my bare feet. My left foot was sticky and filthy with dirt and other things—things such as mouth juice from a corpse.

Man, I needed a shower.

My room didn't have a shower, but I was told by a nurse the hospital was equipped with one large shower room. I discovered it had six shower stalls with floral shower curtains for privacy, three sinks, and a wire basket filled with soap and other toiletry items. It was dim and stone quiet, except for haunted drippy sounds. I cranked the hot water and let the sting take the grime away, paying special attention to my left foot, scrubbing it several times with extra soap.

No matter how much I scrubbed, I still felt unclean, and not just my foot. *All* of me felt dirty, and no amount of washing was going to get rid of the filth. I knew the reason. It was plain to me. My soul was soiled, not my skin.

I didn't see any *Soul Scrubber* soap in the wire basket.

I wiped steam from a mirror and was shocked as I saw my image reflected. Gone from my eyes was my youthful sparkle. It had been replaced with sadness. I saw the bite on my shoulder was healed, but a pink scar would remain as a reminder of my adventure. I touched it, feeling the dimpled skin. I was branded.

The clothes Eunice and Ginny brought to me were suited for a nine-year-old. The sweat-pants were stretchy, so I was able to squeeze into them—major high-water look. But, I ripped a t-shirt trying to fit into it, and gave up on the rest of the shirts. That was all that was in the bag, except for about a dozen pair of mismatched socks. The socks must have been made for gigantic men. At least I could get my feet into them, even if they hung from my calves like old skin.

I walked to my room and was met by a tall stranger. He wore thick framed glasses and had long, bushy hair, and a matching bushy beard. He was twenty-something years old, I guessed.

He extended his right hand to me and spoke with a deep Oklahoma drawl. "My name's Ruckus McGraw, and it looks like we're gonna get to know one another pretty good."

"Mr. Bird told me about you. You're my guardian, right?" I shook his hand. He had working man's hands.

"Yep." He looked at my clothing and my bare chest. "Is that what you're wearin'?"

"I don't have any other clothes here."

"Then I think we ought to head out to your granddad's place and grab some things." He smiled at me and cocked his head. "If you're gonna' be runnin' with me, you can't be lookin' like *that*."

I had not thought of the farm. My heart pounded with excitement. "Yeah! That would be cool, very cool."

"Well, all right. You need to bring anything with ya?"

The old book was resting on the bed. I had a strong feeling I that I needed to make reading it a major priority. I snagged it and held it tight. "I think I'm ready to get the hell out of here."

"Well, all right."

Chapter Ten

Take A Nap, Take A Trip

RUCKUS DROVE A Jaguar. It was forest green and beautiful, shining gloriously. The interior was tan leather and burled wood. Unfortunately, most of it was hidden beneath stacks of bound files, discarded sandwich wrappers, and scattered car parts. A carburetor rolled around in a small box at my feet.

We had only been on the road for a short while, but we were already on highway 75, headed north. At this clip, we'd be back at the farm in twenty minutes.

"It'll be nice to be back at the farm," I said.

"Yeah, I imagine you were getting pretty sick of that hospital."

"You have *no* idea." A thought occurred to me. How much did Ruckus know?

"How well did you know Grandpa?" I said.

"Oh, I got to know him over the years. I've been runnin' his wells since I was eighteen."

"Wells?"

"Yeah, oil wells."

"Grandpa has oil wells?"

"Oh yeah, he did."

He *did*. I was going to have to get accustomed to past tense when referring to Grandpa.

I cleared my throat of the sting that had gathered there. "Oil wells? He never said a thing to me about them."

"Yeah, they're gonna' be yours one of these days. Then, I guess I'll be workin' for *you*."

I thought I knew my grandfather. Turns out I didn't know jack-shit.

"Hey," Ruckus was digging in a small stack of eight track tapes. "What was the deal with all of them cops at the hospital?"

"An old woman died this morning, but she killed a bunch of kids before she passed." I said this nonchalantly.

Ruckus arched an eyebrow and looked at me over the top of his glasses. "The hell you say."

"Yep. I heard that a little girl's head was found in her kitchen sink."

"A head?"

"That's what I heard."

Ruckus shook his head in disbelief. "Goddamn, that's horrible."

"I also heard they were digging up her yard, finding more bodies." The gruesome imagery flashed in my head.

"Where'd all of this happen?"

"I'm not sure." I didn't recognize the murderer while I punched her face. She could have been from anywhere.

Ruckus mumbled something that sounded like "Get me back to the city," then he slid a tape into the stereo.

"Here," he said, "let's listen to some music."

The Allman Brothers Band blasted from the speakers, singing *Rambling Man*. I was ready to change the subject as much as Ruckus.

"These boys here can straight up jam. Ever heard of 'em?" Ruckus said.

"Yeah, I've heard of them. I don't much listen to them though."

"What do you listen to?"

"A little bit of everything I guess. I kind of like Creedence Clearwater Revival."

"They ain't bad. I like 'em all right I guess." He moved the small stack of tapes around, obviously searching for a specific title. "Well, shit. I was hoping to find some Zeppelin. Ya heard of them, right?"

"Yep, but I've never listened to them."

Ruckus looked at me with an authentic expression of shock. "Damn, son."

I was feeling extremely uncool.

"Well, don't worry. We'll get ya fixed on music," he said.

Not much else was said between us for the rest of the ride. Ruckus cranked the volume and we listened to the music, letting our minds pick through private thoughts. I watched for familiar landmarks of home, finding them all, as my excitement grew with each one. When we pulled onto the farm I couldn't help myself, as I cried like a spanked baby.

"I'll meet you on the porch," said Ruckus. It was a kind gesture, and a glimpse of the compassion that lay beneath his carefree manner.

When I was done, Ruckus opened up the old house. The comfort smells were overwhelming. I knew this aroma well. It was home. I almost expected to see Grandpa come out of the kitchen with a cup of coffee, smiling and cracking jokes.

"Nice old place," said Ruckus, running a hand along the bannister.

"Yep, I guess so."

"Well, it's yours. Or, at least when ya turn eighteen."

This lightened my heart considerably. I would have the farm for the rest of my days.

"Any chance of me coming back here...like on weekends?"

"Well, I'm sure we'll get something worked out. Hell, I kinda' like the quiet."

"Could you live out here?" I asked.

"You kiddin'? It's a damn field trip to find a decent bar out here."

Not the response I was hoping for. A shot of irritation

ran through me. "I don't think that's fair."

"What's not fair?"

"Making me live in the city with you, away from my friends. I don't even know you."

"Hey kid, it was the orphanage or me. It's what your granddad wanted." Ruckus began settling into Grandpa's recliner, groaning. "You're gonna' *love* the city. I ain't heard of any old ladies cuttin' off kid's heads in my neighborhood."

"I don't understand why Grandpa picked *you*. I'd never heard of you until today. Grandpa never talked about you."

"He picked me because he trusted me. A couple of the guys he was doin' business with were tryin' to put the scallywag to your granddad."

"What do you mean?"

"They were stealin' money from Theo's company. I put a stop to it, I guarantee you." He said this as he stretched out and reclined.

I didn't argue with him. I was held in this predicament, and I supposed it was clearly better than an orphanage. I'd always heard they served you slop in those places. That wasn't for me.

"Pack some clothes, we'll come back in a few days and grab the rest." His eyes were now closed.

"It's going to have to be a *small* suitcase, if it's going to fit in your car."

"We'll make some room. I'm an expert."

I walked upstairs to my bedroom, pouting, trying not to trip over my bottom lip. Upon entering, melancholy engulfed me.

My basketball lay in the floor with dirty socks and sneakers. I looked into the sensual gaze of Farrah Fawcett-Majors—I had her posters strewn upon a dedicated wall space. And, my unmade bed was the cherry on top on my nostalgic dessert. No matter how much Grandpa chided me for having a messy bed, I habitually failed to keep it made.

I changed into jeans and a t-shirt, then threw some clothes together and stuffed them into a canvas bag. I decided to lie down in my bed. It had been a while since I had slept in a bed of my own, and my expectations of comfort were met. I closed my eyes, just to rest them for a moment.

I dreamed.

In my dream, I was standing in the shade of several trees that lined the embankment of a creek that runs through the farm. I felt the breeze move my hair, and I heard the rustle of leaves. I could smell the sweet, unspoiled air of the country. The creek was running light, gently splashing against the red-clay, lulling me. I sat down with my back resting against an elm tree and watched the movements of the water, feeling like I was going to nod off. Which, I thought was weird. I was *already* asleep.

I heard a loud splashing coming from somewhere along the creek, like it was being walked in. I stood up and carefully made my way down to the water, using overhanging tree roots as foot holds. I stopped my movements and listened. I could still hear someone, getting closer and just around a bend.

"Who's there?" I said.

The splashing stopped. Then, continued.

"Hello?" I said this as I was back pedaling up the embankment. I expected the worst kind of monster to leap on me from the water. It seemed to be the sort of thing that I should expect these days. No matter how implausible, crazy shit could happen.

I was almost to the top when I slipped and slid down, splashing my feet into the creek. I looked to my right and saw a figure come into view and reach for me. "Looks like ya could use a hand."

"Grandpa, it sure is good to see you," I said.

He pulled me to my muddied feet and wrapped me in a hug, and I hung on to him with all my strength.

"We ain't got much time, I'm afraid," said Grandpa. "I'll have to get goin' here in a little bit." He pointed to the top of the embankment, motioning for me to start climbing.

"It ain't but about ten feet up, we can do it," he said.

I laughed and shook my head. Death hadn't changed him one bit.

We made our way out of the creek and started up a grassy hill that was on the northern part of the property. Grandpa talked the entire time.

'Luke, there's a bad lot of people out in the world, a particular lot. They're part of a group that has intentions of spreadin' evil, and these people have a lot of money and power. They're awful dangerous."

"Who are they?"

"Too many to name, and they try to keep everything secret. Some of them are in government. You be careful if ya should run into that mess of folks. I've got a feelin' you ain't goin' to be overlooked."

I sighed. "Yeah, uh…what does *that* mean?"

"It means you'll be troubled with some stuff at times."

"By *stuff*, you're meaning—"

"Demons and murderers, and such."

"Yeah, I figured as much."

"Tommy Bird will be a big help to ya, make sure to stay in touch with him. He knows a lot that you're goin' to need knowin'. There're plenty of folks out there to help ya out, it's a secret society of our own. It's a society that you'll be a member of."

I did *not* want to be a member of his weird club.

I stopped walking and shook my head. "I don't want to have anything else to do with this crazy shit…sorry for cussing. It scares me."

"It can be scary, I reckon."

"You *reckon?* Holy crap, you weren't around to see what I've been seeing."

"I wasn't exactly *around*, but I know about Eunice

and Ginny seein' your ding-a-ling."

Nice.

"I also know about the demon ya fought with. It was an escort for hell bound souls, nasty things." He playfully punched me in my shoulder. "You did pretty darn good. They're tough as a boot heel, and you whupped on it good."

The thought crossed my mind to ask Grandpa why he knew so much if he wasn't there, but I could feel our time together slipping, and I sorely wanted to savor what was left.

"I don't understand why I climbed in the hearse with that dead lady. That's not me, Grandpa."

"I got news for ya, Luke. You're a changed person, and ya ain't the same as you were." He pointed to my shoulder. "Ya got bit."

"I don't understand."

"Well, she…contaminated ya."

"That doesn't sound good." I imagined a horrible affliction of demonic rabies.

"It won't kill ya. In fact, you might like some of the side effects."

"Like what?"

"Well, it'll become more evident as ya get older, but you'll be able to see things, and maybe do things that others can't. On the other hand, you'll be drawn to darkness and vice versa, and you'll probably have some crazy dreams." Grandpa paused for a moment, thinking. "There are folks that would murder to be as up close as you were to a demon."

"Then they're nuts."

"Yep, most encounters don't turn out as good as yours."

Good?

"I've got to switch gears on ya, Luke." He patted my shoulder, directing me to walk in a different direction. "I'm goin' to show somethin' to ya. It's quite a picture."

We started walking down a hill, toward a small valley that was crammed with a wide variety of tree variations. I knew the area. I didn't normally trek this far into the property, due to the thickness of the foliage. A few years ago, as I was exploring, I ran across this area and was unsuccessful in penetrating the woods. Thorny brush skirted the trees, easily thwarting any attempts on my part to go any deeper. The farm was big and full of wonders that were much more accessible than this ugly patch.

Grandpa put his arm around my shoulders as we walked, pointing out spots in the landscape. "Yep, it sure is pretty out here. I used to walk for hours out here, clearin' my head and such, prayin'."

"Is it prettier where you are now? I mean, are you living in Heaven?"

"As pretty as all this is," he said, waving an arm across the scenery. "It just don't compare to Heaven."

"So—"

"Yep, I'm there."

"What's it like?"

"Words won't do it any justice, there's no way I can explain it to ya. "

He comes to me from beyond the grave, and he's still as vague as he ever was. "That's it? Is Mom, Dad—"

"Everyone's there. That's about all I can tell ya."

"Have faith, right?"

"Yep, ya need faith."

Faith, the word I've never quite understood. However, I now *believed*. After everything that I'd seen and experienced, how could I not believe.

I changed the subject.

"What's up with my guardian? Is he for real?"

"Ya mean Ruckus?"

"Yeah, that's the guy."

He laughed and shook his head. "He's quite the character. But, I think he'll look after ya, and I think maybe the two of ya will be good for one another."

"Not sure I see that, Grandpa."

"Give him some time. He's a good man, and I trust him."

My eyes sparkled with tears. "Grandpa, I don't want to be looked after by a stranger. I miss you, and it's not fair for you to be…"

"Dead?"

I nodded my head.

He laughed, sounding extremely amused. "Shoot, I ain't dead. None of us *really* dies."

"Well, you're not around *here*. You're not living in my world."

"You're goin' get along just fine. I got faith in ya."

I wiped my eyes and cleared the snot from my upper lip. "I'll do my best."

"I know ya will."

We approached the thicket of trees. They were compressed and intertwined, creating an opaque fortress of thorns and branches. "How are we going to get in there?"

"I'll show ya." He walked several yards to a scrabble of large rocks and tapped on the biggest one. "How much ya think this rock weighs?"

"I don't know, maybe around—"

"One hundred and eighty-seven pounds. I've weighed it myself."

I looked at him, bewildered, wondering where this was going. He just beamed a brilliant smile at me.

"I don't get it." I said.

"Watch this."

He knelt to a knee and pushed against the rock. It glided along the ground like an ice cube on a plate, coming to rest a few feet away. He motioned to the ground in front of him, and then waved me over. "Come and take a look."

I stood behind him. In the ground was a large metal door, square-shaped, and with a handle. Weeds and grass had grown wild, concealing it from the world. The rock was resting upon a thin, metallic platform that glided on a mini rail system.

Grandpa pulled at the weeds and swept the debris from the door. "Are ya ready?"

"This door takes us inside?"

He pulled and swung the door open, letting it fall to the side. "Yep, just follow after me. There's a ladder that'll get us there."

He faced me as he started down into the hole, humming a hymn as he disappeared. I crawled after him, and the darkness quickly receded, giving way to bright shards of sunlight.

"Wow! This is far out!" I shouted.

"I'd always planned to show this to ya, but I sort of ran out of time. I knew you'd like it."

The ladder ended in a lofty cave. But, beyond the cave, beneath a gentle canopy of trees, was a paradise of lush greenery and small waterfalls that smoothly flowed into a pond. Flowers bloomed in brilliant patches of color, wildly accenting the experience.

We followed a path from the cave that took us farther downward. "This is mind blowing, Grandpa. Just, so *cool*."

He led me to a vegetable garden that looked like it needed some love, but was still hanging tough. Squash, okra, cantaloupes, tomatoes, and other variety grew. He pulled a tomato loose and handed it to me. "You've never had a tomatah so juicy or sweet in your life. Give it a bite."

I preferred salt and pepper with my tomatoes, but it looked delicious. I bit into it, and was dizzy from the flavor. I had to sit down.

"I've *never* tasted anything so good," I said. "But, there's something familiar..."

"It's got the same aftertaste as the pecans, a heavy richness."

"I guess, yeah."

"That's because it's all from the seed that I brought back with me when I was a youngster. My daddy took to crossbreedin' all sorts of plants and such." He pointed to a spot of fruit and pecan trees. "You've had the pecans, but not anything else. I wasn't sure of how it would affect ya, thought I'd start small."

My head was beginning to clear, so I stood up. "The pecans didn't make me feel dizzy."

"I was mixing the pies light. It was mostly normal pecans, but it was a strong enough concoction to make ya see the spell in the sky."

My senses became super-heightened, and I felt as if I were constructed of helium. "Whoa, I'm feeling weird."

"Like how?"

"Like…" I paused and scanned the area, seeing colors and texture as I'd never seen them before. Flowers glowed with vibrant intensity, as did the grass and rocks. The colors looked *alive.* Everything was coated with an aura. "I can see things and—"

A giggle bubbled from me. I was feeling good.

"I think that tomatah made ya high," Grandpa said.

I could taste the fragrances that floated in the air, the soil and the flowers, and I heard the tree branches bend in the breeze. "High?"

"Yep, ya got high."

Blueness surrounded Grandpa. "Is that why I see a blue egg around you?"

Grandpa chuckled. "You're seein' my aura. It's the reason I'm able to be here with ya."

"Do hippies see blue eggs?" I asked.

"I reckon that's an odd question. Why ya askin'?"

"Cause, hippies get high."

"Not this kind of high."

I heard a bird singing, but its song was different. The sound was clearer, and slowed, more melodic.

A hand appeared in front of my face, snapping fingers. It was Grandpa's hand. "You're in la-la land."

"I think you're right. It feels like my feet are made of clouds."

"Yep, that's la-la land."

I laughed like an idiot.

"Listen to the water, Luke. Listen *real* close," he said.

It took but an instant to be tuned to the water. I followed the sounds, walking along a path of sandstone, descending until I stood at the pond's edge. The water had an aura that was blue-violet, and full of pulsing energy that looked like strands of flowing electricity. The waterfalls were sinewy with the effects.

The water's sounds were musical and rich with a strange harmony. Lustrous, psychedelic fish darted in and out of reeds. A rainbow colored trace followed close behind their tails, rippling all through the water.

"Beautiful, ain't it," said Grandpa, as he stood next to me. "There's lots of life in water, Luke."

I was tripping *hard.*

"Luke?"

I was immersed. I wanted to swim with the fish.

"Luke." His snapping fingers made another appearance. "I reckon I shouldn't have let ya eat such a big bite. But, now ya know."

Yeah, I now knew my grandfather used to come here and trip out. I found this strangely bolstering.

"Keep watch over it for me, and be mindful of who ya share it with," he said. "It don't matter how much good could come from this garden, some would use it for bad."

"I gotcha'."

"Ya also need to make sure that no seeds leave this place." He knelt to the water, scooping some into his hat. He held it out for me to take. "Take yourself a good swish, spit any seeds ya run across into the water."

Grinning like a buffoon, I took the hat and drank the water. I'm sure I spilled most of it down the front of my shirt, but what I was able to get into my mouth was cold and sweet.

"Don't forget to swish around," said Grandpa.

I vigorously gargled, and then spat into the water. I

watched the ripples glide the surface, wholly absorbed in the psychedelic effect.

"Feel around with your tongue. A seed'll start to burn like fire if ya don't get it out of your mouth." He pondered what he had just said, scratching his chin. "Unless you're like me, and have been eatin' on this stuff for a good while. I've been feedin' *you* pecans, but nothin' else. I ain't sure if that's enough to make ya immune to the burnin'."

"Did you get heartburn?"

"Nope, that's a funny thing right there. You'd think it'd burn a hole in your stomach, but it never bothered my belly...unless ya count the times I overate."

"What happened?"

"I got sicker'n a dog."

I scooped more water, drinking until I burped. "Man, the water sure is good."

"It's not from the same spring that runs to our well. I reckon there are offshoots of water all beneath us."

I sat down and began playing my hand in the water, feeling tired. Sorrow swooped down on me, summoning stabs of grief. Sniffles and misty eyes once again afflicted me.

My high was teetering on the edge of collapse.

"I'll always miss you, Grandpa. I love you."

"We had some good times, didn't we?" he said, smiling.

"Yep, we sure did."

He sat next to me and lay back on the grass. He pulled his hat down, shading his eyes. "I feel a nap comin' on."

I wiped my eyes and stretched out on the grass next to him. "Wow, even the grass is different. It's more comfortable than my bed."

"Uh-huh..." he mumbled, already slipping into sleep, "...mighty soft."

Chapter Eleven

Villain

I AWOKE TO the cozy confines of my bedroom. I sat up and rubbed my eyes, feeling rested. After a few blinks I stood and looked down at my duffel bag. It was just as I had left it. But, there was something lying on top of it. An object I certainly didn't expect to see.

Grandpa's cowboy hat.

I picked it up and rubbed my fingers against the worn roughness. I smelled it, taking in traces of Grandpa's fragrance. Surprisingly, I didn't become overwhelmed with emotion, no urge to bawl. I instead felt consoled.

I put the hat on and it immediately slid down to my eyebrows. But, it didn't matter to me if it fit or not. Just having such a prized possession was plenty. I slipped into my sneakers and then grabbed the bag, slinging it over a shoulder. I got a few steps out of my room before I stopped and looked back.

I'll be back. No worries. My room ain't goin' anywhere.

I blew a kiss to my pinup girl. "Don't cry while I'm away, Farrah,"

I laughed insanely at my little joke. I slapped my leg and gasped for air, trapped in the throes of laughter. It went on for a lengthy period.

"Everything all right with ya?" It was Ruckus. He was standing at the top of the stairs.

I tried stifling my laughter. I covered my mouth with

both hands, but that was no help. However, it did reroute my hilarity into the tight restrictions of my nasal cavity, forcing a glob of snot from my nose. It adhered nicely to the floral wallpaper, but the colors clashed.

"Damn, boy," said Ruckus.

I put a hand up to let him know that I would be all right, but it would take a minute or two.

"You been up here drinkin'?"

I shook my head, working on my breathing.

"High?"

"No," I lied. I was coming down, but still jacked up.

He came on up and approached me, eyeballing me over the top of his glasses. "Horseshit, son. I could blind you with a piece of dental floss."

"I'm just tired. I took a nap is all, I'm just groggy."

"I got a few hours of beauty sleep myself." He yawned and scratched his wooly head. "But, I didn't giggle and carry on like I was high. I've still got some sense about me." He laughed, then pointed to Grandpa's hat. "Where'd you find that at? That's ole' Theo's, ain't it?"

I pushed it higher on my forehead. "Yep, it was just laying around."

"It's kind of big for ya, but I guess you'll grow into it."

"Yeah, I was hoping to."

Ruckus took my bag from me. "We need to get going. I'll help ya with this."

"Thanks."

"If you need anything else, grab it," he said. "But, make sure it ain't too big."

I saw my basketball and suddenly couldn't live without it. I pointed to it.

"Sure," he said.

I scooped it up and started dribbling down the hallway.

Ruckus said, "Hey, are you gonna' do something

about *that?*" He was pointing to the snot on the wall.

"Yeah, I'll take care of it."

"I can already tell you're a good kid. You remind me a lot of me."

I picked up one of my dirty socks and wiped the mess from the wall the best I could and threw it back on the floor. It was already stiff to begin with.

I walked outside and onto the porch, shutting the door behind me. I jiggled the doorknob, making sure the door locked behind me. I found it to be tricky, letting loose of it. It was the last tangible contact I would have with the old house for a time.

Ruckus was in the shadow of the mimosa tree, leaned over the open trunk of the Jaguar when I arrived. A medley of objects lay about him in the grass, as he sought for a space in which to cram my duffel bag.

"Are you sure there's room?" I said.

"Sure I'm sure."

The sound of gravel and dirt being stirred sounded from the road, and then a cloud of dust rose into the air. We waited to see what was coming.

"Holy crap. It's Grandpa's truck," I said.

Ruckus squinted against the western sun, looking to the road. "It sure as hell is."

The truck slowed and turned into the driveway. I saw the glint from the driver's badge as the truck chugged to a stop.

The good Sheriff Jake.

"Hello, Luke. Good to see you," he said, offering a handshake.

I shook his hand, then nodded to Ruckus. "This is Ruckus McGraw. My...new dad."

"Mighty, pleased to meet ya," said Ruckus, shaking the sheriff's hand. "And I ain't his new dad."

"The truck's been sitting in the impound yard for a good while. I figured it was time for it to come home," said the sheriff. "My deputy *should* be headed here to pick me up."

"Anything new about the killings?" I said.

"Not much I can tell you, Luke. "

"Hell of a deal," said Ruckus.

I noticed the sheriff came from the direction of the Plumes', not from town. Wrong direction.

"Were you looking around the Plume property?" I immediately regretted asking, worried he might start a new line of questioning with me.

"Since I was already out this direction, I figured it wouldn't hurt."

Where did the bodies go?

"We're leaving for the city." I pointed to the mess on the ground.

Why did I say that? Stupid.

"I know how to get in touch with you." He looked straight into my eyes as he said this.

Shit.

It made me nervous, and I surely hoped my discomfort was hidden beneath my boyish façade.

The sheriff rubbed his stomach and glanced at the house. His face looked like he'd swallowed a rotten egg. "Any chance I could use your bathroom? I'm feeling a bad case of the craps comin' on."

"Why, sure," said Ruckus. "We can't have our lawmen shittin' their pants."

"It would be downright unbecoming for an officer of the law," said the sheriff. The two of them busted a laugh before the sheriff raced in the direction of the house. He moved fast for a person running stiff legged.

He reached the door, then shouted to us, panic rising in his voice. "Hey, the door is locked!"

I've never carried a key to the house. There was never a need, as the key to the front door could always be found in the mouth of a ceramic toad that has forever squatted on the porch.

I shouted the location to him, and he carefully bent to

retrieve the key. I hollered the location of the toilet to him, as he worked the key into the lock and undoubtedly puckered his ass.

"I hope that ole' boy don't shit his pants," said Ruckus, chuckling.

I agreed, but I was secretly thankful for the chance to hit the road without having to speak to the sheriff. He could spend as much time in the bathroom as he needed.

"I'll hold the bag in my lap. You don't have to shove it in the trunk," I said.

"You sure? It's pretty big."

"No big whoop."

"How about that ball?"

I still had it tucked beneath my arm. "It won't fit in the trunk?"

"Pretty tight in there."

"Okay, that's fine. I'll keep it in my lap too." I put the ball in the car's floorboard and began to help Ruckus put things back in the trunk, mostly in an attempt to speed along our departure.

"I guess I'm ready to get moving," I said.

"You sayin' you're ready to go?"

"Yeah."

Ruckus shut the trunk and wiped his hands on his jeans. "Then, by God, I'm ready too."

I opened the passenger door. "Hand me the bag once I'm inside the car."

"I will, once the sheriff is finished with his business."

"What for?"

"I don't think we ought to leave him inside."

"He's a *sheriff*. He's not gonna' steal anything."

"I ain't worried about him stealing, it's politer to wait on him I figure." Ruckus looked inside the truck as he spoke, apparently none too worried about my thoughts on the matter. "Ain't a bad ole' truck."

Another vehicle rumbled on the road, its ratty exhaust echoed along the ditches. It sounded like it was wound wide open and coming from the east.

"Damn, someone's haulin' ass," said Ruckus.

"Might be his deputy." I hoped it was. Maybe Ruckus wouldn't mind leaving if his deputy was here.

"I hope it's not one their police cars. Sounds like a pile of shit," said Ruckus.

A strange feeling came over me. Not a residual from my weird and wonderful dream-trip, but a feeling of dread. I was positive it was related to whatever or whoever was traveling on the road.

"Ruckus, I…"

Ruckus walked toward the road. "What?"

"I think you should step back from the road."

"I'm all right."

"I've seen good sized rocks thrown from the road. Seen them smack people in the head." Not entirely a lie. Rocks did tend to fly from traffic, although I'd never actually seen anyone struck.

"Oh, I'll be damned."

It was seconds from arriving. I hoped I was being paranoid.

Cedar trees lined an area between the yard and the road for roughly twenty feet, and then stopped at the driveway. We caught glimpses of a car beyond the trees, before it slowed and whipped into the driveway behind the truck, slinging debris into a cloud

"You know these folks?" said Ruckus.

The car was an old rusty Impala, and I did not recognize it as belonging to anyone I knew. And, I surely did not know the occupants as they got out of the car. It was two men, skinny and straggly.

"Nope," I said, stepping back a few feet.

The driver had dark greasy hair that hung down in his eyes and the other was older, with a gray beard and a bald head. Each was equally dirty in their appearance, covered in tattoos, and each held in their hands an axe handle.

The bald one looked at me and stabbed a finger in my

direction. "You Luke? You the boy?"

"Who the hell wants to know?" Ruckus stepped toward them.

"You'd best stay out of this, motherfucker," said the driver.

"The hell I will." Ruckus took another step forward.

"We come for a book the boy has. Ain't no trouble needin' to happen if he gives it to us," said the bald one.

The book was in the duffle bag, which was lying on the ground next to the Jag. I cut my eyes to it, and the bald one noticed.

"You got it in there, don't ya." He walked to the bag, but Ruckus grabbed his shirt collar, jerking him backward.

"Luke, get in the house," said Ruckus.

The driver ran over to Ruckus, swinging his axe handle and connecting. He struck Ruckus in the middle of his back. The bald one swung and hit Ruckus in the ribs. Both blows sent him crashing against the Jag, which kept him from falling to the ground.

My first instinct was to run into the house, tell the sheriff to wipe his ass and come on. But, I was worried that Ruckus might be dead by the time we arrived. So, I ran and jumped on the driver's back, biting the back of his neck, trying to tear out a chunk of his flesh.

"Ouch! You little son of a bitch!" He sounded like a woman shrieking.

He smelled foul, and unbathed, but his blood was the worst as it poured from his wound. It made me gag.

The bald one punched me in the jaw, but I only clinched my teeth tighter.

The driver fell to the ground, screaming. He rolled onto his back, trying to get rid of me, but I was having none of it. I had my arms and legs wrapped around him like a spider on a fly. "Damn it, Charlie! Get the little fucker off of me!"

"Are you kiddin' me?" said Charlie.

Ruckus took advantage of his attacker being distracted

and landed a haymaker on Charlie's nose. Charlie dropped like the dead. Ruckus then proceeded to kick the other in the balls, repeatedly.

"Whoa, just what in the hell is going on here?" It was the sheriff. He had one hand up and the other on the butt of his pistol. "Everybody calm the shit down!"

Ruckus stopped kicking and stepped back with raised hands. He winced in pain. "What's goin' on is these two boys here took axe handles to me and started beatin' on the kid."

The sheriff looked around at the scene, his face a mask of befuddlement. "Luke, you can let go of that man. Ruckus, you can lower your arms."

I released him and got up, spitting blood. The driver rolled around on the ground, crying.

The sheriff flipped the driver onto his stomach, placing a knee in his back. He roughly placed handcuffs on him. "Is that right? Why did you do that?"

No real response, just moaning. And bleeding.

He then placed Charlie in cuffs and went in the house to use the phone.

"Do you know what they were talking about?" Ruckus asked quietly. "Something about a book?"

I could have lied to him, but I decided not to. Grandpa told me I could trust him. "Yeah, there's a book. Mr. Bird gave it to me."

"The book you brought with you from the hospital?"

"Yep, that's the one."

"Why in the hell did those guys want it so bad?"

I shook my head. "Man, I don't know. I haven't even opened it up yet. I think its stuff that Grandpa wanted me to know."

"Well, it must be directions to a hidden treasure, for someone to want to beat our brains in for it."

I looked at the two men. Charlie was still unconscious, but the other one was wide awake and staring at us.

I made sure the sheriff was nowhere in sight and dragged the bag out of the view of the two men. I reached inside and felt for the book. I found it and stuck it behind the driver's seat of the Jag.

The sheriff had left the house and was walking toward us. He stopped to pick up Grandpa's hat, which had left me during the fracas. He dusted it off and walked to me. "Mighty fine hat."

Chapter Twelve

Bad Buddy

THE DEPUTY FINALLY showed his face—Deputy Buddy Wynn—and after getting his ass chewed by the sheriff for taking too long, he drove Ruckus, the sheriff, and me to the hospital. Ruckus was tough, but it was obvious he was in pain.

The two thugs were hauled off in a paddy wagon to the county jail. The sheriff was excited at the opportunity to question them and search their car. I was not excited. I feared that a connection would be made to Grandpa and me. I didn't know them from Adam, but they knew about the book, and the cops would eventually tie it all together. I would be tried as a murderer, and Grandpa's reputation would indubitably be blackened.

Ruckus told the sheriff that the men started asking for someone named Oscar Dinkowitz, and flipped out when he told them they had the wrong address. Who knew for certain, but the sheriff seemed to accept the story of events.

I sat in the waiting room with the deputy, listening to him giggle over the comic section of the newspaper. It was better than being a patient, but I still hated being there. Something bad was in the air. I could feel it pressing down on me.

"Hey there, boy."

It was Ruckus carefully walking down the hallway.

"So, what's wrong with you?" I asked.

"Cracked ribs. I'm goin' to be sore for a while."

"Man, what a crazy day."

"I'll say," he said.

The deputy got out of his chair and folded the newspaper. I recognized him as the deputy that always handed out speeding tickets and busted parties. He was not well-liked in town. "I guess you're ready to go get your car."

"Hell, yes. I just want to get out of this damn place."

I caught myself thinking the same thing. Things had changed around the ole' hometown. Bad things had moved in.

As we walked toward the exit, we passed the janitor's closet. The door was open with very little light penetrating the darkness. I saw what appeared to be a mop handle protruding from a bucket, and a trash bin on wheels. I also saw small, dark, shapes moving around, sticking close to the corners. Their shining, mean eyes gave their hiding places away.

Bad things had moved in.

On the way back to the farm, the deputy small talked with Ruckus, while I sat quietly in the back of the patrol car. It wasn't hard for me to imagine being cuffed and thrown in there. In fact, being in the back of a cop car can stoke one's imagination plenty. I was unable to imagine a single thing good.

I had somehow managed to fall asleep before we reached Grandpa's place, and was awakened by Ruckus. "C'mon boy. Let's get goin'."

The deputy let me out, grinning. "I don't recall anybody falling asleep back there. Passing out for sure, but not sleeping."

I got out, stretched, and farted.

"Get that out of your system before we hit the road," said Ruckus.

"I think that was it."

He tilted his head. "Well, we're here and a bathroom ain't far. Are you *sure,* you don't have to take a dump?"

"No, I'm good."

"Then I'm good. Let's leave this town before it kills us." Ruckus jingled the Jag keys and shook the deputy's hand. "I appreciate the ride. I'd like to say it's been fun and all, but it ain't."

"I'm sorry you two had such a bad go of things."

"Yeah, *us* too," said Ruckus.

The deputy shook my hand. "You are a tough little guy. I'm impressed, Luke."

As our skin touched, a sensation of light nausea rolled in my stomach. Then, an image of a child flashed in my mind. A little girl, who was crying and afraid.

"You okay?" he asked, still gripping my right hand.

Another flash, and a new picture in my head. A gathering of people, men and women, in the woods. There were children present as well, clearly terrified. Then a new image occurred, a grainy movie of a hole being dug with a shovel. I saw the dirt being piled on the ground. Next to the mound of dirt, a discarded flashlight illuminated a wadded up shirt. Something gold shone from the shirt.

The deputy's grip tightened. "Luke?"

A badge was attached to the shirt, and above it was a shiny name tag. Buddy Wynn, it read.

The scene carried on. I saw a small naked body in the hole being covered with dirt. A headless child's body. My nausea erupted into a generous stream of vomit. Buddy's shoes took a direct hit. And, I might have got some on his pants as well. Maybe, a few flecks of breakfast.

He dropped my hand like a hot plate.

"Oh, shit," said Ruckus. "That's a bad deal, right there."

Buddy wanted to kill me. He grabbed the butt of his gun, but stopped short of pulling it on me.

"Whoa there, Buddy," said Ruckus.

There was a second or two of awkward silence, before Buddy's face broadened into a big smile. "How about a warning next time, huh?"

"Hey, the boy's sick," Ruckus said.

"Yeah, I see that." Buddy relaxed his gun hand and pointed to the house. "Mind I if go clean up?"

I was not going to allow Psycho-Buddy into the house. "You can use the hose over by the horse tank," I said. "That's where I'm going."

Buddy snickered. "I don't see any puke on *you*. Don't see why you need washing up."

"To rinse the puke out of my mouth," I said, deliberately staring into his eyes. I couldn't help myself.

I know what you've done, ole' Buddy-boy.

Ruckus stopped me. "We'll stop by the Dairy Queen and get you a Coke or somethin' to swish out your mouth. Daylight is burnin' and we're leavin' this fuckin' town."

Buddy smiled at both of us and spoke to Ruckus. "Well, I can understand wanting to get back home. I guess it's to the horse tank I'll be going."

"Have a good one, Deputy. And thanks again for droppin' us off," said Ruckus.

I felt a meanness emanating from Buddy. I clearly felt his hateful thoughts. It was very strange, and I did not like how it made me feel.

"Luke," said Buddy, "you really *are* a special boy."

I didn't know what he meant by the comment. Could he somehow sense that I was able to see into his mind?

"Yeah, he reminds me a lot of me," said Ruckus. He got in the car and leaned across to the passenger side to unlock the door.

"You two be careful out there. Take it from someone who's worked his fair share of car accidents. Lots of folks end up injured, or worse out on the road," said Buddy.

Yeah, and you be careful when digging graves in the dark. You might fall in.

Ruckus stuck his bushy head out to me. "Hey, hurry up every little chance ya get."

I tipped my hat to Buddy, told him I was sorry about the vomit and such, and got into the car. I immediately looked into my side mirror for Buddy. He might decide to blow our brains out. Or worse.

"Ruckus, we need to get out of here," I said. My voice was a tad, high pitched.

"Sit tight, we're leavin'."

Ruckus put the Jag in gear and headed to the road. I kept an eye on Psycho-Buddy, and he kept one on us until we were gone from view.

I was far from feeling safe.

"Ruckus, I know this sounds crazy, bu—"

"I thought that ole' boy was gonna' shoot you."

"—uh, yeah. Exactly!"

Ruckus kept glancing at the rearview mirror. "There's somethin' wrong about that guy."

"We need to speed up."

"We can't get goin' *too* fast on this road. This car ain't meant for this dirt road shit, it's too low to the ground. If we end up broke down with a busted oil pan, it won't do us much good."

I put my face in my hands, groaning.

"Hey, you're not gonna' puke again are ya?"

"No."

"All right, just checkin'."

I gasped when a large rock clanged against the under carriage.

"Don't worry," said Ruckus. "We're all right, but I've got to slow down a little."

I hugged the duffel bag like it was a big teddy bear and closed my eyes. Buddy's images clawed at me. The images and the emotions that were attached. He thoroughly enjoyed what he had done. What they *all* had done.

Ruckus interrupted my thoughts with a question. "So, what's the deal with that book?"

"I don't know. I haven't even opened it yet." I kept my eyes closed and spoke in a tired voice.

"Well, first chance we get, we need to crack that thing

open."

I wondered what Ruckus' reaction to the book's contents would be if it was filled with demons, murder, and spells. He would probably think it was all horseshit.

The sheriff would think I was full of it as well, as I explained to him about his employee, Buddy-Boy. Not a conversation I was going to be comfortable with. But these people needed to be stopped. The children needed saving.

I checked the mirror again. "I don't see the deputy."

"If he wanted to do anything, he already would have. He's probably cooled down by now." The car slowed, and Ruckus made a right hand turn. One more mile, and we'd be on the highway.

"What do you think he would do to us?" I knew the answer, but I was curious as to Ruckus' thoughts.

"I ain't sure," he said. "Probably nothing except a ticket, which he'd write *me* up for, even though I ain't the one who puked on him."

A ticket. I wished that were true.

Ruckus laughed. "Damn, boy. You sure got him good."

"Yep, I did."

Ruckus fumbled around his pile of eight track tapes until he found The Allman Brothers. He plugged it in, cranked the volume, and started singing along with the band. I kept an eye on what was behind us until we reached the blacktop, and not seeing a cop car was a wonderful relief. Enough of a relief that I was able to drop off to sleep, even with Ruckus' wailing.

No dreams.

Chapter Thirteen

So Long, Root Beer

I AWOKE ALONE at a gas station, hearing the *tick, tick,* of a gas pump. The sun was almost gone, leaving behind a pinkish-orange sky. The only light to keep me company was the few bulbs that hung loosely from the looming carport. I got out of the car and saw that Ruckus had the gas nozzle in the car, filling it up.

But, no Ruckus.

I wasn't familiar with the gas station, Dorothy's Hilltop. It was a food store, gas station, and feed store that sat back from the highway, having a large graveled area for parking and turn-arounds. Rural Oklahoma was filled with such places. I decided to go inside and have Ruckus buy me a chocolate almond bar and a root beer.

It was a dusty place, with cobwebs hanging thick as drapes in the corners, and a wooden floor that creaked with each step. An old man wearing glasses leaned on his elbows behind the counter, looking me over. The shelves behind him were packed with a mishmash of items. Cowboy boots to saltine crackers.

I found the candy rack next to a stack of out-of-date newspapers. I decided on two bars, figuring I'd surely earned two lousy candy bars. The root beer was in an old-fashioned dispenser. I got two bottles of root beer as well.

I set my treats on the counter, becoming hungrier by the minute.

"That'll be...um, let's see...oh, let's call it a dollar

twenty," said the old man.

I looked around for Ruckus. "Well, I don't have any money."

"Then you can't have these. I ain't runnin' a charity, son."

"I came here with a big guy, he'll pay for it. I just don't know where he is."

"Big guy with bushy hair?"

"Yep, that's him," I said. "So, he's here? You've seen him?"

The old man pointed to a pile of car tires. "He's around them tires, usin' the bathroom. I think he was ready to mess his drawers when he came in. I'll put the root beer and candy in with the gas."

It seemed that bowel movements were destined to dot the day.

"He's in the restroom?"

"I don't expect that he's crappin' on the floor. I hope not anyway." The old man laughed, until a violent coughing spasm came upon him.

"Are you all right, sir?" I was genuinely concerned. His face turned purple, and he stopped breathing.

He nodded and promptly hacked up a sizable knot of phlegm. He spat it into a brass spittoon that sat next to the cash register.

He bagged my items and handed them to me, after he wiped his mouth with the back of his hand. "Don't eat too much, now. It'll make ya sick."

"I'll try not to overeat, sir." I pinched the bag with two fingers, careful to avoid the wet area he left for me.

"Ya'll from around here?"

"Well, sir, I don't think so."

"You don't know where you're from?" His wrinkled face oozed into a frown.

"No, sir. What I *mean* is, I was asleep in the car when we got here, so I don't know where we're at."

The old man nodded his understanding and smiled.

"So, where ya from?"

"Wetumka."

"I know some folks over yonder."

He closed his eyes, deep in thought, working his tongue in and out. This went on for about ten seconds. Then another ten seconds.

"Sir?"

He opened his eyes and smiled at me. "Yeah?"

"Were you going to tell me something?"

"I don't think so, son."

"Okay, then I'm going. Have a nice evening, sir."

"Don't ya want to know?"

"Know, what?"

"Where you're at."

"Oh, sure."

"It depends, ya see. You're kinda' in between Tecumseh and Pink, right off of Highway 9." His face beamed with pride at having shared this information with me.

It did shed some light. I'd traveled with Grandpa on this road. It was his preferred route to Norman for an Oklahoma football game. "We're heading to the city. How much further we got?"

"Oh, I'd say maybe an hour, maybe less."

My new life was close.

I made a saluting gesture toward him with my bagged goodies and started for the door. "Thank you, sir. I think I'll wait in the car for Ruckus."

The door to the store opened, seemingly on its own. But, the door did not open on its own. It appeared that way because the person entering was too small to be seen. It was a dark-haired little boy wearing a tuxedo.

The same little boy from the Plume house. That mean little bastard.

I saw his aura this time. It was black and fuzzy. Not at all the vibrant aura that Grandpa had. But, the rest was pretty much the same as the last time I saw the boy. He had the same creepy smile. A smile that looked to be razor wired in place. His head wounds had healed, so there were no signs of injury from the pistol whipping I put on him. He danced his crazy jig in a small pair of cowboy boots, working his way until he stood in front of me. He growled at me, sounding like a rabid puppy.

"Well, don't that beat all." The old man slowly shook his head.

I slowly backed away from the boy, as if he were a land mine. I certainly didn't want the little creep to bite me again. And, if so, I wondered how the old man would react if I were forced to knuckle upon the kid's head again. Because, there would be no hesitation on my part to smack him.

The boy danced between two aisles, and was gone.

"Well, I swanny," said the old man. "If that ain't peculiar."

Peculiar ain't peculiar anymore, old timer.

"Do you know the little fella'?"

"No, I most definitely do not."

"He kinda' acted like he knew ya."

Ruckus and I needed to be hitting the road. A bad vibe was buzzing.

"Sir, how long has he been taking a dump?" It was time for him to pinch it off.

"You mean the fella' with the bushy head?"

"Yes, that guy."

"Oh, around fifteen minutes or so I reckon. Maybe longer." The old man slid from his stool and walked to where the boy disappeared. "I can't hear the boy back there. He might be stuffin' his pockets."

"Sir, you should be careful."

A breeze came through the screen door, blowing loose receipts onto the floor. It carried the damp smells of a rainy spring with it. And something that wasn't *springy*. A strange smell that didn't fit.

The old man shuffled to the door and peered out,

straining his eyes. "There's a car out by the road. Got its
runnin' lights going. Slick lookin' limousine."

"Oh, yeah?" I'd never seen a *genuine* limousine in
person. So naturally, I peeked around the old man for a
look. And sure enough, out by the road sat a shiny, black
limousine. It was parked next to a hand-painted sign that
read, *One Stop Is All You'll Ever Need.* The rear of the
limo was pointed toward us at an angle, super-elongating
its length. The windows were blacked out, and secretive.

A rear door opened, and a woman's leg stretched out.
It was pale and sensuous, long and lean.

"Holy, shinola." The old man took off his glasses and
rubbed the lenses against his shirt. "I promise ya, I ain't
seen anything like that in a good while."

My right shoulder spiked with pain, burning like a lit
match. It was my demon bite flaring up. It didn't take a
genius to figure out who was in the limo.

"Sir, how do I find the bathroom?" I was going to
pound on the bathroom door.

"Around them tires and down the hallway. It's kinda'
dark, been plannin' on replacin' the light."

I spun around, determined to get Ruckus' ass off the
toilet seat and into the driver's seat. We needed to be
leaving, and in an expedient fashion.

"Mercy, she's getting out. Yep, and she—oh my
goodness, good night would you look at *her*," said the old
man.

Luke, do you think of me?

"What?" I stopped in my tracks. It was the demon
whispering in my head, speaking to me. Smoky and
seductive. Lilith.

I've thought of you often.

"Get out of my head!" It felt like an army of icy
worms were crawling on my brain.

It was required that I roust Ruckus from the crapper.
The sooner we left, the sooner things became better. I
sprinted to the tires, my patience spent, and slipped on a

wet spot just as I rounded the corner. I ended up crashing into a heap of discarded cardboard boxes. My root beer broke on the floor, spraying a fizzy mist into the air.

I've been craving you.

"Shut up!"

"She's walkin' up this way," the old man said. "Whoa, and *holy shit*. She ain't got a stitch of clothes on!"

"Ruckus, hurry!" I was screaming. "We've got to go, man!"

Behind me, I heard the unmistakable sound of small boots. I grabbed an empty box and threw it over my right shoulder, then rolled forward. It was a frantic action, but it worked. I heard the little bastard yelp.

"Hey, what are you doin' over there? You'll have to pay for anything that gets broken." The old man sounded as if he were lost in a dream.

I rolled to my feet and backed into the gloomy hallway, steadying myself for an attack. I quickly located the whereabouts of the monster child. He was rising to his little feet and rubbing a spot on his head. He also held a shiny, meat cleaver.

The sound of a flushed toilet echoed behind me, trailed by a creaky door being opened. Out came Ruckus. "Son, it ain't been good in there."

I pointed to the boy. "Well, it ain't been good out here either."

The boy danced and growled, waving his cleaver around.

"What's his story?" said Ruckus.

The boy looked upward and shrieked in a maddening pitch, stomping his feet.

"I don't know." I was not sure I wanted to know his story.

"Then what the hell is he….is that a meat cleaver he's holdin'?"

"Yep." Behind the psycho-boy was a shiny pile of kitchen cutlery on the floor. It was scattered at the end of an aisle, mixed in with cans of motor oil and baby diapers.

Ruckus stepped forward. "Hey, kid. Where the hell is your mom and dad?"

"I'm not sure he has any parents."

The boy waved the cleaver in arcing slashes, flashing gritted teeth. He was overflowing with hate.

"That boy ain't right," said Ruckus.

He was correct. The boy wasn't right.

Lilith, the she-demon, spoke from beyond our view in a strange language, consisting more of sounds than words. Whatever was said, the boy understood. He turned his head in the direction of the voice, listening intently. He then left us, to follow her voice.

"Luke." Her wiles had an immediate effect on me, as my loin area heated up.

Ruckus brushed past me. "Who's that?"

"You don't want to know. You wouldn't believe me if I told you."

"What, you know her?"

"Mm, not really. I mean, I don't *know* her, but—"

"He is acquainted with me." The demon walked into our view, treating us to her body. It was perfect and on full display. Like the old man said, nary a stitch of clothing. A black mask clung to the left side of her face, hiding the nasty wound the dagger left behind. Her hair moved and wriggled like a nest of snakes. And, she had the same black aura as the boy, except hers was deeper and more defined.

The demon walked toward me, hips swaying, her hands rubbing her breasts.

"Holy shit, son," said Ruckus. His tone was dreamy, sounding the same as the old man. I looked at his face and saw he was under her spell. Drool ran down his chin.

"Please, leave him alone," I said.

"I can't help that humans are vulnerable to my gifts." Her fingers were now probing her pubic area as she approached me.

"What do you want?" I said.

She grabbed the back of my head, pulling me tight against her flawless body, my face against her breasts. She put her fingers in my mouth, forcing me to taste her juices. I found her flavor to be acidic. "I've come to offer you an opportunity, Luke. A chance to leave with me, and to leave this boring life. You could even rule your own slice of Hell."

I pulled away from her, despite my rising lust. "I'm fine with my life. And it hasn't been very boring here lately."

The demon stepped back, revealing a look of surprise. "So, my mistake has strengthened you." She pointed to my shoulder, and then bared her sharp teeth.

I didn't feel strengthened. I was close to popping a load in my jeans.

"Well, I can't force you to leave with me," she said, sounding disheartened. "But, why would you choose to stay in this shitty realm when you can leave with me? There's no one else here for you. Theo is dead, and you're all alone."

"I'm not going with you," I said. "Are you nuts?"

"I could be your girlfriend, Luke. I would fuck you relentlessly. I would be your sex slave."

Ruckus spoke up. "I'll take you up on that offer."

The demon laughed, and then kissed Ruckus, pushing her black tongue into his mouth. She unbuckled his pants and let them drop to the floor.

"Get back," I said. "Leave him alone."

"Hell, I'm all right," he said.

"But, she's not." I grabbed a handful of her hair and gave it a yank, pulling her from Ruckus. "I think it's time for you to leave."

An amused expression appeared on her face. "Well, aren't *you* a wonder."

Her hair coiled around my hand and traveled up my arm, weaving a dark, silken mesh. When I attempted to pull away, the hair constricted. I went to my knees, screaming, and waiting for my arm to be ripped loose.

Lilith squatted in front of me, smiling. "Silly boy."

Yes, I was.

"Lucky for you I like having my hair pulled." She released me and stood. "Care to escort me to the front door?"

She turned and walked away from us, intoxicating me further with her impeccable ass. "I'm right behind you."

"You're a bad boy."

The limousine was pulled up to the storefront, awaiting Lilith with an open door. The little boy sat on the edge of the backseat, glaring at me. He held a wet mess in his hands that was black and fibrous. He ate it with wild abandon.

"What's with the boy?" I had to ask, it was a reasonable question.

She pointed to the boy, and he scooted away, to hide in the darkness. She bent to enter the limo and paused, making certain I got an eyeful—which I did. "He is my little one."

"Like, a son?"

"Yes, he is *mine*. He was a gift from my master." She slithered into the backseat and opened her legs to me.

The demon was painfully tempting. Quite painful.

"Luke, all you have to do is say my name if you should ever change your mind." She playfully worked her fingers. "I promise to be there for you, always. Remember that, pretty boy."

"I'll never call on you." I tried to sound convincing, but my throat was dry, making my voice crack.

She laughed as several small creatures emerged from the dark. I couldn't fully make them out, but they had yellow eyes and scaled skin. They clambered to the warm spot between her legs and huddled. "Never say never, Luke."

A long arm, that looked to be constructed from

leather, stretched from within the limo's shadows and pulled the door shut. I blinked, and the limousine was gone.

I shouted to Ruckus, and he shuffled into view. Thankfully, his pants were pulled up.

I cleared my throat. "How do you feel?"

He cocked his head to one side. "Well, I ain't sure."

"What do you mean?"

"I mean I ain't sure. And, I'm seein' weird colors."

"Colors?"

"Yeah, I'm seein' black and blue all around you."

"Did you eat something from Grandpa's house?"

"I brought some pecans with me. I ate 'em on the road while you slept." He rubbed his stomach and made a sour face. "I seriously thought I was gonna' puke or shit myself to death."

"I'm glad that neither happened."

"Boy, what in the hell is goin' on?" He was bothered, which I completely understood. After all, I too was bothered. Who wouldn't be?

"I don't know what's going on."

"Horseshit," he said.

"Okay, well, the pecans…they're a special brand. Grandpa grew them that way. That's why you're seeing colors."

"What about the woman, and that shitty kid of hers? What happened after the woman showed up?"

"You don't remember?" I found this peculiar. Lilith had her tongue in his throat.

"I remember her walkin' around naked, then me gettin' lathered up like a mad dog. But, everything got hazy after that. I damn sure don't recall droppin' my drawers."

There was no easy way of telling him. I was hoping this most recent incident would at least shine a light. Maybe open his mind to outrageous truths.

"You didn't drop your drawers. Lilith did it for you."

"Ya don't say?"

"Yep."

"So, you *do* know that bitch."

"No, she's just started showing up here lately."

Ruckus slowly shook his head and moaned. "Son, you and me are gonna' have us a real come to Jesus talk, and I mean *real* soon. My life has been out of joint since I laid eyes on ya."

The last part of his comment stung me. I was taking a shine to Ruckus, oddly enough. And, he was all that separated me from a state home. "I'm sorry, Ruckus. I know you—"

"No, don't apologize, boy. It ain't your fault. I'm just tired of bein' in the dark."

The sound of someone choking and coughing cut our conversation short. It came from behind the cash register.

"Oh, crap. It's the old man," I said. "Maybe you should check on him."

"You're closer," he said.

"Are you serious?"

"Just take a look," he said, waving me forward. "What the hell else could happen?"

"Really?"

He mused for a moment. "Yeah, good point. I'll take a look, stand back."

Ruckus leaned his tall frame against the front of the countertop and tippy-toed to get a good view. He waved to the floor. "How ya doin' there, pard?"

More coughing, some wheezing.

"Go around and help him," said Ruckus.

I went to the old man and discovered his pants and underwear were tangled around his feet. I whipped my head around as if slapped. "Shit, he's naked!"

"Yeah, I seen that."

"Well, I'm not touching him."

"Who's there?" The old man blinked. His glasses were missing, and his eyesight was apparently poor without them. He sounded groggy and lost. I felt bad for him, but not enough to dress him and risk brushing against his sagging genitalia.

Ruckus put a twenty-dollar bill next to the cash register and motioned for me to shush. "We're out of here, son."

"Who—what the..." The old man's senses were beginning to swim back, and he was sounding none too happy.

We ran out the door and hopped into the Jag. Ruckus cranked up the engine, and we flew from the gas pumps. We were soon speeding into the night, leaving the old man to wonder what had happened.

"I feel bad for the old man," I said.

"Yeah, well it's better'n havin' to explain shit to him."

"You think he'll remember anything?"

"I don't recall much, so I doubt he'll remember anything either. If he does, then it's bound to be a good memory if that gal screwed him. I'm sure he ain't experienced someone like her." Ruckus shook his head. "I sure wanted her. That much I remember."

"She wanted to have sex with me. Wanted to do it pretty bad." I wasn't bragging, just stating a fact.

"No kiddin'?"

"Yep."

"What stopped her?"

"I told her to leave."

"If *I* were...how old are ya?"

"Thirteen."

"Holy shit, son. If I were thirteen, I would've had her right there on the floor, or blown a wad thinkin' about it."

I was close to the latter during the encounter, but I kept that information close to the vest. It wasn't pertinent.

"So," said, Ruckus. "Are ya gonna' tell me what's goin' on? Do I need to go over everything that's happened today?"

I looked out my window and into the darkness. I was

trying to muster the words that would convince him of the way things are. "You'll think I'm nutso. You won't believe me."

"It's been a nutso day. Try me."

"Okay, but it's sort of a long story."

"We've got time."

"Well, you'd best be ready," I said.

"I was born ready."

He wasn't ready to hear what I had to tell. Nobody was. "Okay," I said. "Here it comes, and *please*, no interruptions."

"I won't say shit." He flashed the scout's honor sign and turned the music down. "We've got about thirty minutes of drivin' left. I'm all ears."

I leaned back against the leather seat, wiggling into a comfortable position. Once I was snug and sunk in, I began to talk. I discovered it felt good, to just let it all hang out. The truth will set you free, and all that crap.

Chapter Fourteen

Whiskey, The Good Stuff

I HAD BARELY stopped jabbering when we finally arrived at our destination. We were parked in a driveway, deep inside a gated community that flourished with lighted water fountains

Ruckus seemed to have been at least entertained by my story. He laughed and shook his head most of the time, but he didn't believe me. Big surprise.

"Horseshit. Are you high, boy?" he asked.

"I didn't expect you to believe me."

"Why, hell no." He opened his door and tried to pull himself out, but yelped in pain, and fell back into the seat. He hugged his injured ribs and groaned.

I said, "Those guys wanted the book bad enough to beat you up for it. I'll bet the book has a lot of stuff we need to know. Oh, and we have to tell the sheriff about Buddy—"

"Hang on there, son. You're gettin' ahead of yourself." He cautiously climbed out of the car, moving warily. "You can't go around accusin' people of killin' kids, based on a fuckin' vision, or whatever. It's horseshit. And there ain't no way Theo and you killed an entire family of freaks. I've known him too long. It ain't in him."

I expected this response from him, but it nonetheless grated against me. I knew exactly how Grandpa felt, all those years ago, when he attempted to explain his wild ride on the devil's side.

"No, it's *not* horseshit." I refused to be defeated. Exasperated, but not defeated. I grabbed my duffel bag and followed him to a monstrously oversized front door. It was made of brushed metal, and had a bronzed bull—horns and all—with a brass ring through its nostrils as a door knocker. "Think about Lilith, and how she looked. Don't you remember the weird stuff about her hair?"

"What about her hair?"

"It *moves*. Like it's alive." I moved my arms in squiggly, snake-like movements.

"Hold on," he said, as he opened the front door. "Let's get inside and talk about this."

We entered the house, which was steeped in total darkness, save for the weak glow of a Bugs Bunny nightlight. Ruckus slid his hand along a wall and flipped a light switch, illuminating the large foyer in which we were standing. A few more lights came to life, revealing an enormous home with a condition of cleanliness that was comparable to his car.

"You'll have to excuse the mess. My maid ain't been in for a while," he said.

"You have a maid?"

"Of course not. I don't need one."

Contradictory evidence was abundant, but I didn't care about his housekeeping. My concern was convincing him of the evil that was running rampant in my home town, and that we had to find a way to put an end to it. I said, "Just like you said, weird stuff has been going on since you met me. I hate that bad stuff happened to you, but you're right. I mean some *really* weird stuff. Can't you—"

"Yeah, weird stuff has happened, *but*, it ain't spooky shit. Weird shit happens without the reason bein' ghosts—"

"Demons, not ghosts."

"Yeah, that's what I meant." He moved to his answering machine, which lay amongst a mess of shuffled mail that seemed magically held together on a small table.

If not for a blinking red light, it would have been invisible. "Time out, I need to check my messages."

I found a couch and tossed my duffel of clothes on it, then sat down to dig for the book. I listened as the machine spewed words into the air.

"Hey, uh, Ruckus, this is Gerald, we need some new hands on this rig. The ones I'm havin' to work with don't know to shit, or go blind. Please, holler at me." Beep.

"I hear ya, Gerald," Ruckus looked at me, as if I had a care about Gerald's whining. "That boy has always got some sort of problem."

"Hey man, give me a call. I think I've got the boat for the weekend." Beep.

"I wonder who the hell that was," he mumbled. "Sounds like a party, though."

"Hey, this is Gerald again. Call me, please." Beep.

"You'll have to hold your horses, Gerald."

"Mr. McGraw, this is Sheriff Sanford. Please call me here at the station...it's urgent." Beep.

"That ain't no good," said Ruckus. "Do ya think he wants to lock ya up for murder?" He said this chuckling, thinking I'd find it humorous.

I didn't break into laughter. What Ruckus passed off as a playful dig was a possibility. Sheriff Jake might have sleuthed some evidence together that tied me to murder.

"Ease up, son. If he wanted ya in jail, you'd be there by now."

"Then, what does he want?"

Ruckus picked up the phone and dialed the operator. "Well, we're about to find out."

I fished the book out and rested it in my lap, gently sliding my fingers along its surface, feeling the aged leather. I breathed in its fragrance and tried to envision the times Grandpa held the book in his hands. At first, I was hesitant to open it. I was nervous and uneasy about learning its secrets. But, I soon found myself fiddling with the brass clasp, as hesitation was replaced with growing curiosity.

"Hey, find out what's so damned important about that book, while you're sittin' there doin' nothin'," said Ruckus. He had the phone pressed to his ear. "It's a good thing this ain't an emergency, cause' nobody wants to answer the phone over there."

I unbuckled the clasp and opened the book. It sprawled across my lap like a wedding album, its yellowed pages finally revealed. I held the book in the air, showing it to Ruckus. "We're ready."

"Good deal. Start readin', see wh—hey, what's goin' on, Sheriff?" He motioned for me to keep reading as he spoke. "We're all good, thanks."

His conversation pulled me from the book, as I was not wholly convinced of the sheriff's ignorance of my crimes. He could be playing a game of possum with me, setting a trap.

"Whoa!" said Ruckus. "Are you shittin' me?"

"What's up? What did he say?" I was sickened with suspense.

He held up a hand as he continued to listen. "How'd it happen?"

"How did *what* happen?" I said.

Ruckus placed a palm on his forehead and sat down in a chair that was tangled with laundry. "Yeah, I understand…but, son of a bitch, that's some crazy shit."

His eyebrows raised, and he cut his eyes at me. "A book? What kind of book?"

I stood next to Ruckus with a finger pushed to my lips. *Not a word about the book.*

"Well, I ain't seen a book. But, I'll ask Luke about it in the mornin', he's already asleep. Yeah, all right…you too. We'll holler at ya tomorrow."

Ruckus placed the phone in its cradle, shaking his head side to side. "Son, you ain't goin' to believe what's happened."

"What happened?"

"Well, it ain't good.

"What ain't good?"

"Well, those two boys that jumped us are dead."

My mouth popped open. "What happened…how?"

"He can't say much to me about it, open investigation and all. *But*," he paused and directed his right index finger at me. "He *did* ask about a book you might have had."

My oxygen left, and then I began to pace. "Crap, crap, crap."

"So, what have ya found out so far?" he said.

"About what?"

"The book, have ya read any of it?"

"I've only had it open for a few minutes. I haven't read anything."

The phone sounded off, ringing like a fire alarm. It jarred us both, but Ruckus jumped out of his chair, cursing and stomping. He was clearly spooked.

The phone rang again, long and irritating. Finally, Ruckus picked it up and spoke into it, sounding cautious. "Hello."

I waited in a cloud of paranoia, believing it was the sheriff calling back, to ask Ruckus to bring me in for questioning.

"Hello?"

"Who is it?" I said, wishing he would hang the damn phone up.

"Hello? Anyone there?" He hung up and shrugged his shoulders.

"Wrong number, I guess," I said, doubting it to be the actual truth. I suspected we were being tracked, but not by Sheriff Jake.

"It sounded like a heavy breather," he said.

"A what?"

"A heavy breather, a pervert."

"Oh, so nobody said anything?"

"Nope, just someone breathin'," Ruckus walked to the front door and locked it.

"Maybe it was Buddy." I said this, fully expecting a replay of his skepticism. But he surprised me.

"Maybe you're right," he said. "Why do you think he'd be callin' here?"

"Well, maybe he's checking to see if anyone is home?"

Ruckus walked to the kitchen area, which was adjoined to the living room by a large, black, granite bar top. Half of the bar looked to be used for storage space, crowded with cardboard boxes. After shoving a few boxes around to make a space, he poured himself a bourbon. "So, why do you think that?"

I recalled the horrific images that I saw in Buddy's mind, and how much glee he took in the vile and wicked acts that were carried out. "I think he means to kill me."

"Maybe he means to kill *us*," he said.

"Does this mean you finally believe me?" I became excited, as hope dared to sparkle. Even if that hope was rooted in the extreme possibility of us being the targets of a psychotic murderer.

"Hell, I don't know." Ruckus drained his drink and poured another. "I ain't sayin' I believe in this hocus pocus shit you're goin' on about. But…"

"But what?"

"I actually *do* remember the weird way that naked chick's hair moved. And, the fact that she walked in the store naked to begin with…and the bratty kid," he said. "None of that shit is what I'd call normal."

"Thank you, thank you!" I fell on the floor, relieved.

"But, it could've been me trippin' from those pecans I ate, for all I know."

I got to my feet, waving my hands at him. "No, no, wait a minute. It wasn't the pecans. What about the old man? He was real, not our imaginations."

He took a gulp of his whiskey.

"Also," I said. "The book! The dead guys wanted the *fucking* book!" I stopped myself when I recognized I was standing a foot from Ruckus, yelling up at his fuzzy face.

"Ain't no need in yellin'," he said. "It won't help."

"Shit, I'm sorry." And not just for my tirade. I couldn't help but feel guilty for his current miseries.

He waved my apology off and killed his drink. "Forget about it." He rushed to the book and picked it up, scanning pages as he stood. "We need to find out what the deal is with this book."

"Mr. Bird said it was something that would help me."

He handed the book to me. "Here, get started. See if you can find some help in there for the *both* of us."

"I'll look," I said. "But, I'm not sure what I'm supposed to be looking for."

"Just do your best. I'm goin' to call Mr. Bird and ask him why he gave you a book that people will kill ya for."

I hadn't thought of that, but it was certainly a practicable question. Surely, Mr. Bird wouldn't have intentionally put me in harm's way by giving it to me.

No. If Grandpa trusted him, then I would do the same. "I don't know why he gave it to me, except that Grandpa wanted me to have it."

"Who else has seen ya with the book, or even knows about the damn thing?" he said, as he shuffled through his wallet. "Hang on, I've got Bird's number in here somewhere. I think."

"The only other person who saw it was a big Indian guy. His name is Bear."

"What was he doin' in the room?"

"I'm not sure, but I think he's Mr. Bird's bodyguard or something."

"Yeah, I've seen him with the old man before. He could have put someone after us, maybe he wants the book for himself."

"I don't think so." I sat on the couch and opened the book. Being mindful of the book's age, I gently fanned the pages, blindly searching for ominous word-clues. I would randomly stop at a page and read a scant few lines of script. I recognized some of what he had written as part of what he had already divulged but, at first glance, nothing seemed worthy of special attention. However, I flipped the pages a bit more and managed to dislodge a folded piece of paper.

I excitedly unfolded it. "Ruckus, I think I found something."

He walked to me, stretching the phone cord from the kitchen wall. "What is it? Money, clues, or something valuable, I'll guarantee ya."

"Nope, it's not money. But, it's a note that I guess Grandpa put in here for me."

"What's it say?"

"It says, '*Luke, you'll need to read and ponder this book in its entirety. However, I believe the immediate information on this page to be the most relevant to your survival. The people named on this list are horrible, and dangerous. But they are devilish charmers, fooling everyone into thinking they are good and caring. There is a detailed account of most of them inside the book.*'" The letter ended. "That's it," I said.

"I'm a little disappointed, to be honest," said Ruckus. "I guess this means no John Wayne to the rescue."

"Nope," I said, moving my eyes down the letter. "John Wayne ain't comin'. But, I recognize two last names on this list."

Ruckus hung the phone up. "Do I know 'em?"

"One of them, kind of."

"I hate riddles, spill the name."

"Wynn." I paused for a moment, waiting for a response from Ruckus, but he was clueless. "*Wynn,* doesn't that ring a bell?"

"Not really, no."

"Buddy *Wynn*, the psycho deputy."

"Oh, *that* guy."

"Well, Buddy's name isn't on here. But, someone named *Leon Wynn* is on here," I said.

"Do ya know him?"

"Nope, but Grandpa wrote *'dangerous'* next to his name, and a page number."

"What's the other name you know?"

I frowned when I said the name aloud, as I was quite shocked. "*Jerry Abbott,* he's a veterinarian. Everyone uses him back home. I think he even teaches at a college."

"And you know him?"

"Yep, I met him a few times. He took care of some of my friends' farm animals. He eats at the café in town all the time."

Ruckus poured another drink and let it rest on the granite. He rubbed his hands roughly through his hair, muttering and swaying his head side to side.

He was in the early stage of denial. A denial of not only the existence of murderous public officials, but also a denial of the existence of demons. I was in a position to be empathetic. "I know. It's crazy."

"Yeah, that's one word to describe this shit." He picked up the bourbon, slaying it in one gulp. He grabbed another highball glass from a cabinet and poured two fingers of whiskey. "Here," he said, holding it out to me. "I hate drinkin' alone."

"I'm only thirteen."

"So, what's your point?"

I had never experienced alcohol, unless one included vanilla extract, and on those occasions it was nothing more than an ingredient used in pies or cookies. Nevertheless, I took the drink and stared at it like it was an alien insect species.

"That there is some high dollar bourbon, son. Ordinarily I'd say sip it, but today I'm recommendin' ya down it."

I sniffed it and nearly gagged, but the smell did nothing to derail my first taste of whiskey. After all, if there was ever a time for my first drink, surely this was it. Wasting no time, I tilted the glass and let the firewater blister its way down my throat. I was immediately stripped of the ability to breathe, and my stomach was a white-hot bed of coals. A coughing spasm served as my whiskey chaser.

Ruckus came from behind the bar and slapped me on my back, nearly knocking me to the ground. "You'll be all right."

I didn't believe him. I felt as if I were on the verge of suffocating.

"Blow air out of your mouth, it'll help with the burn." He demonstrated this methodology to me, narrowing his mouth into an 'o', and blowing his whiskey fumes into my face. "Try it."

I was desperate for relief, so I used his advice and found it to be sound enough. I was able to regain control of my breathing, and lower the burn.

"I told ya you'd be all right," he said. "I'm a pro."

I cleared my throat. "If that's high dollar whiskey, I'd hate to drink the cheap stuff."

Ruckus grabbed the phone and pressed it against his ear. "I'm gonna' try to get hold of ole' Bird again." A puzzled look appeared on his face, and he repeatedly pressed the phone hook.

"What's wrong," I said.

"I can't get a dial tone."

The lights in the house blinked out, and then came the sound of breaking glass. We had intruders.

Chapter Fifteen

Exit Wounds and Tattoos

RUCKUS GRABBED THE back of my shirt and tossed me behind the bar. I rolled roughly along the floor, clutching the book.

"Be quiet," said Ruckus, barely breathing.

We both crouched in the dark, quiet as death. More broken glass sounds followed, then a solid *thump*.

"They're in the house," said Ruckus.

"Where do you keep your guns?"

"I ain't got any guns."

"No guns?" I had never met a person who didn't own at least one firearm. He would have been laughed out of town, had he admitted such a jaw-dropper in Wetumka. "Not even a shotgun?"

He shushed me and pulled open a kitchen drawer. He pulled a pair of butcher knives out and handed one to me. "Here, follow me," he said.

He led me away from the bar, toward the front door. As we moved, a crash cut through the quiet, and a man cursed emphatically from somewhere toward the back of the house. Next came a much louder commotion, as if something large and heavy had fallen. A yelp of pain and more curses ensued.

"I got a lot of shit piled up back there," said Ruckus. "*And,* right around here. Be careful where ya step."

The intruder shouted at us, screaming in a voice that

was thick with hate and pain. "Ya'll might as well give it up! Just hand—*ouch, shit*—just give us what we want!"

"What do you think fell on him?" I said.

"Ain't no tellin'."

As we approached the front door, Ruckus signaled for me to stop my hurried sneaking. He warily looked into the peephole. "It's too dark to see what's out there."

The angry houseguest screamed an obscenity, sounding closer. A new commotion of crashing items affirmed he was pulling himself out from the rubble, drawing nearer. I tightened my grip on the knife. "Ruckus, we've got to hurry."

He was still squinting into the peephole, shaking his head, uncertain of what action to take. "I ain't in no hurry to run into more trouble. I'm bettin' there's more out there."

The intruder laughed, but not because anyone said anything funny. It was a cruel laugh, taunting, and barren of even the slightest touch of humor.

The hair on the back of my neck felt like it was crawling. "Ruckus, something's wrong."

"No, shit."

The man in the dark continued to laugh, but his laughter had changed. The pitch was different, turning guttural and animalistic.

And the room turned icy.

"Ruckus—"

"Yeah, I hear him."

We also heard Ruckus' clutter being waded through, sounding too close for our comfort. A few pieces of junk sailed from the gloom, smashing against a wall.

One of us had to act. I decided it should be me.

I handed the book to Ruckus. "Here, hold this a minute."

He hesitantly took the book from me. "What are ya thinkin'?"

"I've got to do something," I said.

"Like, *what?*"

"I've got to kill that guy back there." I spun and headed in the direction of the man, gripping the knife with both hands.

"Horseshit. You ain't—" As Ruckus protested, the front door was struck several times with gunfire. "Wait up, I'm right behind ya."

I moved as carefully as I could, considering the frantic circumstance I was in. I didn't want to run blindly in the dark, and not just because a maniac was waiting. Ruckus' household landmines were another hitch to seriously consider.

The man made it easy to for us to discover him. He wasn't trying to hide. He was a limping shadow, twenty feet away, moving toward us and swinging a gun in his right hand. His aura was a twisting black hole, standing out against the house's own murk with a dark luminescence.

"Boy, you should have—*blagh, ahgal*—gave us what we wanted!" said the man.

Ruckus grabbed my shoulder. "What the hell is he sayin'?"

"I don't know. I think it's some kind of demon talk."

"Horseshit." His skepticism rang hollow.

The man stopped and pointed the gun at me, flashing a maniacal grin. It was a familiar grin, full of pain, anguish, and hate. It was the same crazy smile that the boy wore.

Ruckus stepped in front of me and let loose with a primal scream. He then threw his knife at the man. "There ya go, ya son of a bitch!" The knife missed its target, sailing well above the man's head, clattering against something metallic in the shadows. "Shit."

The man fired his gun, lighting his ugly features. His eyes were filled with black, and his forehead was grotesquely bulged with skin that was splitting, exposing glistening bone. He did not look human.

Ruckus fell to his knees and grabbed at a spot on the left side of his chest. Blood ran from his fingers. "Shit, fucker shot me."

More gunfire blasted from the front door, but I didn't bother to look at what might be transpiring. I couldn't worry about what was behind me. Not when my new friend, and state appointed guardian, was gunshot and bleeding. Additionally, I was in the middle of a self-proclaimed mission. I had someone to kill.

I took two steps and lunged at the gunman's legs and slid on my belly across a dusty, wooden floor. I banged into his legs, and saw the reason for the limp. His right ankle was broken, and a bone was jutting through the skin. The man was walking on the bone, as if he was unaware of the injury.

"Klagh blagh huhtkal cl—"

I drove the knife deep into his groin area, unleashing a primal scream of my own. "Shut up, nobody understands what you're saying!"

The man produced a sharp gasp of air and dropped the gun. I rolled away from him, literally spinning in place like a cartoon character for a few seconds. I glided on my ass to Ruckus, who was lying on his back hugging the book against his chest. Blood was pooling.

"Ruckus, are you okay?" I realized the stupidity of the question as it left my lips. "We've got to get you to a hospital."

He leaned up on an elbow, ignoring the painful fire that was broken ribs and a gunshot wound. "Get the gun."

The man was still alive. He was on his hands and knees, vomiting and shuddering as if he were being electrocuted.

I saw the gun and quickly scooped it up. Without a scant of hesitation, I pointed the gun at the man's head and pulled the trigger. His convulsions stopped, and he fell flat on his face, splashing into a puddle of blood and bile.

I turned my attention to the front door, pointing the

gun. "What should we do?"

Ruckus spoke in ragged breaths. "Ain't nobody gettin' through that door. It's made of solid steel. We're goin' to have to leave through the back."

Small clicks and ticks came from the direction of the front door, and then it began to slowly open.

"I ain't believin' this shit," he said.

I was weirdly excited about the possibility of killing another monster. I moved forward, foolishly hoping for a confrontation.

"Luke, don't shoot. It's Bear. I'm here to help."

"You're Mr. Bird's bodyguard." I kept the gun trained toward the door and watched as it fully opened.

A large form cautiously moved through the door way. It was Bear. He held his hands open and to the side. "Yes, it's me. And like I said, I'm here to help you. But, we have to hurry."

Ruckus groaned. "You'd best not hurt that boy."

"No harm will come to either of you, at least not from me." He nodded to Ruckus. "You need help."

"How can I trust you?" I said.

"Keep the gun pointed at me if that makes you feel better, but Ruckus needs medical attention."

"Hell, I'll be all right," said Ruckus, although he was sounding weaker each time he spoke. He was steadily losing blood.

"No." I lowered my weapon. "You're not doing so hot."

I motioned to Bear that it was okay for him come into the house. He knelt next to Ruckus and carefully examined his wound. "The bullet went through and through, exiting your back. But, we've got to stem this bleeding. Luke, can I borrow your shirt?"

"Yeah." I took it off and gave it to him. He folded it and wadded it, then pressed it against the wound.

"Luke, I need you to hold this against his shoulder with lots of pressure."

Bear walked to the dead man and rolled him onto his back. "He was sent here to take the book, and do other things. Eventually, killing the both of you."

I looked back at the front door, which lay wide open, and saw the soles of another dead man. He was sprawled across the front porch. "Who's that?"

"He was trying to shoot his way into the house," he said.

"Did you kill him?"

"No, it wasn't me. Apparently, a bullet ricocheted off of the door and killed him. Right between the eyes." Bear chuckled. "There was no way he was going shoot through *that* door. I had to pick the lock."

"Told ya," said Ruckus, as his eyes closed.

"Ah, man, this ain't good," I said. "Something's wrong."

Bear was immediately at my side, attending to Ruckus. He felt for a pulse along his neck.

Oh, God. Please, please, please. Please, don't let him die, don't let him be dead.

"He's alive, but his pulse is weak." He got to his feet and went onto the front porch and dragged the corpse inside. Emergency sirens whined in the distance.

"Do you think that's an ambulance?" I was sick with worry.

"No, not unless you called them. It's more likely the police."

"Shit."

"Don't worry, I've got some help." He left through the front door, out of my view, and came back with a man in a rumpled suit and tie. "This man will handle the situation, but we have to leave immediately."

"Who are you?" I said.

The stranger reached inside his jacket and pulled out a wallet. He flipped it open and flaunted a shiny badge. "Detective Anthony at your service, kid."

He read my mistrust. "Don't worry. I'm a *good* cop,

like most of us are." He pointed to the gun that was now tucked in my pants. "Luke, how about you hand that gun to me. I'll shoulder the chore of shooting folks from this point forward."

I handed it over, and then he shook my hand. I caught a whiff of whiskey, cigarettes, and perfume on the detective.

"What about the dead guys?" I was anxious, as the sirens were steadily closing, and blood lay in pools and rivulets. A lot of explaining to do.

"I have it handled." He nodded to Bear, who had just ripped open the shirt of the man I'd shot.

Bear grabbed the corpse by the ankle—the good ankle—and dragged it to me. He pointed a flashlight beam at the dead man's chest. "Luke, take a look at this."

The man had a large tattoo emblazoned across his torso. It was an owl. Yellow all over, except for the eyes. The eyes were black. There were symbols and letters carved into the body. Some nasty gashes, deep and tearing. "Crap, I bet that hurt."

"The owl represents their organization. The cuts are part of a spell," said Bear.

"Hey, you can educate him later," said the detective. "We need to get Luke's pal over there some help, and get the two of you out of here."

Ruckus raised up, groaning. "Hell, I'm feelin' better."

"You don't look like you're feeling better," said Bear

Ruckus brushed my hand from the bloody remains of my shirt. "Grab the damn book. I've got this part covered."

Bear helped him get to his feet, and then saluted the detective. "Adios, Oliver. Are you sure you got this handled?"

"Does a fish have a watertight ass?"

"I don't know," said Bear. "It might depend on the fish."

The detective pointed to the front door. "Get the fuck *gone*."

As the three of us scuttled onto the front porch, we stepped in brain-goo and blood. This left gory footprints behind, prompting Detective Anthony to chastise us as we hurriedly piled into Bear's white Cadillac, laying Ruckus in back. "Jesus, what the *hell*. Guys, I ain't a fucking miracle worker!"

We were two minutes out of the winding neighborhood when two police cars blew past us, sirens blaring and lights blinding. I wondered how Detective Anthony was going to deal with the mess left behind.

"How is he going to explain all that?" I said.

"Oh, he's probably going to do his best to keep everyone out of the house, say that it was a false alarm from a nosey neighbor."

"Will that work?"

"I hope so."

"Are you okay back there, Ruckus?" He had been quiet, and I was worried it might be because he had bled to death.

"My house is a total wreck now," said Ruckus.

I turned my head sharply toward the backseat, pleased to know he still had a pulse. "Well, it was sort of messy anyway."

"It's a lot worse now."

I thought of the dead bodies, and the blood. "Yeah," I said. "It's worse now."

"Where the hell we headed," said Ruckus, sounding groggy.

"Someplace safe," said Bear.

"He needs a doctor."

"I can patch him up."

"You're a doctor?" I said.

"That would be a negative."

I shook my head in disbelief. "Then, he needs a doctor. I don't want him dying!" I was getting wound up.

"It's all right, kid. He probably won't die."

Ruckus mumbled something, and passed out.

"Probably?" I said.

"He's going to be fine. This is not my first rodeo involving gunshot wounds."

It dawned on me that this wasn't my first rodeo with gunshot wounds either. But, I figured Bear was vastly more experienced in this department, and I didn't have any choice but to trust him.

"Have you had a chance to read the book, yet?" said Bear.

The book sat in my lap. Ruckus' blood had coated the front of it. "No, not yet."

"Hopefully, once we get to safety, you'll have time to."

"Why is it so important that I read it, and why do psychos want to kill me for it?"

Bear made a quick turn and accelerated down an unlit street. "There's no short answer to that question. Once we get to where we're going, I'll give it my best shot."

"Where did you say we're going?"

"I didn't say."

"So, you're not going to tell me?"

"Mr. Bird's house. That's where we're going."

Ruckus sprang up and slurred, "Birdhouse."

Bear nodded at me. "Yeah, he'll be just fine."

Chapter Sixteen

A New Garden

WE EVENTUALLY ENTERED a historical neighborhood of mansions, built in the early 1900's. Most of the homes were obscured by the night, though some had enough light spilling from inside to allow a peek into a world of fireplaces and sweeping staircases. The big car pulled into a driveway marked by two large gaslights and an imposing iron gate. A man appeared from the darkness, allowing our arrival as he opened the gate wide. We followed the driveway as it wound around to the back of the house.

Bear parked the car next to several other vehicles and immediately attended to the task of retrieving Ruckus from the backseat. He was awake but quiet, save for the grunts of pain.

"His ribs are busted up, too," I said. "Be extra careful."

As Ruckus exited, he left a smeared trail of blood on the interior. Bear saw me observing the slick mess. "Can't get blood stains out of leather." He motioned to the man who opened the gate for us and handed the car keys to him. "Burn it," he said, sighing.

The man had an unlit cigarette hanging from his lips, which he quickly remedied with a zippo. "*Burn* it? As in literally?"

Bear pointed to the cigarette. "Yeah, just like that smoke."

The man shook his head as if he had just been asked to bury a family pet, but he didn't hesitate to get behind the wheel.

"Just a few more feet, Ruckus," said Bear. "And then we'll be inside the house."

"I'll make it," said Ruckus. And he actually did appear to be handling his injuries, but not without a goodly amount of grit and determination.

"I'm sorry for all that I caused you." My voice quivered at the end.

"You didn't do nothin' to me."

"I might as well have. If it weren't for me—"

"Hey, why don't ya open the back door for us while you ain't doin' anything," he said. As they passed by, Ruckus patted my head. "You're a good boy." He then collapsed against Bear and closed his eyes.

I SAT IN AN antique chair with my face pressed into my hands. Next to me was a cold fireplace and Thomas Bird, who lounged comfortably in his wheelchair, perusing Grandpa's mysterious and dangerous book. "Much has been added since I last saw this book. Many names, oh yes."

"I don't want the damn book. I wish I'd never heard of it." My comments were muffled, but true to my feelings.

"Sorry, what was that?"

I pulled my face away from the security of my hands. "I said, *I don't want the damn book.* It's brought a lot of bad stuff around. My life has sucked since I met you—sorry, no offense—but it's true. I don't know why it's not locked up in a...bank or some shit. And Ruckus..."

"He's in good hands. He'll be fine, I assure you."

I stood up and paced. "Well, I'll bet that won't make him feel much better. Someone's tried to kill him twice." I furiously pointed to the book that lay in Mr. Bird's lap.

"Again, that, that…fucking book." I threw my arms up in the air, as I was wound up. "I don't *get it*. Why the big fucking deal?"

"I understand your frustrations, Luke. I was in similar shoes once upon a time, yes, *many* years ago." Mr. Bird wheeled to a large bay window that looked over a lighted garden. "You've been thrust into an unknown role, fair or not, but it is now a reality that you're fastened to. I was able to eventually adapt to it, just as I'm certain you'll be able."

"That's just crazy, Mr. Bird," I said, trying to settle my tone. I joined him at the window and looked at the variety of plant life that seemed to ebb with color and life. It reminded me of the garden at the farm. In fact, the similarities were surprising. Some of the flowers were of the type I had only seen in Grandpa's secret garden.

"Mr. Bird, where did those flowers come from?"

"Ah, you've a keen eye."

I pointed to a specific plant that was cropped close to the ground, yet astonishing in its splendorous shades of red and purple. It flowed as a brilliant groundcover, intertwining with other plants. "Grandpa's garden has flowers just like those."

Mr. Bird gently chuckled. "That is where these plants originated from. Theo's garden. Every plant, flower and tree."

"Can I go out there?"

"Of course. You may go anywhere in this house, or these grounds."

Someone heavy could be heard coming down the stairs. I turned and saw it was Bear. I immediately asked of Ruckus' health.

Bear waved me off, smiling. "He's going to be fine. He's a tough son of a bitch."

Mr. Bird said, "Bear, Luke would like to take a walk in the garden. Would you mind showing him the way?"

"No, problem."

"As for me," said Mr. Bird. "I'm going to bed. I'm not built for these late hours anymore."

"Do you need help?" said Bear.

"No, Millie will help me if I need it." Mr. Bird spun his wheelchair around and disappeared down a hallway lined with portraits and antique sconces.

I followed in Bear's footsteps, feeling the old wooden floor heave beneath his impressive frame. We exited through a door that led down some steps to another door. We went through that door and found our way into the garden.

A stone path lay out before me, leading in varying directions, surrounded by beauty. Gaslights lit up the garden and the pathway, and more lights were perched atop a twelve-foot wall that stood as a fortress around the house. I saw a few figures walking about in the shadows, rifles were draped over their shoulders.

Indeed, my life had changed.

"Are there any pecan trees back here?" I said.

"Yep, there is one. I'll walk you to it."

As we walked, I queried him on Ruckus. "Is he *really* going to be okay?"

"Oh, yes. Like I said, he's tough. He's sleeping right now."

"I think I'm going to tell him to forget about me and go on with whatever he was doing before."

"Really?"

"Yep. I'm pretty sure he's been thinking of doing it anyway."

"Why do you say that?"

"C'mon, man. Look at all of the crap he's had happen to him." I shook my head. "It's like a movie, it's all…unreal. Except, it ain't unreal. If he was smart, he'd dump me."

"Hmm, that's not what he told me." Bear stopped to draw attention to a tree. "Here's the tree."

I stared up at the tree's branches, easily spotting the

oddly encased nuts that hung from them. "What did Ruckus say?" I tried to sound disinterested for some silly reason, but I was actually hanging on his every word. Hoping to hear something to contradict me. Fearing I wouldn't.

Bear plucked a handful of nuts from the tree. "He told me that you needed him, and he can't imagine you being stuck in a state home. Also, his word to Theo. That means a hell of a lot to 'em. He loved your granddad."

"Are you sure he doesn't feel *stuck* with me, just because of Grandpa?"

"I didn't get that from 'em."

"I feel bad for him."

Bear shoved the pecans in his jeans and then placed a comforting hand on my shoulder. "Luke, you worry too much. Or, you worry about the wrong shit. Ruckus is going to stand pat with you, no need to waste energy feeling guilty."

"I never used to worry about anything."

"You're too young to start now," he said. "However, with that said…"

"What?"

"You, just like the rest of us, need to be concerned with the events that have been unfolding."

I actually felt a wave of joy ripple through my heart. An emotion I thought was dead and buried. I was finally able to discuss the current lunacy of my life, with someone who would not think me a lunatic.

"Trust me, I've been concerned," I said.

Bear smiled. "Yeah, I'll bet. Let's walk some more."

We strolled along the path, until we arrived at a wooden bench that was parked between two enormous tomato plants. We sat and faced the back of the old house. I had never seen a house so large in person. Three stories high, bursting with grandeur, and spooky with shadows.

"I'm going to start talking, so, please hold your questions. But, feel free to ask me *anything* once I've shut up."

I nodded. "Let's get started."

Bear produced a cigarette from a shirt pocket and lit it up. He took a deep pull and let the smoke unfurl from his body. "That book, I'll start there. Most families of the *Unchosen* have one. It's a record of events—you're considered an Unchosen by the way—and each one is different. The events being the experiences and observations of the Unchosen's life."

"Unchosen—"

He held up a hand. "Wait."

Keeping my mouth shut was going to take a titanic effort.

"What does Theo's book have in it?" said Bear.

"Well, I don't know. I haven't had much of a chance to read it," I said, a little irritated. "People keep trying to steal the book, and kill me while they're at."

"I see," he said. "Well, for now it doesn't matter. But, at some point in the future, you'll have to attend a meeting of sorts. There'll be other Unchosen at this meeting, and all of you will compare stories and notes."

The thought of meeting others who understood my horrific plight was added sunshine for my soul.

Bear drew on his smoke, making it sizzle. The tobacco embers made his face glow, highlighting his high cheek bones. "Those men from earlier tonight had markings on their bodies. Remember?"

I nodded, remembering all too clearly.

"Those were spells invoking specific demons. The demons possess the body, and then murder, rape, torture...whatever their master wants. The men, who are the demon's vessels, know what is to come. They volunteer for it."

"What?" Keeping my mouth shut was never a strong suit of mine. "Why would someone *want* that to happen to them?"

Bear ignored my transgression and answered me.

"These aren't people like you and me. These are some bad folks, Luke."

A chill came over me, despite the night's mild temperature. "Bear, there's some bad stuff going on in Wetumka. The deputy is bad."

"Yes, we believe his coven was responsible for tonight's attack on you two."

"So, you know about him? And he's in a coven?"

"We've known for a bit. And, yes, for lack of a better word, he's part of a coven. Probably more than one."

"Then why hasn't anyone done anything?" Irritation rose again. "He's doing awful things to kids."

"It's not as easy as you think. We need proof to bring it to law enforcement. Proof and witnesses." Bear stretched his legs out and yawned, glancing at his watch. "It's after midnight, we could all use some rest. In particular, you."

"Wait, how can we count on the police when they're the bad guys?"

"Not all of them are bad. Detective Anthony is one of the good ones. I'd venture to say that most are good cops. The problem is when the covens are connected to power. It makes it tough to make anything stick, and there ain't a soul that'll dare turn on 'em. That's what happened to the two men that were arrested in the attacks back at Theo's place." Bear stood up and began to walk back to the house. "They were a weak link and were destroyed before the sheriff could get anything useful out of them."

"Wait, you said I could ask you questions," I said.

Bear crushed his cigarette out on the bottom of his boot and looked at his watch again. "What else do you want to know?"

"Well, how did the guys in jail die?"

"Does it matter?"

"To me it does. Even if it's gross."

"Fair enough," He paused before he spoke. "You won't read this in the newspapers, but, they were found ripped to shreds. I understand it was a bloody mess, with guts hanging—"

"Okay, gotch'a." I yielded to the grisly details. I was familiar with butchery. I was not in need of a descriptive story. But, I was curious to know how the killers were able to walk into a police station and slaughter two men. "How did it happen, who did it?"

"From what we gathered, it was a demon sent to kill them. Of course, the sheriff doesn't know or suspect this. He's at a loss I'm sure."

"Wait," I said, suddenly jolted. "That shit can happen?"

"Not *here*, you're safe from conjured entities." He pointed to the house and stretched his arms over the garden. "It's protected from Hell's creatures."

"That's a relief…I guess."

"But, all bets are off against God's creatures. Meaning, humans."

I watched one of the riflemen move out of the shadows. "So, that's why you have men with guns."

I found myself wishing for a shot of whiskey. The high dollar kind.

"Yep. Anything else?"

"Three things."

"Just three things? I'm impressed. What are they?"

"First thing, what is the *Unchosen*?"

"That's who you are. You're an Unchosen," He dug for another cigarette and heaved a sigh. "Kid, I'll give you the nickel tour, but then you'll have to *read*."

"Gotch'a."

Bear scratched a match and lit his smoke before he sat back down. "Okay, the Unchosen are people who were part of a deal, a pact. A pact with the devil. A parent of a child—mom or dad—can offer up their child in exchange for money, power, sex…whatever their hearts desire."

"Wait, then how can *I* be an Unchosen. My dad didn't do that. He certainly did not."

Bear flashed a dreary grin. "Theo is the reason, not your father."

"I don't understand."

"Theo was promised in a pact to an agent of Hell, but, he was stolen away before he could be handed over. But, that doesn't make things go away, no sir. As far as Hell is concerned, a debt is still owed according to bloodline. Pretty much a curse, Luke."

I quickly called to mind something the devil had spilled to me, something about me being protected from him. Was it true?

"Do you remember when I first met you and Mr. Bird, in the hospital?"

"Oh, for sure."

"So, you know that the devil, uh, paid me a visit—" I unexpectedly exploded into gut-wrenching, knee-slapping laughter. The absurdity of what I'd just said swept over me.

"You, uh, okay?" said Bear.

I regained my poise, stifling any lingering giggles, and continued on without missing a beat. "Anyway, the devil said *he* couldn't harm me. Do you think that is true?"

"I don't know. The devil is the prince of all lies and deceit," he said. "But, there was something different about Theo. There might be something to what you're saying. Even he didn't understand it, but he was somewhat protected I think. Maybe you'll benefit from it." Bear shrugged his shoulders. "Best to be on the safe side, Luke."

"I was bitten by a demon, you know." I reckoned I'd might as well throw all I had on the table.

Bear was clearly stunned by my admission. He stood up and sucked the rest of his cigarette down with a single drag.

"Is something wrong?" Bear's reaction was not what I had hoped for. I was feeling out of place, once again.

He cleared his throat. "No, nothing is wrong. It's just

that…"

"Why is *that* such a big deal?" As far as I was concerned, it was just another demon tale to add to the family scrapbook of horrors.

"I've never met anyone who's been bitten," he said. "In fact, you've experienced some things in just a few days that most Unchosen have never gone through."

I opened my arms and shrugged, feeling that the mood had changed. "So, what are you saying?"

Bear saw the unease I was suffering and tried consoling words. "It's okay, Luke. Sorry to seem freaked out. It's just so remarkable, that is all."

"If you're freaked out, imagine how I feel."

Bear pointed a finger at me and nodded. "Touché."

"I wish it had never happened, you know."

"There's probably a lot that you wish had not happened." he said. "But since you brought it up, how'd that come about?"

I went into my story, delivering every raw detail I could muster. Bear stood with his arms folded, listening and grimacing.

After I was done, he was quiet for a few seconds, thinking.

"There are stories about a demon named Lilith," he finally said. "She's sometimes called a succubus."

"You've heard of her?"

"Yes, she's mentioned in many religions and beliefs. You're lucky she didn't screw you."

Metaphorically speaking, I felt plenty screwed.

"What else you have to ask?" said Bear.

My remaining questions were simple and tied to together. "*Why* in the world did you give me Grandpa's book, and *why* wasn't it kept somewhere safe?"

"That's an easy answer. Firstly, the book belongs to you now. That's how it's always been done, passing it on down to family. And it was kept safe by Theo, for a great many years, until he dropped it off here a few months ago.

He wanted to make sure you received it."

I found it to be strangely healing, learning that Grandpa was keenly aware of his impending doom. His actions proved this.

"So you guys didn't know that people would try to kill me for the book?" I'd been itching to question their decision to drop the book into my lap.

"If you're asking if we used you as bait, of course not. Then again, we suspected that something was going to happen at the hospital due to Agnes Maynard. She's the old lady who was caught with the dead girl's head. We suspect she was a major player in the local coven." He yawned and carried on. "Someone must have been watching Theo closely. Someone who knew who you were."

"Who do you think it was?"

"Not really sure, but I'll take a closer look at those names on Theo's list." Bear raised his arms in the air and stretched. "But that's going to be tomorrow. Time to hit the sack, man."

Sleep began to appeal to me. Maybe I'd be lucky and get to see Grandpa again, in that weird dream state. Or at the very least, sleep dreamlessly. No nightmares that way.

Chapter Seventeen

Natalie and a Side of Eggs

I AWOKE LATE the following morning feeling refreshed, apart from my fuzzy teeth. I did not receive a visit from Grandpa as I slept, but I did dream of the farm. It called to me, using its wiles of waving grass and unruffled vibe. In the dream, I was lazily reclining in the hammock beneath the mimosa tree, sipping on high dollar bourbon.

The smell of bacon and coffee abruptly tipped me away from my melancholy. I sat up in bed, taking in deep breaths of the savory aroma. My appetite became instantly voracious.

I hopped out of bed and went to a window that faced the street. A swaying sycamore tree blocked most of the sunlight, allowing only small snatches of light to flow into the room. I was on the third floor of the house and was able to survey the neighborhood easily. All of the homes were magnificent and old, with each having its own unique quality of architecture. Some looked worn and tired, but even those were grand. It was very different than what I was accustomed to. Not a single dirt road in sight.

I found Ruckus downstairs in the kitchen sitting at a small table with Mr. Bird, the both of them enjoying a beautiful breakfast of pancakes, bacon, eggs, and sausage. Ruckus was shoveling food with his right arm, as the left rested neatly in a sling. I pulled up a chair that had an empty plate in front of it, which was not empty for long. I heaped the food high and drowned it in butter and maple syrup.

"Those pancakes are delicious," said Ruckus. "I've had a few rounds of 'em already."

Mr. Bird pushed his plate away and wiped his mouth with a linen napkin, signaling the end of his breakfast. "Pancakes are one of Millie's many specialties."

After a single bite, I agreed with Mr. Bird's assessment of the pancakes. It melted in my mouth like a chocolate truffle. "Who's Millie?"

A female voice cooed from around a corner. "She's my mama."

Seconds later, a young goddess emerged.

The moment I saw her, a euphoric shockwave moved up and down my backbone, and my demon bite started tingling. I was unable to breathe. I was a captive of her beauty.

"Natalie, good morning," said Mr. Bird. "Meet Ruckus and Luke. They're our house guests."

"Hey there," said Ruckus. "Good to meet ya. I'd stop and shake your hand, but I'm sort of busy at the moment." He pointed his eyes at his plate. "One-armed and all."

"That's okay," she said. "Nice to meet you, too."

All eyes were on me, as it was now my turn to greet the beautiful Natalie. The problem was that I was unable to find any words, because I was too preoccupied with her green eyes and auburn hair. Her hair hung to the middle of her back, darkly rich with strands of spun copper. I also began seeing her aura, as it glowed an intense red. My body began to get hot, particularly my groin area. Something was definitely going on down there.

"Hey boy, what's the matter? The cat got your tongue?" said Ruckus.

"Uh—"

"It appears that your mother's pancakes have cast a spell upon Luke," said Mr. Bird.

Natalie approached me and started to say something,

but she stopped herself. A strange gaze appeared in her eyes, and she slowly looked me over. It made me feel excited and uncomfortable.

Mr. Bird cut through the awkwardness. "Natalie is a few years older than you, Luke."

"Sixteen," she said in a honey coated voice. "How old are you?"

"Thirteen." I was thankful that my voice didn't break into a puberty-stricken pitch.

"Thirteen. So, you're in junior high," she said.

"Yep." In other words, I was comparatively a child. A child wearing filthy clothes that had been slept in, and hair that no doubt needed a serious combing. I was tense with embarrassment.

She extended her hand to me and smiled. I took it, clueless of the required etiquette. But, I needn't have worried as it turned out, because what happened next diminished such mundane worries. When our hands touched, the room instantly became blindingly white, drowning out Ruckus, Mr. Bird, walls and furniture. The only thing visible was Natalie and her red aura. It was blotted against the whiteness like pooling blood on snow.

My ache for her increased. I wanted to feel her body's warmth, and I wanted to kiss her lips. The demon bite burned with a sensation, egging my desires forward. I also had an erection as hard as a quinine bottle.

"Luke," she said.

Hearing my name said from such sensuous lips was more than I could stand. I felt I was going to explode. And then, I did. In my pants.

I became racked with orgasmic convulsions. I shuddered and made ridiculous, strange sounds. Then the whiteness went away.

"Damn, boy. What in the hell is wrong with you?" said Ruckus.

I heard him speaking to me, but not from across the breakfast table. I was flat on my back, lying on the floor alongside my pancakes. Eggs were literally on my face.

"Are you okay?" It was the goddess speaking.

I immediately whipped my hands to my crotch. In doing so I displaced my plate, sending it skittering across the floor to wobble like a dying top.

"What happened?" I said.

"You're askin' *us*?" Ruckus was now standing over me. "You looked like you were having a seizure."

"Um, a seizure?"

"Kinda' looked like one." He extended his arm to me, grinning in amazement. "Here, let me help ya."

I was reluctant to reach for his hand, for fear of revealing my erection.

"Why ya cuppin' your balls?" he said. "Did ya hurt 'em?"

I rolled and maneuvered onto my hands and knees. "Yep, that's right. Hit my balls."

"You've got egg on your face," said Natalie.

"Ain't that the truth," said Ruckus.

Mr. Bird laughed.

I stood up—careful to keep my back to the gawkers—and cleared my throat. "Yep, some sort of seizure," I waved goodbye over my shoulder and slinked away. "I'll be back after I clean up. I'll take care of the mess down here."

"It's been weird," said Natalie.

"Bingo again, girl," said Ruckus.

I mumbled and made my escape, climbing the stairs like an Olympian. That is, until I slipped in my stocking feet. My knees and shins were dealt a painful ordeal as I tumbled. I'd might as well have been wearing a clown nose and floppy shoes.

I rolled onto my back and rested my shoulder blades against the steps. My stiffy was chased away by humiliation.

Ruckus was abruptly at the foot of the staircase. "Holy shit, son. You break anything?"

"I don't think so." I began rubbing my injuries, hoping I was correct in my diagnosis.

"What's goin' on?" he said.

"I wish I knew."

"I might have an idea." It was Mr. Bird. "Go on and get cleaned up first, then we'll talk."

I took off my socks and carefully got to my feet. "Yep, a bath would be crazy fun. But, I don't think you can help me with my problems. Nobody can."

"We shall see, Luke," said Mr. Bird. "Bear spoke to me this morning, regarding your unusual circumstance."

I assumed he was referring to my demon bite, but I didn't know how much Natalie knew, and I didn't want to sound any crazier or appear any weirder in her eyes. I was careful with my words. "He told you what I told him…about Lilith?"

"Oh, yes."

"And you can help me?"

"Take a hot bath, then we'll talk. Get yourself refreshed," he said. He then deftly wheeled his chair around and scooted away.

"I'm going to wash my breakfast off," I said to Ruckus.

"Good idea, ya look like a derelict."

Before ascending the stairs, I took a hard glance around for Natalie. She was not within my line of sight, but I could feel her. She wasn't far.

I HAD TAKEN notice of the incredible amount of posh that inhabited the upstairs bathroom, the previous evening as I used the toilet. The crown molding was a rich, dark wood. It framed the space nicely, overlooking a marble floor and marble countertops. Sprawled upon the floor—a ridiculously large floor—was a bearskin rug. I was no expert, but I figured it was a grizzly bear. It was huge.

An enormous chandelier hung from the middle of the

ceiling. It shined with twinkling jewels that dangled from strands of gold. The faucets were of gold. It was all fairy tale stuff. Admittedly, it was impressive to be soaking in a clawfoot bathtub and to be surrounded by such opulence. But truth be told, I'd have much rather been in the horse trough back at the farm. A chandelier was a poor substitute for the stars.

As I lounged in the steamy water, I took the time to torture myself with the embarrassing events of breakfast. Not my finest moment. Having Natalie think me a fool and a buffoon was mortifying. I would be able to explain away my strange behavior to Ruckus and Mr. Bird, but not Natalie.

"Screw it." She was older anyway, and I didn't stand a chance with such beguiling beauty. Besides, if being around her caused me to react as such, then it was best to stay away from her. I'd be just fine, nothing to it.

Mercy, but she's so beautiful.

A horrific thought came to me. What if I spiraled into my strangeness every time I came into contact with women? "Crap."

Doomed to be a freak. *Gee, thanks Grandpa. Thanks for dragging me into this wonderful new life.* A spike of anger and frustration ground into me, but it was momentary. I couldn't blame Grandpa. I *wouldn't* blame him. He was—and is—the single most wonderful person I'd ever known. He certainly didn't ask for his life to unfold as it did. He got a raw deal.

"Grandpa, I sure do miss you. It'd be nice if you could visit me, in a dream just like last time." My eyes stung as tears began to seep. "I think I need some help."

A gust of wind battered against the house, whistling through a bathroom window that was open a crack. The breeze seemed to linger even after the wind died down, swirling around the room. I sat up straight, splashing water and suds onto the floor. "Grandpa?" I listened closely for anything that might signal his presence, while my eyes darted and searched. This went on for several minutes, but in the end, he didn't appear to me.

I finished my bath and wrapped myself in a shining robe that hung from the door. As I padded to my room, I heard the sound of hearty laughter from downstairs. It sounded like company had arrived.

A new set of clothes were laid out on the bed for me. Jeans, new sneakers, and a Rolling Stones t-shirt.

Cool.

I anxiously dressed, enjoying the feel and the smell of clean clothes. It was good to be rid of blood-spattered—maple syrup-spattered—jeans. And of course, the dried gore of two dead guys.

It just felt *nice.*

I immediately went to the kitchen area, back to the scene of the incident. I felt bad about the mess I'd left behind and wanted to make amends. However, the floor was wiped clean with nary a sign of my spasmodic episode, and I saw no sign of Millie.

And blessedly, no sign of Natalie either.

I followed voices to a large sitting area that was toward the front of the house. Mr. Bird, Bear, and Detective Anthony were sitting in leather chairs, leaned forward and in intense conversation. I heard Ruckus speaking somewhere, sounding like he was on the phone.

"Luke, good to see you," said the detective. He stood and shook my hand.

"What happened after we left, Detective?" I said.

"Firstly, call me Oliver. And I was able to cover your asses, so don't worry."

"Luke, have a seat," said Bear. "We have some news."

"What kind of news?" I was beginning to subscribe to no news is good news. A cynical view, but in my case it seemed at least a somewhat acceptable—if not forgivable—disposition.

"It seems the FBI have taken an interest in the child murders," said Oliver. "I'm hearing that they're finding some kids that have been missing for several years, some from other states. That means they'll be digging for more dead bodies. They might get lucky and tie the deputy...what's his name?"

"Buddy Wynn. He's a creep," I said. "He has to be stopped."

"There's no evidence," he said. "Is he the only one you think is involved?"

"In my grandpa's book. He left me a list of people he said were bad. I personally know one of them from Wetumka."

The detective's eyes narrowed. "Who is it?"

"Dr. Abbot. He's a vet from around there."

"Anyone else?"

"Not that I know. But there were more names on the letter he wrote me."

"Where is this letter now?"

I looked to Mr. Bird. "I'm not sure. It's folded up in the book."

"It's locked in a safe," said Bird, motioning to Bear. "Bear, would you mind?"

"Nope, I'll be right back. Minus the time I'll need to stop by the crapper." He rubbed his stomach as he left the room.

"We could have done without that information," said Oliver.

"What are you going to do with the list?" I said to the detective. "Give it to the FBI?"

"Maybe anonymously, and hope they stumble across something useful," he said. "What about the sheriff? Is he on the up and up?"

"I think he's all right. But, I don't know for sure."

"The key is the old woman," said Mr. Bird. "I feel certain of this."

"Yeah well, unfortunately she's dead," said Oliver. "It's still early, but so far the only information on her is that she owned and ran a greasy-spoon café in Henryetta, and by God, she was the nicest, sweetest little thing you ever did want to meet according to the locals."

I thought of the incident I had with her in the Hearse. It gave me a shiver. "Uh, I sort of…met her. Sort of."

"Oh, and when was this?" Oliver's eyes were bright with inspective intensity.

"Well," I said, shaking my head and chuckling, "It was after she was dead."

Mr. Bird rubbed his hands together and leaned forward. "How very interesting."

"Huh?" said Oliver.

"Yep, it's crazy, but what ain't these days." I gave them the nickel tour of the skirmish, but nothing useful could be gleaned. She was still dead, after all.

"Man, that's messed up," said Oliver. He leaned back in his chair and made a clucking sound, but he didn't appear to doubt me.

Mr. Bird pointed a bony finger at me. "Yet another reason to pay The Crone a visit today."

"Crone?" I knew what a crone was. It was what my buddy Eldon's grandfather called his wife, which she generally did not appreciate.

"Crone. I don't know her name, and as far as I know, no one else does either. Crone is apt enough, trust me." Concern flickered across his face. "We'll have to watch our p's and q's while in her company."

"Hey there, boy." Ruckus burst into the room, eating a sandwich. "You're lookin' better now that you're all cleaned up."

Seeing Ruckus was bolstering. I had grown fond of him, despite the short amount of time together. There was something intangible about him that was comforting to me. I was beginning to see why Grandpa picked him to be my guardian.

"I've got to check on some of Theo's wells over close to his property," said Ruckus. "I'm thinkin' of goin' in a few minutes. I thought you might want come with me to pick up some clothes and such."

"What time are we going to the Crone," I said to Mr. Bird. I was torn between potentially finding some cures and answers for my weird afflictions, and going back to Grandpa's place.

"Crone? What in hell are you talkin' about," said Ruckus. He then held up his hand, waving us off. "Never mind, I don't want to know."

"Might you be able to delay your trip a few hours, Ruckus? I believe it's pertinent that Luke speak to someone today. I believe it's someone who might help him with some issues he's having," said Mr. Bird, squinting up at Ruckus.

Ruckus took a generous bite of his sandwich and mulled the possibility of a compromise. "All right," he said, with a food-muffled voice. "I guess a few hours won't matter."

"I'm not sure that's a good idea," said Oliver.

"What ain't a good idea?" said Ruckus.

"The two of you going back. I think it would be dangerous."

Ruckus chewed his food for a few seconds, then swallowed. "Hell, I was goin' to make you go with us."

"I've got a job here in Oklahoma City. You know, doing stuff like protecting, serving, solving crimes."

"I'll buy ya a drink later at my favorite waterin' hole when we get back."

"What's the name of your watering hole?"

"Butterfield's, where they pour 'em stronger than a garlic milkshake and the baby dolls all love me."

"Hell, I'll drive them for free drinks." It was Bear. He had silently entered the room, which was impressive considering his size and the age of the old wooden floor.

"Sorry, big fella'. You're too late, he offered the free drinks to me," said Oliver. He pulled a silver flask from his blazer and took a sip. He grimaced as it went down.

Mr. Bird took the book from Bear's hands and opened

it up to the letter. He gently handed it to the detective. "I, for one, would feel better if perhaps the *both* of you would escort them."

"I guess I could make the time today," said Oliver. "But, that doesn't change fact of the matter that's it's still a *very* bad idea. I believe there's a heavy potential for bad shit going down." He pointed at Ruckus. "It didn't take them long to search you out and find out where you live."

Ruckus burped and said, "Speakin' of my house, I ain't in no hurry to go back, but I've got some shit I've got to grab."

I certainly understood his hesitancy to go back to his home, which was now tainted with the blood of two dead men. I wondered if I would have felt the same if the events had happened at the farm instead of at Ruckus'.

"Oliver and I will go there with you while Mr. Bird and Luke are doing their thing," said Bear.

"Man, I'd appreciate it." Relief flooded Ruckus' face.

Oliver stood up. "Then let's get this party started. Daylight's burning."

"I'll get Junior to run you guys out to the Crone's place," said Bear.

"Excellent, I feel *much* better," said Mr. Bird.

I, too, was relieved. Relieved—selfishly, yes I know—to have new friends that were entwined in the same tangled mess as me. Friends that were willing to die alongside me. Friends that didn't think me nuts, even if it's because they were nuts.

Chapter Eighteen

Junior's Tale

THE THREE MEN left in a pickup truck, heading toward Ruckus' defiled home. I watched them travel down the street, as I sat in an aged wicker chair that hid in the shadows of an immense wrap around porch. I was waiting for our driver and Mr. Bird to pull to the front curb, and I was hoping to further avoid seeing the goddess Natalie.

But, she found me.

I first heard the approaching roar of a car, and then the sound of screeching rubber. A vintage Mustang, shining canary-yellow with the top down, was pulling into the driveway. I tensed, easily expecting the worst—demon possessed hit men, violent hicks—but, I was instead treated to the transfixing beauty of my goddess. I would be lying if I said my anxiety was lessened by the absence of mad-dog killers. Natalie's presence set my heart racing just as similarly, and left me even more breathless.

Don't see me. Please, I don't want to make a fool of myself again. I closed my eyes and tried to make myself invisible, trying to sink deeper into the shadows. I heard the determined clack of her shoes as she strode along the driveway, until they stopped.

"Who's up there?" she said.

I opened my eyes and saw that she could see me lurking. I cleared my throat. "Uh, me."

"Luke?"

"Yep."

"What are you doing up there?"

"Oh, just waiting for Mr. Bird."

She walked toward me, climbing a brick staircase that reached to the porch. Initially, I could only see her face and shoulders from I was sitting, but she was now coming into full view. She was wearing cutoff jean shorts, open-toed high-heels, and a tight-fitting concert jersey that read, *Led Zeppelin.* A pair of aviator sunglasses added a touch of sexiness to her, even with them hiding her delightful green eyes. She sat opposite me and stretched her long, tanned legs out, wiggling her painted toes.

I wished for a pair of sunglasses myself, because I was incapable of ignoring such golden beauty.

"Take a picture it'll last longer," she said, smiling mischievously.

I began to stammer a response, but gave up. It wouldn't have come out sounding clever or witty. I instead sat red-faced, wearing my clown nose.

"Relax," she said. "I'm only kidding."

"Uh, okay." I was again paralyzed and breathless.

"So, are you okay? I mean, are you sick or…" She made a circular motion with a finger while pointing to her head.

"Uh, no. I'm not crazy." I wasn't offended. It was a legitimate question considering this morning's event.

"Hmm." She bit her bottom lip, thinking. I found it to be a thrilling gesture that heated my loins. I also began to see her aura, burning with red-hot fire. I closed my eyes, shaking my head.

"Something wrong?" she said.

I opened my eyes and saw that she had taken her sunglasses off. Her eyes instantly intoxicated me. I suddenly felt emboldened to do something stupid. "No," I said excitedly. "There's nothing wrong at all." I leaped from my chair and gently took her face in my hands. I kissed her goddess lips, with vigor and passion. I expected a punch to my face, if not a slap, but something unexpected happened. She pressed back against my lips and slipped her tongue into my mouth. A most foreign experience on my part, as I'd not yet even had the pleasure of an old-fashioned peck on the lips. But the effect on me was like a wind of ecstasy, fanning my flames of desire.

"Whoa, what the shit...?" She abruptly ended the kiss, pushing me back. "Just, *whoa*, Luke. Like, *wow*."

I sat back in my chair, feeling dizzy and idiotic. "Crap, I'm sorry."

Natalie stood up and stepped back. "Wow, so fucking *trippy.*"

As she stood there I still wanted her. I even considered trying to kiss her again, but it was a fleeting thought. I had to look away from her as her aura continued to ebb. "Actually, something *is* wrong with me. I just don't know how to explain it to you. I don't usually do what I just did."

"You sure could've fooled me." She put her sunglasses back on and fanned her face with a hand. "And how old are you?"

"Thirteen."

"Oh, my God." She click-clacked back and forth. "Just so you know, *I* don't usually do what I just did either."

A voice called to Natalie from outside, sounding from the backyard of the house. It was her mother, Millie.

"Look, I've got to take my mom shopping. And, just forget about...this weirdness. Because, that's what I'm going to do."

"Whatever is wrong with me won't let me forget about this. I'll keep thinking about you."

She bit her bottom lip again, which remained a profound turn on. "Luke, you're just a kid—"

"Natalie!" Millie was at the bottom of the porch, slightly out of my view. "We need to get moving, we're blocking Mr. Bird and Junior in."

Natalie waved to me. "I've got to go, Luke."

I waved back and sighed, feeling dejected and rejected. "Okay, I understand."

"Okay, then see ya, man," she said, turning to leave.

I was going to let her go without me saying anything else, but I had a question for her, and I would regret it later if I didn't ask it. Keeping my voice low, I said, "Natalie, why did you kiss me and stick your tongue in my mouth if I'm just a kid?"

She stopped and whirled around at me, saying nothing.

"Well?" I said.

"I don't know." She came a little closer to me. "I don't know, but it was way, way, wrong. I'm sorry, okay?"

"Natalie, what the hell are you doing? Didn't you hear me?" Her mother was ascending the porch steps, coming closer.

"Gotta' go, man." Natalie quickly went down the steps to meet her mother, sending a parting word of advice to me over her shoulder. "Stay weird, Luke."

"I don't think that'll be a problem," I said.

When I heard the Mustang fire to life, I went to the end of the porch to watch Natalie and her mother drive away. I must have looked like a lovesick collie.

A blasting car-horn made me nearly jump out of my skin. I looked down from the porch and saw a longhaired hippie with a scraggly beard behind the wheel, who I assumed was Junior, and Mr. Bird in a cherry-red supercab pickup. The passenger window lowered, and Mr. Bird poked his head out. "Are you ready, Luke?"

"Yep, I reckon so."

AFTER DRIVING SEVERAL miles north, we exited onto Route 66 and headed east. The old highway was winding with sharp curves, in addition to trees that pressed against the sides of the road in some places. However, Junior drove as if we were on an airport runway. He paid no mind to the blind curves. He pushed the truck to a brisk pace, stressing the tires to the point of squealing and riding the outside lines on a few occasions. I was grateful for the random farmer that clogged the flow of the road with a rustic tractor or slow moving hay truck.

Junior was a talkative sort, apprising me of how he came to know this odd bunch I was now affiliated with. I found out he served as a Marine in Vietnam with Bear, and that they remained in touch with one another after the war. But, not because of the fierce battles they'd experienced and conquered together—although they did, in fact, weather such incidents. It was because of an inexplicable event that they bore witness to. Something that made the horrors of the war almost pale by comparison.

"It was downright freaky, man," said Junior, digging in a cigarette pack.

"How was it freaky?" I said.

He popped a bent smoke in his mouth and lit it, then rolled down his window a few inches. "We were on an offensive, pushing into Cambodia through the jungle when the weird shit first started. It was a few hours after a nasty firefight, and we were licking our wounds, checking on how many of us were dead or wounded." He flicked an ash out the window and drew more smoke, taking delight in the flavor. "We had some dead, and plenty of wounded. But, Charlie took worse casualties than us before retreating deeper into the jungle."

He stopped talking and looked over at Mr. Bird, who was staring out the window.

"It's okay, you can tell him," said Mr. Bird. "Luke has seen more than most."

He pulled on his cigarette, burning most of it up. "So, anyway, our CO didn't make it. He got riddled with machine gun fire right from the get-go and died—which didn't bother any of us a bit because he was a cowardly asshole." He shook his head at his last statement and continued. "So, Bear was now in command of us, which most of us didn't mind. We respected him, and trusted him.

"Some of the men wanted to chase after Charlie, but Bear ordered us to stay put since nightfall was closing in. He made sense, since the jungle was crawling with the enemy, and it was their own backyard." One last drag killed the cigarette. "And, we were in the middle of collecting our dead brothers."

"Man, that must've been awful," I conjured the bloody scene in my head.

"Yeah, it was awful. War turns men, changes them. When we were done with our own, some of the men started collecting trophies from the dead VC."

"What do you mean?" I asked the question, but knew what he meant. My morbid curiosity wanted details.

"Oh, some of the guys cut off the ears and made necklaces out of them—and brother, did it ever start to stink after a few days. Sometimes I'd see someone keep a skull, or pull out the teeth of a dead man and keep them in a pocket for good luck." He looked at the rearview mirror and grinned at me. "I didn't see much use in doing such things. I kept my weapon close at hand for good luck."

It was good to know he didn't partake in the hideous mutilation of corpses. I would have found it hard to like him.

"Anyway, when nightfall did arrive, Bear put me on night watch, along with a couple of other fellas—Bama and Lamar. Bear said he'd help too." Junior halted his tale briefly, as if he were steeling himself for what he had left to say, then charged forward. "It was probably three or four hours after dark that the weird shit started. I was hunkered down in a hollow spot of a tree, looking down on the boys, when I heard some rustling going on like someone was walking through the bush. I first heard it on my left, but then I heard it on my right, then…all over the damn place. I thought Charlie was back, ambushing us. But it wasn't Charlie, not really."

A hairpin curve was suddenly upon us. Junior violently swung the steering wheel, hugging the outside line at a speed I found to be reckless and dangerous. The momentum of the turn sent my butt sliding across the backseat, putting my shoulder against the door with considerable force. I felt the rear-end slide from the pavement and bump onto the grass for a moment before it straightened up.

I expected Mr. Bird to say something to him, but he was unperturbed. In fact, he was looking out the window at the scenery, admiring it with a smile.

Junior continued, equally collected. "So, anyway, I think I fired first. I wasn't sure what I was shooting at, just firing into the dark at the noise, and hoping I wasn't killing our own. Then all hell broke loose, men started screaming, gunfire all over the damn place. Somehow, amongst the noise we were able to hear Bear's voice commanding us to stand down. It wasn't instantaneous, but we all managed to ease up on our triggers. And once the smoke began to clear, we all saw 'em crawling and limping toward us."

I became excited, thinking he was surely to describe the horrific, scaly creatures I'd experienced with Grandpa. However, I was wrong. It was a different sort of horror.

"The fucking dead VC were *moving,* man. And they were speaking some weird-ass language, walking right at us from all over. Yeah, and something else freaky was the temperature. It got fucking *cold,* I mean can you dig that shit? In the middle of a steamy jungle, and I can see my breath."

"I know exactly what you're talking about," I said, fully engrossed. "What happened next?"

"Well, Bear's orders to ceasefire went straight to shit, as you can imagine. We opened up on 'em and they went down, but some tried to get back up. It was pretty much a slaughter, except that what we were slaughtering wasn't dying."

"Did you shoot them in the head?" I was recalling the time I shot the possessed man in the head. It ended his animation instantly.

"Bear caught on to that, and so did the rest of us when we saw him charging them with his Colt handgun." Junior made his hand a gun, firing it at his temple. "Pow, man. Pointblank to the head."

"Yeah, I know."

"Bear had us retreat, and then he called in an airstrike. Burned the bastards."

Junior popped another smoke in his mouth and curiously eyeballed me as I looked at him in the rearview mirror. "Kid, how old are you?"

"Thirteen."

He shook his head and lit his smoke. "And you've shot someone in the head before?"

"Yep." I looked out the window, as if viewing something out there would cancel out what I'd just said.

"That sucks," he said. "But, it explains why you don't smile."

"Well, not after a story like that."

Junior laughed, which poked a chuckle from me. It felt good.

"How did you meet Mr. Bird?" I said.

"Lamar claimed to know about this spooky shit, said he'd grown up around this sort of thing down in Louisiana. So, after the war, Bear and I met with him and talked about what we'd seen. No surprise, it's a small world when it comes to people who know about this shit, because it didn't take long for his kinfolk to contact Mr. Bird."

"What about the other men, have they met Mr. Bird yet?"

"Not many. Some prefer to forget about it, or least try to." Junior's tone turned somber, "Suicide, homicide, and madness has haunted most of us. And, trust me when I say that the war alone was more than enough to push a man to the same troubles."

"But, surely they told *someone* about what ya'll saw."

"Sure, some did. In fact, a few got to go home on account of the military thinking they were looney. Free ticket home, man."

The theme music of the television series *MASH* played in my head, accompanied by an image of Corporal Max Klinger in a blue-chiffon dress, with matching hat. It made me grin.

"Bear and me, we kept our mouths shut until we were approached by the CIA," Junior said. "They asked us about it, wanting the full skinny. They said nobody would think we were crazy."

"What did they say about all of it?" I found it exciting to know of others who had experienced the supernatural as I had. It made me curious as to how many in the world there actually were.

"Not much, I got the impression they thought we were under the influence of a drug, or some kind of gas. They advised us to keep quiet about it, which was not a problem." Junior looked ready to add something else, but let what was on his mind go. In fact, he went silent and watched the road through suddenly vacant eyes.

Mr. Bird pulled his attention away from the window. "Luke, your episode this morning. Was it sexual in nature?"

I was aghast.

"Don't pay me any mind up here," said Junior. "I've seen and heard enough to not judge, especially anything that's been said in this truck."

"I don't mean to embarrass you," said Mr. Bird. "But, I suspect that you might be experiencing some sort of side effect from the demon bite. Specific effects from a demon of lust, which Lilith most certainly is."

"Still not judging, but that's a new subject for this truck," said Junior.

"Okay, yes. Yes, it was *very* sexual." It felt good to confess my perversion. "She drove me totally, crazy. I could see her aura—it was bright red—and I…" I pointed to my crotch with both hands.

"Understood," said Mr. Bird. "No need to divulge

further."

I rubbed my face with my hands, as frustration seeped. "Good Lord, am I going to go all funky every time I'm around a girl? That will totally suck."

"Don't jump to the worst conclusions," said Mr. Bird. "I remain confident that the Crone will shed some light."

"Man, my life is so *not* groovy," I said.

"I can dig it, man," said Junior.

Chapter Nineteen

A Bumpy Road

THE WAY TO the Crone's was a slender ribbon of road, and a considerable distance from the highway. It was thick with weeds and quite bumpy. Trees—mostly dead—crowded what little space there was, scraping against the truck's paint and blotting out large sections of the sky.

After ten minutes of driving, Junior stopped the vehicle. "Man, I'm gonna' set the four-wheel drive. The road's starting to feel mushy."

Mr. Bird touched Junior's forearm. "Be careful, and be quick. We're far enough onto her land to expect a bit of strangeness."

"Copy that," he said.

Junior got out of the truck, disappearing for a moment as he knelt to attend to his task. Meanwhile, Mr. Bird fumbled with the radio dial, listening to the static.

"What are you doing?" I said.

He slowly turned the dial, moving past stations with a signal and lingering on the ones filled with static and white noise. "Sometimes, it's possible to hear a witch's familiar on the radio. Something about electricity and sound waves."

I was tired of always asking questions, but I assumed I should know what a familiar is. "And a familiar…"

"A person, animal, or demon that protects, and informs the witch it is tied to."

Yet, another hideous fun fact. "Are you hearing

anything?"

He held up a hand and pointed to the radio. "Listen closely."

I listened and didn't hear anything more than annoying static. He then turned up the volume and told me to close my eyes. At first, I heard a loud ticking. It was distorted and fuzzy, then the ticking sped up and I was able to discern some sort of gibberish being spoken. "Wow, that's a trip."

"Indeed, quite a trip," he said.

"Can you understand it?"

"No. The Crone is the only one." Mr. Bird scanned the narrow road ahead of us. "It must be close by, watching us."

The gibberish was strange and disturbing, having a rather mean quality to it. It made me feel uneasy.

Junior let out a yelp from outside and popped up on the driver's side of the truck. "Damn trees, poking me. They're right up against the truck."

Mr. Bird rolled down his window to keep a close watch on Junior, and to listen. "Junior, are you hearing anything out there?"

"No, it's weird man. I'm not even hearing birds." Junior hurried along, forced to break a number of sharp twigs to get to the passenger side wheel. "Something is starting to stink though. Can you smell it?"

I caught a whiff of something rotten.

"Are you nearly finished?" said Mr. Bird, pinching his nostrils.

Junior stood up. "Yeah, I got it."

The sound of breaking and groaning trees could be heard amongst the woods. Junior pulled his gun, looking in all directions. After a quick assessment, he got back in the truck and started us moving. "Something big is moving around out there."

"I've no doubt the Crone knows we're coming," said Mr. Bird.

"How much farther?" said Junior.

"We're getting close," said Mr. Bird.

The road suddenly narrowed even more, as a canopy of tangled trees pushed down on us. Large boughs hung low, scraping against the top of the cab. "Man, the paint is history on this truck."

"The paint is the least of my worries," said Mr. Bird.

The gibberish began to sound deep and syrupy, having less static to it. "What the hell are we listening to, dudes?" said Junior.

"A familiar." I said this, as if I had known of such things all my life.

"Right on." Junior fiddled with the radio dial and searched until *Love Train* was blasting from the speakers. "That other shit was grating on me, man."

So, we bounced and fishtailed our way down the treacherous road with the sound of the O'Jays ringing in our ears. Junior sang and thrummed his fingers to the beat on the steering wheel, seemingly oblivious to our current situation. Even Mr. Bird seemed to be tapping his fingers on the dashboard to the tune. I watched them, somewhat awestruck at their ability to cope with less than normal circumstances. However, it was conduct I had seen before. Grandpa lived and acted in the very same manner, right up to the moment of his demise.

A large branch appeared out the blue, striking the windshield with sizeable force. Junior put on the brakes and reached for Mr. Bird, yelling at him to duck. I rolled onto the floorboard.

After the truck was stopped and some seconds had passed, I raised my head and peeked up front. "Everyone okay?"

Mr. Bird said, "I was buckled in, so I'm fine. But, Junior is bleeding."

"Am I?" Junior searched the windshield for the rearview mirror, but instead found it laying in the front seat. After a quick look at his reflection, he proclaimed himself fit. "Ah, that ain't shit."

He had a cut on his forehead, and it was dripping blood at a decent clip. "It looks bad to me," I said.

Junior had found a dark cloth and was applying it to his wound. "Nah, I'll be fine."

"What about the truck?" I said, as I regarded the damaged windshield. The top was partially caved in, and small fragments of glass were scattered along the dashboard.

"The truck's fine, it's just a windshield," said Junior. "Our problem is that we're blocked by a giant tree limb. We can't go any farther." He turned in his seat and looked out the back glass, shaking his head. "And there is no way to turn around. I'm going to have to back this bitch out of here, ya know."

Loud crashing sounds came from the woods on Mr. Bird's side of the truck, and then the disgusting smell returned. I looked as deeply as I could into the thicket of trees, but it was too dense to see anything but a gray darkness.

"Our music has been replaced," said Mr. Bird.

The O'Jays were no more. We were instead subjected to the strange babbling once again. It was growing in volume and buzzed in my head like a bee hive. I felt as if it were trying to infect me and drive me mad.

Junior turned the radio off, mercifully releasing me from its bothering effect. The sudden quiet allowed me to hear the violent thrashing that was growing nearer to us.

"What do you want to do, Mr. Bird? I can back our asses out of here, or I can try to locate whatever is out there." Junior cocked his gun. "I'll kill it."

Before Mr. Bird could offer his opinion of action, the tree limb began to shake and rub against the truck. And then, with a loud crack, it was pulled away to reveal an open road with a small, stone shack at the end. There appeared to be an area of water surrounding it, with a connecting bridge. It was no more than fifty yards from us.

"And there you have it," said Mr. Bird.

"Is that where the Crone is at?" I said.

"Yes." He faintly smiled, as if he were amused.

Junior stomped on the gas, sending mud in a spray behind the truck. When we neared the shack, he whipped the truck around to face the road. Mercifully, the landscape was much improved so that he was able to set us upon solid ground. The suffocating trees and sloppy road gave way to a black stone slab that stretched for miles. It was an empty, stone prairie.

Junior immediately got out of the truck with his gun drawn. "You dudes stay tight for a minute. Let me check shit out."

"It'll be fine, Junior," said Mr. Bird.

Junior didn't show any signs of agreement, as he continued to skillfully sweep the area with his gun. "Begging your pardon, sir, but something's out there. It's watching us."

Mr. Bird waved to him, trying to get him back to the truck. "I don't smell it anymore. I'm reasonably certain we're clear of any danger it would pose to us."

Junior shrugged his shoulders and holstered his gun. "Well, as long as you're *reasonably* certain. I trust you, sir."

The cut on his forehead was swollen, and the blood was still streaming down his face. I left the truck and brought his bloodstained cloth with me. "Here," I said. "You're kind of grossing me out, ya know."

"Thanks, man." He wrung the blood out and tied it in place like a bandana. "I'm gonna' get Mr. Bird loaded in his wheelchair. Hang here for a minute."

As I waited, I took the opportunity to examine the Crone's dilapidated hovel. It was a lonely looking structure, just squatting in the middle of nowhere with neither tree nor shrub to keep it company. Even the encircling water seemed dead and devoid of life, as there was nary a ripple. Two misshapen chimneys jutted from a sloped roof, with each one billowing a glowing smoke that changed colors. The front door was some sort of wood and tin concoction with a small window.

The terrain of the site was unnatural. The stone ground was flat and even, and went on and on into a barren horizon. "Mr. Bird, where are we?"

"Some sort of mystical realm," he said. "With the exception of the road, her location changes each time I visit."

Junior wheeled him next to me, and then playfully slapped me on the back. "Freaky, huh."

"Yep."

"Junior, I need you to stay here with the truck," said Mr. Bird. "Luke and I will be crossing the bridge together."

"Are you sure?" said Junior.

"Quite sure. We need you to stay and guard against vandals."

"Vandals?" Junior's eyebrows drew together.

"Oh yes. The truck could possibly attract some unwanted attention."

"Way the hell out here?" I said.

Mr. Bird chuckled and nodded his head. "Yes, but not the usual sort of vandal that brandishes a can of spray paint, or a carton of eggs. These would be small imps, or some other such being, having a more destructive nature."

Junior lightly touched the butt of his gun. "Wow, that's far out."

The front door of the shack opened and a small, blonde-haired girl walked out. She was attired in a yellow dress and wore a blue ribbon in her hair. The door shut behind her, and then she walked toward us, holding an object in her hands.

"Is this normal?" said Junior.

"Nothing is ever normal out here," said Mr. Bird. "I have not the foggiest idea of who this child is, nor do I know what she's bringing us."

"Shit, I'm not gonna' have to shoot her, am I?" It was the first time I'd detected unease from Junior.

"No way, man." I hoped the girl wasn't the same sort of horror as the boy. Even if she was, I wanted no part of killing a child. "I'd rather leave and never come back."

"I don't believe killing the girl will be necessary," said Mr. Bird.

The girl caused a small wiggle in the bridge as each of her tiny footfalls fell upon its surface. She was halfway across and would be reaching us in a matter of seconds.

"Luke, if any weird shit happens, I want you to jump in the back of the truck," said Junior. "I'll get us out of here."

The girl stopped short of coming over to our side and stood behind a pair of short, rock pillars that marked each side of the bridge's entrance. She held out both hands and showed us what she had brought. It was a leather pouch. "Here," she said. "It's a poultice for Mr. Pickett's head."

"Whoa, what?" said Junior.

"Who's Mr. Pickett?" I said.

"Me," said Junior.

"Go on, take it," said Mr. Bird.

Junior stepped back, eyeing the girl. "Man, I'm not sure about—"

"It is important to apply it quickly," said the girl. "Or, it won't work."

"Go on," said Mr. Bird. "It will be fine."

Junior walked to the girl, and guardedly accepted it. She smiled sweetly at him. "Go on, it's okay. I promise, it will make the boo-boo better."

Junior held the pouch, deciding whether or not to open it. He finally succumbed to the girl's and Mr. Bird's wishes, and reached inside. He pulled out a mossy looking substance and showed it to Mr. Bird and me. "What do you think?" he said.

"It couldn't be worse than that gross looking rag on your head," I said.

Mr. Bird made a sour face. "He has a valid point, Junior. Your dressing does look rather unsanitary, to say the least."

Junior removed the bloodied rag and gently placed a handful of the poultice on his cut. "Cool, man."

"Is it working yet? Does it feel better?" said the girl anxiously.

He weighed her question for a moment. "Actually, yeah. The pain is almost gone."

Joy swept over her face. "Oh, good. I prepared it myself."

"Well, then thank you," said Junior.

"You're welcome, Mr. Pickett."

"Yes," said Mr. Bird. "That was very nice of you."

"Thank you, Mr. Bird." She then turned her pretty little face toward me, beaming a smile as sweet as honey. "And your name is Luke."

"Yep."

"Luke," she said. "Will you come to me?"

I nervously cleared my throat and walked in her direction until she motioned for me to stop. "Luke, you can't pass through until you spill some blood on the rocks."

"Um, what was that?" I hoped I did not hear her correctly.

She patted a pillar. "You have to spill blood. Right here."

I looked to Mr. Bird for some sort of counsel. "That doesn't sound like something I want to do."

"It's not nearly as dramatic as it sounds. A simple pin prick of your finger will suffice," he said.

"Here." The girl held a gleaming, silver needle in her hand. "It won't hurt, I promise."

I had little faith in her promise, but I offered her my left index finger nevertheless. "Okay, whatever."

"Close your eyes if you want to. That's what I do," she said.

"Just hurry, please." I didn't close my eyes, but instead looked away. I found it very surprising and silly that I would shy from something as simple as a tiny drop of blood, considering all that I had seen and underwent.

She patted my hand. "All done."

I again, did not believe the girl. But when I looked at my finger I saw a small well of blood begin to drip. "Wow, I didn't feel a thing."

The girl smiled at me, proud of her feat. "Now, wipe your blood on the rocks."

I smeared a small amount of blood onto the pillar and was immediately shaken with a dizzying sensation, but it died when I pulled my hand away. Blood began to seep and cascade from both of the pillars, running down onto the ground. I had to step back to avoid being splashed.

"Come along," said the girl. "She's waiting."

I took over the reins of the wheelchair and began pushing Mr. Bird through the gateway, but he had me stop for a moment as he spoke to Junior. "If you should experience any issues during our absence, don't hesitate to leave."

My head jerked to Mr. Bird and then to Junior. "What do you mean *leave*? Please, tell me you won't leave us out here."

Junior pulled a gold chain with a crucifix from beneath his shirt. He kissed it and said, "Hey man, don't worry. I'll be just fine, which means I won't be splittin' on anyone."

"Hurry," said the girl. She grabbed Mr. Bird's hand and gently tugged. "We have to get across the bridge."

"Come along, lad," said Mr. Bird.

We followed the girl onto the bridge, which was unstable and creaking with age. Curious, I looked into the calm water. What I saw was terrifying.

The water was clear as window pane, revealing hideous creatures swimming at the bottom of the moat. They were gelatinous and transparent, with triangular heads that were predominantly gaping mouths filled with pointed teeth. I was able to see their organs moving and convulsing, as they swam with webbed hands and feet that were tipped with claws. Yet, despite their grotesque appearance, I found them to have human characteristics, such as their arms, legs, and torso. However, I did not see anything on the monsters resembling eyes, and I hoped that meant they could not see us.

"Luke, make sure to keep your boo-boo finger from dripping in the water," said the girl.

"Okay, but why?"

"Because they would probably try to eat you."

"Oh." I wished the bridge were shorter. As it was, I guessed it to be twenty yards in length, and we were less than halfway across.

"Sound advice, Luke," said Mr. Bird.

"Yep."

"Young lady, what is your name?" said Mr. Bird. "I don't recall ever meeting you."

"Constance." She sang her name and began to skip and hum a playful tune. She certainly didn't appear to be bothered by the fact she was surrounded by carnivorous monsters.

"That's a pretty name," he said. "So, tell me how you came to know this place and the Crone."

"I'm training to be a witch."

My heart broke a little upon hearing this. She was such an innocent little thing to be involved in such darkness. "Wow. Why do you want to be a witch?"

"Because my mom is a witch."

"Ah, you're a hereditary witch," said Mr. Bird. "And do you like it thus far?"

"I like learning how to make poultices and other things that make people feel better."

"And what else do you learn?" said Mr. Bird.

"Oh, lots and lots of things." Constance reached the end of the bridge and stopped. "Some things, I don't want to learn." She then hopped along a small path that led to the front door.

I turned to check on Junior and to give him a wave, but I saw only a whirling mist. The truck, the road, and the ragged trees were all gone. Even the sky was missing, replaced by a vast darkness that was dotted with sparkles of multicolored stars. "Mr. Bird, I don't see Junior anymore."

He looked with wonder at our new backdrop. "We've travelled far away from our realm. I believe we are now in another dimension."

A strangled roar rolled through the mist, echoing strangely. "Mr. Bird, maybe we should go inside," I said.

"Yes," said Constance. "You shouldn't stay out here."

The front door suddenly opened, and then a scratchy voice from within spoke. "Ya'll best git in 'ere."

And so we entered the abode, and I met the Crone for the first time.

Chapter Twenty

The Crone

THE SHACK WAS much larger than I had imagined. So much, that I deciphered on my own that the outside was a façade. The ceiling was vaulted—not at all associated with the sunken and leaned roof visible from outside—with most of it lost in the shadows being cast by a countless number of black, wavering candles. There were lengthy tables butted end to end, jumbled with jars of clay, and specimen glasses with weird little creatures inside that were suspended in a whitish liquid. Trees grew from sunken areas, with some of them ascending into the overhead darkness.

"Follow me closely, please," said Constance. "And don't touch anything."

She held a candle in her hand to push away the shadows and led us along a carpet runner that turned its way past a number of elongated tables. I observed many items that I guessed to be spices and herbs, haphazardly placed on some of the tables, while some were more organized with bins and names. Here and there, I would see a wooden crate on the floor that shook as if something alive was trapped inside.

We stopped at a table that was round, with the base being that of a tree that grew out of the floor. Burning black candles sat on top, dimly illuminating wood carvings of symbols and letters. A couple of tree stumps looked to be the seating arrangement. "You can sit down. She'll be here very soon," said Constance.

I sat down, and Mr. Bird rolled up close to me. "Luke, tell me what you think of all this." he said, waving his hands in the air.

"I don't know what to think," I said, quite truthfully.

"Sometimes people go crazy in here," said Constance.

"Too late," I said. "I'm already crazy."

She came to me, smiling, and gave me a hug. "I have to go now."

I searched her eyes for sadness and despair, as I considered her dark situation. But, there was no darkness to be found, only purity and kindness. "Thanks for your help," I said. "And good luck, with all of this…witch stuff."

"It's been a pleasure meeting you," said Mr. Bird, extending a wrinkled hand.

Constance kissed his hand and blew her candle out, further dampening what little light there was. She walked toward a particularly shadowy corner and reached into it. Amazingly, what I saw as a shadow was actually a door. She opened it up and was swallowed by darkness.

"Is she okay?" I was troubled by the girl's circumstances. I wanted to play the hero and plunge in after her.

"She'd be good, she is," said the Crone. We both jumped upon hearing the haggard voice, and I was again startled when I saw she was mysteriously sitting across the table from us. She was leaned back in a rocking chair, covered in shadows, smoking a pipe. "Ya ought not to be worryin' on her."

"You scared the crap out of me." I clutched at my heart for dramatic purposes.

The Crone drew on her pipe, which cast an orange glow onto her face. I was able to see a patch covering her left eye, and the brim of a fedora, before the embers died. "Boy, you got thangs hangin' o'er yer head that ain't blessins, I mean to tell ya."

"What do you know of his condition?" said Mr. Bird.

"Not everythang, I don't." She leaned into the soft glow of candlelight, showing me her face. Her right eye was the size of an egg yolk, lidless and pale as the moon. "But, I knows him be touched by somethin', 'cause the boy sendin' lust to me."

I cocked my head to the side, shocked and bothered. "I hope that doesn't mean—"

"It mean you makin' me slick betwixt my legs, boy." Her mouth was a toothless black hole when she spoke, spewing breath that made me want to vomit. Coupled with her unveiled sexual remark, I nearly did.

"Behave, damn it," said Mr. Bird.

The Crone puffed on her pipe and cackled, leaning and rocking in her chair. "What? You a'fearin' I'm gonna' pull his britches down and have my way wit' the boy?"

"We've come a long way, Crone. We don't have time to listen to your vulgarities." Mr. Bird's voice had an unfamiliar edge to it, revealing he wasn't always unflappable.

I ignored her repellent comments and tried to make the most of this meeting. I didn't care to stay here any longer than was needed. I got to the bone of things. "So, you're saying that I'm…turning you on?"

The Crone laughed, shaking her head in amusement. "Yep, you got mah' cooter a' twitchin' like a cricket in a spider web."

"Crone, you know why we've come. So, get to it," said Mr. Bird.

The Crone's taunting laughter stopped. "You ain't one bit o' fun, old man."

"If fun were what I was after, I most assuredly would not travel here in search of it." Mr. Bird stabbed a finger at the Crone. "Furthermore, this young man is the grandson of Theophilus Morgan. An air of respect is demanded."

The Crone's face softened at hearing Grandpa's name. Even the sagging skin on her face seemed to lift a bit. "So, you be Theo's kin."

"Yes."

She adjusted her hat and tapped an unkempt fingernail on the table. "He done me a spot o' help, some years ago."

"He was good like that," I said.

"His faith were somethin' to behold, boy."

"Yep, it was crazy."

"How 'bout you? You got faith?"

"Yes, I have faith." I hoped.

"It ain't strong like yer grandpappy's was. Don't be foolin' yerself by thankin' it is."

"I'm not fooling anyone over here."

She gurgled a small laugh, and licked her lips and chin with a freakishly long tongue. "You a funny boy. It makin' me want ya more."

"Damn, it," said Mr. Bird. "I told you—"

"Don't be worryin' on such," she told him. "We fixin' to remedy."

"And how do you intend to do that?" he said.

"Ain't sure yet," she said. "I has to taste the rocks."

"If you're talking about my nuts, you can forget about that shit." I was fed up.

She again choked out an intended laugh. "Nah, not that. I meanin' *rocks*." She pointed into the darkness behind us, "I'm meanin' them yonder rocks ya bled on."

I was immediately calmed.

Shuffling sounds began to take place in the gloom behind the Crone, as if something were being dragged by someone—or *something*—with a peculiar gait. The sound of doors being opened and shut echoed in a circle around us, and then bestial breathing huffed around in the dark until it came to rest directly behind Mr. Bird and I.

"Ya'll jes' keep a'lookin' at me." She held her arms up and received a small, burlap sack from the creature. I was able to observe it had three fingers, was hairy, and equipped with claws. It also stank of the beast from the road.

"Thank ya, ole' girl," said the Crone. "Now, off ya go."

The odor became eye-wateringly foul, and I felt hot breath on the back of my neck.

"No, ya cain't have the boy," said the Crone. "So, git."

It snorted a spray of moisture on top on my head, and then whined like a disappointed dog before shambling away. I lightly touched my hair and found a sticky mess that clung to my fingers in beads of dripping yellow.

"I'd not be advisin' ya to sniff none of that," said the Crone.

"Don't worry, I'm not." I was doing my best to fling the glop from my hand.

The Crone pulled several bloodstained stones from the sack and set them upon the table. She then licked them with her abnormal tongue and smacked her lips, like a child eating honey.

"So," said Mr. Bird. "What can you tell us?"

Something trying to be a smile spread across her face. "Jus' as I figgered. The boy been close with a demon. I thought I seen it in his life glow, but I weren't shore."

"Life glow?" I said. "I think that's what I see sometimes."

"You be seein' a red glow, right, boy?"

"Yes, sometimes."

"You meanin' when you roun' women."

"Yes."

"Other colors, too?"

"Sometimes."

"That not a bad thang. It'a help ya in seein' what folks is hidin' from ya."

"Also worth mentioning is, he appears be a rapid healer," said Mr. Bird. "The doctors marveled at how quickly he recovered from his injuries, which were quite substantial."

"I ain't doubtin' on it."

"And what of his carnal affliction," said Mr. Bird.

"You mentioned a remedy."

A row of candles suddenly came to life behind the Crone, revealing a large shelf full of clay jars and small chests. She grabbed a jar and set it down in front of her. "I cain't make the lustin' leave the boy. But, I can stomp it down some." She held the jar out to me. "Here, ya got to drank it."

I took it from her and sniffed the contents. Naturally, it was horrid smelling. "So," I said, "This will help with my problem?"

"It'a help ya, not cure ya," she said. "It'a keep ya from traipsin' around with yer stiffy a'showin'."

"Down the hatch," said Mr. Bird.

"Yep, down the hatch." I took a large gulp of the brew and gagged horribly.

"Don't be a'wastin' it," she said.

I fought against my rising bile and handed the jar back to her. I used Ruckus' whiskey method to try and dislodge the aftertaste in my mouth, but it was to no effect. "Is that it?"

"Somewhat, I reckons," she said.

"What does that mean, Crone?" said Mr. Bird.

"It mean his lustin' ain't as bad as it were, but him gots more thangs goin' on." The Crone raised a candle to her left eye and lifted the patch, baring a bulbous eyeball that looked to have a will of its own. It moved crazily in circles. "I sees a coldness in ya, boy. I felts it when ya got close." She pulled tobacco from a pouch she had slung around her neck and began to load her pipe. "So, tells me how many men's ya done kilt."

"I think three or four, something like that," I said.

She chuckled and lit her pipe. "And here ya is, talkin' like it were nothin'. How'd the killins come about?"

I told her of the circumstances, which led to the lives I'd snuffed out. She knowingly nodded her head and smoked the whole time I spoke.

"You was scared when ya kilt yer neighbors, and you

was helpin' Theo. That there ain't the coldness I talkin' on, but you has yer grandpappy's blood in ya. You has his gift o' judgement when it come to knowin' evil." She stopped speaking long enough to summon a clump of phlegm, which she spat on the floor. "But, you enjoyed killin' the demon-man."

"No, I didn't enjoy it all."

"Boy, you's a liar," she said. "But, yer lyin' to yerself more'n to me."

"I only killed that man because he was trying to kill us."

"Time'll tell the truth to ya, boy. Time'll tell ya." The crone reached below the table and withdrew a small, wooden box with a lid. She opened it and let several gems of fluctuating color spill onto the table. "These here'll help figger' yer power, boy."

"I imagine his power is quite sizeable," said Mr. Bird. "Particularly, as one considers the name of the demon who bit him."

The Crone froze and cocked her head at Mr. Bird. "He been bit?"

"Oh, yes," said Mr. Bird.

"And ya knows the demon's name?"

"Lilith," I said. "Her name is Lilith."

The Crone shook her head back and forth, making the skin from her face and neck flap. It reminded me of hung sheets in the wind. "Ya'll should'a tolt me!" She stood up and began walking in and out of the darkness, mumbling and pulling on her hat as if she was in a windstorm.

Mr. Bird opened his arms in confusion. "Is there a problem, Crone?"

"Oh, hells yes," she said. "Lilith ain't no plain demon. Ya know'd that ole' man, ya tricks me."

Mr. Bird sighed. "I'll admit to withholding some details, but I hardly *tricked* you into anything."

"It surely a'splain why he sends lust so strong." The Crone grabbed a burning candlestick and got up from the table. "We needs us a protectin' circle, a real strong'en," She walked in a circle around the seating area, wobbling weirdly with each step, and dripping wax onto the floor.

"Crone," said Mr. Bird. "What do you have planned?"

"I ain't got no time for a'splainin' thangs to ya."

She continued to put the circle of wax around us, speaking strange words and sprinkling a shimmering dust onto the ground. When she was finished with her magical task she joined us back at the table, and scooped up the gems. "Pays close attention, boy."

I watched as a fuzzy radiance began to form out of the gems. It writhed and sparkled until the semblance of a ball took shape, and then we were able to see shadowy shapes within. "Looks close, boy."

"I have a name, you know," I said. "You don't have to keep calling me *boy*."

"Ya sayin' yer not a boy?"

"Uh, no—"

"Then quits yer sassin', boy."

I surrendered peacefully, as she utterly terrified me.

"Looks close, both ya'lls," she said. "Thangs tied to ya is goin' to visit us. Some thangs be good, but most I figger'll be bad for ya."

The fuzzy nature of the glow left and became a tightly formed sphere that floated like a bubble. Inside of the sphere were moving forms that grew clearer, eventually becoming a live look into Ruckus' home. We were able to see all three men, as they stumbled and stepped around the ruling clutter.

"Them's friends of ya'lls?" said the Crone.

"Yes." I was awed by the floating ball. "That's where I killed the possessed man."

"Hmm, so's that where ya first relished a killin'."

"If you say so."

"I does fer sure."

"Why are we seeing them?" said Mr. Bird.

"Ya'll fates is knotted together."

"Are their lives in danger?" said Mr. Bird.

"They's good for now, but not for later."

"Then we need to leave and warn them," I said uneasily.

The Crone gently pulled on the loose skin beneath her chin, stroking it as if it were a beard. "Boy, yer darkness is the reason they in danger. This somethin' ya best be git'n used to fer the rest of yer life."

"So, they're safe as long as I stay away from them?" My heart broke at the possibility.

"They ain't nobody that live fer ever, boy."

I turned to Mr. Bird, as a lump in my throat began to singe. "I'm done with this. What's the use if everyone around me is gonna' die?"

"You *must* fight against this," he said with passion. "You cannot simply give in to the darkness, Luke. Trust me, hope is worth battling for."

"I don't want everyone to freakin' die. I'm nothing but a—"

"Bleedin' cooter if'n ya ask me," said the Crone. "Ya ain't a'actin' like ya has a drop o' Theo's blood runnin' in ya. Ya sound more like a cowed dawg a'whimperin' for his supper."

Her comment was a stinger. It angered me and made me want to violently clear the table of its contents. I visualized my fist smashing into her crooked, bent nose. But I was also embarrassed and ashamed. She was correct in labeling me a *bleedin' cooter.* Particularly the genetic backbone comparison. Grandpa would have relied on his faith and leaped headfirst without hesitation.

"Your lack of finesse is truly remarkable," said Mr. Bird.

"She's right," I said. "I've been acting like a pussy."

"That the first true thang been said by ya, boy."

It was this very moment that I finally accepted my new life. It was useless to fight against it. Grandpa's life and history summed up my future. It was time I did him proud.

"Okay, what do I do?" I said.

"I cain't tell ya what to do, boy. But I tell ya that if'n yer as strong as I figger ya to be, then you can overcome the darkness that chasin' on ya," she said.

"I don't even know what power you're talking about."

"Use yer coldness, boy," she said. "Yer coldness saved that big fella' there, when ya kilt the demon-man."

"You mean Ruckus," I said.

"Ya got to learn how to entwine Theo's blood with the darkness that Lilith bestowed in ya, make 'em work for ya in union. Yer grandpappy was full o' love, but he didn't have the darkness like ya got." The Crone dropped the gems onto the table and cracked the gnarled knuckles of her hands. "Ya kilt the demon-man on accounts of Ruckus bein' in danger. That were love, pure and simple. But listen to me, boy. The darkness a be tuggin' on ya from now til yer endin'. Try to git yerself some faith."

"I have faith."

"Ya ain't soundin' convincin', boy."

The candles on the table began to waver as an unexpected breeze swept through the Crone's home. It was cold and caressing as it grazed my neck.

"Ya'll gits ready," said the Crone. "The dark comin' to take a look at ya, boy."

I raised an eyebrow. "That doesn't sound good."

"That cause it ain't good."

Ruckus and the other men disappeared from the sphere and were replaced with a swirling blackness. The candles beyond the protective circle followed suit, winking out one flicker at a time.

"Git ready, ya'll."

I felt a stabbing pain in my shoulder, and I yelped my discomfort. "Oh, crap."

"What ailin' ya?"

"It's her," I said. "Lilith is here. My bite hurts when she's around."

"Good Lord, where is she?" said Mr. Bird.

Lilith's unmistakable laughter echoed and taunted. "Thomas Bird, you old fool. I'm nearer than you think."

From the blackness I heard horrible snarling from a goodly number of unearthly creatures. Their eyes were unblinking and yellow, circling us like a pack of wolves.

"Crone we *are* safe within the circle, correct?" said Mr. Bird.

"I'm hopin' so."

"I was hoping for a more confident response," he said.

"You're correct in doubting her magic," said Lilith. "She's too old and weak to protect any of you."

"Shush yer whore-hole," said the Crone. "Ya ain't doin' nothin' to the boy. Ya craves him too much."

"And you do not?" said Lilith. "Think about how succulent he must be. Wouldn't you like a taste?"

"You can't do anything to me," I said to Lilith. "You should leave."

"No, but the ugly bitch can," she said. "Crone, wouldn't you like to have your beauty back? All you need to do is kill the old man, and then have your way with the boy. Perhaps you can share him with me, and we fuck in a threesome?"

I did my damnedest to push such an image from my head.

"Is ya sayin' you can make me purdy again?"

"Oh, yes. Your beauty is waiting for you to claim it," said Lilith.

"It been a long while since I turned a head on account o' me bein' purdy."

"Whoa, you can't listen to her," I said.

"He's correct," said Mr. Bird. "She's full of lies, surely you—"

The Crone laughed hideously. "Ya'll so funny. I ain't a listenin' to that bitch."

Lilith roared, and her demonic minions joined in. The sound was chilling, and unlike anything I'd thus far experienced. And then her face appeared in the magical ball, full of hate and cruelty. Gone was her supernatural beauty, as it was replaced by sharp, reptilian features. Her eyes locked onto my own. "I'll take all that you cherish, Luke. All that you love, and crush it."

"Why?" I found the question to be practical if nothing else.

For a fleeting moment, I believe I was able to see a touch of compassion in her eyes just as her face became beautiful again. "Because, my sexy boy—it's my nature."

I stood up and looked around in the darkness, daring the fiends of Hell to make a move. "I won't let you hurt them."

Lilith laughed wickedly, mocking me with her hypnotic voice. "Darling, the only way you're saving your pathetic friends is if you willfully commit to coming away with me. Agree to walk in the shadows with me, and to be my lover."

"I'm only thirteen years old. That's pretty sick." I cast an accusatory glance at the Crone, to which she found humorous. She tried to wink at me, but was unable due to the lidless nature of her eyeball.

"I'm not bound by such trivial distinctions," said Lilith. "And neither would you be, if you joined me."

The Crone retrieved a twisted, wooden staff from behind her chair and laid it across her lap. "I'm a'thankin' ya'll cain't handle the boy down yonder in Hell. I thankin' he too powerful fer even yer likes."

"Your mind is full of rot if you actually believe that, hag," said Lilith.

"Well, I figger him and his grandpappy was strong enough to put ya to a'wearin'a mask," said the Crone. "And that was a'fore yer demon affliction was in 'em."

Lilith pointed to the mask on her face. "This had nothing to do with them being superior to me."

"I'm thankin' yer's wrong on that. Theo were too strong for ya, and I thank the boy is too."

Lilith bared her fangs and hissed. "It was blind, fucking luck that caused my wound."

"I'm thankin' not," said the Crone. "Theo and his kin is blessed."

"If Luke's grandfather was blessed, then why is he dead?"

"It were his time I reckons."

"Are the two of you going to stop this spatting anytime soon?" said Mr. Bird. He looked at me apologetically, shaking his head.

"Yep, I reckons so." She then surprised me—and certainly Mr. Bird—by taking the staff and placing one end of it against Mr. Bird's chest, and then pushing him outside the protection of the circle. "Okay, boy. It up to you to save his ole' skin."

Chapter Twenty-One

A New Weapon and Stiletto Heels

I DIDN'T HESITATE in joining Mr. Bird. I was immediately at his side, nervous, scared, and angry. Yes, *very* angry. "You old bitch! I'll kill you for this!"

"That good, boy. Use yer coldness." She held her staff out to me. "Here, take it. Kill them demons with it."

"Crone, have you finally gone off the deep end?" said Mr. Bird.

I began rolling him back to the safe confines of the circle, determined to kick the Crone's teeth out of her head—if she possessed any—once we were both safely within the protected area. But I quickly discovered we were unable enter back into the circle. There was an invisible barrier that pushed back against us.

"Once ya leave, ya cain't come back in unless'n I lets ya."

"Is this how you're going to show your appreciation to Theo?" said Mr. Bird. "By having his grandson murdered?"

The Crone waved the staff in a circle, which set several candles and torches ablaze. "Quit yer belly achin', ya damn titty-babies."

The candle light pulled back the covers on the demons, revealing the nasty lot of them. They were in different shapes and sizes, but equally gruesome and frightening. A creature with hoofed feet was closest to Mr.

Bird, standing over him with its drawn-out gooseneck. It looked ready to devour him with a grotesque mouth that rapidly snapped at the air.

The witch held the staff out to me, beyond the protective circle. "I reckons it'a be a good thang to take this."

Without any forethought, I snatched the staff away from the Crone and swung it at the monster. I connected cleanly with its rotting head, causing it to scream in pain. As I swung again, I noticed the staff glowing a brilliant amber color, which intensified upon contact with the beast's head.

An explosion of gore rained down upon Mr. Bird.

"Sorry." It was all I had time to say, as the rest of the demons moved in for the kill.

A demon with scales and feathers lunged at me and was quickly met by the staff. It was sliced in half, and its entrails splashed onto the floor. "Crone, let us in!" I said. "What is your problem, man?"

"Don't be a'git'n yer panties in a wad, boy. Yer a'doin' fine if'n ya ask me."

A rage, born of frustration, filled me, and I began to seek out the demons. Keeping Mr. Bird at my side, I shrieked like a madman and swung at every monster I saw. Each one exploded into a shower of bits and gore when I connected. But they were closing in, moving too fast for me. I began to feel a bit on the doomed side, particularly when a group of large spider-like creatures showed themselves. I say *spider-like*, but they weren't spiders. They actually had more legs than a spider, and had black spikes at the end of each leg. Each of them had bulbous heads with one cyclops-eye, and two drippings fangs that snapped together. Their bodies were white and gelatinous, similar to the aquatic creatures beneath the bridge. If they had been the actual size of an everyday spider, even tarantula-sized, I would not have been so concerned. But these things were as big as a prize calf.

"Wonderful ally you have there, Luke." It was Lilith, still speaking from the confines of the magic ball. "I would never put you in such a dilemma."

The Crone picked the gems up from the table and placed them in the palm of her hand. "Watch close, ya whore." She dropped the gems back into the box. "Once I close this here lid, yer goin' to be gone."

"Hag, has your decrepit mind finally rotted to the point of no recovery?" said Lilith.

"Nope, not yet it ain't." The Crone shut the lid to the box, and the ball with Lilith's face disappeared. Any remaining demons also vanished. If it were not for the floor being slick with demon intestines, there would be no evidence they were ever here.

"Damn fine mess ya made," said the Crone.

"Is that your response for such foolhardy actions?" said Mr. Bird. He had his glasses in his hand, wiping the demon-goo from the lenses. "Both of us could have been killed, due to your little stunt."

I wanted to unload my own fiery objections to her insane methodology, but my mind went to the staff I held in my hands. I hadn't noticed during the fray, but now that the dust had settled, I was able to feel a familiar thrum of power. "Crone, what's the deal with this staff?"

"Why ya askin'?"

"It feels weird in my hands, and it totally demolished the demons."

The Crone dipped her tongue into the tobacco pouch and pulled out a wad. She then, still using her tongue, packed it into the pipe. "It were yer grandpappy's."

"What?" My mouth opened in surprise and joy.

"How did you happen to come into possession of it?" said Mr. Bird.

"Right after he whittled it, he give it to me."

"It feels just like the dagger," I said. "Kind of like electricity in my arms."

"Lilith felt the pow'r in ya. That's why she's a'wantin'

ya," said the Crone. "That, and she wants ya to diddle on her."

"Grandpa made this and gave it to *you*?" My curiosity was bristling. I hardly knew where to begin with my line of questioning.

"It were a long time ago, I ain't rememberin' on the exact amount of years."

"Do I get to keep it?" I had already decided that I was.

"I reckon's it's yers to keep."

"This is quite remarkable," said Mr. Bird.

"Mind blowing, man." Even at my young age, I knew destiny was playing a game with me.

"Does ya have yer grandpappy's book?" said the Crone.

"No, not with me," I said, feeling suspicious. "Why?"

"Settle down, boy. I ain't got me no designs on it."

"I haven't read it yet."

"Ya needs to read, boy. It'a tell ya the history of thangs," she said. "Thangs on yer grandpappy's life and such. They's folks that'll want it for they ownself, and they'a kill ya fer it."

"It's in a secure place," said Mr. Bird.

The Crone puffed on her pipe, making it billow with thick, white smoke. She appeared to be contemplating a subject. "Birdman, theys a darkness risin' out yonder in yer world, and it aims on takin' thangs over. All o' them books that yer Unchosen folks has got, is goin' to be hankered fer."

"What's in the books that is so important?" I said.

"It depend on whose book it be, but all'em books has got secrets on the folks who intends to spread the darkness."

"People with power and money," I said. "That's what Grandpa told me in my dream."

"In a dream say ya?"

"Yeah, it was pretty trippy. He showed me a secret garden, and got me high…uh, I mean I ate a tomato that got me high."

The Crone shook her head and cackled a wretched laugh. "Yer a dream traveler, boy. Yer' spirit goes to other worlds and such."

"That must have been wonderful," said Mr. Bird.

"It was." My eyes stung as I relived the moment, recalling the sadness I had felt. But I realized I was being selfish and silly at the time. I was now fully aware of just how blessed I was. Not many—if any—have experienced such a thing. How many times have people hoped, prayed, and wished for one last time with their loved ones? Just one more embrace, to express how much they've meant to you, and how much you love them.

"Here, dab on yer eyes," said the Crone. She handed me a silk handkerchief, which surprised me, but her showing an actual emotion that could be construed an act of *kindness* was the real shocker. "What else? Did ya brang anythang back from the dream?"

"Well, his old cowboy hat." I turned to Mr. Bird, alarmed. "Crap, I don't know what I did with it!"

He patted my arm, smiling. "Don't worry, it was resting upon one of your pillows as we left the house, according to Millie."

"Anythang else?" she said.

"Um, I was still pretty high when I woke up."

"Well, ain't that somethin'."

I dried my eyes with the hanky and handed it to Mr. Bird. He was in more need of it than I, as he was dripping with demon juices. In fact, he needed more than a tiny handkerchief to rid himself of the mess he was covered in. A fireman's hose came to mind.

"Ya'll needs to step all the way in the circle," said the Crone.

"Why is that?" I said, following her instruction. "Are they coming back?"

"Nah, they's cleanin' that need a'doin'."

Neither Mr. Bird nor I understood what *that* meant,

but were immediately enlightened when a group of large worms sprang from trapdoors that were littered throughout. Instead of squirming, they scuttled along the floor on insect legs, shoveling the demon innards into mouths that did not seem to ever close.

"My dear God," said Mr. Bird.

"Purdy ain't they?" said the Crone.

"Oh, yeah. Real *purdy*," I said.

I was startled by the odd, humanness of the beasts' heads. They were roughly the same size and shape as a grown man's head, but with multiple eyes across their foreheads. The nose appeared perfectly humanoid, but the ears were elfin and the mouth was extra-large. And as I looked closer, I was able to see a pair of small hands reaching from within the mouths to pull the guts inside. The hands were oily and black, with twitching claws.

I had to look away.

"What sort of monster are they?" said Mr. Bird.

"They ain't got no name. They's just thangs I trapped fer my likens."

Sometimes people go crazy in here. I didn't doubt Constance's words for a second. "We need to go, Mr. Bird."

"Yes, we certainly do."

"It just as well. I got me thangs a'goin' on that needs tendin' to," She stomped her foot on the floor, and the monsters darted into the darkness. "They ought to leave ya'll alone, now."

I gripped the staff. "They'd *better* leave us alone."

The Crone grunted out a fart that immediately gripped me with its noxious waft. A literal green fog circled around her. "Don't be a'gettin' cocky with me, boy."

"He didn't mean any offense, Crone. He is merely telling you that if any of your...pets become aggressive he will, ah, destroy them."

Her gastric attack induced a surge of vomit from me. I turned my head and let it loose. As it splattered onto the floor, one of the Crone's cleaning crew inched in from the darkness. "Git on back!" she said to the creature. Fortunately, it obeyed her and hid itself once more. "Puke be a favorite thang for'em,"

The sound of a creaking door, being slowly opened, boomed throughout the surrounding murk. It conjured memories of every Vincent Price movie I had ever watched.

"Hello, Mr. Bird and Luke." It was Constance. She was standing behind Mr. Bird and me, wearing the same pretty dress and bow. Her purity was blooming and out of place in such an environment.

"Constance, it's good to you see again!" I was so overcome with happiness that I picked her up and hugged her. Mr. Bird's face lightened with her presence as well.

She giggled and kissed my cheek, and then I set her down. After hugging Mr. Bird, she walked to an aisle that was between two enormous tables. "I'm going to lead you back."

I clasped my hands and looked Heavenward. "Yes, how excellent."

"Ya got a hug and a sugar fer me?" The Crone stretched her veiny arms to me, and waggled her tongue.

"No."

The Crone hee-hawed lustily.

"Crone, thank you for your time," said Mr. Bird.

"Yeah, it's been..." I held the staff up high. "Thank you for this."

"Don't be a'tarnishin' yer grandpappy's mem'ry by a'bein' a cooter."

"Gotch'a." I took her last pearl of wisdom and began pushing Mr. Bird, as we followed Constance. After a few steps, I was unable to resist the temptation to look back at her one last time, as impossible as that might seem. She was bent over and looking inside of a box. She was not wearing underpants, and her rag-like garb had hiked up in the rear. I was prepared to unleash an unearthly scream of disgust, but was strongly taken aback when I saw the derriere of a much younger woman. She wore a pair of stiletto heels and sported, I dare say, a perfect ass, legs and *cooter.*

"Weird, man," I said, as I wheeled along.

"Yes," said Mr. Bird. "Weird is one word amongst a plethora, that would describe today's activities."

I agreed with him, but I wasn't referring to the goings on of the day. No, what I found weird—and quite disturbing—was that I became aroused upon seeing the Crone in all her glory. In truth, I wanted another peek.

Constance led us to a door that was not the same as the one we entered through. This one was made of a light colored stone and covered in hieroglyphics. "Here you go," said Constance. "All you have to do is push on the door, and it will open for you."

"Strange place for a young girl to be," said Mr. Bird. "I hope you are happy."

"I am happy, thank you."

I took her little hand and held it. "I don't see how you could be happy here. It's an awful place." Slithering, wet sounds from overhead reinforced my statement.

"I'll be just fine," she said, patting my hand.

"Why not leave with us?" I was pleading with her. "We can all three leave together, and you'll never have to come back here ever again."

"I can't leave yet. But when I do, I'll come visit you." She beamed a smile of innocence at me and walked to a dark corner, again disappearing into a door made of shadows.

Mr. Bird gestured toward the door that was to be our exit. "Shall we?"

"Yes, we shall," I said.

The door opened upon contact with my hand, swinging outward. I rushed us out, feeling as if something vile and evil might snatch us back at the last moment. Luckily, nothing of the sort occurred. We were instead treated to warm sunshine and a partly cloudy sky.

"Are we in our world?" I said.

Mr. Bird inhaled deeply and then let the air out slowly, as if savoring a fine cigar. "Yes, we are back." He sounded very relieved.

We were on the path that led from the bridge to the front door, and we were able to see Junior as he leaned against the tailgate of the truck. I looked for the door that we had just exited from, but it was either gone or invisible. The shack looked to be the same shack, except it was now surrounded by lush greenery and Spanish moss trees.

"Don't bother yourself by trying to understand," said Mr. Bird. "Or, it will truly drive you insane."

As we crossed the bridge, I was unable to resist the temptation to look into the monster infested water. However, I didn't see monsters. I instead saw carp swimming to the surface, sucking at the air and expecting to be fed

After we had crossed the bridge, Junior greeted us and took over the duty of rolling Mr. Bird. "Did you guys change your minds?"

"About what?" said Mr. Bird.

"About seeing...the Crone."

"No, we most definitely saw her," I said, brandishing my staff. "She gave me this."

"I guess she didn't have much to say," said Junior.

"She said a *bunch*."

"She couldn't have said too much. You weren't gone for more than five minutes."

"Whoa," I said. "That's not right. We were there forever, at least a couple of hours. Right?"

"Time is different when playing with metaphysics," said Mr. Bird, wagging a finger. "Again, Luke try and keep your sanity."

"Gotcha."

Junior studied the drying fragments of demon parts on Mr. Bird. "Uh, so..."

"I'll tell you on the way home. It will help pass the time," said Mr. Bird.

I looked the truck over for signs of vandalism, as Junior loaded Mr. Bird into the truck. I saw only the scrapes and bruises left by the trees, nothing that would qualify as defacement by imps—whatever those were. "So, nothing happened while we were gone?" I said.

"Like I said, you weren't gone long enough for much to happen," said Junior. "But, with that SID, I was beginning to hear some shit moving around in the trees and brush. I was hoping it was squirrels."

I wondered what a squirrel out here looked like. Probably had horns and fangs.

"I believe we should make haste in leaving," said Mr. Bird.

"Right on," said Junior. He put the truck in gear and floored the gas, getting us moving in a manner that was definitely hasty.

I fastened my seatbelt and steadied myself. "Do you get many speeding tickets?"

"Nah, I don't know if I've ever had one."

"Now *that*," said Mr. Bird, "is truly a thing to wonder upon."

Chapter Twenty-Two

A Circus in Wetumka

WHEN WE ARRIVED back at the mansion, the first thing I did was shower. Two bathing experiences in one day was unnatural for a country boy like me, but I felt filthy, and it was not altogether because of the demon matter that clung to me. I felt dirtied by an unnamed foulness that was beyond skin deep.

Millie was there to attend to Mr. Bird, who was in greater need of a shower than I. She didn't ask any of us questions, just did her duty of caring for Mr. Bird. "My good Lord, you're a frightful mess."

"Yes," he said. "It has been quite an eventful day."

She looked me over and pointed to my feet. "Luke?"

"Yes."

"Make sure to kick your shoes off before going into the house."

I understood her concern, as my shoes were coated with nastiness. "Yes, ma'am."

I watched as she entered the house with Mr. Bird, and wondered if she was aware of the strangeness that encircled her as the do-it-all caretaker to Mr. Bird. Surely, I thought to myself, she must know *something*. And what of Natalie? How much did she know?

I shook my head and went inside, minding to leave my shoes outside the door. As far as I was concerned, the shoes could be burned. I didn't want them touching my feet ever again.

I again found a clean change of clothes lying on my bed, when I had finished with my shower. The short pile rested alongside Grandpa's hat. After I was dressed I put the hat on, and looked into a full-length mirror that was hung on the bedroom door. It sat crookedly on my head, but I liked the way I looked in it anyway. I was hopeful to be able to eventually grow into it.

I heard Ruckus' booming voice from downstairs, which filled me with anticipation of seeing the farm once again. I wanted to rummage through the house more closely, curious as to what sentimental treasures I might uncover, and I still had clothes to pack. I took off the hat, and took a moment to inhale the aroma of sweat that was rooted in the hat band, before hanging it on a bedpost. The smell had an element of sweetness that was assuring.

"Hey, boy," said Ruckus from downstairs. "You ready to roll?"

I yelled to him that I was ready. But, I wasn't ready for what was to come later that day. Nobody else was either.

We took Highway 9 back to Wetumka, travelling in separate cars. I rode with Ruckus in his Jaguar, while Bear and Oliver followed in a black Lincoln sedan. Mr. Bird stayed at the house, stating he was going to watch *Hee Haw* and then retire for the evening. Junior stayed behind to keep watch over the house.

We were halfway to the farm, pounding our eardrums to death with the sounds of The Allman Brothers, when Ruckus fished a crooked looking cigarette out of the car ashtray. He cracked his window and lit it up. It smelled strangely sweet. "I didn't know you smoked," I said.

"I don't smoke," he said. "Cigarettes, that is."

"So, that's not a cigarette?"

"Yes, and no."

"I don't know what that means."

"It means it's a marijuana cigarette."

"That stuff's illegal," I said. I was naïve, but I knew about pot. I knew it was what the *hood* kids smoked at school. A small crowd usually gathered around lunchtime and smoked out behind the building where shop class was held.

Ruckus inhaled and tried to speak as he held the smoke in his lungs, but ended up coughing and making sneezing sounds. After he'd gathered himself, he said, "Are ya goin' to call the cops on me?"

"Well, no."

"That's good to know."

I rather enjoyed the euphoria of the tomato and was curious to compare the high. "Can I try it?"

"Hell, no. You're too young."

"Kids my age smoke it at school all the time."

"They sound like a bunch of derelicts to me. Don't be hangin' around them kids." He drew on the joint and made more sneezing, barking sounds as he tried holding his breath.

"Why are they derelicts and you're not?"

He blew out smoke and crushed the joint out in the ashtray. "Cause I'm an adult."

"Mm, gotch'a."

He looked at me and then at the extinguished joint. "Don't be gettin' any ideas."

"I won't."

"Speakin' of school," he said, turning down *Midnight Rider*, "I'm responsible for gettin' ya enrolled in one."

"Enrolled where?" School had not crossed my mind for a long time. I wasn't opposed to attending, but I was nervous about starting over and having to make new friends. The very thought almost terrified me as much as The Crone.

"Probably a private school back in the city, and you'll probably have to take summer classes to catch up."

"Man, that'll suck."

"Hell, you'll be all right." His voice had a relaxed

tone. "My dad was in the Air Force for a while, I had to move around to a different school all the time."

"It'll still suck."

"At first, yeah."

He became quiet as a shiny gaze affected his eyes, and we rode in silence for a considerable time. I decided to take the opportunity to doze, since both he and the music were muted. I was just sinking into a deep stage of sleep when he spoke to me, jarring me awake.

"Hey, what happened over at…where did ya'll go?"

"Her name is Crone—"

"Crone?"

"—and it was totally weird and scary shit."

"How do ya mean?"

I sighed. "You won't believe me." Which irked me. Despite what he had already witnessed with his eyes, he refused to believe. I wished it was as easy for me to dismiss.

"Try me."

"All right, first off…Crone is a witch." I waited for his typical '*horseshit*' response, but he remained quiet and allowed for me to continue. "Okay, and she had me drink some nasty shit that's supposed to help me, but not cure me."

"Cure ya? What the hell's wrong with ya?"

"Remember, I told you that Lilith bit me, right?"

"The chick with the weird-ass hair?"

"Yep, that's the one. Well, her bite infected me, and it's caused me to kind of lose it around girls."

"Lose it how?"

"Makes me…super horny, and makes me see weird shit. Colors, and…"

"What?"

"Gives me a hard-on and makes me come in my pants." I said the latter part as fast as I could and awaited his remarks.

"Is that what happened at breakfast?"

"Yes." My face flushed with embarrassment.

"You *came* in your britches?"

"Yes," I said, looking straight ahead.

He erupted in laughter and slapped the dashboard. "I was a little worried about ya, boy. At least ya have an excuse for actin' the way ya did."

"Are you saying that you believe me?"

"Hell, I guess. I've tried explainin' shit away, but I can't."

I almost cried with relief. "Finally."

"Is that where ya got that thing?" He pointed to my staff, which was poking three inches out of my rolled down window.

"Yep. Grandpa made it."

"The hell ya say."

"Yep, he made it and gave it to Crone." I cleared my throat and continued. "And it's a good thing I had it when Lilith and her demons showed up, otherwise…I'm not sure what would've happened."

"Horseshit," he said. "Are ya kiddin' me?"

"Nope, no horseshit."

"I sure as hell hope that don't happen around me."

"Me too."

"Get some rest there, boy."

I folded my arms and lay back in the seat, but sleep was not going to happen. My mind was wandering down too many avenues, and not strictly related to supernatural thoughts. I was hoping to make time to say hello and goodbye to my friends, and to make plans to come back for visits. But, I also worried that my friendship might also endanger them. According to Crone, it was a reality I'd best become acquainted with. Regrettably, I decided against seeing any of my old pals.

Before arriving at the farm, we made a stop at a small, mobile home that was just off Highway 9. It was scruffy with weeds and cluttered with oil field equipment. Next to it was a rust-streaked, tin garage that appeared to be housing a few cars and trucks. It was junked out, and familiar. However, directly behind all of that was a vast peanut field, which I found to be beautiful. The plants were perfect, uniform rows of greenery that hugged the terrain as it became wavy with rising hills.

"All of this crap everywhere reminds me of your house," I said. "Why'd we stop here?"

"It's a satellite office for the company. I ain't takin' the Jag out on dirt roads again, figure I'll use a company truck. Also, I've got to check on the rig hands at some of Theo's wells. I'll meet ya'll back here this evening."

"You're not going out to Grandpa's?"

"Nah, too much shit to do," he said.

"How are you going to do any work with your arm in a sling?"

He moved his shoulder and grimaced. "To tell ya the truth, it ain't even hurtin' that much anymore."

I had noticed his movement was strangely sinuous, as if he had not been shot, but was merely nursing a soreness. I immediately chalked up his speedy recovery to the pecans he had eaten.

Bear pulled up alongside us and rolled down his window. Cigarette smoke billowed out like the car was on fire. "So, what's the game plan?" said Bear.

Ruckus bent to look inside the car and had to wave smoke out of his face. "Damn, are you boys on fire?"

"Yeah," said Oliver. "We're all hammering on coffin nails."

"Well, ya might want to put 'em out before Luke jumps in there," said Ruckus.

It was subtle, but he showed to me that he was concerned about my well-being. Of course, if it was marijuana they were smoking, it might have been okay. But it was the effort I appreciated. It's the little things.

I approached the car and stood next to Ruckus. "I don't understand how you can smoke those things."

"I don't know about Oliver's reasons, but I smoke

because it makes me look cool," said Bear.

"Ditto for me," said Oliver.

They got out of the car and opened all of the doors, allowing for the smoke to leave. "So, what are we doing here?" said Bear.

"I've got stuff to do. Luke'll get ya'll to the farm from here. It's about five miles or so," said Ruckus.

Oliver pulled his flask and flipped the lid. "I'd feel better if we all stuck together."

"I think it'll be all right," said Ruckus, pointing to the flask. "How about a pull on that thing?"

Oliver took a few sips and handed it over. Ruckus took a liberal dose before giving it back. "Hey," said Oliver. "There's no prize at the bottom of that thing."

Ruckus went through his post-whiskey-drink routine. "Damn," he said, making a sour face. "That's good shit."

"Seeing as how you're being so generous, I might as well get in line for one of those," said Bear.

Oliver rolled his eyes and gave the flask up. "You guys are buying me a new bottle."

"Ruckus already owes you drinks," I said.

"I haven't forgotten," said Oliver.

"Hey, you ain't got to remind him," said Ruckus.

"It's about half past three," said Oliver. "Let's agree on a time to meet."

"I ought to be done by five thirty or six," said Ruckus. "Let's meet at six, right here where we're standin'."

"It's a date," said Bear.

"Be here, or be talked about," said Ruckus.

Ruckus went into the mobile home, and I jumped into the backseat of the car with my staff. I immediately crinkled my nose at the bitter smell of smoke. "It smells like an ashtray in here."

"That's the smell of money," said Bear, as he launched us onto the highway.

"Money? I don't get it," I said, rolling down the window.

"Yeah, money going up in smoke. Cigarettes ain't getting any cheaper."

"Hilarious," I said.

"Before going to the farm, I'd like to stop by the police station. I'm curious as to how the case is going," said Oliver.

"It's on Main Street, I'll show you," I said. "But, I'm nervous about going near the station."

"Why?" he said.

"The Plume family."

He shook his head. "I wouldn't worry too much. They've got their hands full with the child murders, and from what I've been told, everyone seems to think the tornado whisked your freaky neighbors away."

Whisked away, yes. But to where? What goes up, must come down. My imagination allowed me to believe it was only a matter of time before their bullet riddled bodies rained down upon some poor, unsuspecting farmer as he plowed his field. Or even more ghastly; a group of children enjoying their lunchtime recess.

"Since you're here, you might as well tell them about Buddy," I said.

"Look, I get you, and I don't doubt you, but I can't walk into another town's police station and accuse an officer of the law of being a child murderer," he said. "We've got to have a little better tact than that."

"Like what?" I said.

"Why don't we find this Buddy character, and follow him?" said Bear.

"The idea has been crossing my mind," said Oliver.

"We'll be coming into town soon." I lowered myself in the seat, just in case ole' Buddy-boy was parked along the highway nabbing speeding drivers. "Hang a left at the stop sign and follow Main. The police station is next to the town hall, on the right."

"Isn't Buddy a county sheriff?" said Oliver.

"Yep."

"Then wouldn't he be at the county jail?"

"He's always hung out here, in Wetumka."

Oliver pulled Grandpa's list of names out and started looking it over. "How many of these people do you know?"

"Just Mr. Abbott, but not very well. He's the local veterinarian, I've seen him around."

"Your grandpa didn't use him on your farm?"

"It's not really a farm. We used to have cows and horses, but Grandpa sold 'em off. We didn't even have a dog or a cat. But we still called it a farm."

Oliver turned and faced me. "Okay, so you've never seen him at your…farm? Correct?"

"Yep."

"Have you ever seen Buddy and Abbott together? Think hard," he said.

I couldn't recall a single instance. Not at first. But then a small memory buzzed me. "Actually, maybe once."

"Maybe won't work. Did you, or didn't you see them together?"

"Yes, I definitely saw them talking in Buddy's cop car. It was during the county fair, and they were parked behind the livestock barn, Mr. Abbott sat in the passenger seat."

"How long did they talk?"

"I don't know. I was just walking with some friends when I saw them."

He became quiet and began working his jaw back and forth. "I don't suppose you know how your grandpop came to possess this list of names?"

"He wrote the names himself. But, I don't know how he knew about them."

"Do you think he might have some information stashed away at the farmhouse?"

I shrugged. "I don't know."

"We'll do some digging once we're there," he said. "I've got some people looking up some information on the others. It'll be a few days before I get anything though."

"We're here." I pointed to the four way stop, where Highway 9 and Highway 75 cross. Before turning left into town, we all gawked at the Rancho Motel & Restaurant that was across from us. It was a sight that I never expected to see in this quiet little town. News trucks and vans with perched satellite dishes were squeezed into the horseshoe parking lot. Reporters were scattered, moving up and down Main. "Holy Crap."

"It will be a long time before this town fades from memory," said Bear. He pointed out major television networks, along with the countless local media. "The paper said Wetumka's police station's going to be the command post for a while."

Main Street was slow moving, mostly due to the parade atmosphere. Clusters of people were walking in and out of the street. Many were on the sidewalks in front of businesses, sitting in lawn chairs beneath canopies and enjoying a cold drink. The parking was nonexistent. Fortunately, one of my school chum's parents owned a corner gas station, and we were able to find parking in the alleyway behind the business. It was within two blocks of the police station, with easy access to the adjacent neighborhood.

"I'm going to the police station. You guys hang here," said Oliver. "I won't be too long."

"Not to get all conspiracy theory on you, but how long is *too* long?" said Bear. "I mean, what if you get grabbed?"

Oliver patted the gun beneath his jacket and pointed to a gun he claimed was strapped to his ankle. "If for some reason the FBI and OSBI has been infiltrated, I'll shoot my way out of trouble."

"All right, as long as you've got it covered," said Bear.

"But, I seriously doubt that is the situation. So, give me half an hour, tops," said Oliver. "If I see it's going to take longer, then I'll come back and let you know."

Bear wasn't entirely sold on the plan, but he agreed to

go along with it. So, the two of us sat in the comfort of the car with the windows rolled down and waited in the alley. At least it was shady and cool, guarding us against what was a warm day with temperatures in the high 80's.

"I've ridden my bike down this alley millions of times," I said.

"Oh yeah?"

"Yep." And not just this alleyway. Eldon and I had logged a great many miles on our bike treks, usually ending at the drugstore with frozen Cokes in hand. "I know this town like the back of my hand."

Bear yawned and stretched his legs out of the passenger side window. "That's good to know. I'm sure it will come in handy."

"Are you crashing?"

"I was thinking of it. I guess I could smoke instead."

"Sweet dreams," I said.

"I'm just going to rest my eyes."

"Sleep tight." He was snoring in less than a minute, no doubt sleeping off his shots of whiskey. I got out of the car and used a ladder, which was hidden amongst an untamed honeysuckle bush, to gain access to the roof. It wasn't the first time I'd done this. My pal Lynn Jensen and I used to climb onto this roof every weekend. His folks, who also owned the gas station, were unaware of our daring antics. On more than one occasion, we've lain flat on our stomachs while his father searched and yelled for him. We thought it was good fun. But that was before the town was racked with child murders. I now found such behavior to lean toward being cruel.

I light-footed it to the large sign that rested on the roof. It read, *Jensen's Gas and Garage*, in bright red letters. I peeked over the top to study the hubbub that was afoot, and most importantly to keep an eye peeled for Buddy-boy. If he was within the vicinity of the police station, I felt confident I would be able to spot him. I had already decided what I would do, if I actually did see his sorry ass. I would beat him to death with Grandpa's staff.

Ya gots a coldness about ya.

I saw many people I knew, bustling about the town, chatting about the murders. I also saw a large number of news media people who were interviewing the locals, digging for information that might be news worthy. I kept a closer eye on the police station, however.

I didn't see Buddy, but I saw Sheriff Jake. He got out of a patrol car, donning his good-guy white hat, and entered the station. I wondered if he really was a good guy. I tried to see his aura, but it either would not show, or I didn't know how to make it visible. It was a question I should have asked Crone, because I damn sure wasn't going back to her. I hoped to never see her again.

I stayed on the roof until I became concerned about the time. I had not checked before I climbed on the roof, but I felt certain Oliver was overdue.

I climbed down to look at the clock inside the car. Bear was still *resting* his eyes and snoring, sounding very much like a real-life bear. "Hey," I said. "What time did Oliver leave?"

He opened a groggy eye and looked at his watch. "Forty minutes ago."

"Aren't you worried?"

Bear got out of the car and began rubbing stiffness from his neck. "Not sure."

"You don't *really* believe the cops'll nab him to you?"

"Oh, probably not."

"How much longer should we wait?" I said. "We still have to go to the farm."

"It's four-thirty," he said. "Maybe I ought to stroll on over to the police station."

"That's probably—"

Bear held up his hand, shushing me. "Someone's coming. Get behind the car."

I pointed to the ladder and then to the roof. "Even better," he said.

Halfway up the ladder I heard the footsteps. It sounded like two sets, and they were close. I rushed to the top just in time to see Oliver and the sheriff come around the corner. "Is that Luke I hear scrabbling on the roof?" said Oliver.

"He's no Indian," said Bear.

"Luke? This is Sheriff Sanford," He looked up at me. "What in Sam Hill are you doing up there?"

I thought of leaping onto the adjoining rooftop, to jumpstart my getaway. To go on the lam. "Oh, just checking things out."

"Yeah," he said. "It's a circus out there."

"Come on," said Oliver, signaling me down. "It's all cool, man."

"Yeah, I know it's cool." I started down the ladder, trying to be normal and not show my apprehension. The ladder shook with my nervousness.

"Sheriff, the big ape is the consultant I told you about," said Oliver, referring to Bear. "He's okay to bring in on any information."

Sheriff Jake shook Bear's hand and introduced himself. "I'm the one who found that young man." He pointed to me. "He was in bad shape, covered in mud and blood." He sized me up with sharp eyes. "But you seem to be doing all right for someone fresh out the hospital."

"Yep."

"Well, the reason I'm over here is because of Detective Anthony's concerns about Deputy Wynn."

Bear passed a look to Oliver. "What concerns did he…relate to you?"

"Concerns relating to the recent murders. He told me an informant passed it along to him that Buddy should be looked at." The sheriff shook his head and then laughed humorlessly. "If he'd brought this sort of story to me this morning, I would have told him he was crazy."

"But not now?" said Bear.

"No, not now," he said.

"Why? What happened?" I said.

"Some photos came to light. Photos with Buddy involving young children." The sheriff looked down at the ground. "Right under my own nose, all this time."

"Is he in jail?" I said.

"I'm afraid not. He's missing, along with two more kids."

"That's not good," I said.

"Luke," said the sheriff. "How is it that you're involved in a conversation with police officers about a murdering pedophile ring?"

"Uh…" I almost stumbled as I searched for a reasonable explanation. But I allowed for the truth to set me free—some of the truth. I skipped over countryside tales of demons, and the devil. "I think Buddy wanted to kill me yesterday."

The sheriff crossed his arms and frowned. "Why do you think that?"

"He was mad at me for puking on him."

"You puked on him," said the sheriff. "Okay, so what happened after that?"

"He reached for his gun, and almost pulled it out. He looked at me…" I recollected the moment, remembering the vicious look on his face. It was filled with hate. "If Ruckus wasn't there, he would have shot me."

"Where did this happen?" he said.

"At the farm, when he dropped us off."

"But the primary reason for Luke being here is to go back to his old place, to grab some clothes and such. The Buddy thing is circumstantial," said Oliver. "Ruckus is working around here today, and we offered to give him a lift out to the farm."

"I understand," said the sheriff. "Luke, how well do you know Dr. Abbott?"

"I don't."

"Your grandfather never used him at your farm?"

"It's not a real farm," I said tiredly. "We stored hay for

some people in our barn, but we didn't have any animals."

"Is Abbott also MIA?" said Bear.

"No, he's teaching today," said the sheriff. "Your accusation is the first I've heard of him being a suspect, and I'm not keen on letting anyone else know."

"Why is that?" said Oliver.

"Well, I need more than your say-so—which is not to say I don't believe you. He holds some sway in this county, and is well respected. I'm afraid that if I drop his name, it might get back to him." The sheriff took off his hat and fanned his face. "But, if we find incriminating evidence in his possession, well, that's a horse of a different color."

"Find Buddy, and he'll probably spill the beans," said Oliver. "Men like Buddy have brittle spines. I've dealt with too many scumbags to know any different."

"We're looking for him," said the sheriff. "The feds, right down to the local cops. I expect the media to be alerted any minute." He straightened his hat and held his hand out to Oliver. "Thanks for your concern and your help, Detective Anthony."

"If there's anything I can do, you can reach me at the OKC station," said Oliver.

The sheriff held onto Oliver's hand, gripping it a few seconds longer than was necessary. "I wouldn't be doing my duty, if I didn't tell you that Luke needs to be kept away from this mess. And, I don't suppose I need to remind you that you don't have any jurisdiction here. I also didn't just fall off of the back of a turnip truck. I know there's something you're not telling me, but I'm going with my gut that I can trust you." The sheriff released Oliver and patted his shoulder. "I'd expect the same lecture from you, if I was in your neck of the woods."

"No offense taken," said Oliver. "We're going to the farm for a quick trip, and then we're on our way."

Sheriff Jake looked left and right, being very cautious of who might be near. "Now, with all that said, there's some things not right about this case. Things that ain't jibing with me."

"Such as…" said Oliver.

"A man from Nebraska walked into my station at four in the morning, with a pair of government goons and a lady in a suit. The lady handed a warrant to my desk sergeant that was signed by a federal judge, ordering us to turn over any and all evidence as relating to this case. But my department isn't running this investigation, it's the FBI and OSBI. My deputy rang me from bed, and I showed up to take a look at the paperwork." He paused as he thought about the information he was about to relay to us. He looked shaken. "Well, Buddy's name was on the list as a person of interest. I asked them why, and they pretty much told me to stick my questions in my ass. They wanted to know where Buddy was at, and I said to try his house."

"So, this was before the pictures were found?" said Oliver.

"Yeah, that's right," said the sheriff.

"And Buddy's gone MIA," said Bear. "Do you think his disappearance is connected?"

The sheriff shook his head. "I don't know, truth be told. But, it's damned strange to me how this Nebraska fella has suddenly been calling shots in the investigation. And it's not just me that feels this way. The state bureau is up in arms about it."

"What's your gut telling you?" said Oliver.

"Cop to cop gut?"

"Yeah, cop to cop."

"I think they're trying to cover something up." Sheriff Jake glanced up and down the alley, appearing nervous.

"High level shit?"

The sheriff nodded.

Oliver frowned and seemed to be studying him. "Is there anything else, Sheriff?"

"You're a good cop, Detective," said the sheriff. "Yeah, there's something else." He lowered his voice, despite there not being anyone within earshot of us. "Something about this asshole scared me, and not in a normal way."

"Like how?" said Bear.

"Like he was somehow responsible for the murder of my two suspects yesterday, and he could do the same to me and my family."

"What's this guy's name?" said Oliver.

"I didn't ask, Detective. I was too scared, and there ain't much that scares me." Sheriff Jake took a step back, awaiting a response from Oliver. "And before you label me a chicken-shit hick, remember you weren't the one who found those two boys ripped to pieces."

"Sheriff," said Oliver. "Not one of us will judge you."

Bear and I said as much, agreeing with Oliver.

"That's not all." The sheriff continued. "The cell that they were murdered in is, uh, not right. It's got everyone spooked. We keep hearing sounds, and the lights don't work down that hallway."

I wanted to speak up and tell him I saw a leftover residual of creepy critters at the hospital from my evil visitation. But I remained in my cautious mode when it came to the sheriff. I merely nodded my head at his comments.

"Be careful, Sheriff," said Oliver. "And expect the unexpected."

"Sheriff, don't begin to doubt yourself, and don't start thinking you're wacky in the head," said Bear. "Because everything you just said, is stuff we've *all* experienced."

The sheriff shook his head, as if it was all too crazy, and he didn't actually harbor such eerie thoughts and beliefs. But we knew better. His eyes revealed his fear.

He looked down at his feet and sighed. "Guys, I've got a wagon load of shit to do. Nice meeting you, Bear, and good to see you doing so well, Luke." Without another word, he tipped his hat and abruptly made his way around the corner of the gas station and was gone.

Oliver said, "I hope this doesn't ruin him. He seems to be a good guy."

"Hope in one hand, shit in the other," said Bear.

Oliver leaned back, staring at Bear. "You got that from a bumper sticker, right?"

I got into the car. "We need to hurry to the farm," I said. "I'd like to grab a few more things." I also wanted to take another stroll into Grandpa's secret garden, to test and collect the various fruits and vegetables. I didn't have a good look at everything the last time I was there, and I was also in my dream travelling mode during my last visit. I was curious to experience it in the flesh.

Chapter Twenty-Three

Home Again

THE FAMILIARITY OF the dirt road to the farm was lifting, as it kindled memories of better days. It was also a tremendous help in aiding Bear down the old road, in being able to point out and predict the low spots, which prevented damage to the Lincoln.

"I don't get why all you city people always drive fancy cars out here," I said.

"Hey, cut me some slack," said Bear. "I *am* a city boy, after all."

"The kid has a point," said Oliver. "It is a *farm* we're headed to."

"Which is coming up at the top of this hill. We'll hang a right," I said. I couldn't have been more excited if a pile of money was waiting for me.

When we pulled into the driveway, I didn't wait for the car to come to a complete stop before jumping out. The smells and sights were an old friend's embrace.

"Nice place," said Bear. He and Oliver walked to the middle of the yard and looked at the natural beauty that was all around them. It was a reaction I had seen plenty. There was a special wonder to the farm that left many spellbound.

"Yeah, I can see why you miss it," said Oliver. "If only there was a rustic bar down the road."

"I think Ruckus feels the same way," I said.

"I knew there was a reason I liked him."

Bear walked to Grandpa's truck that was still parked in the driveway and looked inside. "The keys are still in the ignition. Do you usually leave it parked out here?"

"No." I pointed to the mimosa tree. "It's been parked over there forever. Sheriff Jake left it there when he delivered it from impound."

"I'll put her back for you."

I ran to the house and found the front door unlocked. "Hey, Oliver. You guys come on in."

Oliver walked toward the house, taking in the scenery and looking for signs of trouble. "I'm coming."

When I entered the house, I was welcomed by the same creaky floor and bouquet of scents. The items on book shelves and the hung pictures were family to me. Corny, yet true.

I walked directly into the kitchen and looked in the refrigerator, a habit I've never outgrown. I found several items covered in mold, and the milk was curdled to the point of being cottage cheese. "Disgusting."

I scanned the countertops for garden items and found a few coffee cans of pecans, as well as a bowl of apricots that were on the cusp of being overripe, but were surprisingly still edible. I picked one up and sniffed it.

"How is it that those haven't gone rotten?" said Oliver.

They should have been a sticky, black mess. But these weren't ordinary fruit. "I know why."

"Oh, wait," said Oliver. "Are these the same type that Mr. Bird grows?"

"Theo is the one who brought the seeds to the mansion garden. It all started here." It was Bear, who once again impressed me with his stealth, as he seemed to have suddenly appeared next to me. "Although, Theo's harvest is always more potent."

I thought of Ruckus and how his gunshot wound seemed to be healing unnaturally fast. "Did you feed

Ruckus anything from the garden?"

"That's why he's doing so well."

Oliver nodded toward the fruit. "This stuff kills my stomach."

"Speaking of stomachs—I'm famished," said Bear.

"Well, there's nothing in the fridge that's close to being appetizing." Oliver's tone held disgust.

Bear grabbed the apricot from me and began eating it. "Holy shit, that's sweet and delicious."

"Uh, you should be careful." I held up a cautionary hand.

"I know what to expect." Bear spoke around a mouthful of apricot.

Oliver took a swig of his whiskey and offered it to Bear.

Bear shook his head. "No thanks. In a few minutes I'll probably be high as a kite."

I hadn't given much thought to Oliver's drinking. I certainly didn't judge him because of it, but I was now curious. However, Grandpa had raised me to know better than to inquire of such matters.

"I don't see a garden out back." Oliver looked out of a kitchen window. "I see a few fruit and pecan trees. Is that it?"

"Those are normal trees," I said. "And we grew some normal tomatoes around behind the barn. The…other garden is…" I hesitated as Grandpa's words spoke to me. *"Be mindful of who ya share it with."* But, I knew I could trust them. I was suddenly able to see beautiful, blue auras emanating from them. They glowed with it. I didn't know what it meant, but I was struck with a strong sense of trust and loyalty. "You guys up for a walk?"

"Hell, yes," said Bear, smiling. "As long as the two of you can keep me from floating away."

WE TOOK OUR time as we walked to the garden, mostly

due to Bear and Oliver. They were caught up in the beauty and the peacefulness, slowing several times to inquire about certain parts of the land, or to simply stop and stare. Bear was giggly and easily distracted by birds and other things. We waited for at least fifteen minutes on one occasion, as he studied a patch of wild flowers crawling with buzzing bees. When we eventually reached the garden area, Oliver looked confused, as the view was suddenly less picturesque. The fortress of twisted thorn bushes and trees loomed before us.

"So, you're saying we're at the garden?" said Oliver.

"Pretty much. It's beneath that rock." I showed him the sliding rock, but left it in place. "Go ahead, move it."

"The garden is under that rock?" He frowned. "How is that—"

"Jeez, just move the rock," I said.

"Yeah," said Bear. "Move the rock." He was grinning ear to ear, moving his hand in front of his face.

Oliver went to the rock, shaking his head. "I think *both* of you are stoned if you think I'll be able to move this big-ass rock."

"Just give it a little push," I said.

He gave the rock a slight push and it moved effortlessly, revealing the hidden trapdoor. "Well, fuck me with a duck."

"Man, that would be a funny and disturbing sight." Bear giggled.

Oliver moved the slide latch and pulled open the door. "Wow, I can smell the scent of flowers already."

He started the downward climb, excitement beaming from his face. "I hope that smelling the air down here doesn't make me all goofy."

I was reasonably certain of that not being an issue, but I was feeling quite goofy and happy about sharing the garden with my two new friends. That, and it was damned good to get back to where my roots began. I thought of Grandpa and hoped he approved of me letting them in on the secret. Secrets, after all, aren't meant to be secrets forever.

I followed Bear down the hole and joined him and Oliver in the garden. I took a deep breath of the sweetness and found a rock to sit on. "So, what do you think?"

"I think I've stumbled onto paradise, amigo," said Oliver.

"Yeah, this is a trip." Bear sniffed a patch of unkempt flowers.

"The colors," said Oliver. "I've never seen such a…brightness."

"Mr. Bird said he's been here at night and seen the plants and flowers glow in the dark," said Bear. "Man, I'd love to see that sometime."

"That would be cool." I made a mental note to make certain I indulged myself with the experience.

Grandpa had only exposed me to the nickel tour, so I ran to the places that appealed to me the most. The main point of interest for me was the waterfall. It was quite incredible as it poured from large rock crevices into the pond.

"Simply amazing." Oliver walked to the edge of the pond and watched the fish swim in the crystal clarity of the water. "Do you fish out of here?"

"No, we've got two other ponds for that."

Bear erupted in laughter. "Can you imagine the effects of a fish fry?"

Oliver shook his head in amusement. "Like at a church social. My God, they really would see the light." He retrieved his flask and took a nip of whiskey, and then looked at his watch. "Guys, I honestly hate to poo-poo on this party, but if we don't get a move on we'll be late to meet Ruckus."

I had wanted to sample more of Grandpa's garden wares, but decided that I would wait. "Okay, but let me take a few of these tomatoes and things."

Bear was silent, staring into the water as if it were

another universe. Who knows, maybe he was in fact seeing another universe brought on by the effects of the apricot.

"Hey, partner," said Oliver. "We're leaving."

Bear still seemed lost in his world. I stretched a hand to his face and snapped my fingers, which brought him back to earth.

"Whoa, I was out of my mind for a minute," he said.

"Grandpa calls it being in la-la- land."

"Yeah, him and most everybody else." Oliver dangled the car keys. "*I'm* driving back, for obvious reasons."

"Says the man hitting the whiskey." Bear pointed to Oliver's flask and giggled.

"I'm not drunk, and I'm a professional drinker. But, touché."

"I'll be fine by the time we get to the car," said Bear. "The effects only last an hour anyway."

"We'll see." Oliver grinned.

"Yeah, about an hour is right," I agreed.

Oliver slowed and looked at me. "Kid, I'm somewhat bothered that you partake in this fruit thing."

I plucked a few cherry tomatoes and gently placed them in my pocket. "It's not like I'm doing heroin. Eating tomatoes isn't illegal."

He made a hand gesture like a talking mouth. "Whatever, let's get moving."

The walk down the hill was considerably faster. Mostly because Bear paid less attention to the wondrous world of nature, and we were pressed for time. We saw Ruckus' work truck parked in the driveway as we arrived back at the house, which was a complete relief. There was no need to rush anymore, which meant I could pack more things to take back. As was my nature, I went immediately to the kitchen and found Ruckus prowling through the cabinets.

"There's not shit to eat, except for some fruit," I said.

"No, kiddin'," said Ruckus. "We've got to stop and eat somethin' in town before headin' back."

"I'd rather not stop in town."

"Hell, I've got to eat somethin' soon. My stomach thinks my throat's been cut."

Bear plopped down at the kitchen table and picked up an apricot. "You could eat one of these."

"No, thanks. The last time I ate somethin' out of this kitchen I damn near shit myself to death."

"And we don't need *you* eating any more of this trippy fruit either." Oliver pointed a finger at Bear.

"I'm done. In fact, I'm in need of a bit of evacuation, if you follow."

"The crapper's down the hallway and to the left," I volunteered.

"Much obliged." Bear moved quickly.

"His colon is amazing," said Oliver.

Ruckus looked at me with bloodshot eyes. "Get what ya need, and I'll help ya load up the Lincoln."

"Gotch'a." I bounded upstairs to my old room and sat on the edge of my bed. Before I started to gather my things I wanted to soak up the goodness of the house. I allowed my mind to silence itself, basically turning off my internal dialogue. I closed my eyes and let the energy of the house embrace me. My breathing became soft and rhythmic, sending me into a light trance. It was wonderful to be back, despite how much it pained me to be here without Grandpa.

"Don't get too comfy," came the voice.

My eyes opened, and I jumped straight up. "Holy crap!"

"You're jumpy as a cat in a room full of rockin' chairs."

"You would be too if you'd been through what I have, Grandpa."

"I reckon I would."

After we embraced, he had me sit back on the bed. He pulled up a stool I used as a table for my comic books. He glanced at my *Amazing Spiderman* and set the rest of the comic books on the bed. His aura was not as bright as the last time I visited with him, but it nonetheless was impressive. "What do you mean by not getting comfy?"

"Ya cain't go back just yet. There's still some work to be done up to the Plume property."

I shivered at the thought of stepping onto that accursed land. "Why?"

"Buddy's hidin' out up yonder."

"Where? The sheriff said the house was burned and wiped out by the tornado."

"There's an underground system of tunnels beneath where the house stood. You'll find 'em there, but it'll take some lookin'. But be careful. He ain't goin' to be alone, he'll have some of his sorry lot with him."

My head was spinning, and my stomach was queasy from dread. "Why can't I get the sheriff to come get him?"

"That won't work, Luke. There needs to be more than him bein' locked up. He's ate up with evil, and is infected with demons. I ain't sure a prison cell would hold him for long."

"You mean he needs to be killed."

Grandpa patted my shoulder, comforting me in the way he'd always done. "I know killin' is an awful business, but he ain't like other folks."

I sighed and fell back onto the bed. "I'm only thirteen. Doesn't it bother you that I've already killed...jeez, I don't how many."

"I surely don't like the predicament I've put ya in. But, it's somethin' that needs to be done. There's an evil that's comin', Luke, and it'll be plenty bad when it arrives. Buddy and his sort are the first part of it."

"Crone told us about something bad coming," I said. "Whoa, and speaking of *her*. How do you know her? She said you helped her or something." I sat up.

He ran his hands through his hair and smiled. "There's more to her than ya might think."

"Grandpa, I don't get why you're smiling. I feel like

getting sick, just thinking about the whole experience." I was unable to keep my mind from drifting to the parting glance I had of Crone. The woman—or whatever she was—was grotesque and appalling. And I loathed the quick pang of desire that came over me when I saw her nakedness. I hoped Grandpa wasn't privy to the event, and I wasn't going to bring it up.

"Well, ya ain't done any readin' in the book yet. After ya read up some, you'll feel less in the dark about such things."

It was obvious to me that he was not going to be forthcoming with any of the information I wanted to know. So, I went to the subject matter at hand. "Okay, so I murder—"

"Not murder."

"Uh, *kill* Buddy and—"

"Remember, he ain't a natural human anymore, it'd be the same as puttin' down a dog with rabies."

"Like Old Yeller, gotch'a."

Grandpa slapped his knee, finding humor in what I'd said. I can't say I found it funny, but Buddy Wynn was actually less than a rabid dog. At least the dog was out his mind with infection, not understanding or knowing of his actions. But Buddy tormented and brought terror to children, due to him being outright evil. He had no virus to blame his actions on.

"Ya need to go to the barn before headin' over to the Plume place. There might be some weapons in there ya'll can use."

"Like the dagger?" I had assumed that the weapons had been scattered by the storm. I hoped there would be something we could use.

"Maybe."

I was again baffled as to how he got a pass from Heaven to visit me, yet he was unable to tell me what was in the barn. I hoped the dagger was available, but if it wasn't, I still had Grandpa's staff. "Your staff, the one you made for Crone. I like it, thanks."

"She gave it to ya?"

"Yep, and it was a good thing. Lilith and her demons showed up, and I was afraid that Mr. Bird and I were toast."

"How's ole' Tommy doin'?" He smiled.

"He's good." I was curious about his knowledge on some events, but not on others. "I don't understand why you don't know some of these things. I mean, why don't you know how he's doing? And why didn't you know that I had your staff?"

"Some things I know, and other stuff I don't," he said. "But, I'm knowin' less and less ya see. Ain't nobody in Heaven supposed to know everything about what their loved ones are goin' through. There ain't no worries in Heaven."

"That must be nice," I said. "All I ever do is worry down here."

"Bide your time, and be patient, and kindle some sort of faith."

"Everyone keeps telling me to have faith. Even Crone preached it to me." I had faith, surely, by now. My dead grandfather was in my bedroom, speaking to me of Heaven and how wonderful it is. I've battled creatures from Hell. If I didn't believe, then I was a rather dense individual.

"Remember, faith ain't all about believin' in the Almighty."

I knew better than to expect an explanation of what he'd just said.

His demeanor changed quickly, from carefree to serious. He took me by my shoulders and looked me in the eyes. "Ya need to be awful careful of Lilith, Luke. She's taken a shine to ya."

"I am careful."

"But…ya don't seem to understand somethin', and as your ole grandpa I need to drill a disturbin' fact into ya."

He leaned back, and then stood. After a bit of pacing he said, "Because of ya bein' partly like her, you'll have a weakness in ya."

I became bothered. "Partly like her?"

"Ya got demon in your blood. You know this, Luke."

"Yeah, but I'm not like her. Jeez."

Grinning he said, "No, you ain't evil like her. You're a good boy—no, make that a good *man*. But, what I'm trying' to get across to ya is you'll be easily tempted by her. She'll pull out all the stops, and she'll use the people ya care for to get to ya."

"Grandpa, I've also got *you* in my blood. You're the best person I've ever known, and I figure that'll help me."

"That's mighty nice of ya to say, Luke." He walked to a window in my room that faced north, toward the hilltop with the hidden garden. It was easy for me to see that he was troubled, and I felt bad that he was here with me instead of being in paradise where he belonged. "Ya ought to know that it ain't normal for so many demons to be runnin' loose and to be seen by mortal folk. Not even for our bloodline."

"You mean the Unchosen?"

"That's right," he said. "It's only goin' to get worse."

"How many do you think are like us?"

"There ain't no tellin'. Folks have been makin' deals with the devil for centuries. I was one of the lucky ones that got stole away from my daddy, or otherwise…things would've been different."

"Did you ever find out who your daddy is?"

"Nope, and it don't really matter, I reckon."

"Can't the angels, or whoever, in Heaven tell you?" I thought he surely must have at least a minutia of clout with the Heavenly beings he now resided with.

"Nope, it don't matter up there."

I heard footfalls upon the staircase, ascending. Ruckus, I assumed, coming to hurry along my packing and to tell me he was near death because he was starving. "Are you going to stick around for the other guys?" I was excited for the possibility, as I was certain that Ruckus and Bear would enjoy the experience.

"Nope, I'm afraid not. Truth be told, I've got to get goin'."

"But, you just got here." I was set to plead for him to stay a little longer, but those selfish thoughts quickly left. He was meant to be in Heaven, walking streets of gold and hanging out with Jesus. Or, whatever people did in Heaven. He didn't need to be involved in this gothic drama of evil and darkness.

"Come on over here," he said, opening his arms. "Give your ole' grandpa a hug."

I embraced him and rested my cheek against his chest. It was remarkable how he felt and smelled the same as I'd ever recalled. The aroma of soil and sweat would forever be a wonderful reminder of Grandpa and all things comforting and good.

"Hey, boy," said Ruckus from the staircase. "Try to hurry every chance ya get."

And my eyes opened.

Ruckus appeared in my doorway, raising his eyebrows at me. "Hey, we ain't got time for you to be nappin'. We need to get on the road."

I was hugging my pillow, reeling from my experience. "Oh man, you aren't going to believe what just happened."

"What, that ya took a nap?"

I shook my head, attempting to loosen the lingering effects of my sleep. "I didn't know I was sleeping, but Grandpa was here."

"Come again?"

"I fell asleep—not *meaning* to—and Grandpa visited me. He must've somehow sent me to sleep or something."

"The hell ya say."

"He told me that we need to go to the Plume's."

"Are ya sure ya ain't high or somethin?"

With the exception of seeing Grandpa, I wished

Ruckus was right. That I was hallucinating, and there was no need to go back to the Plume's. "No, I'm not high."

"You were sleepin', are ya sure it wasn't just a dream?"

I thought about it. Maybe, but I was doubtful. "I've got to go to the barn. There might be something to prove I wasn't imagining the whole thing."

"Like what?"

"I'm not sure."

I ran downstairs and spurted my intentions to Oliver and Bear. "Gotta' got to the barn, Grandpa said there might be something in there for us."

"Like what?" said Bear.

"I'm not sure, probably weapons."

"Uh, when did you learn of this?" he said.

"A few minutes ago."

"Another letter or note?" said Oliver.

"Nope, he paid me a quick visit." I ran out the front door and continued running until I reached the barn. It was murky inside due to the fading daylight, so I flipped the overhead light on, which exposed a scene just as familiar and rustic as I'd ever recalled it being. But, I didn't allow for nostalgia to hook me. I looked to the darkened corner beneath the loft, the one that Grandpa pulled the golden weapons from. I had not forgotten the teeming spiders that covered Grandpa.

"Ah, damn," I said to nobody.

"Hold up, Luke!" It was Bear, jogging to the barn. Behind him was Oliver and Ruckus, they were talking and grinning.

"I'm not moving, trust me," I said.

I waited for Bear to join me, and then I pointed to the corner. "I *think* there are some things over there for us."

"Weapons?"

"Yep."

Bear cleared his throat. "And…Theo told you this just a few minutes ago?"

"Yep."

"What's that boy sayin?" said Ruckus, as he and Oliver arrived.

"He's saying that there are some weapons for us over there." Bear pointed to the corner, and then started walking to it.

"Wait," I said. "A bunch of spiders jumped on Grandpa the last time. I'm talking a *bunch.*" The hair on my arms rose as I relived the horrible moment.

"I'm still trying to get caught up here," said Oliver. "Now, did I hear you correctly when you said your grandpa paid you a visit?"

"Yep."

"I've seen some weird-ass shit lately, but are ya sure about seein' Theo?" said Ruckus.

"Pretty sure."

"Well, I'm going in," said Bear. "I've survived worse things than spiders." He didn't hesitate as he walked into the darkness and disappeared.

I grimaced in anticipation of a repeat performance, feeling foolish to be jarred by clusters of spiders when I'd faced much worse adversaries as of late. But, I just *hate* spiders.

However, my worry was for naught. Bear came out of the corner spider-free, holding the golden dagger in one hand and a double barrel sawed-off shotgun in the other. "Is this what you were expecting?"

"I guess so." I walked in a circle around him, searching for spindly-legged varmints. "The dagger is what Grandpa and I used to take down the Plumes." I took the shotgun from him and looked it over. "He normally kept this in the truck, or whatever he was driving."

"And Theo told you to come out here?" said Bear.

"Yeah, but he wasn't sure I would find anything."

"It would've been nice for 'em to stick around," said Ruckus.

"You believe me?"

"Hell, why not."

Oliver held up a hand and waved it, frowning. "Okay, just so we're on the same page, you're saying your...deceased grandfather came to you and told you to grab these things?"

I looked the other two in the eyes, just in case I needed some support. "Yes, and I know it's crazy—"

"No, no. I'm not saying you're crazy, or that I don't believe you—I mean c'mon," he said. "I haven't been exactly blind all these years. I only ask because I'm curious as to *why* he asked you to do this."

"Pull up a bale of hay," I said. "You may want to be sitting down for this."

Chapter Twenty-Four

Oliver's Demon

"SO, YOU'RE SAYIN' that the ole' boy you puked on is up there hidin'?" said Ruckus.

"Yep, that's what I'm saying." I walked to the west side of the barn and opened the doors, to point out the direction of the Plumes'. There was a small amount of sunlight left, more darkish and orange than shining. But, there was enough to highlight the black hole in the sky, with its attached tendril wiggling like a black snake. "Oh, no."

"That sounded ominous," said Oliver.

Bear stood next to me, and stared into the sky. "I see it, too."

"What are you seeing?" Being a detective and not knowing all the facts, was obviously irking Oliver.

"Someone's conjuring. It must be Buddy."

Ruckus stood on a crate and searched. "I ain't seein' sh—wait a minute. What in the hell is that thing in the sky?"

"I don't know, but it has something to do with conjuring," I said.

"It's supernatural," said Bear. "It forms when the incantation has been completed. It has to form in the sky, away from the earth."

Oliver threw his arms up in defeat and sipped from his flask. "Well, I don't see anything except for fading daylight."

"That's because you don't partake in the fruit. It somehow allows for some people to see things that are normally hidden away," Bear abruptly looked away, and then threw his hands in front of mine and Ruckus' eyes. "Don't stare at it."

I averted my eyes, remembering the time Grandpa asserted the same advice. Ruckus turned, and I hastily shut the two doors. "Grandpa said there might be some weapons in here for us, and he was right. So, I guess that proves I'm right."

"All right, so let me get this straight," said Ruckus. "We're supposed to go to this place and kill this Buddy character."

"Yes, that's what Grandpa told me," I said.

"As your official guardian, I can't say that I think any of this shit is a good idea." Ruckus was clearly distressed by the situation, pacing and shaking his head. "The proper thing to do—the *right* thing to do—is to get the sheriff's ass over here. It's his job to deal with this shit."

"Certainly can't argue with what he's saying, Luke," said Oliver. "And remember, you're already paranoid about the last time you, uh, visited your neighbors."

They were both right, but Grandpa felt it pertinent that I participate. "Ruckus, I know this is bad," I said, lowering my head. "But, this has to be done this way. Grandpa doesn't think prison will hold him."

"Luke, you don't have to be a part of this," said Bear. "I'll take care of the son of a bitch."

"According to Grandpa, I have to do this."

Ruckus sat down on a hay bale and leaned on his knees. "Your grandpa saw somethin' in me a long time ago, when I was just a rig hand. I ain't sure what it was or why, but he treated me damn good. Shit, he entrusted me to look after his only grandson, and I ain't even owned a cat."

Oliver extended a shot of whiskey to him. "Here, this

might help."

He took it and tilted it back, letting it bubble several times before handing it back. "Thanks."

Oliver flipped the flask upside down, and a small drop fell to the hay-littered ground. "There goes that," he said.

"With everything you and I have been through together…I know it's jacked up shit. But, you have to trust me," I said.

"You really believe Theo came to visit you? It was him?" he said.

"Yes, it was him."

"And he was okay with you doin' this?"

"I don't know why, but yes."

He looked up at me, and I saw in his eyes that he had finally given in. "Then fuck it."

"Fuck it, indeed," said Oliver.

"Lead the way, lad," said Bear.

I went to a sagging set of cabinet doors and opened them wide, searching for shotgun shells. I found a stack of boxes and handed them to Bear. He immediately began loading the shotgun, but paused for a moment to study the cartridges. "The caps on these have some weird inscriptions."

"They're probably special then. I bet they kill demons," I said.

"I've seen similar stuff, here and there," he said. "There's an old church in Arkansas that comes to mind. It's deep in the woods and has this sort of writing around the doors and windows."

Oliver pulled a .357 from beneath his jacket and spun the cylinder. I took the dagger and tucked it into my front pocket.

"Damn, you boys look like Butch and Sundance before they took on the Bolivian Army," said Ruckus.

Oliver and Bear exchanged looks, and then Bear said, "Ruckus, there's no need for you to join in on this hunting expedition. In fact, I'd feel better if you stayed here.

Things could go bad."

"I ain't scared," he said.

"I know you're not, but I've been trained for combat and have killed a goodly amount. And, Oliver here is a cop who's seen plenty of action himself."

Ruckus pointed to me. "Luke ain't trained."

He was wrong on that point. I was no longer a snot-nosed teenager. I had a number of kills.

"Ruckus, my friend, Luke has killed several times over." Bear cleared his throat, trying to cover the fact that what he'd just said disturbed him.

"And, you're too good of a man to have something happen to you," said Oliver. He placed a hand on Ruckus' shoulder. "I can't put a finger on it, but I can see what Theo saw in you. Luke's going to need you on down the road."

That was for certain. The mere thought of losing him caused me feelings of grief and anxiety. In an odd way, I felt just as obligated to protect him as much as he wanted to protect me.

After a few seconds he nodded his head. "Shit, all right. I'm more of a lover than a fighter anyway."

"I'll have to take your word on that," said Oliver.

"I guarantee it, son."

Bear clapped Ruckus on the back, grinning. "When we get back to the city, I'd like to see you in action."

"Bring a notepad," said Ruckus. "Ya just might learn somethin'."

"If our lovefest is over, then perhaps we should get the task at hand done and over with?" said Oliver.

"I'm driving," said Bear.

Oliver looked at me in disbelief. "Is he serious?"

"I think so."

Oliver pulled the keys to the Lincoln from his front pocket and jingled them. "Follow me, gents, 'cause this train is pulling out."

"Do you know where you're going?" I said.

Oliver pointed to the west. "Um, that way. Right?"

"I've got the shotgun," I said.

AS WE TRAVELLED up the bumpy road, I was unable to stop reliving the last time I was at the Plumes'. My emotions welled inside my chest, and my breathing was quick and shallow. I closed my eyes, trying to get control, but that only caused images of the past horror to appear in my head. I couldn't understand why I was being affected, as I was no longer a rookie when it came these horrors.

"Hey kid," said Oliver. "You all right?"

"Yeah." It was all I could do to keep my voice from wavering. I wanted to appear strong and able in front of the guys, and not look like a *bleedin' cooter.*

"Well, you're looking white as a sheet. And the way your chest is heaving, well, it looks like you're likely to start hyperventilating."

Bear motioned to Oliver. "Pull over for a minute."

With ditches on both sides, Oliver settled on stopping in the middle of the dusty road. "Are you about to get sick?"

"No." Although my stomach suggested it was a possibility.

"It's all right to feel nervous," said Bear. "Hell, you don't even have to go through with this."

"Yes, I do have to do this."

Bear said, "Let's get out of the car for a minute."

"Yeah, maybe that'll help," I said. "Get some fresh air."

We all three got out, and I paced back and forth in front of the car. Bear and Oliver leaned on the hood, watching me and sucking down cigarettes. "I think I know why you're feeling so distressed," said Bear.

"I'm listening," I said.

"First of all, and probably most important, you're going back to the place where you lost Theo. That's big. But, I also think your new abilities are maybe trying to tell you something."

I stopped moving and considered what he said. "You think so?"

"I think so, probably."

"Like, what?"

"Shit, I don't know," he said. "You visited the old hag. What would she tell you?"

"I don't know what that freaky old lady would say." Indeed, the more I thought about it, the more I considered the trip to see her as an utter waste of time. Nothing she divulged to me was suddenly flashing into my head. Nothing rushing to me as a helpful antidote during my time of crisis.

"She didn't offer you *any* advice?"

I shook my head, hoping for a useful nugget that I knew wasn't there. "She was mostly a pain, she told me to have faith. But, nothing much—"

"There you go," said Bear. "Have a little faith."

"I'm pretty sick of hearing that."

"Look, just try to muster enough to believe we'll make it out of this crap alive."

"I don't think—" Oliver and Bear began to glow in rainbow colors. "Wow, man."

"What's up?" said Oliver. "You're looking at us like we have an extra set of eyes."

A vision seized me, and I began to see a flickering, grainy movie in my head that looked like an old silent film—except it was in living color. I saw winding and shadowy corridors, lit with flaming torches along the walls. One of the hallways was marked with hieroglyphics, which led to an open room filled with several large cages. In one of the cages there were two children, a boy and a girl. They were dirty, looking half starved to death, and scared out of their little heads. Someone was screaming at them. Someone named Buddy.

The vision left me, and I fell to my knees, puking.

"Are you trippin' on any fruit?" said Bear.

I shook my head no and spit. "It's awful, man."

"Yeah, vomit was never high on my list of favorite flavors," said Oliver.

"No," I said. "I saw kids held in cages. It's so bad, man." Sadness gripped me, as I thought of what those poor kids must be going through. "It's Buddy. He's got 'em down there."

"You saw this?" said Bear.

"Yeah, it was in my brain," I tapped my head. "Shit, I've got a bad headache."

Oliver helped me to my feet, and then looked to Bear for an explanation. "Do you know what in the hell just happened?"

"I think he just had a vision."

"Which means…"

"Which means we need to hurry," said Bear. "Luke was able to see where Buddy is hiding."

"And he has two kids with him." I jumped into the car and waved at them to get moving. "C'mon, man!"

Oliver got behind the wheel, and Bear barely made it into the backseat before we were fishtailing up the dirt road. "How much farther?" said Oliver.

"Not far, a few miles more," I said.

"You feeling better?" said Bear.

"Yeah, my headache is getting better. And I don't feel like puking anymore." Although, I did have a bad feeling in the pit of my stomach. I feared we weren't going to make it in time to save them.

"So, what's a vision like?" said Oliver.

"It's like a TV in my head."

"And you saw kids?"

"Yep. There were two, a boy and a girl."

"How old do you think they are?"

"I don't know, maybe eight or nine."

Oliver pressed the car faster, pushing us to over seventy miles an hour. The car moved as if on patchy ice, slipping and threatening to slide out of control. But Oliver held dominion over the road and the Lincoln, moving us purposefully toward the awaiting evil. His face was void of expression as he pushed us forward. He appeared to be undaunted by it all. But, his aura revealed that he was not calm on the inside. His years working as a homicide detective had calloused him enough that he was able to hide his true feelings.

But, his aura raged.

It was red and pulsing, but not the same red I associated with Natalie. Whatever I felt for Natalie was wild, rebellious and exhilarating. *True* red, whatever that is. But Oliver's aura was more like a muddied red, giving me the sense that he was infuriated. I was also aware of a feeling of supreme confidence. It ebbed just as strong as his anger.

Out of the blue, I said to Oliver, "How did you get tangled up in this stuff?"

"Oh, that's a long story," he said.

"What happened?"

"Well, I once saw something during a murder investigation that…freaked me out."

The ruins of the Plume house were fast approaching, much faster than I had anticipated. Oliver's tale would have to wait. "Whoa, start slowing way down or we're going to miss it. It's on the right."

He slowed the car, but not enough. We whizzed past it, which would have been easy enough to do at a slow speed since the house no longer stood, and the sunlight had winked out. "That was it, back there," I said, pointing.

Oliver slammed on the brakes, and the car slid on the dirt, causing a huge cloud. "Hold on, boys," he said, as he threw the car into reverse and stomped the gas. "I'll get us there."

"In one piece?" said Bear.

"Bitch, bitch, bitch," said Oliver.

I tapped on my window. "There, right there. Stop already." Oliver stopped in front of the tall columns that marked the entrance to the property. Not even the tornado's force was able to topple the twin towers.

"Thanks for the ride, Starsky," said Bear.

"I'm more of a Baretta guy, but you're welcome, Hutch."

We stayed in the car until the dust settled, and then we got out and surveyed the remains of the Plume house. A broken chimney rose above a battered, wooden floor that was marked with small piles of boards. Gaping holes were in the floor, which I assumed was our only way of gaining entry to the darkness below.

"Not much left," said Oliver.

"Nope," I said. Most of the trees that were closest to the house had been uprooted and taken away by the storm, and the few that still stood were void of leaves and splintered. It was eerily desolate.

"C'mon," said Bear. "I've got some things in the back." He opened the trunk, and the inside light showed a pair of revolvers and a couple of flashlights. He tucked the biggest of the guns in the front of his jeans and handed me the other. "It's a snub-nose .38, in case you need more than your stick."

I tucked the gun in my front pocket, and then held the dagger out to Oliver. "You'll need something to use against demons."

"My .44 Magnum won't work?" he said.

"If it's Buddy you're shooting at," I said.

He looked the dagger over, unable to hide his skepticism.

"This is a new animal, partner," said Bear. "We're about to go up against some mind-blowing shit."

"All right, I'll hang onto it." He took the weapon from me and nearly dropped it. "Whoa, that's weird."

"Yeah," I said. "It sort of vibrates."

"Let me see." Bear held out his hand. "I didn't notice anything when I found it in the barn."

Oliver gave it to him, but Bear showed no signs of

feeling the power. "Nothing."

"Grandpa didn't feel it either," I said.

Bear handed it back to Oliver. "I guess you're special."

"Damn right."

Bear bent and spoke to me. "Luke, Oliver and me will hang on to the flashlights. Stay behind us, let us do the wet work," said Bear.

"Gotch'a," I said, although my plan was to kill Buddy myself.

Oliver walked to the edge of one of the holes in the floor and shined his flashlight. "Shit, I don't suppose there's another way in."

"I don't know," I said.

"If we're supposed to go underground, then this looks simple enough," said Bear. "I'll go first, then Luke, and then you."

Oliver squatted and looked closer at the darkness. "I can see the ground, so it's not that far down."

"I hope nothing is down there in the dark waiting for us," I said. "You know, like a trap or something. We haven't exactly been quiet."

"That's why we're letting the big guy go first," said Oliver. "If something starts eating on him, it'll take longer. The perfect diversion."

I chuckled, despite the actual possibility of something taking a bite out of him. "Man, that's messed up."

"Yeah, that's Oliver," said Bear. "He's messed up."

"Are you going to go already?" said Oliver.

Bear sat on the edge of the hole, letting his legs dangle in the darkness, while Oliver shined the light. "I was born ready." He leaned forward and held onto a remnant of the floor, slowly lowering himself down into gloom. Then, just as his head dipped below the floor, the old boards gave way to his bulk. A large chunk of the flooring fell with him, creating an echoing rumble.

"Holy shit!" said Oliver. He shined his flashlight into

the hole, moving the beam crazily. "Fuck me."

"Someone had to have heard that," I said, nervously.

"I'm okay." Bear's voice filtered up faintly.

Oliver shined his light again and was able to locate Bear. He was lying on his back with several boards across his chest, covered in white dust. "You sure?" said Oliver.

"No, but I'm alive."

"We've got to get down there," I said.

"Copy that shit, amigo," said Oliver. "You first."

He hugged me from behind and lowered me into the basement by my armpits. Bear grabbed me once I was within his reach, and then set me atop a pile of rubble. "Give me your flashlight," I said.

"I dropped it," he said. "It's somewhere...around here."

"Great." I gripped my staff with both hands and looked for movement in the darkness. I listened for menacing shuffling and sniffed the dank air for anything foul.

"We might as well be ringing church bells, announcing our arrival," said Oliver.

Dinner bells, more like it.

Oliver started his climb down, moving slowly, as to avoid bringing any more of the flooring down. Bear grabbed his feet and helped to guide him down. He immediately shined his light around the basement. "I don't see any doors, or tunnels."

"I don't even see a staircase," said Bear.

"I don't see shit," I said. But, a sweep of Oliver's light caught something that made me curious. "Hang on, move the light to the left."

"Here?" he said.

"Yeah." I moved closer and discovered a set of shackles and chains, stained with something dark and rusty.

Bear joined me and nudged the chains with his boot. "Looks like dried blood."

A wicked howl followed by a chorus of horrible laughter came to us, sounding as if it were just on the other side of a wall. It was very close.

"Demons," I said.

Oliver swung his light away from the chains and toward what looked like a part of the chimney. A hearth, cold and dark, sat at the bottom. "It sounded like it came from around here," he said quietly. "Demons, huh?"

"Have you ever seen one before?" I said.

"Not exactly," he said. "But, that case I started to tell you about was, uh, well, there was a demon involved."

"How do you mean?"

"A young boy was possessed."

"You said it was a murder investigation…"

Oliver sighed heavily. "Yeah, it was a murder investigation. The boy killed his parents and his baby sister."

I was horrified to hear of such an awful crime, even as we stumbled around in a demon's lair. You see, true evil isn't numbing. One does not get used to such atrocities. It's the opposite, as it is always pushing us to the edge of fear and madness, escalating the shock.

"The boy's aunt made contact with Mr. Bird. That's when I first met Oliver," said Bear.

Oliver stared into the dirt, shaking his head. "I thought they were nuts at first."

"What changed your mind?"

"I saw the boy rip a man's head off, during an exorcism."

"That might do it."

The air quickly became icy, and a raspy cackle and a growl moved in stereo around us. A voice, thick with cruelty, spoke in a ragged hiss. "Inspector, it's so good to see you again."

Oliver gasped and spun around. "What the…no way." It was clear to me he knew who the cryptic voice belonged to.

"What's going on?" I said.

"Ignore it, Oliver," said Bear.

"We need to find our way to the kids," I said, hoping to help Oliver find mental footing.

"Shine your light around the fireplace," Bear told Oliver.

"Yeah, got you, man." He searched the charred hole with the light, sticking his head into the darkness.

"Oliver," said the awful voice. "You're too late. We're going to cut the children's heads off and eat them."

"Fuck you!" said Oliver.

The voice said, "Hmm, the younger the sweeter."

The flashlight flickered, and then died. There was no light to filter down from the sky, as there was no moon to assist us. Oliver tapped the defunct light against the chimney, but it was useless. We were blind.

"The boy, Luke Morgan," said the hissing voice. "He is not one of you, he is us."

"Grab the dagger," I said to Oliver. The thought came to me quite unexpectedly. In fact, it felt more like someone else was whispering in my head. But, I was confident in my suggestion.

As soon as Oliver's flesh came into contact with the dagger, the entire room was suddenly ablaze with a golden luminosity. Oliver's tormentor screeched, and then a large portion of the flooring exploded upward. He waved the dagger around, grimacing a warrior face. "Like I said, *fuck you.*"

"An old friend of yours?" said Bear.

"Un-fucking-believable. It's…the demon from the kid." Oliver's body was trembling.

Bear placed a steadying hand on Oliver's shoulder. "I sort of figured that out."

Oliver shook his head, obviously disturbed. "I mention the case, and it shows up here talking shit? Man, it's been ten years or more since all that happened." His hardened exterior showed a sign of being cracked. The horrors he faced during the case with the boy still lingered within. "Why is it here?"

I knew why the demon came to Oliver. "It's because of me," I said.

"How do you figure?" said Oliver.

"I'm like a magnet for 'em. Crone and Grandpa said as much."

"How do you figure that?" said Oliver.

"He's probably right," said Bear. "He's got a touch of their blood."

He is us.

"But," said Bear. "Your demon-pal is gone now. So, let's get humpin'."

Angry, scratching sounds came from the other side of the chimney. It was an inclination that we were digging in the correct location, even if our progress was sloth-footed. However, worry for the children begin to tingle in me. What if the demon was being truthful about the boy and girl? Were their heads, indeed, gone and eaten? No.

"Demons are dirty-ass liars," I said. "I think we still have time."

"I tend to agree with you." Bear looked around the room. "We need something heavy enough to bust through the chimney wall."

Oliver pointed to a bent steel rod that stuck out of a heap of lumber, which Bear immediately began to pull from the rubble. In doing so, he moved several pieces of debris out of the way, which unearthed a grim discovery of countless children's clothing.

Chapter Twenty-Five

Tunnels, Demons and One Mercy Killing

NO ONE SAID a word.

Bear ripped the rod loose of the rubble and went to the chimney. With a growl of sorts, he rammed it into the mortar and rock with a reverberating clang. Bits and chunks broke loose as he continually struck the rock. "Stand back, here it goes."

Bear broke through, and a fetid wind shot out of the hole he'd created, carrying with it moans and screams of torment. The whispering of demons was also in the wind, buzzing in our ears like bees, until the Holy light of the dagger sent them hissing and yowling away. Then the ground began to shake, and the chimney trembled. "Shit," said Bear. "It's coming down."

We ran toward the farthest wall from the chimney, stumbling as we picked our way around the mess. Oliver slipped and fell onto a board lined with ragged nails, piercing the arm that held the dagger. It fell from his hand, bouncing just a few feet away from him. I started to run to him, but Bear ordered me away. "Get the hell back!"

I watched in horror as the chimney collapsed and fell onto Bear as he leaped onto Oliver's back. Filth and soot filled the room, and the dagger's light quickly began to wane. "Bear!" I screamed his name, knowing the worst had just happened.

"Oliver, shit, *somebody* fucking answer me!"

Neither of them answered me, but something in the dark did. It was the demon from Oliver's past. "Luke, let them be. You are destined for more than this pitiful existence. You are *us.*"

I remained silent and held my staff in a sweaty grip, slowly making my way to where I thought Bear and Oliver were, fighting back tears of loss.

The demon was relentless in its goading.

"Leave your sorrow behind, Luke. They are dead, soon to be rotting sacks of meat for the maggots to feed on. But, that doesn't have to be your fate. Lilith is ready to claim you. Just ask for her, and you'll feel no more pain, no more sorrow. She will introduce you to a domain of infinite pleasure. You are us." I felt the demon's icy breath in my left ear as it spoke. "Such sweet, physical pleasure awaits you. Go to her, and stop your pretending."

"Fuck you," I said.

Taunting laughter ensued.

"Luke," said a weak voice. Oliver's voice.

I nearly tripped and fell over with excitement. "Where are you?"

"Walk a little to the right," he said. I detected a voice strained with pain.

The demon hissed and growled, and a strong gust of wind blew debris and dirt into my eyes. The air was arctic with cold, and stinking of rotting flesh. "There is no hope for the inspector," said the demon. "He knows it, *yes.*"

"Don't listen to that asshole," said Oliver.

I got down on my hands and knees and moved forward against the cloudy darkness. I stopped when a hand shot out and grabbed me around the wrist. Thankfully, it was Oliver.

"You scared the shit out of me," I said.

"I can't reach the dagger, get it," he said.

"Where?"

"Right fucking close, a few feet from my face."

I felt around but was unable to locate it, and began to

feel anxious and useless. "Son of a bitch, I can't find it."

"Keep your cool and keep looking, it's there."

I heard the unmistakable sound of the smallish, slithering creatures that I had encountered the first time I was here. They whined evilly, no doubt having just finished feeding on whomever was sacrificed for the current conjuring. They sounded like babies, and maybe they were for all I knew. Ugly-ass crybabies from Hell, who sounded like they were still hungry.

"What the hell is that?" said Oliver.

"You don't want to know." My hand scraped against the dagger, and I was able to grab it and control it. "Got it, thank God!" The area once again lit up like an inferno, cutting through the grimy cloud and darkness. And not a moment too soon, as the crying demons were nearly upon us. Larger, bony demons were also creeping into the room via the cave that was created when the chimney tumbled down. They were quite displeased.

The baby-like demons rolled as if on fire and screamed with high-pitched squeals of pain. The others ran away from the light, back into the darkness, voicing their discomfort with ferocious roars. Alas, the little monsters had no legs and were forced to drag themselves from the light, with most of them not making it to safety. They turned black, and indeed, caught fire. The wailing was ear piercing.

"Are...whatever they are gone?" said Oliver.

"Yeah, for now."

Oliver groaned his relief. "I don't hear that asshole demon anymore. Damn, it sure loves the sound of its own voice."

"I think the light chased it away again."

"How's Bear looking?"

He didn't look good.

Bear's head was laying against the middle of Oliver's back, and a large slab of mortar and rock was lying on him from the shoulders down. A trickle of blood ran from the corner of his mouth.

"Well," said Oliver.

"There's a lot of crap piled on him."

"No, shit. It's piled on *both* of us." He wiggled his body, trying to dislodge himself, but had little success. "I need you to move what you can."

"Here." I laid the dagger in his good hand. "It only protects us if one of us is holding it." I looked closer at his wound. It looked as if the board had been hammered onto his arm. "Your arm looks like shit."

"It feels like shit, too."

I began pushing the rocks loose of the pile and used my staff to pry the larger ones away. I was able to get rid of a large amount, but not the slab that was the relevant piece. "Try to get loose again," I said.

"Check on Bear first," he said. "And this time, tell me what's up."

I looked at Bear, not feeling confident of a good prognosis. "Okay, hang on."

I leaned my head next to his and listened for breathing, but didn't have much luck. "Aww man, I don't think he's breathing."

"Slap him," said Oliver.

"Slap him? I don't know—"

"Just slap the living shit out of him."

I came down on Bear's cheek with the palm of my hand, but I pulled up just as I made contact. I couldn't help it. I felt bad for hitting him.

"I barely heard that," said Oliver. "Try a little harder."

"Okay, okay. I'll smack him harder." On the second try I struck him with more force, but he didn't show a sign that he felt anything.

"Jesus, are you kidding me? Slap him!"

"All right, shit!" This time I used more force than before, slapping him repeatedly. "Wake up, wake up, wake up, wake—"

"I'm awake." Bear's eyes rolled open. "You can stop

slapping me."

"Thank, God," I said.

"I can't breathe. Get this off me." He spoke in gasping snatches, sounding starved for air.

"I'm going to try and get loose again, hang tight, buddy," said Oliver.

"Hang on." I jammed the end of my staff into a small gap beneath the block of stone and pried upward with all I could muster. It worked beautifully. The slab moved enough for Oliver to scoot out.

"Keep holding it, kid," said Oliver.

Surprisingly, it was an easy task. The staff held strong, and the weight seemed to be much lighter than I anticipated. But, just as I thought I had somehow tapped into some sort of adrenaline pool of strength, I was corrected. It was Bear pushing up against the weight that was the real support. His arms were fully extended in an impressive pushup. However, it was easy to see he was laboring, and close to losing his battle. I leaned into the staff even harder.

"I need something to prop underneath the slab," said Oliver.

I looked at his injured left arm with the protruding nails and winced. "Will that work?" I pointed. "That's a big board stuck to your arm."

"You're smarter than you look." He slid the blade of the dagger in between his skin and the board. It took him several attempts, but the board finally fell free. Paying no mind to the blood that poured from the holes, he grabbed it and jammed it beneath the slab. He then got down next to Bear. "Okay, let it down slowly. I'm going to pull your big ass out of there." He held the dagger out to me. "Here, I can't pull on Bear and hang onto this. The board should be enough to hold it up, you can stop with the stick."

Bear relaxed and lay back on his belly, letting the weight rest on the board. There was less than an inch between him and the slab, but it looked to be enough to allow him to breathe easier. Oliver pulled on Bear's arms, but his wounded arm was struggling.

"Do you need my help?" I said.

"Yeah, but I'm out of whiskey." He carefully braced his feet against the block of stone and pulled with all he had. Bear wiggled some and came out a few feet. "Good job, brother. Keep wiggling."

I heard a sound from the cave that sounded like voices. Human voices, not demonic. This meant the dagger would not protect us, as it only casts its power amongst demonic entities. The most it could do now was provide light. This new danger would require protection of the old-fashioned type.

I pulled my pistol and pointed it into the mouth of the cave. "Uh, I think someone's coming."

"Shoot first, ask questions later." Oliver didn't bother looking my way. "I've almost got him free."

I slid the staff down my pants and into a pant leg, holding the dagger in my left hand and the gun in the other. Just like old times.

"He's out," said Oliver.

Bear groaned in relief and rolled onto his back. "My leg is fucked up, man."

"How bad?" Oliver inspected the leg and turned his head in revulsion.

"You tell me," said Bear.

"Fuck me, it ain't good."

I looked and saw that his leg was broken about four inches below the kneecap, with a bone sticking through his jeans. "No, it ain't," I said.

Bear sat up and studied his leg. "We need to pop the bone back in place."

"Are you shitting me?" said Oliver.

"I wouldn't shit my favorite turd." Bear gestured to Oliver's arm. It was gushing blood and was swollen. "You aren't looking so hot yourself."

"Ah, merely a flesh wound."

They could joke and be a couple of nervous comedians, but we all knew they were perilously injured and could suffer serious consequences without medical attention. The two children, it appeared, were doomed.

I then noticed a wetness in one of my front pockets. For once, it wasn't an embarrassment. "Wait, this might help us."

"What do you got?" said Bear.

"Garden tomatoes." I pulled out four beautifully-red, cherry tomatoes. One of them had been squished a bit and was leaking.

"Ollie," said Bear. "Be a good lad and fetch those. Luke, keep a close watch on the cave. I'm pretty sure that's how to reach the tunnels."

Oliver took three tomatoes from me and then sat on the dirt next to Bear. "Are these the trippy kind?"

Bear took the soppy one from him and popped it into his mouth. "Yeah, but they do more than cause giggles. They heal, man."

"Screw it," said Oliver, and he began chewing one as well. His face lit up with enjoyment as the flavor overtook him. "Wow, this is delicious. But, it's gonna' take more than vegetables to fix your leg, brother."

"Fruit," I said. "Tomatoes are actually a fruit because they have seeds."

Oliver said, "Thank you, Farmer Luke for the agricultural lesson."

I heard voices again, closer. "Shh, someone's coming."

Bear pointed out two large chunks of the chimney to Oliver. "Okay," he said. "We've got to do this in a hurry. I need you to place them next to one another, so that they form a *v*."

"I've seen this movie before," said Oliver. "You're really going to reset the bone?"

"I've got to do something."

Oliver quickly assembled the rocks and set them next

to Bear's broken leg. "Are you ready?" said Oliver, slightly smiling.

"I'm assuming the tomato is taking effect, and you're not seeing humor in my predicament," said Bear.

"God, I'm sorry, man. But, yeah, it's doing something…" Oliver's voice trailed off, and he stared intently at Bear's leg.

"He's going into la-la-land," I said.

"Hey," said Bear. "I need you to pay attention. Put my leg between the rocks, man."

"Yeah, yeah, got you. Sorry, but your leg is…glowing."

"I don't doubt it," said Bear.

Oliver gently gathered the leg and placed it between the rocks. Bear didn't utter a single syllable of pain. "Didn't that hurt?" said Oliver.

"Shit, probably," he said, laughing.

Oliver joined him in laughter. "Well, you ain't seen nothin' yet, brother."

"Guys," I whispered. "Get a grip, man."

"Copy that," said Oliver, still struggling to contain a titter. He ripped Bear's jeans up to the kneecap and pulled the material away, fully exposing the wound. "Ooh," said Oliver.

Bear shook his head, obviously dreading the pain that awaited him. "Okay, here goes." With Oliver holding his ankle locked between the rocks, he pulled his leg until enough space was created for the bone to snap back into place. Oliver helped, by pushing on the bone. I felt my stomach go queasy.

Bear breathed heavily and slapped the ground during the procedure. But, he did not express or show his pain. He giggled a little, sounding a touch crazy.

"I'll be all right if I never have to see that done again," said Oliver.

Bear made the okay signal and then covered his face with his hands. With a muffled voice, he said, "Help me get to my feet."

"Luke, I need that staff," said Oliver.

Keeping an eye on the cave entrance, I tossed it to him. He caught it with his injured hand, showing no signs of pain.

"Are you still bleeding?" I said.

"No, it's stopped." He gave the staff to Bear, and he stabbed it into the ground. Oliver then gripped one of Bear's arms. "How's the leg feeling? I mean, considering."

"It's throbbing, but I can't really feel any pain."

"If people find out about Luke's garden, it'll put whiskey out of business," said Oliver.

"You guys should split a tomato," I said. "After about an hour it'll start to wear off."

Oliver bit the tomato in half and gave the other piece to Bear. It took a matter of seconds for Oliver's face to become a smile. "Here, big fella'," he said. "Upsy daisy."

They both laughed like a pair of idiots as Oliver pulled Bear to his feet. Then, I heard a loud bang and felt heat zip past my left ear.

"Get down!" said Bear.

I did as ordered and heard two more shots just as I landed in the dirt.

"Drop the dagger," said Oliver.

I understood why he wanted this done—the dagger lit us up like golden fish in a barrel. But I was hesitant to allow the demons back on the attack. I instead fired my pistol numerous times into the darkness. I got lucky with a shot, as I heard someone yelp in pain.

"Move out of their line of fire," said Oliver. "And kill the fucking light for a minute."

I darted behind a sagging shelf filled with dusty mason jars and extinguished the dagger's light by sticking it in my pocket. The darkness was sudden, and suffocating. It didn't take long for the unnatural cold to settle upon us, marking the arrival of evil entities.

From my hiding spot, I was expecting to be blind in

the darkness. But, something strange occurred. I was able to see the creatures as they began creeping into the basement. They had a black aura, so pure with evil that it somehow glowed in the murk. I at once thought of the conjuring blackness in the sky. It was the same shade of deep black.

I also saw two men with handguns walking slowly, sneaking their way in. They were bare chested with each having blazing symbols carved into their skin. One of them was bleeding from a stomach wound, no doubt due to a bullet from my gun. I could see a transformation in them, as their eyes turned shiny black and their faces became vicious and beastly.

The demon-kind who came in ahead of the men were bony, hunched over, and walked with spasmodic movements. They carried a horrible stench—as most all of their kind did—and had skin that was patchy with fur and rotting skin. Long faces, similar to a horse's, and rattling teeth that constantly snapped. They made wheezing sounds, which I believe was actually their language and how it was spoken. A few of the smaller monsters came crawling back, dragging their bodies along the ragged floor. I decided to give them the name of *The Eaters*, rather than crybabies. After all, eating flesh seemed to be the only thing the awful bastards craved. They ate themselves free of a human form when called upon, and cried when there was nothing left to eat. Always looking for a bite.

I watched as Bear leaned against a wall, essentially propping himself up with my staff. He held his shotgun low, and ready. Oliver was next to him, with his gun trained toward the cave entrance. "Okay," said Oliver. "Do it!"

I pulled the dagger free and held it up high. Shrieking again arose from the monsters, as the bright glow set their flesh on fire, including the men—who were no longer men in the sense of the word. As expected, they attempted to retreat back into the darkness of the cave, which is what Oliver had anticipated. He opened fire on them, ripping them with bullets as they came near to the cave. Bear had moved away from the wall and was blasting with his shotgun, spraying rank chunks of meat that caught fire and blackened.

I splayed myself as flat as possible onto the floor, in an effort to avoid being shot. I was forced to scoot on my back as I distanced myself from the fray, all the while I held the dagger tight with both hands. As I moved, I looked up through an open area of the dilapidated floor and saw a swirling, shapeless blackness. It appeared to be hovering above the basement, fleetingly taking the form of something with wings. In some way, I knew it to be the demon from Oliver's past. It circled, as if it were a fiendish hawk.

A demon leaped at Oliver, screaming from a widening mouth and flinging long, hooked arms. Its skin had melted away, to reveal a disjointed skeletal structure that had turned black. I didn't see a way for him to avoid the creature's last gasp attack, but Bear quelled my fear as he blasted it in half with the shotgun.

In less than a minute the battle was over. The demons had melted into nonexistence. The men were still alive, writhing and flopping like animated mannequins. One of the men still clutched a gun, firing it uncontrollably and screaming. Bear hobbled over to him and raised the staff above the man's head. The man's eyes continually flashed between the blackness of a demon, and the humanness of bright blue. Both shades were chockfull of hate.

"I'm doing you a favor," said Bear. He drove the staff into the man's head with a sickening crunch. "The brain, man, always the brain."

Oliver approached the other and pointed his gun. But, an aura suddenly erupted from him, bursting with colors.

"Wait," I said. "Before you pop him."

"What's on your mind?" said Bear.

"Yeah," said Oliver. "You're taking all the fun out of this."

I went to the thrashing man and squatted next to him. I looked into his eyes and saw them turn to a normal brownish color. I touched his forehead and felt an immediate jolt of energy as his thoughts and emotions struck me. He was communicating with me.

He has my daughter, stop him, God, please stop him! I felt his anguish and torment as if it were my own, as I lived the man's last few hours in a matter of minutes. I knew his name was Eddie, he worked at the co-op, he has an eight-year-old daughter named Sharla, and a beautiful wife named Dean Anne. Buddy stole their beloved daughter two days ago, and Eddie suspected something was wrong about Buddy-boy. He followed him here last night, reckless with anger and revenge, which worked against him and got him beaten and captured. Tied up to a chair and defeated, he was forced to look upon his daughter in a cage, all the while Buddy told him what was in store for her. He told him in detail of what he would do to her. What others would do.

In clear view of his dear, sweet Sharla, Buddy began carving symbols into Eddie's flesh, cutting brutishly and deeply. Buddy then began to recite strange words from an old book, and cast a demon into Eddie that inflicted constant mental and emotional pain upon him. The force was too powerful to fight, as it possessed him fully, rendering him to nothing more than wounded flesh to do the demon's bidding.

Kill me! Set me free!

"Eddie, we'll find her, and I'll kill Buddy," I told him. "We'll make all of this right." I brought the dagger down with both hands into his temple, burying it deep. A cold wind shrieked and spun in the basement, and something dark left Eddie's mouth. It was in the form of mist and quickly dissipated in the Holy power of the dagger's light.

"Did you know this guy?" said Bear.

"No." I felt wetness on my cheeks and wiped them dry with my shirt sleeve. "But, the little girl in there is his daughter."

"How do you know that?" he said.

"I don't know. He somehow told me."

"You were stuck in a crying jag there for a minute," said Oliver. "We couldn't get you to snap out of it. In fact, you didn't seem...all there until after you jammed the dagger in, uh, Eddie's head."

"It was horrible," I said. "I felt his sadness, and his shame at not being able to help Sharla."

"Sharla?" said Oliver.

"Yeah." I got to my feet, feeling determined and stirred up. "His daughter's name."

"You had another vision," said Bear.

"I don't know if that's what it was or not, but we need to get going."

Oliver held up an index finger, and then covered his mouth with his other hand. "Wait, I've—oh shit."

He vomited onto Bear's boots, spitting and spraying. "Shit, sorry. My stomach is not..."

"It's the tomatoes," I said.

"Yeah, I know *why*," said Bear. "But it doesn't make me feel any better about being puked on."

Oliver bent over and hung his tongue out. "Fuck me. Shit, sorry brother."

"It's better than being shit on, I suppose," said Bear. "By the way, don't shit on me."

Oliver shook his head and stood upright. He started to say something but stopped and stared into space.

I snapped my finger in front of his face. "La-la land."

His eyes began to focus. "Thanks."

Bear pointed to the cave entrance, and then looked down at dead Eddie. "Let's go. Let's get this poor son of a bitch's little girl out of here."

I took the lead and started toward the cave. I stopped just short of entering, and then turned around to face my fellow warriors. "Time to go cold."

Chapter Twenty-Six

A Deal Is Made

WE ENTERED THE cave and found it to be narrow and confining, with less than six feet of available headspace. An obvious inconvenience to Bear. The cramped conditions also forced us to walk single-file, a situation that made the men nervous. "Luke, give me the dagger and get behind Bear," said Oliver. "I don't like us being lined up like this. We're sitting ducks."

"I can handle it," I said.

"No doubt of that," said Bear. "But, with us being the grownups in this fucked up situation, we'd feel better if you were better protected from a frontal attack."

"And, with Bear's leg all jacked up we can better protect him," said Oliver.

"Oh, shut up," said Bear.

I glanced back at Bear. He was hunkered over and bent, utilizing the staff as a makeshift leg. He was big and bad, and was flying high on homegrown tomatoes, but his injury left him woefully less than one hundred percent.

"All right." I handed over the dagger and squeezed my way to the back. "That staff is more than just a big stick," I said to Bear. "It clobbers demons pretty good."

"Good to know," he said.

"Luke, how far back does the light travel?" said Oliver.

We had only travelled twenty yards or so, and the light did not reach the cave entrance. But there was plenty enough to keep the rear secured from creeping demons. Unfortunately, the light would not deter or wound the human type of evil, unless possessed of a demon. I would have to keep a close watch.

"This is strange, having so damned many demons out and about," said Bear.

"I would hope that just having *one* of these assholes running around would be strange," said Oliver. "Or at the very least, worrisome."

"And I'm seeing weird shit," I said.

Bear stopped and rubbed his leg above the break. "Weird shit?"

"Are you all right?" I said.

"Yeah, man. Still high as a kite, and pain free," he said. "But, back to you—what do you mean *weird* shit?"

"I'm seeing auras, and I can see in the dark."

"It's your new blood. Whatever is the cause of so many demons, is also affecting you."

"Oh, that's Buddy," I said. "He's got a book, and he's using it to conjure."

"How do you know that?"

"Eddie showed me."

"You mean during your *Vulcan* mind-meld thing," said Oliver.

"Yep."

"This sounds crazy, but I hope Buddy knows what he's doing," said Bear. "Because if he's winging it, and just spouting shit out of a spell book...well, he could lose control."

"What would happen if he lost control?" I said.

"Oh, he could open up a portal to Hell."

"Well, I'm gonna' go out on a limb and say that's probably not a good thing," said Oliver. "So, what would the ramifications be if such a thing occurred?"

"Off the cuff, I'd say that it would allow demonic entities to come and go as they please. This particular bit of countryside would be terrorized with madness, murders, and failed crops."

"So, you've dealt with this before?" said Oliver.

"On a small scale. It was on my first trip to New Orleans, Mr. Bird was with me."

"How'd that turn out?" said Oliver. "Or, do I *really* need to know?"

Bear paused a moment before answering. "We got the gate closed."

A sound from behind drew my attention. I turned and pointed my gun into the dark.

"What is it, Luke?" said Bear.

"I heard something."

"Fire a few rounds, see what happens," said Oliver.

I popped off two and waited for a response, but nothing explosive or dramatic occurred. The only thing that changed was my ears were now ringing, and held the sensation of being stuffed with cotton.

"Save your ammo, and save our hearing," said Bear. "Damn, that shit is loud."

"If I'm reading your lips correctly, I agree," said Oliver. "My fuckup. Probably not a good idea to fire a weapon in here...unless needed."

We kept moving forward, and I kept glancing back, spooked and wary. I didn't hear anything—*couldn't* hear anything—but thought I was seeing subtle movement in the dark. Turns out, I was right.

THE CAVE ELEMENTS soon gave way to actual constructed hallways with wooden flooring and concrete walls. Torches wavered with flames that were nearly invisible against the dagger's light. It was less cramped, allowing for Bear to stand fully upright, and for us to not be so huddled.

"Does this look familiar, Luke?" said Bear.

"Yep." It wasn't the exact location, but I knew we were getting close. I could feel their presence growing nearer, which allowed me the ease of knowing they must still be alive. "We need to keep going, we're getting closer."

"Any sort of a vision trying to happen?" he said.

"I don't think so." I closed my eyes, hoping one would hit me, but I scrapped the idea after a quick moment. Visions found me, not the other way around.

"We've got a door," said Oliver.

It was to our left and made of metal, with a bean hole for passing food, and was secured with a wooden slide lock. Oliver moved the dagger close to the door and looked inside the slotted hole.

"Anything newsworthy?" said Bear.

"Take a look at this," said Oliver.

I moved ahead of Bear and peered into the hole. What I saw was shocking, but not out of the blue—I wasn't expecting to see a pile of frolicking kittens rolling around with a ball of yarn.

"What the fuck is it?" said Bear.

"Piles of human limbs," said Oliver.

"*Small* limbs," I added.

An angry grimace passed over Bear's face. "I don't need to see that shit."

I again heard something to the rear of us. "Guys, something's back there."

Oliver moved toward me and signaled for me to stay. "I'll check it out, hang loose a minute," he said.

"No." I knew who was back there, or rather *what* was back there. "She wants me, not you."

"Uh, she who?" said Oliver.

I was now able to see her, despite the deep darkness she was shrouded in. Her evil darkness glowed and shimmered like water beneath a full moon. She was staying beyond the light, watching us. Watching me. "Lilith."

"Say what?" said Bear.

"Yeah, it's her."

"Wait, she's the one who bit you…right?" said Oliver. "Isn't she a demon or something?"

I started walking to the darkness. "Yep, that's right."

"Luke, you need to stop," said Bear. He hobbled after me, moving quite well for a man who fifteen minutes ago had a leg bone jutting through his skin.

"I'll be all right."

"Bullshit," said Oliver. "Sorry, brother. But we can't let you go into the dark without us."

"I promise you, I'll be fine."

"No—"

"I won't harm a single pubic hair on his body," said Lilith, in her intoxicating voice.

Bear and Oliver were instantly affected by her smoky tone. They both stood slack-jawed, looking drugged. Finally, Oliver said. "She sounds so horny, man."

"She's Hell's whore," said Bear.

"I am the Queen of Fucking," she said. "And yes, I am *always* horny. If you'll put down that silly knife and come to me, I'll show you."

They were again silenced by her charms.

I said, "Don't listen to her. Hang onto that dagger super-tight, Oliver." They didn't appear to be as severely afflicted with her charms as Ruckus, or the old man from the store. I was sure the dagger helped to dull her full power, and I was certain she would dearly love to somehow acquire it. It was a potent weapon against her kind, and was also the cause of the blight upon her beauty. She was no doubt plenty pissed. And me, being an idiot, had decided to walk straight to her.

"No way are you doing this," said Oliver dreamily.

I continued to walk from the shelter of the light. "Guys I need to see what the hell she wants, and you'll be safe as long as you stay in the light."

"Luke," said Lilith. "You know what I want."

Yeah, I knew what she wanted. She wanted me in a psychosexual, perverted way. That was no secret. But a gut feeling was letting me know there was something else that warranted the risk of meeting her head on.

I ran into the dark knowing Bear would not be able to keep up with me, and Oliver would not leave his pal without the protection of the light. "I'll be back, I promise." I hoped.

I reached the cramped area of the tunnel and felt her presence before I actually saw her. Meaning, my groin area was excited with blood, and my old bite wound was tingling.

"Luke, my pretty, pretty boy." She was suddenly before me, looking more beautiful and entrancing than ever before. She was naked and had her hand between her legs, rubbing gently, moaning. Her alabaster skin shone like the moon itself in the stark darkness, lending even more sensuality. And her mystical, magical hair writhed and moved over her body, caressing her like a lover.

My heart sped up, and my breathing became labored. And, my erection felt capable of breaking bricks.

"What do you want?" I said in a winded voice. "To hurt my friends?"

She quickly closed the space between us, standing inches away from me. Unlike other demons, she carried a scent that was pleasant and intoxicating. It made me want to kiss her neck and lick her all over. "What do *you* want, Luke? Hmm?" She smiled wickedly and then flicked her black, serpent's tongue. "Let me answer that for you; you want to stick your cock inside of me."

Yes, I certainly did.

"No," I said, closing my eyes. "I want to know why you're here."

I heard a rattling from behind her and a small growling sound. I glanced past her and saw the little boy with the asshole attitude. He was in a small cage shaking the bars with his little hands and glaring poison-tipped arrows at me.

"Why does he hate everyone?" I said. "I mean, what's

wrong with him?"

Lilith moved to the boy and stroked his head, which seemed to calm him somewhat. "He was bred from hate, and there is nothing wrong with him. The Master believes him to be perfect." She then bent over and spread herself open for me to see. "Want a taste?"

I had to turn away. I felt close to losing control. "Lilith, please answer my question."

She walked back to me, looking pleased. Again, she almost had her flesh pressed against me. "Luke, you said my name."

"Haven't I said it before?" My throat was dry, causing my voice to click as I spoke.

"Not like this. This time you sounded as if you might have a care about me. It's making me wet." She knelt down in front of me and leaned back, spreading her legs. "If it weren't for you and me sharing the same blood, you would have already succumbed to my power. You're stronger because of it."

I was dizzy with desire and on the edge of jumping between her thighs. I wasn't sure if my new blood would be enough for much longer.

"I'll tell you why I'm here...besides the obvious reasons of wanting you to fuck me. The Master is not happy with what Buddy has done, and he needs this situation amended."

I assumed the *Master* was the devil, which was easy. "The devil isn't happy with what happened to the kids?"

She threw her head back and laughed. "The Master has no issue with his actions toward the children. No, very much to the contrary—he is ecstatic with glee in that regard."

"Then what?" A surge of anger arose in me, momentarily distracting me from Lilith's sexual guile.

"Buddy has become reckless and has created a doorway between our two realms."

"I don't know why the devil would think that's bad."

"Because the devil has control over this world, not that silly, pitiful mortal mispronouncing spells and incantations. It's wrecking the principalities of Hell."

"I don't get it."

"You're so pretty," she said, smiling. "It means there are gatekeepers in Hell, high ranking demons, who are responsible for dispatching specific and lesser demons for...tasks. A rank and file of sorts. But, if these demons are loose and rampant then no plan can be set in motion." She tightened her thighs around her probing hands, and began squirming around on the floor, breathing heavily. She wasn't the only heavy breather. I felt myself becoming more aroused.

"Stop that shit!" I started to loathe myself for giving in to her allure. I dug for the memories of what she looked like beyond her beauty facade, recalling her reptilian monster features. It began to work, but not as easily as one might think. Not when she was in this current state of magnificence.

She sucked on her fingers and then stood up, smiling mischievously. A pair of elongated, scabby arms appeared from the dark and placed a shimmering, black cloak around her. As soon as her body was wrapped, the mysterious arms zipped back into the dark. "I'll finish myself off later."

I was instantly relieved as she turned off her charms and hid her splendid body. It allowed for me to think clearly and to catch my breath. And of course, to soothe and quell my throbbing discomfort. "Lilith, why are you telling me this stuff?"

"Because the devil wants Buddy dead, and out of the way. You can help by handling the task yourself."

"That was already my plan."

"But, you've now the assistance of Hell, which is a guarantee of ultimate victory."

"I don't need any help." It was a prideful lie, of course. I needed help, but not from Hell. I had Oliver and

Bear to back me up, and I was willing to travel the entire road with them. Win, or lose.

"The big one, Bear," she said. "He's barely able to walk. And the other one is just one man, and he's haunted by his past tonight. He will break, I promise you."

"Never."

The little boy became agitated again and began to shake his cage like a wild animal. He bared his teeth at me and reached through the bars. "That kid's a butthole, but I still feel sorry for him," I said.

Lilith once again calmed the boy, scratching him behind his ears as if he were a pet dog. "Do not feel pity for him. He would rip your throat out if given the chance."

I didn't doubt her.

"How do you plan on closing the gate to Hell?" she said, as she continued stroking the boy's ears. "The big man is right, in regards to the repercussions of leaving it open. The creatures will spread, and they will cause much mayhem."

"Bear will know what to do." At least I hoped so. My primary concern, thus far, had been aimed toward the children. A doorway to Hell was a new pain in the ass.

She threw her head back and laughed. "Mm, so pretty."

"He's not new to this. He knows a lot."

"Stop being so stupid, Luke. It's a turn off." She sat on the boy's cage and surprisingly crossed her legs. "He's never dealt with *this*. Not even old man Bird has trod down this path before, so don't be *stupid*. If you really have a shit's worth of care for your ragtag band of friends, then you'll shut the fuck up and listen to me."

My pride was stung from being spoken to in such a manner, but I readily, if not begrudgingly, agreed to listen to what she had to offer. Circumstances had changed, a trend that I feared would continue. And, most importantly, I didn't want any more harm heaped upon Oliver and Bear. Yet, on the other hand, I was speaking to a demon. A being full of lies and malicious intent. "You threatened to hurt my friends when I was visiting Crone. I don't think I can trust you."

"I certainly do not wish good fortune and health upon your pathetic associates. You are correct, handsome boy. But the situation has, for the moment, changed. If I can use your...love for them to help me, then I will not hesitate. I'm a selfish bitch, I know."

"What do I have to do?"

"Well, it's simple in a way."

"Okay..."

"You have to retrieve the spell book from Buddy, after you've killed him. And then you hand it to Paimon."

"Who's Paimon?"

"Paimon is not nearly as frightful as The Master. He runs most matters in Hell and is currently suffering the wrath of The Master due to this chaos. So, I would expect he'd lend a helping hand if needed."

"How would I get him the book?"

"Once it's in your hands, he will appear, and you will simply hand it over to him."

Too damn tidy. "What do you want?"

"To be in the good graces of Hell."

"Why don't *you,* or one your freaks, get the book from him?"

"Because Buddy is inside a protective circle. Our kind cannot reach him." She adjusted the mask on her face and smirked. "Meaning *our* kind. *You.*"

"I'm not like your kind."

"Maybe not fully pedigreed, but you have my substance in your veins."

"Then, how am I going to enter the protective thingy?"

"Circle. Protective *circle*. And you probably won't be able to, but your friends...they certainly can."

"What about the kids?" The children sprang to the front of my brain. I wondered if this was all a ploy to hinder us in reaching them. "Are they all right? Lilith—"

"They're safe, locked away in their cages. Buddy wouldn't dare leave his protected area to get at the children, and we are not to touch the little ones."

"So, how is it you're helping us?"

"Paimon will close the gate and destroy the remaining demons and imps. This is no small favor."

"Luke, we're coming for you!" It was Oliver.

"Hang on," I said. "I'll be right there."

"Screw that shit, buddy," he said.

Lilith backed away, and her unseen helper dragged the cage farther into the dark. "Buddy has more of his brutes scattered down here. I'll personally see to it that they will cause you no trouble, which will clear the path for rich success. Otherwise, I fear the alternative will be assured deaths for Oliver and Bear. You are outnumbered down here. Buddy and his little coven had big plans until everything went awry. Quite a gathering."

I didn't see any other recourse. The three of us would either die down here, or we wouldn't. Priority one was getting the boy and girl to safety, and if that entailed getting help from a horny demon then so be it. "Screw it," I said, sighing. "Okay, I'll do it if you do your part."

Lilith said, "I look forward to it." She blurred into the murk, and was gone.

"Luke!" Bear sounded nervous.

"I'm right here," I said.

The light found me before they did, and I fell to my knees, basking in its cleansing purity. Tears ran from my eyes, as I was cleansed of my contamination from being so close to Lilith. She was cold and harsh, with a blackened heart devoid of love or compassion. I took comfort in realizing that my heart must have something worthwhile to offer, otherwise, the dagger's glow would have been wounding me instead of cleansing and protecting. Because, I too, am demon. Even if not *pedigreed*.

Oliver got down next to me and looked into my eyes.

"Hey, man, you all right?"

I looked at the two of them, relieved and thankful to be in their presence. "I am now, dudes."

"What happened?" said Bear.

"Nothing happened," I said. "But she told me you were right about Buddy screwing up and opening a doorway."

"She told you this? Why would she do that?" he said.

I told them of the reasons she offered, and of the agreement I'd made. They were rightfully skeptical. But, they also didn't see the harm in accepting a helping hand.

"If she's willing to take out Buddy's goons for us, then cool beans," said Oliver. "It'll make things easier, but I think it would be wise to assume that she's full of shit."

"Nobody's in Hell for telling the truth, or for good behavior," said Bear.

"Yeah, she ain't a girl scout." My mind flashed to her sexual antics. "Definitely not."

"Then, shall we continue?" said Oliver.

"We're waiting for you to start walking," I said.

Oliver took the lead, and we followed him deeper into the tunnel, and, quite literally, into Hell.

Chapter Twenty-Seven

Charlie Bronson Ain't Here

THE TUNNELS WERE quiet and absent of roaming demons. It was nice, but we knew it was the quiet before the storm. And, sure enough, the stillness was interrupted with a strange harmony of music.

It had the sound of screeching violins and mad wind instruments being played out of tune. And instead of background vocals, the sound of moaning and screams. It gave me a bad vibe.

"Where's that coming from?" said Bear.

Oliver stuck his fingers in his ears. "Up ahead. The tunnel bends to the right, so that must be where it's coming from."

"It's making me crazy." It was insane asylum music.

"Yeah, it's fucking weird," said Oliver.

Bear cupped his hands around his mouth. "It's music from Hell."

Oliver agreed. "Yeah, I get it. It sounds like shit."

"No, I mean is it's actual music from Hell. The devil doesn't create music; he perverts it just as he does everything else."

A vision took charge of me, feeling like it was searing a blister on my brain. I saw Sharla and the little boy in their cages. They were terrified and bunched into a corner, as spectacularly frightful demons circled them. The monsters were agitated at their powerlessness to attack the children and tore at their own flesh and began eating it in frustration. I saw women and men run screaming as Lilith ripped open locked doors to allow the creatures access to them. Apparently, they had sought shelter when Buddy let things get out of hand and were hiding in rooms that were usually intended for the abuse of children. Some of the demons raped the women and the men, before tearing into their intestines and gobbling the goodies. And ole Buddy-boy's eyes were huge with fear, as he cowered and cried inside his protective circle, clutching the book of spells.

I pushed the scene from my mind and took control of my thoughts. "Buddy's right where we want him."

"You had a vision, didn't you?" said Bear.

"Yeah."

"We thought so. You stopped in your tracks, and your eyes rolled up in your head," he said.

"It was either that or you were having an epileptic seizure," said Oliver.

"How long was I like that?"

"A few minutes," said Oliver. "You good now?"

"Yep, let's go," I said. "But brace yourselves, man. Some trippy shit is going down."

Oliver upped the pace. "Trippier than what we've already seen?"

"Uh, it's pretty bad."

"I can hardly wait."

Bear's wounded gait was much more pronounced. If the pain was affecting someone as tough as him, then it must have been plenty bad.

"Here." I handed him my last tomato. "This'll help."

"You should hang on to it for yourself," he said. "You might need it."

"I've got to agree with Luke on this," said Oliver. "You're the badass here, and we might need your badass skills. I'll keep the kid within the dagger's range, or let him hang onto it if it's needed."

Bear ate the tomato without objection and appeared to feel the effects in no time. So much, that he began to move without a limp. "This shit is amazing, man. Oh, wow. The dust in here looks like little birds, floating—"

"Like I said, we need you. So, try not to join your little bird friends and fly away on us," said Oliver.

"I'm flying, but I ain't goin' anywhere."

We rounded the bend almost running and were hit head on by the crazy music and the stench of demons. Oliver drew away from it, gagging. "Shit, give me a sec."

We were nearly upon the portal. "C'mon Oliver," I said, even though I was bent over and retching.

"I smell lots of blood," said Bear. "Like buckets of it, dudes."

Olive regained his stomach and kept us moving until we came to a widening of the tunnel that entered into a cavernous room, with a pit as long as a football field, and thirty feet deep. There were numerous rooms lining the area above, set in a circular pattern, with most of the doors missing or hanging from damaged hinges. Looking down, we were able to see numerous cages and burning torches. And, of course, Buddy, wide-eyed and jabbering like an idiot in the middle of his protective circle. It was similar to the Crone's, but it had some differing symbols scattered in it. I knew next to nothing when it came to such things, but it was easy to see that it was doing the trick, as the rest of his group were not fairing so well.

Oliver stood at the opening, clearly shocked at what he was seeing. It was a sight that one did not forget. "Oh, my God. That man is being gangbanged by…oh my God."

"Wow, man. Brother, you weren't kidding when you said it was trippy," said Bear. He then pointed into the pit. "I see the kids."

I followed his finger and saw them as well. They were about ten feet away from Buddy, balled up together with their heads hidden from the evil that surrounded them. I shouted to them. "Sharla! We're coming!" She heard me and dared to peek her head up. But, she didn't see us. Not with all that was going on around her.

There were two sets of metal stairs that led into the frightening scene below us. We chose the set closest to the children and hastily made our way in that direction, staying tightly within the dagger's light. The demons scattered and ran to the darkened areas, or they got caught in the glow and suffered and burned. We reached the staircase with no resistance and began our descent. My heart was pounding with anxiety as we got closer to the kids. "Hang on, Sharla!"

She again looked up and, again, she did not see us.

"Holy shit, look at that," said Oliver.

We felt the portal as it emanated a powerful dark power, and then we saw it. It was beneath the area we entered through, and it was a whirlpool of glowing darkness. The familiar black mist was rolling from it and then spilling onto the floor of the pit. I was able to see the inhabitants of the mist. They were creatures with a multitude of eyes and needle teeth.

I noticed Oliver had stopped and was staring into the portal. "Don't look at it, Oliver," I said.

He didn't respond.

"Oliver, stop looking at it!" Bear looked ready to belt him.

Oliver wavered, looking as if he would tumble down the remaining steps. He then shook his head and looked around, as if he was just now arriving. "Whoa, whoa, whoa," he said. "I'm cool, holy shit. I'm cool."

"Are you sure?" said Bear.

"Yeah." He brought the dagger to his lips and kissed it. "It almost had me, man. Weird thoughts…but the dagger stopped them, but I'm not sure how."

"I'm the one who's high," said Bear. "I'm the only one allowed a bad trip."

Buddy spotted us and screamed at me. "*You!* What the fuck are *you* doing here?"

"We came to kill your sorry ass, Buddy!" I had to shout, because the volume of the insane music had reached a rock concert level, and the wailing of the demons only added to the awful sound.

Buddy laughed, but it was the laughter of the insane.

We hurried to the bottom of the stairwell and ran to the kids—all of us doing our best to stay within the confines of the dagger's radiance. "Sharla," I said, waving my arms.

She looked up and this time, she saw us. "Stay away from us, just please stay away."

"We're here to help you," said Bear. "We're getting you out of here."

Buddy ran toward us, full bore, screaming and spraying saliva. "She's mine! Stay away!"

Everything went red for me. Oliver, Bear, and the kids. Red. It wasn't the good red, it was the *rage* red. And it enveloped everything within my sight, ebbing and glowing. And the music became dulled, as if it were in another room made of cotton. I left the protecting light and ran toward Buddy. He had to pay for his damage.

To reach him I had to climb a podium staircase, which I did with ease. I moved with speed that was unnatural and new to me. I initially had my gun drawn, but I tucked it away. I wanted to kill him with my bare hands. I leaped for him with clenched fists.

A foolish decision, looking back.

His protection was a sledgehammer to my midsection. I was thrown backward, and into the dirt. Too much demon in me to get past the barrier.

They rushed to me, and Bear said, "That looked like a bad deal."

My whole body felt sore and tingly, and I was dizzy. "I'm such a dumbass."

"Buddy isn't going anywhere," said Bear. "Let's concentrate on getting the kids out of here."

I had let my disgust of Buddy overshadow the wellbeing of the children. "You're right. I'm sorry."

"Don't worry about it," he said. "Are you all right?"

"Yeah, I'm cool." The madness of the aura had left me, and I was able to concentrate on matters at hand. I placed Buddy on the backburner for the time being.

Oliver used the dagger to bang on a massive padlock that hung from the children's cage. It took a single blow to bust it loose, and for the door to swing open. He reached for the kids, pleading with them to come to him. "Sharla, right? It's okay, we're not going to hurt you. I'm a cop."

Sharla spoke through a choked voice. "So is *he.*" She pointed at Buddy.

"Well, I'm not like him. I am the opposite of him, and I promise you that we'll make Buddy pay for everything that he's done." He held his hand out to her, willing her to take it. She latched onto it, and he pulled her and the boy from the cage. Their eyes were blank with fear as they looked upon the horrible creatures that surrounded us. Oliver understood their fear. He too was afraid. "If you stay in the light, you'll be okay," he said. "Do you understand?"

Sharla nodded her head, but, it was obvious the boy's mind had escaped to some other place. A place, I assumed, where monsters were mere shadows mixed with imagination. A place in which, the monster in the closet was nothing more than a disheveled winter coat, hanging awkwardly from its hanger.

"Okay, so now we snag the book from shithead, right?" said Bear.

Oliver and I looked around at the mass of evil beings that had us surrounded and outnumbered. Each one enraged and frustrated that they couldn't get to us. They crawled over one another, staring intently at us, growling wickedly. "If we're going to keep our end of the deal, yes," said Oliver.

"I don't think it's a good idea to renege," I said. "That would be...bad, I'm thinking."

"I'm with you on that," said Bear. "So, let's do this and get it done." He pointed at Oliver and me. "Oliver, stay with the kids. Luke, don't be a dumbass. I've got this. I'll get the damn book."

"We need to stay together," I said. "You'll be out of the light." Demons were crowding us, growing bolder. I began to wonder if one of them could do any of us damage. Maybe, if one were able to ignore the agony of the light for a split second, before exploding into flames...

"Hey man," said Oliver. "This ain't a Charlie Bronson flick, right?"

"You're right" said Bear. "Bronson would have already shit his pants." Without notice or inclination, Bear sprang toward Buddy. He climbed the short steps in quick fashion—busted leg or not—narrowly escaping hideous claws and snapping teeth. He let loose with an impressive war cry, just as Buddy pulled a pistol and shot him. Blood burst through the back of Bear's right shoulder, but he didn't slow down. He continued his momentum and leaped in the air with a kick that connected with Buddy's chest. It sent him sprawling to the edge of his protective circle. The book and the gun were no longer in his hands. They were both lying in the dirt.

Bear took an end of the staff and pressed it against Buddy's chest.

Buddy looked shocked. "What's happening? Who are you people? And that kid...what's your fuckin' deal?"

"Do it, man." I felt cheated. It should have been me up there.

Bear kicked the gun away and grabbed the book. "I have a better idea."

"Just *do* it already," said Oliver. "I mean, you've been shot—you *do* know this, right? And, I'm tired of this loud-ass music, and these fucking demons."

Bear looked down at his bullet wound. It was bleeding, but not gushing. "Oh, yeah." He snatched Buddy by the foot and began dragging him.

"You ain't got a clue Injun-boy," said Buddy, in an excited squealy voice. "This is bigger than anything you can imagine. You're a stupid, blanket-ass, piece of shit. We're everywhere, I mean fucking *everywhere*." He started laughing and couldn't stop. It wasn't exactly a fun-filled laugh, though. Not punchline laughter. It was crazy laughter.

Bear deftly broke Buddy's ankle with a quick, little twist. When Buddy opened his fat mouth to scream, he shoved the end of the staff into it. Just hard enough to snap his teeth, and create a thick flow of blood.

"Kill him!" It was Sharla.

"I'm gonna' let *them* have the honors," said Bear.

"Them?" said Oliver.

"Yeah," said Bear. "Them." He pointed to several areas that were thick with demons.

"Do this now, damn it," said Oliver.

With the tiniest effort, Bear threw Buddy in the air. The monsters were on him before he hit the ground. They gibbered and growled as they ripped off his clothes and raped him.

"Holy shit, hide the kids' eyes," said Bear. "Damn, I didn't see that comin."

Oliver wrapped his arms around the kids and buried their heads against his chest. He nodded. "Neither did Buddy."

It was a punishment none of us would have dished out, or thought of. But it was suitable and satisfying, as long as he died during the process.

Bear jumped from the circle, resembling a comic book hero as he landed and rolled to his feet next to us—again he showed no signs of effect from his injured leg. He handed me the book, frowning. "Where's Paimon?"

"I have no idea." I didn't know what to expect, now that we'd held up our end of the agreement. Time had slowed to dripping molasses and to wait much longer would be near impossible. It was too claustrophobic, the music was maddening and, of course, we had to get the kids above ground.

"We've got to get these kids out of here," said Oliver. "I get that we need to shut the portal, but we can come back."

I eyeballed Bear's gunshot wound. "You're bleeding, too."

"I feel fine," he said. "It was a through and through shot, and the tomato is doing its job."

"It won't for long." I glanced down at his leg, shuddering. "*That* is going to hurt like a bitch."

Oliver held up his arm. "He's right. My arm is beginning to throb."

The portal quickly changed from dark to multicolored, turning the murk psychedelic, and the music's volume ticked higher. Cymbals and trumpets joined the mix of atrocious sounds. Then drums. And not a single note was on key, or in rhythm. It was creepy and gnawing.

The demons were now pulling off Buddy's arms and legs.

"Hide their eyes," said Bear, pointing to the kids.

A trumpet blast escalated above the current din of noise, and then several demons entered from the portal. Each had a musical instrument in hand and moved in odd, jerky movements. They appeared more human than the rest, having the same size and build. They wore matching black uniforms that sported top hats, tux, and tails. Yet, there was no mistaking them for anything more than disgusting demons. Their eyes were too big, and they had no whites to their eyes. Just shiny blackness.

And surely, no human was capable of playing an instrument so badly.

"Please, use your damn shotgun and kill those fuckers," said Oliver. "I seriously believe I'll lose my mind if I have to listen to this shit anymore."

The music abruptly stopped as another figure emerged from the portal. It wore a crown filled with gems and was riding a camel. "I am Paimon."

Chapter Twenty-Eight

Shovels, Pricks and Rope

PAIMON APPEARED HUMAN, having an effeminate face and voice, despite having an obviously male form. His blacked out eyes confirmed his evil deity.

"I'd always heard you were difficult to understand when you spoke," said Bear.

"Normally that is the case," said Paimon. "But, I was not conjured. I am here of my own accord, due to this unfortunate chaos."

"So, Luke gives you the book and what?" said Bear. "You shut the door to Hell, and everyone goes home?"

"Yes."

"Why do you need the book?" said Oliver.

"To keep it from the hands of fools." Paimon waved his arms over the drooling creatures. "Buddy wasn't meant to open the book, let alone attempt to conjure. He stole it from his master, thinking he would be able to summon a personal demon to do his biddings. However, he was an idiotic buffoon and truly unworthy of seeing the words."

"Who's his master?" said Oliver.

"Ah, always the detective," said Paimon. "But, unless conjured, I am not obliged to indulge you with answers. So, let's move this along."

"That's not fair, you know," said Oliver. "Apparently, you know something about me, but I don't know anything about you."

"Summon me some time, and I'll dispense many mysteries to you. Otherwise, please gently piss off."

Oliver just shook his head. I figured it was a smart move on his part to *gently piss off*, so we could conduct our business and get the hell out of there.

I eyed the book for the first time, studying it. The cover was leather with glyphic symbols.

"You like books, Luke," said Paimon. "Correct?"

I loved books. I had a paperback library in my closet at the farm. They were Louis L'amour westerns and Mickey Spillane mysteries. Nothing as dark as this shit. "Yep."

"Then I find it strange that you've not read your grandfather's book. In the end, it's a part of your legacy."

"Why do you give a shit about Luke's legacy?" said Bear.

"I don't actually give a shit. But, as one who holds a vast library of books that contain secrets and mysteries of the universe, I would think that his grandfather's book would hold many answers, and secrets." Paimon trotted his camel toward us, pushing demons out of his path. He stopped several feet short of the dagger's glow. "If you're not interested in reading it yourself, I know of particular parties who would gladly take it from your charge."

"Who?" I said.

Paimon wagged his finger. "Tsk, tsk, you should know better than to ask by now."

I held the book out to him. "This is the only book I'm giving up."

He daintily pointed to the dagger in Oliver's hand and moved his camel back a few feet. "Despite me being more powerful than any demon you've thus far encountered, I am not invulnerable. That dagger—the one that none of you have a trace of information about—is a weapon that could do me serious injury. So, I shall not be entering your huddled mass of purity." He waved at the kids and winked.

I tossed the book at the feet of the camel, which happened to be standing in a juicy pile of human intestines. The book plopped onto the mess and slid to the rear of the animal.

Paimon slipped a long, slender instrument from a scabbard that hung from his saddle. It had three prongs at the end, which he used to stab a pale demon with. He thrust it into the back of its head, igniting a show of excited wiggling and thrashing. Kind of like a grasshopper on a fishhook.

He guided the creature to the book, forcing it to retrieve it. "Many thanks." Paimon then drove the device through the creature's mouth and twisted its head off. He held it up for display. "Something for the den, perhaps?"

"No thanks," said Oliver. "I've barely got room for my bigmouth bass."

Paimon laughed heartily, which was in sharp contrast to his feminine characteristics. "Inspector, it's good that you have a sense of humor. You'll need it." He rocked back in his saddle and laughed some more. "Hell be fucked, I'll break a rule today—Oliver, there is a demon that wishes to do great harm to you. I'm sure you know of the one I speak."

"I'd say there's more than one." Oliver pointed out the collection that surrounded us.

"Amen there, brother," said Bear.

"Yes, but this little devil is far different from these brutish creatures. It's devious, and is a creative bastard. It even tried to set fire to…" Paimon pointed upward. "*His* kingdom. It was an act that strongly contributed to the rest of my kind being cast out."

"Well, what can you say except that he's an asshole," said Oliver.

Paimon grinned. "He is a demon of second rank, with a strong spirit and a destructive nature…and yes, he is quite the asshole."

Oliver pointed the dagger at Paimon and took a small step in his direction. "The talk has been nice and all, but it's time for you to take your freaky cousins back to Hell with you."

Paimon nodded to us and raised his hands in the air. "You beasts have had your fun, but it is now time to leave." He moved his hands in odd gestures and then turned and entered the portal. Upon his heels arrived a howling draw of wind that began pulling the demons back to Hell, bouncing and rolling them like gruesome tumbleweeds. I also felt the pull and feared we would be sucked into Hell alongside the demons.

"Get going up those stairs," said Bear.

Oliver led the way, with the kids clinging to him as he hunkered down low and moved up the steps. I stayed as close to them as I could, trying to keep the kids on their feet. Bear had my back.

"We're almost done," said Bear.

I nodded, but I didn't want to curse us by being cocky. We were still in a bad place.

"It gets better as we get higher," said Oliver. "The wind isn't as strong."

"Is it clear behind us?" I said to Bear.

"We're good, don't worry."

"Hey, Bear," I said.

"Yeah."

"How are we getting out of the basement?"

Bear chuckled and slapped me on the back. "Anyone ever told you that you think too much?"

"Yep, they have."

"They were right. Don't worry about it, we'll figure it out."

"It's kind of a deep basement is all I'm saying, and we don't have a ladder."

"Hey, Luke," said Oliver.

"Yeah?"

"You think about too much shit."

It seemed a perfectly logical concern to me, but I let it go to the wayside and concentrated on getting the kids someplace safe. And, it eventually paid off. We made it to the top.

As we scurried to the tunnel, I looked down into the pit. It was not much more than a glance, but I could see that most of the demons were gone. Only a few were left, and they were vainly clinging to rocks in an attempt to survive.

We entered the tunnel to freedom, relieved and thankful that we were still alive.

The tunnel seemed more cramped than before, but I knew it was anxiety brought on by being so close to the end. I longed for the openness that was outside this underground horror, and it was taking too long to get there. "Man, I can't wait to smell some fresh air," I said.

"What, you don't like subterranean demon stench?" said Bear.

"Nope."

"I'm with you there," said Oliver.

"Hey Oliver," said Bear.

"Yeah?"

"I'm curious as to what you thought about your old demon pal from the past, still having a hard-on for you."

Considering the sights and scenes from earlier, I would have preferred not hearing demon and hard-on in the same breath.

"I have no thoughts on the matter," he said. "Except, maybe you shouldn't use the word *hard-on* in front of children."

"Point taken, and I'm sorry, kids."

The kids didn't mind the language. They were silently fighting for their sanity. They were way past being traumatized by bad words.

"Well, I hate to sound like a Debbie-downer, but Paimon was giving you a warning," said Bear.

"No worse than my ex-wife's rants."

"You were married?" I said.

"Oh, yeah."

"Wow."

Oliver forced a chuckle. "Shocking, right?"

"There is no comparison, my friend," said Bear. "Your ex is good-looking."

"This is the demon from that murder case, right?" I said.

"The very same," said Bear.

"I saw it earlier tonight," I said.

Oliver stopped. "When?"

"In the basement, after the last time it talked to you. Uh, actually it was outside the basement, flying around."

He started walking again, but with a faster pace. "I know its true name, so it'd better not fuck with me."

"That's good," said Bear. "That protects you somewhat."

"By the way, thanks for the gloomy pep talk," said Oliver. "You really *are* a Debbie-downer."

A refreshing breeze swept across me, raising my energy level. It had the smell of night-time country air.

"You guys feel that?" said Oliver.

"Oh, yeah, baby," I said. "We're almost out of here."

It was then that Sharla spoke. "Have you seen my dad?"

An uncomfortable silence fell over us, lasting a few seconds but feeling like half an hour. *Yeah, Sharla. We saw your dad and I jammed a dagger into his head. But hey, he was possessed so we did him a favor.*

"We sure did. That's how we found you guys, he told us where you were. And, he also spoke of how much he loved you." Oliver to the rescue.

More air was reaching us, which meant we were close to entering the basement. Exciting stuff, but not so much for Sharla if she saw her father's mutilated body with a hole in his head. I silently mouthed to Bear, *her dad's body*, and made a stabbing motion toward my temple.

"Good thinking," said Bear. "Ahem, guys I'm going to make sure the path is clear up ahead."

"I follow you, man," said Oliver. "But, if you do that you won't have the protection of the light."

"I don't think I'll need it. Paimon took all of the demons with him." Bear flaunted his sawed off shotgun. "And I've got shit covered, in case I'm wrong." He handed me the staff and slapped me on the shoulder, grinning ear to ear. "Theo would be very proud of you."

I hoped so.

Bear squeezed his way to the front, so we followed him for several minutes until he held up his hand for us to stop. "Hang onto the kids, I'll only be a few minutes."

Bear disappeared into the dark, and we waited. I impatiently shuffled my feet, while Oliver sat down with the kids and rested his back against the dusty wall. He closed his eyes and breathed in the fresh air.

"Is my dad okay?" said Sharla.

She looked at me, and I looked down at my feet.

"Is he dead?" she said.

"Yes, honey," said Oliver. "I'm sorry to tell you that."

She didn't cry, but I saw her sorrow deepen. It was heart wrenching. "Your dad really, really loved you. He saved your life and the boy's," I said.

"Do you think he's in Heaven," she said.

"Yes, I do." This I firmly believed. When I was connected with her father I was able to know his heart, and I didn't feel anything that would keep him from Heaven. Certainly nothing that would earn him a trip to Hell.

The unexpected white beam of a flashlight began to bounce along the hallway, growing ever closer to us. It came from Bear's direction. Oliver got to his feet and drew his gun. "Get between us kids," he said. "Luke, get your gun ready."

I already had it pulled and was ready to face any difficulties head on. "We're all good here."

Bear emerged just seconds later, flashlight in hand. "I literally stumbled across this light."

"You almost got shot again," said Oliver, with a touch of irritation

"How's your leg," I said. It was obvious to anyone

watching that he was beginning to struggle with his leg injury. The numbing effect of the tomato was gone.

"Oh, it's not bad."

"And your gunshot wound?" said Oliver.

"I'll live."

"Can we get the crap out of here?" I said. "Is it…you know, clear?"

"Yeah, c'mon," said Bear. "It feels great out there."

"All right, kids," said Oliver. "You're going home."

Home. I didn't know what or where home would be for me tonight, but I liked the sound of the word. I just wanted to get there, wherever it might be, without incident.

I actually thought it was possible.

Bear was right. Being out of the tunnel was, indeed, great. The night air cooled our sweating bodies and replenished our lungs. Hope was alive and well. The only task left to accomplish was to crawl out of the basement and leave this abominable place.

"I wish we had a ladder," I said.

"So, we've heard," said Oliver.

"I've got something almost as good," said Bear.

"Cool," I said. "What is it?"

"A rope. It's big enough and long enough to get us out of here."

I looked around, baffled. "We didn't bring a rope down…did we?"

"No, we did not," he said. "It's in the trunk of the car."

"How's that help us?" I failed to see why he even mentioned it. It was almost cruel.

"You're going to get it out of the trunk, and then tie it to the bumper of the car before you drop it down to us."

"Shit, how am I going to do that?"

"You're a beanpole, kid," said Oliver. "We can throw your skinny ass out of here if we need to."

"Whatever," I said. "I don't give a shit." Even if it meant I would be tossed into the air, it was as good a plan as any. Seeing as we didn't have a ladder.

Luckily, I was able to stand on Bear's shoulders instead of him chunking me into the air. He stood on a pile of boards, elevating himself another three feet. I was able to reach the edge of the old flooring and pull myself out. I then rolled onto my back and let my body go limp for a moment, as I enjoyed being alive.

I stared into the sky, expecting to see darkness and glittering stars, but all I saw was darkness. However, a flash of lightning broke the dark's dominance and revealed a sky thick with storm clouds. A rumble of thunder also arrived.

I got to my feet and peeked down at Bear. "It's going to storm."

"Then I guess you need to hurry," he said. "Remember, the keys are in the ignition."

"Oh, hey," said Oliver. "Grab my pack of Camels while you're in there."

"No kidding," said Bear. "I could smoke a cigarette as long as my arm."

"Right." I trotted to the car and found two packs of cigarettes, but no set of dangling keys. I looked on the floorboard and in the cracks of the seats, but came up empty. "Shit."

I ran to the edge of the basement and threw my arms up in the air, expressing my annoyance. "Hey, check your pockets. The keys ain't in the ignition."

"They have to be," said Bear. "I remember leaving them."

"Smokes?" said Oliver. "Did you happen to snag a pack?"

"Yeah, I got your smokes." I tossed both packs down to them, and then the rain started. Big, giant plops. Lightning sizzled the atmosphere, and sharp thunder punctuated the moment.

"You got a light?" said Oliver.

"Are you kidding me?" I said.

"I only wish," he said.

"Look for the keys again," said Bear.

I rolled my eyes and shook my head. "It's a waste of time."

The distinctive click of a pistol being cocked sounded from behind me. "Yes, the boy is right. The keys are in *my* pocket," said a male voice. My head was yanked back by my hair, and the gun was pressed against the base of my skull. Whoever had the drop on me pulled me away from the edge of the basement, but not far enough to obscure me from Bear and Oliver's view. They pulled their weapons and pointed them in my direction.

"Sharla," said Oliver. "Take the boy to a safe corner."

"You don't want to do this," said Bear. "Not unless you're ready to die."

"You got a bead on him, brother?" said Oliver.

As much as I wanted out of my predicament, I was not ready to do so at the expense of a well-intentioned bullet from either Oliver or Bear entering *me* instead of the gunman. I had my gun tucked into the small of my back, which made a smooth grab for it impossible. I would probably get shot in the head if I made a play for it. I was rather fucked.

"I'm a good shot, Luke," said Bear.

My unknown captor moved me farther back. "Let's all do a good thing here, and let this young boy live. All I'm wantin' is the book that Buddy stole from me. Even-steven, boys."

I laughed. "You're shit out of luck on that. Paimon took that book to Hell with him."

"What? You're lyin'!" He pushed the barrel roughly against my head and screamed in my ear. "You don't know shit about Paimon!"

"Oh, I know Paimon," I said. "I was the one that handed him the book. Yeah, he was riding a camel."

He was quiet, but for his worried breathing. I figured he was mulling over what I'd told him, wondering if it was true. He pulled back on my hair and leaned his cheek against mine. "Why would Paimon show himself to *you*?"

"Wrong place, wrong time, I guess."

He scraped the barrel across my skin until he came to my temple, and then he tapped the metal against my skull. "Who the fuck *are* you?"

I heard a metallic sound in combination with a solid thud, and then I no longer felt a gun at my head. I spun around and pulled my gun, ready to empty it into the first person I saw. It's a good thing I didn't, or I might have shot Ruckus.

"Just what in the hell's goin' on around here, son?" He held a shovel in his hand. "And who's this prick I just knocked the shit out of?"

The man was face down in the new mud, so he was thus far a stranger to me. "I don't know. But, he knows…*knew* Buddy."

Ruckus rolled him over with his boot and pointed the end of the shovel at his face. "Recognize him?"

I had to wait a few seconds for the rain to wash the blood from his face, but I knew who the man was. "Yeah, it's Jerry Abbott." I wasn't surprised. I guess I suspected it the whole time he had the gun to my head.

Ruckus picked Abbott's gun up from the mud and stuffed it into the front of his pants. "The veterinarian guy?"

"Yep." Looking down at Abbott, I thought of the times I'd seen him participating in community projects. Chili cook-offs, softball games, school fundraisers. A pillar of the community.

"Hey," said Bear. He had managed to reach the floor and was hanging from his elbows. "How about a little help."

"Well, since I'm here I'd might as well," said Ruckus.

"Ruckus, my pal. Please, tell me you've got a light on you," said Oliver.

"Sure, but I'd be lyin'," he said.

"Shit."

"I'm gonna' keep a gun on this dickhead while you help Bear," I said. If Abbott were to awaken while we were assisting Bear, I had no doubts that he would take full advantage of the situation. And, I was too tired to drag Bear out of the hole.

Ruckus stood with his hands on his hips and looked down into the basement. The dagger's glow lit up his wooly beard, turning it golden. He shook his head. "Why ain't ya'll got a ladder?"

Abbott's eyes fluttered and opened. He looked confused at first, shocked even. But, then I saw a flicker of recognition in his eyes.

"I'll shoot you if you try any shit." I cocked the hammer for emphasis. "I'm pretty sure nobody would miss you."

He sat up and wiped blood and rain away from his face, still acting as if he was in charge of the situation. I was having none of it. I fired a round in the ground next to him. "No," I said. "You stay flat on your back, or I'll shoot you in the head next time."

Abbott covered his face with his arms and laid back down. "Okay, okay. I understand your anger. I acted…inappropriately, and that's on me."

"Ya think?" I said.

Bear dropped his knee onto Abbott's neck. Abbott screamed in pain. "Which pocket are the car keys in?" said Bear.

Abbott pointed, and Bear dug them out. "Here." Bear handed me the keys. "Get the rope out. We need to get Oliver and those kids out of that hole."

"That would be appreciated," said Oliver, sounding exhausted.

"Who are you people?" said Abbott.

"Shut up," said Bear.

"What are your plans for me? Are you goin' to kill me?" said Abbott.

We were willing and determined to kill Buddy. Why not Abbott? He was the local mastermind, after all, while Buddy was nothing more than an ambitious, weakling follower.

I was jolted with a remembrance of the last time I was standing on Plume property. I was terrified and tormented with the anticipation of what was to come. I was horrified at the thought of taking another human being's life. That sort of thing just wasn't in my nature.

Things had since changed.

I dragged the rope out of the trunk and tied it to the bumper of the Lincoln. It was a big rope with knots tied throughout its length, perfect for climbing out of a dilapidated basement. Bear dropped it down to Oliver, who then tied it around the little boy's waist. Bear and Ruckus hoisted him up and then repeated the process with the girl and Oliver. It was left to me to watch over Abbott as this went on. I did so with a gun pointed at his head.

"Are you goin' to shoot me if I talk?" said Abbott.

"Keep talking, and you'll find out," I said.

Abbott flinched against the rain, which was being whipped into liquid needles. "You're just goin' to leave me on the ground in this shit?"

"Yep."

"You're a mean little shit aren't you?" he said.

I didn't say a word. I just stared him down with my pistol.

"So, is it safe to say that Buddy's dead?"

I gave him the silent treatment again and studied his face. It was kindly with late sixties wrinkles and gray five o'clock shadow. He looked as normal as anyone else. Nothing stamped on his forehead that read, *monster*.

"C'mon, is he dead?" he said.

"Yeah, he's definitely dead," I said. "So, shut up."

Abbott closed his eyes and smiled. "At least there's a little bit of good news."

When he smiled he looked like a wolf, which was

oddly poetic. Because, he actually was a wolf in sheep's clothing. He preyed upon the most innocent of lives, pursuing his twisted perversions beneath the guise of an upright citizen. But, he wasn't the only wolf. Apparently, they were scattered and hidden amongst all of society. The thought of it nearly caused me to shoot Abbott in his evil-filled brain.

From the corner of my eye, I saw movement within a ragged tree line that was just north of us. Despite the thickening downpour, I was able to discern what it was. It was the entity that sought revenge against Oliver. It was in a tree, watching us with unblinking, red eyes. I decided to keep this information to myself, as I did not see how telling the others would help our situation. It would only be an added worry.

Just as Oliver reached the surface, an explosion of lightning and thunder rocked the sky. The wind spiked substantially, nearly blowing Ruckus into the basement. "Hey, we've got to shag our asses," said Ruckus.

"What about him?" I waved my gun toward Abbott.

"Good question, Luke," said Oliver. "What *should* we do?"

I walked closer to Abbott and stood over him, pointing my gun pointblank at his face. "I know what to do."

Chapter Twenty-Nine

A Dog, The Devil and a Girl

I SAT SIPPING hot chocolate in Sheriff Jake's office, wrapped in a blanket. Along with me was Ruckus, Bear, and Oliver. We had just told the sheriff our version of events, but withheld the supernatural tidbits. We told him that Abbott shot Bear, and then held a gun to my head and confessed to murdering Buddy. Seconds later, Ruckus clocked him. And we also fudged on the place of the incident, telling him that it all happened at Grandpa's farm, and the kids were found in the trunk of Abbott's car. The last part was easily fabricated when we discovered his car and having also found suspicious items in the trunk. Items such as rope, handcuffs, duct tape, and lurid photos of kids.

Sharla and the boy were immediately transported to the hospital, where the boy was reunited with his parents and she with her mother. Sharla went along with the bullshit storyline, knowing full well that nobody would believe the truth. The boy was the only possible fly in the ointment. But, he wasn't talking and even if he did, it was the wild hysterics of a traumatized boy.

Jerry Abbott and his followers destroyed many lives, and the FBI was digging deep to find out how high the number went. Apparently, someone called in a list of names to them anonymously, which was quickly leading to some eye-popping names in government. From the state level, all the way to the White House. Crazy shit.

We talked Ruckus into the phone call.

Abbott deserved to die for his fiendish deeds. A few shots to his kneecaps, before the finishing touch of a bullet to his brain. He deserved it all. He *earned* it.

But none of those things happened.

"Has Abbott lawyered up yet?" said Oliver.

"Strangely, not yet," said the sheriff. "But, even more strange is his request for extra security. He claims his life is in danger."

"And is it?" said Oliver.

"Probably," he said. "There's a lot of people that don't want him to talk. And…well, as you all know, we had an incident with a few prisoners not too long ago."

"How's the investigation been into that?" said Bear, playing dumb.

"A whole lot of head scratching so far, but I'm determined to find out how they were murdered," said the sheriff. "I plan on keeping some extra men outside his cell, until he's the FBI's problem." The sheriff took a huge gulp of coffee and stared at a snow globe on his desk. It depicted a scene of a hunter taking aim at a deer as it grazed beneath a tree. Then, out of the blue, he said, "It gets creepy here late at night."

I was going to ask him to elaborate, but he had already moved on. He leaned on his elbows and pointed at Bear. "I've got an ambulance on its way to take your ass to the hospital."

Bear shook his head and held his hand up in protest. "There's no need, Sheriff. I'm really all right, but I appreciate your concern."

"Bullshit on that," said the sheriff. "You've got a bullet hole in your shoulder, and I can see the bone in your leg."

"He's got a point," said Ruckus. "Your ole' leg is lookin' pretty nasty."

"It's gross," said Oliver.

Bear threw his arms up in surrender. "All right, shit. But, no ambulance. I'll just have the good detective here run me by."

Oliver stood up and lit two smokes and handed one to Bear. "Then let's get moving now, amigo."

"You never explained how you hurt your leg," said the sheriff. "How'd that happen?"

The question caught him off guard, and he searched for a lie. It caused a hesitation in his response. "Oh, this?"

"He fell from the hayloft," I said. "We were gonna' take him to the hospital, but all of this other stuff came up."

The sheriff tapped a pencil on his desk. I was sure that each *tap* represented a hole in our story that he intended to expose. He was just giving us rope. *Tap, tap, and tap.*

"What in the world were you doing in a hayloft?" said the sheriff.

"Well, it's a little embarrassing, but I'd never been inside of a barn before," said Bear. "I slipped on some hay. I feel stupid about it."

Tap. Tap. Tap.

"Your friends are right," said the sheriff. "You look like shit. I'll call off the ambulance, but be careful out there. There's some bad weather out and about."

"Come along, *Hop-a-long*," Oliver said to Bear. "Maybe I'll meet a nice country nurse while they bandage you up."

Bear and Oliver each shook the sheriff's hand and headed out the door. Ruckus and I stood up from our chairs, ready to do the same.

"Luke," said the sheriff. "How are you doing?"

His aura appeared to me. It was a beautiful, orange egg that flamed all around him. It gave me a vibe that he wasn't trying to fleece me for clues, but was genuinely concerned for me. "I'm doing better, thanks."

Such a lie.

We shook hands, and he said, "You guys have a safe trip back. I'll stay in touch, I promise you."

I had no doubts of that.

"Thank ya," said Ruckus. "He's in good hands."

It was no small feat to exit his office and the building in a casual manner, but, we maintained our cool all the way to Ruckus' truck, in the middle of a pounding rain. I'm not even sure we were breathing.

"He believes us, right?" I said.

"Ah, no I don't think so," he said. "He ain't no dummy."

"Then why'd he let us go?"

"Because he trusts us."

"Do you think?"

"Based on how much information he spilled to us— and one of *us* is a thirteen-year-old kid keep in mind—I'd say he trusts us plenty."

"Or, he's being sneaky."

"He *knows* he has the right guy behind bars, regardless of the bullshit. He don't particularly like the bullshit, but, him and those feds got a case against that ole' boy that's stronger'n a garlic milkshake."

I thought about that for a moment. "You know, that would be a strong milkshake."

"Damn right, think about it."

I burst into laughter, and then Ruckus joined in. It was almost spooky to suddenly feel joy. But then Ruckus had to bring reality into things. He stomped on my moment of mirth.

"Well, ya know those FBI boys ain't done with us either. I figure they'll still want to talk to us now and then. They ain't gonna' to be as easy as the sheriff."

"Thanks, for the gloom," I said.

"Don't mention it."

I assumed this was what I was to expect for the rest of my life. Teasing, snippets of happiness. "How and the crap did my life end up here?" I said.

"Beats me."

"Thanks, again."

"Sure, anytime.

But, I knew how I arrived here. This nightmare was set into motion the moment Grandpa was placed upon Chester and Lucille's doorstep. We are all powerless against destiny.

"Hey, I been meanin' to ask ya somethin'," said Ruckus. "Do you know a gal named Constance?"

"Uh, I met a little girl named Constance," I said.

"This wasn't a little girl, son. She was a full grown gal and a fine lookin' little thing, blonde-haired and pretty."

"I don't know anyone like that," I said.

"I think you know her."

"Nope."

"She told me to tell you that she met you at Crone's, and to tell you hi next I see ya."

"Huh?"

"She's the only reason I showed up to save ya'll's asses."

"It can't be the same Constance...when did you see her?"

"That's the weird part, ya see," he said. "I was nappin' there at the house when someone came beatin' on the door like they had a sledge hammer. I thought it might be some more of those redneck crazies, so I grab a lamp and open up the door."

"And was Constance standing there, holding a sledge hammer?" I said.

"No smartass, but she was wearin' a yellow dress."

This was sounding familiar. "A yellow dress?"

"That's what I said."

"And a blue ribbon in her hair?"

"That's her all right."

"But she was only five years old this morning," I said. "I don't see how she could have grown up in one day." I remembered Junior saying that Mr. Bird and I were inside Crone's home for five minutes, when it seemed an eternity to me. Maybe this fell under that sort of weirdness.

"Hell, maybe it was her big sister. All I know is she

told me to follow her to the Plume place. She said ya'll were in bad shape and were goin' to die if I didn't get movin'. And then she takes off runnin' across the yard, headed for the road. I start after her and…then I'm layin' on the couch, just wakin' up."

"That's trippy," I said.

"Tell me about it."

"Was she gone?"

"Yeah, she was gone. But, the front door was wide open, and a dog was sittin' on the porch barkin' at me." Ruckus shook his head.

I twisted my mouth, thinking. "What did the dog look like?"

"Some type of hound. It was black and tan, and one of its ears was missing."

"Whoa, Ole' Ace," I said, grinning. "What happened then?"

"Well, it kept barkin' and ran out to the road. So, I followed it out there, thinkin' maybe it was hurt or somethin'. That was when I saw the light coming from up the road, and it started to storm. That's when I knew."

"Knew what?"

"That ya'll needed your asses saved."

It came to me that I'd not thanked Ruckus for his help. "By the way, thanks man," I said. "You were my hero today. Uh, everyone's hero."

"All in a day's work."

"What happened to the dog?" I was feeling happy about the news of Ace, and for a moment considered telling Melvin of the miraculous resurrection. But, I canned that idea quickly. Melvin wouldn't believe me, and I feared I might upset him. He truly did love that dog.

"I don't remember, exactly. One minute it was there, and then it wasn't."

We came to the flashing red light at the intersection of Highway 9 and 75. To my right was a gas station with an array of neon signs advertising cigarettes, beer, and minnows that lit up the small parking lot. A weathered picnic bench was off to the side, somewhat protected from the rain by an a-frame roof that clung loosely from a gazebo. Someone was sitting on the bench, making the most of a precarious refuge from the storm.

It was the devil. Old Nick.

He smiled at me with his coal-black teeth, and then tipped his hat. "Hello, hayseed," said the devil, ever so smoothly. However, his lips didn't move. But, they didn't have to. His words were appearing in the middle of my brain, each one feeling like a wasps' sting. "You and your dolt of a companion take care. It's quite nasty tonight."

"Get out of my head, butthole," I said.

"Not without me first thanking you for retrieving our book. It's been in the hands of you idiots for too long."

The pain in my head became like icy spikes. I was near the point of screaming. "You can thank me by shutting up."

The devil laughed, which intensified my agony. I was now screaming.

"Luckily for you, I have something I must attend to on the other side of the world. So, I'll be leaving you soon enough."

I looked over at Ruckus, but he was oblivious to my howls. He was just sitting behind the steering wheel, staring at the flashing lights of the intersection.

"Ruckus!" I shrieked his name, but he acted as if he didn't even see me, let alone hear me.

The devil got up from the bench and walked toward us, his smile growing with each step. He left a trail of blackness behind him that twisted with life. "Ready yourself, Luke. A darkness is coming, and it's coming specifically for all humans. It will be a terrible time."

"Please, shut up!" I said through tears of excruciating pain. My brain was throbbing.

"However, you can avoid having to see your loved ones suffer and perish," said the devil. "Just give in to

Lilith and allow yourself to be taken. You would have the opportunity to be risen to a place of power in this world. You could, potentially, be one of my greatest agents."

I grabbed fistfuls of my hair and screamed at the devil. "You've got to shut up! My head…"

The devil pushed his face against my window. "I don't have to do anything," he said. "I am Lucifer."

Mad with pain, and feeling I was on the brink of death, I grabbed my staff and stabbed it at the devil's face. It broke through the glass and struck him between the eyes. Old Nick—Lucifer, whatever he called himself—looked surprised.

I got out of the truck and swung at the devil again. I missed him, but I was able to knock his hat off. I watched as it bounced and rolled into a puddle of rain, moving in slow motion. Indeed, everything seemed to be moving in slow motion except for the devil. The rain barely fell, almost becoming suspended in animation, and the electronic hum of the neon became distinct and drawn out.

And then I was back in the truck with Ruckus. Warm and dry, and headache free. My staff was still lying between Ruckus and me, and the passenger window was fully intact.

"Holy crap," I said.

"Nice of ya to join me, son," said Ruckus.

I saw that we were on the highway, approaching the first lights of Oklahoma City. "I've been sleeping?"

"Yeah, you've been sleepin' all right. You slept right through a hail storm."

"Wow," I said, shaking my head.

"Hell, I pulled over to make sure you were still breathin'," he said.

"And was I?"

"Apparently," he said.

A stretch limousine, black and shining brilliantly, pulled up alongside us. And, even before my Lilith bite began tingling, I knew it was her. It travelled with us for a minute or two, running parallel to the truck, before it sped off at breakneck into the driving rain.

"Who do you think that was?" said Ruckus. "A rock star?"

"Probably someone who *thinks* they're a rock star." I didn't see a reason to let Ruckus know who was in the limousine. I wanted to give his body and mind a break from the things that Lilith represented. It was time to give normalcy a shot, and see if it would hold.

Ruckus opened the glove box and pulled out an 8-track tape. "Speakin' of rock stars," he said. "You ever heard of Alice Cooper?"

"No," I said. "Is she a rock star?"

"Good God, son."

"What?"

He showed me the tape cover, and I saw that Alice Cooper was a man. The name on the tape read, Alice Cooper and below his name was a photo of Alice himself. He had long black hair and wore a tuxedo, and held a top hat in his right hand. And below that was the title of the 8-track—*Welcome to My Nightmare.*

"I've got a lot to teach ya," he said.

I chuckled and popped the tape into the player. "Yep, I reckon so."